CW01024492

THE
GREATER
GOOD

A WARHAMMER 40,000 NOVEL

Ciaphas Cain

THE GREATER GOOD

Sandy Mitchell

BLACK LIBRARY

For Liz. Not before time.

A BLACK LIBRARY PUBLICATION
First published in Great Britain in 2013 by
Black Library,
Games Workshop Ltd.,
Willow Road,
Nottingham,
NG7 2WS, UK

10 9 8 7 6 5 4 3 2 1

Cover by Clint Langley.

A CIP record for this book is available from the British Library.

UK ISBN 13: 978 1 84970 287 4
US ISBN 13: 978 1 84970 288 1

This is a work of fiction. All the characters and events portrayed in this book are fictional, and any resemblance to real people or incidents is purely coincidental.

See the Black Library on the internet at
www.blacklibrary.com

Find out more about Games Workshop
and the world of Warhammer 40,000 at
www.games-workshop.com

Printed and bound by CPI Group (UK) Ltd, Croydon, CR0 4YY

It is the 41st millennium. For more than a hundred centuries the Emperor has sat immobile on the Golden Throne of Earth. He is the master of mankind by the will of the gods, and master of a million worlds by the might of his inexhaustible armies. He is a rotting carcass writhing invisibly with power from the Dark Age of Technology. He is the Carrion Lord of the Imperium for whom a thousand souls are sacrificed every day, so that he may never truly die.

Yet even in his deathless state, the Emperor continues his eternal vigilance. Mighty battlefleets cross the daemon-infested miasma of the warp, the only route between distant stars, their way lit by the Astronomican, the psychic manifestation of the Emperor's will. Vast armies give battle in his name on uncounted worlds. Greatest amongst his soldiers are the Adeptus Astartes, the Space Marines, bio-engineered super-warriors. Their comrades in arms are legion: the Imperial Guard and countless planetary defence forces, the ever-vigilant Inquisition and the tech-priests of the Adeptus Mechanicus to name only a few. But for all their multitudes, they are barely enough to hold off the ever-present threat from aliens, heretics, mutants - and worse.

To be a man in such times is to be one amongst untold billions. It is to live in the cruellest and most bloody regime imaginable. These are the tales of those times. Forget the power of technology and science, for so much has been forgotten, never to be re-learned. Forget the promise of progress and understanding, for in the grim dark future there is only war. There is no peace amongst the stars, only an eternity of carnage and slaughter, and the laughter of thirsting gods.

Editorial Note:

This latest extract from the memoirs of Ciaphas Cain is of interest in several respects, not least in the insights it gives into the workings of tau diplomacy, a weapon in their arsenal at least as potent as a cadre of battlesuits, if rather less liable to make a mess of the carpet.

Although the tau empire is currently co-operating with the Imperium in a joint campaign against the tyranid hive fleets, they can hardly be considered reliable allies, given their notorious opportunism and their obsessive pursuit of the so-called 'Greater Good.' Which, let us be clear, would be rather more accurately translated into Gothic as 'the Greater Good of the Tau, and the warp take the rest.' I leave drawing any parallel with our own attitude towards the arrangement to those more cynical than I.

Which brings us back to Cain who, if not instrumental in the forging of the pact, undoubtedly played a major role in preventing its premature dissolution, which would have been to the ruination of us all. His motives for so doing were, of course, entirely personal, at least by his own account. As ever, I leave it to the reader to weigh how far he may be taken at his word.

As has become my habit over the preceding volumes I have left his narrative as close to how I found it as possible, doing little more than breaking it down into chapters for ease of reading, and inserting additional explanatory material whenever required to elucidate the occasional obscure reference, or provide the wider context generally lacking in his woefully self-centred account of events.

Amberley Vail, Ordo Xenos.

ONE

SAY WHAT YOU like about the tau, and I've said plenty myself over the years, they know how to put on a good war. In fact, if you ask me, they were making rather too good a job of it in the closing phases of the Quadravidia campaign; I'd been expecting a hard fight, having butted heads with the little blue[1] blighters on more than one occasion, but they were giving us a lot worse than that. By the time I arrived in the capital, dodging plasma bolts every foot of the way, our defences were crumbling all over the planet, and it was clearly only a matter of time before they overran the last remaining Imperial enclave altogether.

'Quadravidia cannot be allowed to fall,' General Braddick insisted, in flat-out contravention of what everyone crowded into the command

---

1. *Tau skin shades actually vary as much as human ones, though the majority appear somewhere in a range between pale grey and an even paler cerulean, a result of the role cobalt seems to play in their metabolism. Anyone interested in the physiological details can find more than they would ever wish to know in Magos Gandermak's pioneering paper* Some Preliminary Conclusions Concerning the Haematology of the Tau, Imperial Journal of Xenobiology, Vol. MMMCCXXIX, *Number 8897, pp 346 - 892, Rasmussen's* Tentative Results of the Analysis of Tau Haemoglobin Free of Obvious Methodological Errors, *Vol. MMMCCXXIX, Number 8899, pp 473 - 857, and the ensuing century and a half of increasingly acrimonious correspondence with the editor.*

bunker beneath what was left of the local Guard garrison already knew to be inevitable, the febrile glow in the depths of his slate-grey eyes making the unhealthy pallor of his skin even more noticeable. You can only substitute recaff and stimms for sleep for so long, and the time to redress the balance in his case was well and truly past. He raised his voice over the distant rumble of exploding ordnance, which, to my distinct and well-concealed alarm, was noticeably louder than it had been that morning. As if to underline the fact, dust motes jarred from some recess near the ceiling tumbled lazily in the shafts of setting sunlight sneaking in through the firing slits. 'If it does, the entire subsector goes with it.'

Which was why the tau had struck at Quadravidia in the first place, of course, its position at the nexus of several warp routes making it the natural conduit for Imperial military transports on their way to prop up the steadily eroding buffer zone between the two powers.

'That may be overstating the case a little,' I said, brushing my sleeve free of the specks which had settled there, and trying not to sound as if retreat was the best option I could think of by a long way. 'But the general is quite correct in considering the ramifications of an orderly withdrawal.' Which were more than likely to include a firing squad for cowardice and incompetence, at least so far as he was concerned. Hardly fair, given that he'd hung on grimly in the face of overwhelming odds for months; but someone would have to take the blame for the fiasco, and it certainly wasn't going to be the morons from the Munitorum who'd sent the Guard in under-strength and under-equipped in the first place.

'You think we should pull out?' one of the senior staffers asked, spotting a potential lifeline: if the celebrated Ciaphas Cain recommended turning tail, they could hardly be blamed for following my advice. That was what commissars were supposed to be for, after all, considering the wider picture.

'I'd be on the first shuttle,' I said, completely truthfully, with just enough of a smile to make them think I was only joking. 'But as General Braddick has just pointed out, that isn't, unfortunately, an option.' Not because I was having an uncharacteristic rush of noble self-sacrifice to the head, you understand, but because anything larger than a servoskull taking to the air would be shot down by the tau before it had time to clear the pad, and we didn't have anything left in orbit capable of making warp in any case.

As if to underline my words, and because the Emperor sometimes shows a taste for the dramatic as well as a nasty sense of humour, a faint tremor shook the command bunker, and another rain of dust pattered off the peak of my cap.

'Reinforcements are on the way,' Braddick said, in the tone of a man who hopes to make it true by saying so with sufficient conviction, and I nodded.

'They were certainly due to be dispatched,' I agreed, clinging to the faint shred of hope even more tightly than the general. I'd been assured of that just prior to my own departure, aboard the small relief flotilla which had arrived about six weeks before, and which my old dining companion Lord General Zyvan[1] had hoped would prove sufficient to bolster our defences until he could pull a large enough task force together to raise the siege and send the tau scuttling for home. And so it would have done, if the tau hadn't had the same idea, and sent a relieving force of their own to match it.

On the plus side, I suppose, we'd managed to deprive the xenos of the easy victory they'd hoped for, and would undoubtedly have seized by now if the extra division of Catachans I'd arrived with hadn't proved so tenacious, but from where I was sitting it looked uncomfortably as though all we'd managed to do was delay the inevitable. I was sure Zyvan was doing his best to get a proper relief force together, but the tyranid hive fleets had been striking ever deeper into the heart of the Imperium over the past few years, and all too many of our resources were being diverted to contain them; the promised reinforcements could take months to arrive, if they even got here at all.

---

1. *Though their relative positions in the somewhat tangled skeins of military protocol precluded anything as firm as out and out friendship, their relationship was somewhat warmer than Cain's words might imply; particularly by this point, in the last decade of the millennium, only five years from Cain's official and frequently interrupted retirement. They socialised as frequently as possible given the pressing nature of their respective duties, and undoubtedly enjoyed one another's company on such occasions.*

'Then we hang on,' Braddick said, his shoulders slumping with weary resolution, at odds with the sharp creases of his typically ornate Mordian tunic, and I nodded soberly.

'I don't see that we've any other choice,' I agreed, all too conscious of the irony.

The thing was, you see, that I needn't even have been there in the first place. My current position, Commissarial Liaison Officer to the Lord General's staff, had left me in a position to pick and choose my assignments to a far greater extent than I'd ever dreamed possible in the earlier stages of my long and inglorious career, where circumstance and the long arm of the Commissariat had kept shoving me into harm's way despite my best efforts to let it gallop past unimpeded. Of course my entirely unmerited reputation for dauntless courage and flamboyant derring-do meant that I was hardly in a position to follow my natural inclination and remain indefinitely on Coronus[1], watching my aide, Jurgen, deal with most of the paperwork passing through my office while I wondered how soon I could slope off for lunch. Maintaining it meant showing my face at the front line from time to time, to encourage the troops and remind Zyvan how lucky he was to have me around, while keeping as far from the enemy as possible in the process.

With this in mind, a quick jaunt to Quadravidia had seemed just the ticket; as I said, we'd expected the relief flotilla I'd hitched a ride with to tip the balance of the war there decisively in our favour, so I should have been able to keep out of trouble without too much difficulty once we'd arrived. More to the point, it would keep me comfortably out of the way of the encroaching hive fleets. I had no desire to end up as a blob of goo in a reclamation pool somewhere, which seemed all too likely if someone decided they needed a Hero of the Imperium around to keep the troops steady in the face of so many scuttling horrors. So, making myself scarce while the high command drew up their plans for the latest attempt to contain the tyranid menace was only prudent.

---

1. *An Imperial Guard staging world, where many of the campaigns Cain was involved in over the course of his career were planned and the forces for them assembled.*

To cut a long and dismal story short, we arrived in good order, and disembarked by drop-ship, the orbital side of the starport facilities having failed to survive the first tau onslaught[1]. We were harried a bit on the way down, of course, but the Navy had enough fighters still in the air to keep most of the fleas off our backs, and we took only a few losses, digging in around the planetary capital for the most part. Braddick and his Mordians were delighted to see us, especially once our first counter-attack had thrown back the enemy forces to the outer hab ring, and for the first week or so it really looked as if we had the xenos on the run; although I was seasoned enough a campaigner to realise that reclaiming the entire world would be a long and arduous process.

So much the better, I'd thought, envisaging a long spell comfortably behind the firing line, while Zyvan and the Navy got ready to tackle the 'nids. With any luck I could spin things out here long enough to get back to Coronus well after their departure.

So the appearance in orbit a fortnight later of a fleet of tau 'merchantmen'[2] came as a pretty unpleasant surprise. By luck or base cunning, probably the latter knowing them, they popped into the system a couple of days after the Imperial flotilla had left for Coronus, and had a clear run for the planet, the gunboats of the SDF[3] having been swept from the sky in the course of the first incursion.

All of which left me without the proverbial paddle. I wasn't dead yet, though, and I'd been in tighter spots than this before now, so I dispensed a few encouraging platitudes, bade everyone in the bunker a good night, and withdrew, ostensibly to go and make sure the troopers on our perimeter were keeping up to the mark. I was by no means certain the final assault would come tonight, but if it did the

---

1. *In fact most of the orbitals were still substantially intact, but the amount of debris around them made docking a starship problematic at best.*

2. *Despite Cain's clear cynicism, that is indeed how the tau themselves refer to their larger capital ships, which combine as much cargo space as a dedicated Imperial troop transport with the firepower of a battleship. An uncomfortable combination in planetary assaults, to say the least, although, as the Navy like to say, at least the defenders get to concentrate their fire against fewer targets.*

3. *System Defence Fleet.*

command bunker would be a singularly unhealthy place to be. I had no doubt that the technosorcery of the tau would have pinpointed it to the millimetre, and that it was top of the list for a visit from one of their strike teams.

'Good meeting, sir?' Jurgen asked, materialising from the shadows, his unique and earthy aroma greeting me a good three seconds before he had time to open his mouth.

'I've had better,' I admitted, with more candour than I'd normally employ. But Jurgen had served with me for nigh on seventy years by that point, saving my miserable hide more often than either of us could count, and I owed him as much honesty as I ever gave anyone.

Our brief exchange was punctuated by heavy weapon discharges flickering in the distance like a gathering storm, lacerating the grey overcast of early evening, stark against the red-tinged sky. Not all the red was due to the sunset either; hab blocks were ablaze in a dozen places throughout the beleaguered city. Unfortunately the firestorms hampered our movements as much as the tau, if not more so: the xenos were able to hop about in their anti-gravitic vehicles pretty much as they wished, instead of having to grind their way along laboriously cleared routes like our Chimeras and Leman Russ were forced to do, only to end up in the middle of an ambush as like as not.

'Tanna, sir?' Jurgen said, producing a flask from somewhere among the tangle of webbing he was habitually festooned with, and I took it gratefully. The evenings were chill here in the equatorial mountains, where the capital had been founded, although why they hadn't put it somewhere a little more clement was beyond me[1].

'Thank you,' I said, sipping the fragrant beverage, and savouring the tendril of warmth which oozed its way down into my stomach. 'Shall we go?'

'Ready whenever you are, sir,' my aide assured me, scrambling into the driving seat of the Salamander we'd requisitioned from the

---

1. *Because, given Quadravidia's value to the Imperium as a transport hub, cities on the ground were less important than the orbital docks above them. Which, in turn, meant that they were built beneath the footprints of structures in geostationary orbit which, by definition, were positioned above a point on the equator.*

transport pool shortly after our arrival. The engine was grumbling quietly to itself already, Jurgen being far too seasoned a veteran to risk even the second or two's delay that firing it up would take if we were caught flat-footed this close to a combat zone.

I clambered into the passenger compartment, returning the salutes of a squad of Guardsmen double-timing it past us in the direction of the main gate as I did so. With reflexes honed by decades of exposure to Jurgen's robust driving style, I grabbed at the pintle mount for support an instant before we jerked into motion.

It was as well that I did, for in regaining my balance my eyes drifted skywards. Black shapes were moving above the buildings the fading light had now reduced to stark-edged silhouettes; etched against the crimson glow, the gracefully sinister curvature of their surfaces betraying their origin unmistakably.

'Incoming!' I voxed, opening fire with the storm bolter as I did so, quietly cursing my luck. The attack I'd anticipated, and come so close to avoiding, had arrived.

Editorial Note:

It will hardly come as a surprise to most of my readers that, beyond a few desultory complaints about the air temperature, Cain says little about Quadravidia itself. The following extracts may go some way towards remedying this deficiency.

From *Interesting Places and Tedious People: A Wanderer's Waybook*, by Jerval Sekara, 145.M39.

QUADRAVIDIA WILL BE a familiar destination for most seasoned travellers in and around the Damocles Gulf, since it has the great good fortune to be situated at the confluence of no fewer than four warp currents of unusual swiftness and stability. Unsurprisingly, therefore, this is a world, or, to be more precise, an entire planetary system, which tends to be passed through rather than visited. Indeed, it is quite possible to transfer between vessels aboard one of the many orbital docks and void stations which ring it about without ever setting foot on the planet at all.

Nevertheless, it can be worth breaking a longer journey here for a prolonged sojourn, or even making it the intended destination of an indefinite stay. Though it's true to say that at first sight the principal cities around the equator offer little to the discriminating wayfarer, consisting as they do almost entirely of starport facilities, the vulgar commercial institutions deemed necessary by those engaged in trade, and the habitations of the artisan classes apparently required in depressingly high numbers to ensure the efficient running of both, Peakhaven is as gratifyingly cosmopolitan as any planetary capital in that region of space.

Set high in the mountain range which sprawls along the equator, bisecting the western continent, its streets and avenues cling to the sides of peak and valley alike, the highest ramparts of which wall off the worst of the noise and bustle of the starport. This is thus confined to a broad depression, some three or four kilometres across, surrounded by higher mountains. It goes without saying that lodgings should be sought on the outer wall of the rim, since the intervening mass of granite effectively muffles most of the sound of the constant shuttle traffic. The sight of it is quite spectacular, however, particularly at night, when the engine glows make a constant vortex of light in the darkness, like the sparks above a forge.

Smaller towns and villages are, of course, to be found elsewhere on the two continents, but contain little of interest.

From *The Crusade and After: A Military History of the Damocles Gulf*, by Vargo Royz, 058.M42.

THOUGH CHECKED BY their first confrontation with the Imperium's might, the expansionist ambitions of the tau were far from blunted. The next two hundred years were marked by periodic clashes between the two powers, as frontier worlds were annexed, defended, reclaimed, and in many cases lost again. Indeed, Semplaxia was to change hands seven times in all, before ultimately being lost to both sides as the outliers of Hive Fleet Kraken smashed into the Eastern Arm, although such a case was exceptional. For the most part, what the tau gained by subterfuge or the force of arms they kept, although the Imperium made them pay a heavy price, and were even able to claim some notable successes of their own, such as the reclamation of Gravalax in 931.

Had the forces of the Emperor been able to concentrate their full might on the upstart usurpers, things would have been very different of course, but the last quarter of M41 was riven with conflict on every front. To the ever-present menace of the orks and the fell designs of the Traitor Legions was added the gradual awakening of the necrons, who began to attack human outposts in ever-increasing numbers, while the eldar continued their piractical raids seemingly at will. Perhaps fortunately the tau, too, were beginning to fall foul of these enemies and others more and more frequently as their sphere of influence expanded, preventing them from engaging in an all-out invasion of Imperial space.

The stalemate was eventually broken in 992, when a tau fleet striking deep inside the Imperial border appeared in orbit around Quadravidia, rapidly overwhelming the planetary defences, and landing an invasion force. Once in uncontested control, denying Imperial access to the vital warp currents which flowed together there, they would have effectively blockaded eight of the disputed systems in the border region, cutting them off from reinforcement, and leaving them free to be picked off at their leisure.

Fortunately for these imperilled worlds, the second relief expedition was led by Ciaphas Cain, the renowned commissar who had been so instrumental in foiling the tau designs on Gravalax, and was to prove more than equal to this fresh and more urgent threat to Imperial interests.

TWO

WHETHER THE WARNING I gave made any difference I couldn't say; but mine wasn't the only finger on a trigger as the first wave of the tau assault burst over the jagged reef of airstrike-shattered buildings surrounding the compound, and which had masked their approach from detection by our auspexes. Ragged small-arms fire sparked and popped against the smooth rounded armour of the troop carriers circling above our heads, and the bright streak of a rocket from a man-portable launcher slashed the sky for a moment before detonating against one of the blocky engine pods attached to the rear of the closest. The Devilfish lurched and pulled up, aborting its descent, but the respite was short-lived; a pair of platter-like drones detached themselves from its hull almost at once and swooped in search of vengeance, plasma rounds from the guns mounted beneath them bursting around the sandbagged emplacement from which the rocket had come.

How the Guardsmen crouched within it fared against this unexpected attack I never saw, though a flurry of las-rounds replied with commendable alacrity, for by that time my attention was entirely taken up with the matter of my own survival. The Salamander lurched, as Jurgen made a hard turn to evade a crater gouged into the rockrete ahead of us by a far bigger plasma burst from the main gun of another circling troop carrier, and I suddenly found a small, fast-moving shadow drifting across my sights.

The storm bolter bucked against its mount as I squeezed the trigger reflexively, stitching a row of impact craters along the belly of a skimmer which screamed overhead, low enough for the backwash of its passing to snatch the cap from my head. I must have found a weak spot, for almost at once smoke began to seep from its starboard engine, and it flipped over, ploughing into the ground. It kept going on pure momentum, raising a bow wave of pulverised rockcrete, and smearing its luckless crew along the hard surface as it did so, before coming to rest embedded in the wall of the officer's mess.

'Ouch,' I said, feelingly.

'They were asking for it,' Jurgen opined, triggering the forward flamer, and immolating a couple of swooping gun drones before they had a chance to open fire on us in return. 'What sort of idiot flies around with an open cockpit in the middle of a firefight?'

'Good point,' I said, ducking behind the thick armour plate, as debris from a nearby explosion rattled against it. One of the Hydras spitting streams of tracer rounds at the descending invaders had just taken a direct hit, the intense heat of the tau plasma bolt cooking off its ammunition, and a section of hull plating whirled through the space I'd just vacated. If I hadn't ducked when I did, it would have taken my head off.

Finding my cap in the bottom of the passenger well I jammed it back on my head as firmly as possible, feeling that I might as well look the part, and peered cautiously over the rim of the armoured compartment. We were the only Imperial vehicle still moving through the blizzard of descending fire, although a Leman Russ with its track blown off was traversing its turret, scanning hopefully for a target, and the crew were bailing out of a second Hydra, which had no turret left at all that I could see. Clearly the tau had prioritised the targets most capable of harming them, although I had no doubt that they'd get round to picking off our lightly-armed Salamander before long.

'Get us under cover!' I ordered, despite being pretty sure Jurgen would have worked that out for himself by now.

'Right you are, sir,' he acknowledged, and spun the vehicle on a coin, slamming the right-hand track into reverse with a speed which elicited an alarming sound from the gearbox, although that would have been as nothing compared to the fuss any of our enginseers would have made if they'd been around to hear it. Once again I clung to the pintle mount for support, while we took off in a completely different direction, plasma bolts boiling the rockcrete where we would have been if Jurgen hadn't swung us about.

The first of the attacking troop carriers hit the ground about a hundred metres ahead, its shock absorbers flexing against the rockcrete; even before they'd fully extended again, the boarding ramp dropped. Instantly, another pair of lethal drones soared into the air to provide fire support for the pathfinder squad disembarking from it. The xenos moved with remarkable agility despite the body armour they were encased in, their faces rendered curiously insectile by the glowing red lenses embedded in their faceplates.

Undeterred, I opened fire on warriors and vehicle alike, scything a hail of bolter rounds through the air they occupied. A couple of compact plasma bolts from the ground troopers' carbines burst against the armour surrounding me in reply, gouging deep craters in the ceramite, but it held. Then a solid armour-piercing projectile slammed right through the passenger compartment, punching holes in both sides I could have pushed my fist through.

'One of them's got a rail rifle!' I shouted to Jurgen, although the noise of the engine and the firefight surrounding us meant that he could only hear me over the vox-link anyway, so there was little point in raising my voice. I tried to depress the storm bolter to engage the ground troops, but a piece of debris from the exploding Hydra was jammed in the pintle, and I couldn't swing it down far enough. 'Frak!'

'I'm on it,' Jurgen assured me, and triggered the flamer again, adding a burst from the hull-mounted heavy bolter for good measure. The pathfinder squad scattered from the gout of blazing promethium, which hosed up inside the transport through the still open passenger ramp. 'That'll give 'em something to think about.'

It certainly did: a moment later the upper hatches popped and the crew bailed out, becoming easy targets for the vengeful lasgun fire of those Guardsmen still in the fight.

At this point I began to hope that the balance might tilt the other way. The tau had a definite edge when it came to long-range shooting, but they had no stomach for getting up close and personal, while the Guard had no such qualms. In fact the death worlders making up the majority of the garrison here[1] seemed to prefer it, wading in with bayonet and lasrifle butt at every opportunity, their ork hide capes swirling about them with almost as much ferocious energy as if they were still attached to their original owners. Which didn't mean they fought with all the finesse and tactical sense of Khornate berserkers; quite the contrary. Where they came from, survival meant using their wits as well as their weapons.

'All units pull back,' General Braddick voxed, just in time to rein them in. 'Defend the bunker.'

I couldn't fault his tactics, our priority was clearly to deny the tau their objective, but from where I was standing (or, more accurately, rattling around like a pea in a can), we'd just handed them the initiative again[2].

'Hold on, sir,' Jurgen urged, triggering the forward-mounted heavy bolter again. Another sleek and deadly troop carrier was drifting in from out of the darkness above our heads, cutting across our path as the pilot brought it in to land. The explosive bolts chewed away at the hull armour, doing little damage that I could see, but at the very least we must have startled the crew as the Devilfish grounded hard, buckling its landing gear; although I found myself vindictively hoping we'd done a great deal worse than that. The shock of impact had clearly come as an unwelcome surprise to the passengers too:

1. *From the aptly-named Settler's Bane, a planet teeming with inimical life forms among which the tribes of feral orks rate no higher than a minor nuisance.*

2. *An opinion shared by a number of later historians, although others assert with equal fervour that under the circumstances Braddick had little choice in the matter: any attempt to counter-attack at that point could just as easily have overstretched the defensive line, breaking it altogether.*

instead of disembarking in good order, securing the boarding ramp as they went, they boiled out as though abandoning the vehicle, and I was pleased to note that at least a couple of them were limping. The Salamander jerked violently, as Jurgen swung it round to keep the weapons bearing for as long as he could. 'Oops.'

'Oops indeed,' I agreed, hanging on for dear life as my aide kept us lurching from left to right in an attempt to evade as much of the incoming fire from the xenos as he could, or possibly to run a few of the stragglers down. It was hard to be sure which, as I was more than a little preoccupied with trying to remain on my feet.

Mindful that there were probably a few Guardsmen still around too tardy or sensible to have rejoined Braddick in the middle of a closing trap, and that I had a reputation to live up to, I squeezed off a few rounds from the storm bolter too. I failed to hit any of the scattering pathfinders, the explosive projectiles simply hissing over their heads due to the damaged pintle mount, but I was pretty sure I'd put them off their aim at least.

'Some good cover over there,' Jurgen said, doggedly sticking to the last order I'd given him, and completely disregarding Braddick's[1], which was fine by me. Another burst from both heavy and storm bolters was enough to shred the chain fence which, in happier times, was supposed to keep lowly civilians from trespassing on the hallowed rockcrete of the Guard garrison, and with a lurch which almost broke my spine we bounced over the masonry footings and onto the road beyond. Our gallant Salamander's tracks bit deep into the surface of the carriageway separating the perimeter of the barracks from an abandoned industrial facility, and Jurgen rammed the throttle lever as far forward as it would go. 'That smelting plant's still standing. Mostly.'

'Keep going,' I said. Now we were clear of the combat zone I saw

---

1. *Though an Imperial Guard soldier, and therefore obliged by regulation to follow the orders of a superior, Jurgen remained convinced that his position as the personal aide to a commissar was a* de facto *secondment to the Commissariat itself, removing him entirely from the chain of command, apart from on those occasions when he could see some advantage to being lost within it. Needless to say this was a position Cain was perfectly happy with, and few Guard officers would have been inclined to dispute the point.*

no reason to linger, and become a footnote in Braddick's Last Stand.

'Commissar Cain, respond,' the general's voice echoed in my comm-bead, as if in reproach to that fleeting thought. 'Are you there?'

'We're cut off from the bunker,' I told him, truthfully enough, as it would have been suicide to try fighting our way back to it though the rapidly deploying tau. 'The xenos have it completely surrounded.' Which may have been a slight exaggeration, but if it wasn't true by then it soon would be. Their preferred tactic when faced with a static defensive position was always to surround it, relying on the superior range and firepower of their weapons to wear down the defenders. The bloody business of actually taking an objective they preferred to palm off on their kroot vassals[1], which I could hardly blame them for, especially as the kroot seem to enjoy that kind of thing. 'I'm going to head for the southern enclave, and try to pull some effectives together before it's too late.'

Most of the units we had left were concentrated in the southern quarter of the city, which made it the best place to be so far as I was concerned; the more bodies I could put between me and the tau the better. With a bit of luck we'd be able to hold out long enough for Zyvan's task force to turn up and evacuate the survivors, which I was determined would include me, and if the worst came to the worst it would be easy enough to go to ground on my own more or less indefinitely. I hadn't forgotten any of the lessons I'd learned dodging orks on Perlia, and the tau would be far less inclined to waste time and resources hunting down stragglers who didn't do anything stupid to attract their attention, like shooting at them or blowing things up, than the greenskins had been.

'Good idea,' Braddick said, clearly believing that the situation meant I'd be bringing a relieving force back with me.

---

1. _A common misapprehension among Imperial citizens, who generally consider the relationship between the kroot, demiurg, and other races incorporated into the Tau Empire, and the tau themselves as something akin to that of the gretchin among orks: slaves or servants to do the dirty work their masters are unwilling to sully their hands with. In fact both the tau and their client races, which, let us not forget, includes a disturbingly high number of renegade humans, seem to consider them as equals; albeit the tau are clearly a little more equal than any of the others._

'Just hold out as long as you can,' I voxed back, not having the heart to disabuse him, and sure he'd do that anyway whatever I said. 'The Emperor protects.' Although, so far as I could see, He was going to have His work cut out keeping Braddick in one piece for much longer.

Come to that, He didn't seem to be doing that good a job for me either. Shadows were moving at the end of the street, too quick and fluid to identify, but some of them seemed uncomfortably big. All of a sudden the abandoned smeltery looked a good deal more attractive than it had done, but it was far too late to worry about that; whatever was lurking up the boulevard would have registered our approach by now, and be locking its weapons on our auspex trace as like as not.

'Hit the lights,' I told Jurgen, wrestling with the damaged pintle mount again, once more to no avail. Nothing was going to free the mechanism short of the benedictions of a tech-priest, and there's never one around when you actually need one.

'Right you are, sir,' my aide responded, and I squinted reflexively as the powerful spotlight kindled, the beam knifing erratically through the darkness in response to every jolt of our abused suspension. Then the breath seemed to solidify in my lungs, as the dancing ray of light picked out a cluster of vaguely humaniform figures, more than twice the height of a man. Dreadnoughts, or the tau equivalent at any rate: just as heavily armed as their Imperial counterparts, and a lot more manoeuvrable.

'Second wave's incoming,' I voxed to Braddick. If I was about to die, I supposed I might as well be remembered for some heroic last words. 'I'll delay them as long as I can.'

Which wasn't likely to be more than a second or two, especially as I hadn't actually said anything about trying to engage the towering battlesuits in combat. Attracting their attention just long enough for them to be sure I was heading for the horizon and not worth wasting the ammo on would be good enough for me.

'Can you give us an estimate of their numbers and disposition?' Braddick asked, determined to get his currency's worth out of my noble sacrifice, and I gritted my teeth. Clearly 'Lots, and surly,' wasn't going to be an acceptable answer. Throne alone knew who might be monitoring the vox-traffic, and if by some miracle I did get out of this with a whole skin, the last thing I needed was an auditory record of me appearing to panic and run for it popping up in time to prevent me enjoying the benefits of another boost to my fraudulent reputation. (Not that I've anything against panicking and running for it; on the contrary, it's worked for me every time. The trick is to not let anyone else realise that's what you're doing, otherwise you'll have all that tedious business of tribunals and potential firing squads to put up with afterwards[1].)

'Wait one,' I said, hoping to buy a little time, and hoping even more fervently that the next sound on the vox-record wasn't going to be an ominous burst of static followed by silence. I gestured to Jurgen. 'Get us off the street!'

'Very good, sir,' he responded, as phlegmatically as ever, and swung the vehicle hard over. A railgun round howled through the space we'd just vacated, the sonic boom of its passage shaking the air and making the Salamander rock on its suspension. I ducked, as he took us through the side of a warehouse without bothering to look for a door, the wall exploding around us in a shower of shattered brick as he rammed his way through it.

'Battlesuits,' I told Braddick, protecting my head from the blizzard of masonry as best I could, while Jurgen carried on demolishing interior walls in our headlong dash towards some semblance of safety. The searchlight beam had swept across the whole Crisis team just before they'd opened fire, and I tried to recall what I'd seen in as much detail as possible. Which wasn't much, if I'm honest, I'd been too busy ducking. 'A full squad, but there are probably more behind.' At least I thought I'd seen three of them, but they were hellish fast and agile, and in the dark it was hard to be sure. 'They've got railguns,' I added, as an afterthought. At least, the one which had shot at us did, and I wasn't about to go back for a look at the rest.

'Then we haven't got long,' Braddick concluded, remarkably calmly

---

1. *Probably a reference to the incident on Adumbria, where malicious accusations by another commissar led to a formal enquiry into Cain's conduct which, ironically, only added lustre to his reputation.*

under the circumstances. We both knew the hypervelocity projectiles would punch through the reinforced ferrocrete of the bunker like Jurgen through a meringue, and with an equal amount of scattered debris.

'I think we've shaken them, sir,' Jurgen said, giving me some good news at last, ramming a large wooden cargo door as he spoke. We plummeted about a metre from a raised loading dock, not even slowing, our spinning treads slamming into the rockcreted yard in a shrapnel burst of pulverised gravel. The Salamander's floor shot up to punch me in the face, driving the breath from my lungs, and I tasted blood, where my teeth had lacerated the inside of my cheek.

'Good,' I gasped, feeling the relatively minor discomfort a small price to pay for our deliverance; but of course I was speaking too soon. Hardly had I staggered to my feet again, leaning on the much-abused pintle mount for support, than one of the towering battlesuits landed right in front of us, shaking the ground with the impact of its arrival. My elevated perch in the rear of the Salamander brought my head almost level with the pilot's[1], and I flinched as a targeting beam swept across my face, blinding me for a moment.

'Hang on, sir!' Jurgen called, as though I'd been doing anything else for the last ten minutes, and triggered the weapon mounts. A hail of bolter rounds and a gout of promethium roared towards the giant warrior, but the pilot triggered its jump jets at the last possible instant, and it hopped nimbly over the devastating barrage like a child with a skipping rope.

Blinking my dazzled eyes clear, I tried to track the soaring silhouette with the storm bolter, but the mounting had seized up entirely by this time; which I suppose was hardly surprising, given the battering it had taken. Then I took in the battlesuit's trajectory with incredulous horror. 'Jurgen!' I yelled. 'Jump!'

Suiting the action to the word I scrambled out of the passenger compartment and leapt for my life, praying to the Throne to grant me

---

1. *Not quite true, as the pilot sits in the heavily armoured torso; but given the anthropomorphic design of the tau battlesuit, it's easy to forget this, and assume it's up in the head, like the princeps of a miniature Titan.*

a soft landing. I didn't get one, of course, the Emperor having more urgent business as usual, but Jurgen had slammed on the brakes to avoid colliding with our towering assailant, no doubt appreciating that the impact would break our necks however much damage it did to the battlesuit, so at least we were moving a lot slower than we had been. I struck the rockcrete of the yard no harder than required to crack a rib or two, which was uncomfortable enough, but I'd had worse, and felt that if I was well enough to complain about it I'd got off pretty lightly, all told.

An instant after I'd hit, the tau dreadnought landed squarely atop the Salamander, crushing it into the rockcrete with a squeal of rending metal as though it had been no more robust than a cardboard box. Rivulets of promethium gushed from the ruptured fuel and flamer tanks, spreading out around the crippled vehicle like blood from mortal wounds.

'Jurgen!' I called. 'Where are you?'

'Over here, sir.' My aide rolled to a sitting position, half hidden in the shadow of a wall a dozen metres away, and tried to haul himself upright, one hand pressed to the side of his head. 'I'll be right… right with…' Then his knees folded, and he slithered back down on his haunches. A dark stain was visible beneath his fingers, which admittedly was nothing new, but this one was spreading slowly; had it not been for his helmet, the impact of landing would probably have crushed his skull.

'Stay down!' I called to him, as though either of us had any choice in the matter. 'Just got to see off this pile of unsanctified scrap, then we'll get you to the medicae.' And right after that, I added under my breath, the necrons will take up flower arranging. I tapped where my comm-bead should have been, hoping to summon help, but just got an earful of finger for my pains; somewhere along the way the tiny vox-unit and I had parted company. We were on our own.

The tau battlesuit stepped back off the mashed remains of the expiring Salamander with one foot, leaving the other where it was, looking for all the world like a beast-hunter with a trophy, posing for a pict. Its head turned, scanning the yard, and I looked round frantically for some vestige of cover, only to find there wasn't one. I was surrounded by nothing but bare rockcrete, a sitting target.

I scrabbled for my sidearms, feeling better for the weight of the chainsword in my hand, even though against the heavily armoured battlesuit it would be worse than useless. Then the acrid odour of spilled promethium scratched my nostrils, and a desperate idea began to blossom, fertilised by panic. The laspistol in my other hand would barely scratch the thing's paint, but…

The looming figure raised an arm, a vicious-looking rotary cannon swinging towards me; even a single round from it would be enough to vaporise me where I stood. With no more time to think, I pulled the laspistol's trigger.

My aim was true, the las-bolt sparking off the sundered metal of the Salamander, although by this time there was so much promethium vapour in the air it hardly mattered where the round impacted. It detonated at once, a fireball boiling out from the wreck in all directions, close enough to shrivel my eyebrows. A wall of furnace heat arrived with the shockwave, slamming me back to the ground and sending my chainsword skittering off into the shadows. I hung on to the laspistol though, the augmetic fingers on my right hand slower to relinquish their grip, for which I was suitably grateful.

For a moment I dared to hope that my desperate gamble had paid off and that the battlesuit had been immolated in the explosion or, at the very least, damaged enough to discourage the pilot from pursuing us. But of course I'd reckoned without the jump jets. They kicked in at once, allowing the huge machine to ride the shockwave in a single balletic leap, with no more ill effects than a faint charring around the ankles.

I clambered to my feet once more, only to stagger again as the battlesuit crashed back to earth. This time I remained standing, however, my footing rendered no more unstable than during a typical drive with Jurgen, as the armoured giant plodded relentlessly towards me, shaking the ground with every stride. Raising my laspistol, I sent a desperate couple of ricochets bouncing off its torso plates, but didn't even manage to slow the thing.

Then, by the light of the burning Salamander, I finally saw a way
out of the trap, a second loading door further down the wall of the
warehouse, this time at ground level. Without another thought I
sprinted for it; but before I could get anywhere close the corrugated
metal sheet bulged and tore, ripped aside by another of the towering
machines as though it was no more substantial than a curtain. It too
began to plod unhurriedly towards me, and I retreated a few paces,
firing as I went, but for all the effect I was having I might just as well
have been throwing feathers at it. After a dozen or so steps I stumbled
against something yielding and almost fell, being brought up short
by the stout masonry wall behind it as a familiar odour assaulted my
nostrils.

'Run for it, sir. Don't mind me,' Jurgen slurred, already halfway to
unconsciousness.

'Not an option,' I assured him, certain that by now escape was
impossible. I raised my hands, and let the laspistol drop to the
rockcrete. Perhaps they wouldn't just gun us down out of hand, if
they thought we were harmless. At least we weren't dealing with
vicious brutes like the orks, or refined sadists like the eldar reavers, in
whose hands we'd be far better off dead anyway.

Then the targeting beam swept my face again, and I flinched, cursing,
wishing I'd chosen to go down fighting after all. At least that would
have left me with the illusion of possible escape right up to the end,
instead of the crushing certainty of imminent ignominious butchery.
I braced myself, hoping the Emperor would be in a good mood when
I arrived at the Golden Throne, or at least willing to listen to excuses.

'You are commissar hero Ciaphas Cain?' a voice asked, in halting
Gothic, the curious lisping accent of the tau amplified by an external
vox-system somewhere on the battlesuit facing me.

'I am,' I said, fighting to keep a sudden flare of hope from inflecting
my voice. If they wanted to talk, they weren't going to pull the trigger
right away, although I was damned if I could see that we had anything
to discuss. 'And you are?'

'Ui-Thiching, of the shas'ui ka'sui[1]. In the name of the Greater Good, we ask of you to convey a message to your fellows.'

Better and better. They clearly weren't about to shoot the messenger; I just had to hope Braddick didn't either[2].

'What message would that be?' I asked, not wanting to seem too eager. For all I knew they were recording this and the last thing I needed was to be accused of collaborating with the enemy to save my own neck.

'We wish the negotiation of a truce,' the tau told me, as though that were the most reasonable thing in the galaxy, just as they were about to snatch the entire planet out from under us regardless.

'A truce?' I repeated, not entirely willing to trust my own ears. 'Are you sure?'

'Completely,' the amplified voice assured me. 'Hostilities must cease at once on this world. The Greater Good demands it. For both our empires.'

---

1. *Literally 'battlesuit unit fortuitous gale,' no doubt one of the semi-formal honourific titles tau units acquire to commemorate notable successes on the battlefield.*

2. *Completely impossible, of course, as Imperial Guard officers, however senior, don't have the authority to execute a commissar; although I suppose Cain can be forgiven the impulse to indulge in some obvious wordplay.*

Editorial Note:

One of Cain's more annoying idiosyncrasies as a chronicler of events is his tendency to gloss over periods of time in which he feels nothing of interest to have happened from his singularly self-centred perspective. Just such an elision now occurs, picking up his narrative after a gap of several weeks.

I have accordingly inserted the following extract, which I hope will go some way towards making up the obvious deficiency.

From *The Crusade and After: A Military History of the Damocles Gulf*, by Vargo Royz, 058.M42.

THE TAU'S OFFER of a truce was regarded with a fair degree of suspicion at first, not least by Commissar Cain, to whom it had been delivered. Nevertheless, with the Imperial forces poised on the brink of annihilation, the defenders had little option but to accept it.

Accordingly, when the relief flotilla arrived, accompanied by a hastily-assembled diplomatic mission and no less a personage than the Lord General himself, they found General Braddick in uncontested control of Peakhaven, to no one's greater surprise than his own.

Before long the Quadravidia garrison had been reinforced by the new arrivals[1], of sufficient strength to deter all but the most determined of assaults. But such a precaution scarcely seemed needed, as the tau remained behind the lines to which they had withdrawn immediately upon the declaration of a ceasefire.

Thus it was, with a fair degree of suspicion, that negotiations began, and the tau's motives for such an unexpected move became clear.

---

1. *Primarily composed of Vostroyan and Harakoni regiments, supplemented by others raised from neighbouring worlds.*

THREE

'THEY'RE UP TO something,' I said, delighted to feel the deckplates of an Imperial vessel underfoot once again. The fact that it was Zyvan's flagship, and therefore the most heavily armed ship in the flotilla, only added a little zest to my relief at finally making it off Quadravidia in one piece.

'Of course they are,' Zyvan agreed. He'd met me personally as I'd stepped off the shuttle in the hangar bay, much to my surprise; but it was pleasant to see him again, and he seemed to feel the same about me, although the purpose of my visit was far from social. 'They've said nothing else since they first spoke to you?'

'Nothing about their reasons for calling a truce,' I said, raising my voice a little over the clatter the boots of his personal guard were making as they trotted ahead of us, clearing the corridor like a braid-bedecked dozer blade. Light from the overhead luminators ricocheted from their polished helms and hellguns, held ready for use despite the fact that we were among friends. I doubted that the captain and crew were all that happy about heavily armed Guardsmen waving guns about in their vessel, but protocol demanded it, and I for one was hardly going to complain, given the number of assassination attempts Zyvan had already survived[1]. 'Just the usual bickering about the details.' Details which Braddick and his staff had dealt with, leaving me free to seek more congenial diversions. 'I'm afraid I can't fill you in on those, I'm a bit behind on the paperwork.'

'How is your man, by the way?' Zyvan asked, as we reached the door to his personal quarters. 'Recovering well, I trust?'

'I'll convey your good wishes,' I told him. Jurgen was probably still sulking about being left behind, but the medicae had recommended light duties for a while, and being jolted around in a shuttle would hardly have helped his convalescence. Besides, I wanted him back in the bunker, so I'd know at once if Braddick did anything rash, like turning his newly-acquired firepower on the tau while their backs were turned. Throne knew, I'd be tempted in his shoes.

'I heard what you did, going back for him like that. Not many men would,' Zyvan said, leading the way into his state room while the storm troopers took up position outside to guard the corridor.

'He'd have done the same for me,' I said, truthfully enough. Evidently the tau diplomats had been talking to their Imperial counterparts already, and another spurious tale of my gallantry was doing the rounds. I settled into a comfortably padded seat, and accepted the goblet of amasec which Zyvan's steward had already poured for me with a nod of thanks; it never hurt to get on well with the servants, particularly in my covert avocation as Amberley's eyes and ears. I'd gleaned quite a few nuggets of information that way over the years, to my own benefit as well as hers.

'No doubt,' Zyvan said dryly, taking my modesty for granted, and firmly cementing the story in his mind as he did so. He accepted his own drink, and the steward bustled out, closing the door with a satisfyingly resonant thud. No chance of anything we said being overheard now. 'I'd like you to sit in on the initial meeting.'

'I could do that,' I agreed, readily enough. The Commissariat would expect a report anyway, and if I didn't agree to be their observer, one of the other commissars attached to the task force would be handed

---

1. *A couple due to Cain's direct, if reluctant, intervention, which no doubt went some way towards explaining the warmth with which the Lord General regarded him.*

the job. I hadn't met many, but most of the ones I'd conversed with would cheerfully urge a full-scale invasion of Quadravidia if the tau didn't pack up and leave, a course of action which was bound to end badly. Besides, I'd had dealings with the tau and their vassals before, and couldn't quite shake the feeling that something wasn't right about all this; when the other boot dropped, I wanted to be there to hear it.

'That would be most helpful,' another voice put in, and I turned, to find a face I recognised; narrow, serious, and sporting a faint scar inflicted on a night I'd rather have forgotten.

'Donali.' I rose to shake hands, both surprised and pleased to see the senior diplomat I'd first met on Gravalax, the same night as Amberley, some sixty years before. 'You're heading the delegation?'

'So it seems.' He smoothed a non-existent crease from the front of his immaculate robe, regarding me with the air of calm deliberation I recalled so clearly. 'You look well. Surprisingly so, for a man in your profession.'

'I've been lucky,' I said, with rather more sincerity than I'm used to. 'And I could say the same about you.' His hair was a lot greyer around the temples than I remembered, but then so was mine; hardly surprising, given the number of times something had tried to kill me since the last time we'd spoken.

'I'd say we've all been lucky,' Donali said. 'If you hadn't been on Quadravidia, the tau might well have decided against opening negotiations.'

'Me?' I said, in honest astonishment. 'I'm sorry, but I don't see what I've got to do with it.'

Donali settled into a seat between Zyvan and myself, and reached for the decanter the servant had left on the polished obsidian table, laid siege to by the chairs. 'The tau still remember your part in resolving the Gravalax incident,' he said.

'Do they?' I asked, an uncomfortable chill overtaking me. The stand-off there had ended in humiliation for the xenos, and if they were still carrying a grudge about it, I'd have to start looking over my shoulder.

'Indeed. They speak very highly of your integrity, and your

commitment to the Greater Good of the Imperium.' Donali sipped at his drink, at just the right moment to mask any facial expression accompanying the words.

'So they had every confidence that you would relay their message, and get someone in authority to listen to it,' Zyvan added.

'Couldn't they just have voxed?' I asked, 'instead of chasing me across half the city?'

'At that point they had no idea it was you,' Donali said. 'Fortunately their vox intercepts had made them aware of your presence somewhere among the Imperial forces, and the on-board cogitator of the battlesuit you encountered had instructions to look for an officer who matched the facial features of an old pict from Gravalax.'

'I see,' I said, recalling the targeter beam sweeping across my face, and trying not to think about how close we'd come to the xenos machine spirit having nothing recognisable left to read. 'But voxing would still have been easier.'

'I'm not sure General Braddick would have listened,' Zyvan said dryly, and I had to concede the point. By the time I'd got back to the bunker, Braddick had concluded that the sudden cessation of the tau bombardment was the prelude to an all-out assault, and it had taken a fair amount of persuasion, not to mention shameless trading on my inflated reputation, to argue him out of sallying forth in a glorious do-or-die, pre-emptive counter-attack; which would have had precious little of the 'do' about it, given the forces ranged against him.

'So where are we supposed to be meeting them?' I asked. 'Peakhaven, or somewhere in the occupied zone?' Given the choice I'd have opted for the latter, as the tau held most of the temperate areas and I'd got heartily sick of the bracing mountain air in the capital by now. Besides, it never hurts to get a good look at your enemy's resources while they're not shooting at you. I had fewer qualms about venturing into the stronghold of the foe than I normally would, as, by and large, the tau can be trusted to observe the terms of a truce; they're devious little buggers right enough, but hoisting a white flag to lure you into a crossfire doesn't sit well with them[1].

'Neither,' Donali said, to my surprise. 'The Lord General has expressed some disquiet about the opportunities for intelligence gathering afforded by a tau presence within the Imperial zone, and my opposite number from the water caste[2] has similar concerns.' Which, as I'd been considering precisely that myself, I could hardly quibble with.

'Where, then?' Zyvan asked, leaning forward to pour himself a refill.

'One of the abandoned orbital docks,' Donali said. 'We can secure it easily enough, and it's not as though it's needed for cargo handling at the moment[3].'

'Works for me,' I said, assessing the pros and cons, and settling instantly on the major advantage from my point of view. If the whole thing went ploin-shaped and the war kicked off again, I'd be sitting comfortably above it for once.

'Me too,' Zyvan said. 'I'll ask the Navy to station a warship alongside then we can blow the whole thing to scrap at the first sign of treachery.' An idea I liked the sound of a lot less, but Donali was already nodding in agreement.

'The tau have already indicated that they're taking a similar precaution.'

Both men looked at me, and I plastered a wry grin on my face, wondering if perhaps I should find some pressing reason to palm the job off on one of my commissarial colleagues after all but even before

---

1. *There are, indeed, few if any instances on record of out and out treachery by the tau in their dealings with other races, although they're not above a little self-serving confusion about the exact terms of whatever arrangement has been come to.*

2. *The tau who specialise in diplomacy and administrative tasks, maintaining social cohesion within the Tau Empire, and overseeing the smooth integration of conquered species. The closest Imperial equivalent would be a cross between the Administratum and the Ecclesiarchy, although the caste's responsibilities and remit go far beyond anything which that would imply, touching almost every aspect of life among the septs.*

3. *Word of the tau invasion had spread quickly, and the dozens of civilian vessels which would normally have arrived or departed each day changed their routes to avoid the Quadravidia system. Their new paths through the warp were, of course, far slower, and the resulting economic disruption was to continue rippling through the sector for over a decade.*

the thought had time to form fully, I dismissed it. Zyvan and the tau both wanted me there, and if I pulled out, chances were the xenos would pick up their ball and go home, we'd all start shooting at each other again, and I'd get the blame for snatching defeat from the jaws of compromise. 'That should keep everyone honest,' I said instead, resolving to make sure I knew where the saviour pods were before anyone had a chance to open their mouths.

IN THE EVENT I didn't need to make sure of an escape route, as everyone was on their best behaviour; although that didn't stop me from doing so anyway. By this stage in my career, finding the quickest way out of any new place I found myself in had become second nature, which rather accounted for the fact that I was still around to be paranoid.

Both warships assigned to what was euphemistically referred to as 'diplomatic protection duty' were stationed several kilometres from the orbital, due to the high concentration of debris still clustered around it. The cloud of detritus was so dense, in fact, that nothing much larger than an Aquila could approach the void station without being pounded to pieces; accordingly, as we approached the huge, and somewhat battered structure, our transport bobbed and weaved like an inebriate, as the pilot was forced to make constant course corrections to avoid a collision.

'That'll take some clearing up,' Jurgen commented, peering through what seemed to me under the circumstances to be a pitifully thin sheet of armourglass at the spiralling chunks of jagged metal beyond. Many were rimed with frost, where some residual atmosphere had frozen around them, and I tried not to think too hard about the explosive decompression that had undoubtedly accompanied its deposition. Finding myself morbidly wondering how many of the motes of flotsam catching the light of the sun rising from beyond the edge of the world below were the cadavers of those too slow to have reached the closing bulkhead doors, I nodded, hoping a little conversation would distract me[1].

---

1. *An uncharacteristic moment of introspection; presumably he was reminded of his own near-death in this manner during the First Siege of Perlia.*

'I imagine it will,' I agreed. I'd been in two minds about bringing him, but was grateful by now that I had. His recovery was almost complete, and if the niggling little voice in the back of my head was right and the tau were up to something underhand, there was no one I'd rather have watching my back. Besides, he'd been grumpy enough about being left behind for my little chat with Zyvan and Donali; another perceived slight would have prolonged the sulk for weeks. 'But at least it'll make it hard for anything to sneak up on us.'

'Anything big,' Jurgen replied, after a moment's reflection. 'But it'd make it really easy to slip one of those drone things through without anyone noticing. Auspex'll be well clogged.'

'Quite so,' I said, not best pleased to have been handed something else to fret about. Offhand, I couldn't see any reason the tau would bother to do something like that, of course, but then I suppose that would have been the point. 'Can you see the void station yet?'

Jurgen shook his head. 'I thought it was on your side.'

'Your side was my side a minute ago,' I reminded him, just as the pilot tucked us into another roll, this time around a larger than usual piece of junk, which looked as though it had once been a pressure vessel from a fabricatory, or possibly a storage tank for liquids of some kind. Either way, it was longer than our Aquila, and eclipsed the sun for a moment. When the light returned it was from a new and unexpected angle, dazzling me. As I blinked my eyes clear, the orbital finally came into view.

I'd seen plenty of similar structures over the years, of course, although since our crippled starship had glanced off the anchorage above Nusquam Fundumentibus in its headlong plunge to the surface, the sight of one always brought with it a momentary surge of unease. I waited for the unwelcome sensation to pass off as it usually did, but the sense of disquiet refused to leave me, and after a while I realised it wasn't going to. Not until I had a much better idea of what was going on, anyway.

'It's a bit of a mess,' Jurgen said, unconscious as always of the irony; but on this occasion I had to concede that he had a point. The tau had attempted to board the orbital during the first wave of their initial attack, hoping to deny the SDF the chance to resupply and refit there[1], but had underestimated the defenders' resolve: vastly outgunned, and faced with certain annihilation, the captain of the last surviving gunboat rammed the primary docking arm, reducing both it and his vessel to high-velocity shrapnel and taking a respectable tally of tau Mantas with him[2]. The resulting mess had forced both sides to abandon the structure, although I gathered that the tau had been making diligent efforts to repair it prior to their unexpected offer of a ceasefire.

As our shuttle drifted closer, the full magnitude of the damage the void station had suffered became progressively clearer. What had appeared from a distance to be nothing more than minor blemishes on the hull gradually grew, revealing themselves to be vast chasms torn or burned through the sheathing metal, or blown out by internal detonations. Through these jagged rents the equally ragged edges of interior decks could be seen, the damage going deeper than our running lights would penetrate.

Uncountable firefly sparks moving in and around these stricken areas puzzled me for a moment, until, as we approached the small lighted region on one edge of the city-sized structure where warmth and air awaited us, one drifted close enough for me to recognise it. It was a smooth-sided drone, of the kind I'd become all too familiar with on the battlefield, although this particular specimen was equipped with a welding torch instead of armament; it floated past the viewport, followed a moment later by a couple more, carrying girders and flat sheets of construction material in articulated manipulator arms.

'That must be where we're going,' I concluded a few moments later, spotting a bay door cranking open to admit our approaching Aquila. The habitable zone stood out clearly now, enough to discern a few details even from this distance: the warm, golden lights blazing from viewports and docking bays standing in stark and poignant contrast

---

1. *Though an undoubted goal of the invasion fleet, it was probably a secondary one. Tau planetary assaults make great use of assets in fixed orbit, and, more likely, they hoped to use the orbital as a gun platform, and to speed up the deployment of their ground forces by using it as a staging post.*

2. *For a fuller account of this incident, see Royz, chapter 17.*

to the dark, dead bulk of the station to which it clung. Welcoming as it looked, I still felt a shiver of apprehension. Smooth, curving, tau-constructed surfaces clung to the solid Imperial structure beneath like fungus to a decaying tree trunk, where the xenos had repaired and replaced the original architecture, tainting it with their inhuman presence. Clearly they'd intended to stay, claiming the entire orbital for their own, before whatever it was they were concerned about had prompted them to sue for peace on the very threshold of victory.

There was little time for such dispiriting reflection, however, as before long we were on our final approach, the great portal looming up to swallow our tiny shuttle. The hangar beyond was absurdly large for so modest a vessel, it having been intended for heavy lift shuttles capable of lugging a Titan around[1], and able to accommodate several at once to boot, so the Aquila seemed dwarfed by the cavernous space surrounding us. A few moments later the hull reverberated to the clang of our landing gear making contact with the deck, and the whine of our engines died away.

So great a volume took several minutes to pressurise, and I spent the time gazing at our surroundings as best I could though the haze of frost which formed instantly across the viewport as the thickening atmosphere met a hull chilled to near absolute zero by the vacuum of space. The tau renovations didn't seem to have spread as far as the interior of this particular hangar, and I took heart from the familiar sturdy girderwork surrounding us, the oppressive sense of wrongness I'd felt at all those smooth curves clinging to the surface of the station receding a little. There was even an Imperial aquila dominating the far wall, its spreading wings poised to enfold the vast chamber in the protection of the Emperor.

About a dozen other shuttles stood in serried ranks nearby, the Imperial ones close to our own, while the unmistakable rounded hulls of their tau counterparts were stationed on the opposite side, ironically appearing to receive the benediction of the Imperial icon behind them. Through the gradually melting rime obscuring the viewport I could see movement, which at first I ascribed to vacuum-hardened

---

1. *Big, certainly, but hardly* that *big.*

servitors tending the air pumps, or perhaps simply wandering vaguely in search of the cargoes they used to lug about. But as the temperature rose and the armourglass cleared, their true nature became apparent. Void-suited Guardsmen, their heraldry and the hellguns they carried marking them out as members of Zyvan's retinue.

'The Lord General must be here already,' I remarked, confirming my guess almost at once as I caught sight of his personal shuttle, half-hidden behind an adjacent Arvus, and Jurgen nodded.

'And he don't trust the xenos any more than we do,' he added, with every sign of approval.

'I think that's mutual,' I said, catching a glimpse of similar movement among the xenos shuttles across the wide expanse of clear decking between us. 'They've posted guards too.' The armoured figures seemed unusually squat for tau, and a moment of further observation revealed the reason. 'Demiurg, by the look of them.' Which finally confirmed the long-standing rumour of a contingent of the blocky xenos accompanying the tau fleet.

'Doesn't matter who they are,' Jurgen said, reducing the political complexities to their most basic as readily as he usually did. 'If they get in the way they're kroot fodder.'

'Quite so,' I said, hoping it would turn out to be that easy. Then the hiss of the pressure seal breaking informed me that the atmosphere was now dense enough to breathe, and that it was time to disembark. I adjusted the angle of my cap to one I hoped my reception party would consider appropriately heroic, and began to descend the ramp.

FOUR

Outside the confines of the shuttle, the hangar seemed bigger than ever, a bleak metal plain stretching into the distance for roughly a kilometre[1], unrelieved by anything other than the occasional protruding fuel line or deactivated loader. The residual chill, which had seeped in along with the vacuum accompanying our arrival, hardly made the place seem any more welcoming, although Jurgen seemed happy enough with being able to see every breath we exhaled.

After exchanging salutes and a few words with the Guardsmen we'd observed through the Aquila's viewport, my aide and I began to trudge towards the hatchway they'd indicated, leaving them and their opposite numbers to glower at one another across the echoing void.

Even though I knew there was little risk of active hostilities breaking out before we reached it, the veteran storm troopers assigned to Zyvan's personal guard being far too disciplined to start anything, I must confess to feeling a distinct sense of relief as we approached the

---

1. *Almost certainly an exaggeration for effect, although it's possible,* pace *his earlier remarks about the size of the vessels intended to use it, that he was simply misjudging the scale of his surroundings. A space that size could hardly be opened to vacuum and repressurised as regularly as required for commerce without considerable difficulty.*

airlock set into the wall ahead of us[1]. The demiurg could be touchy, especially if the tau weren't around to keep an eye on them, and standing around in the open made me feel dangerously exposed even at the best of times.

The temperature rose to more comfortable levels almost as soon as the hangarside door thudded closed behind us, which improved my mood no end, although my renewed equanimity lasted no longer than the time it took for the further door to open. Instead of the solid metal bulkheads I'd been expecting, the walls of the corridor beyond were of smooth, blue-white polymer, reflecting the pale refulgence of tau luminators. Clearly this part of the station was firmly in enemy hands.

'Commissar Cain?' A young woman in a pale-grey kirtle was waiting for me, an elaborately braided scalplock reaching halfway down her back. If anything, her appearance was even more disconcerting than the decor. 'The other delegates are waiting for you in the conference suite.' Her Gothic was flawless, though marred by the peculiar lisp with which the tau inflected it.

'Then I must apologise for my tardiness,' I replied, masking my discomfiture with the greatest of ease. If nothing else, I've had plenty of practice of doing that over the years. In truth, though, I was profoundly shaken. I'd known intellectually, of course, that the tau had annexed a number of human worlds in the last couple of centuries, and that their inhabitants had embraced the insidious creed of the so-called Greater Good, but I'd never thought to meet one of the heretics in the flesh, unless it was at the business end of a chainsword.

'No apology is required,' the woman said, with a courteous inclination of her head. She was damn good at her job, I had to give her that. She hadn't even blinked at her first sight of Jurgen[2]. 'Please follow me.'

---

1. *Enabling personnel to enter or leave while the hangar was decompressed, to speed up the arrival or departure of traffic.*

2. *Probably because the humans assimilated by the tau generally regard Imperials as uncouth barbarians, and she would have expected all Imperial Guardsmen to be like that.*

'With pleasure,' I assured her, with rather more gallantry than accuracy, as I fell into step at her elbow. Were the tau hoping to put us at our ease by her presence, or was it supposed to rattle us, leaving us more inclined to make an error? Either way, I was damned if I'd give them the satisfaction of reacting in any way other than the appearance of perfect calm. 'May I present my aide, Gunner Jurgen?'

'Of course.' She nodded at him, as though I'd just introduced an item of furniture. 'Pleased to make your acquaintance.'

'And you are?' I asked, convinced now that she was as practised a dissembler as I was.

'Au'lys Devrae, Facilitator of External Relations.'

'Tau personal name, Imperial family one,' I said. 'Interesting combination.'

'Quite common where I come from,' she assured me, with a smile most men would have taken for genuine. 'A blend of both, to remind us of the Greater Good.'

'And where would that be?' I asked, trying not to sound as though I meant to earmark it for virus bombing. Clearly her home world was well past due for liberating, although whether a population where heresy had taken such firm root could ever be guided back to the light of the Emperor seemed a moot point to me.

'Ka'ley'ath,' she said, before apprehending the name meant nothing to me. 'Our ancestors called it Downholm[1],' she added helpfully.

'Still doesn't ring any bells,' I admitted. While we'd been talking, we'd progressed deep into the heart of the station, finding the same patchwork of tau and Imperial systems wherever we went, which I suppose applied to Au'lys too.

'It's a big empire,' she said, failing to take offence, and provoking the first genuine smile from me; but I suppose most of its denizens must have been ignorant of just how small and insignificant the tau holdings were compared to the scale of the Imperium, or they would

---

1. *One of the Imperial worlds whose annexation led to the Damocles Gulf Crusade; after a quarter of a millennium, it was hardly surprising the population had become as thoroughly assimilated as it appears here.*

never have dared to challenge us in the first place[1]. 'Just through here.' She gestured to a doorway, no different to my eyes than any of the others we'd passed, apart from some inscription in the blocky, rounded sigils of the tau alphabet.

'You're not joining us for the briefing?' I asked, and the woman shook her head.

'I'm no warrior,' she told me, with a hint of amusement. 'I happened to be on my way up here, so I offered to escort you.'

'For the Greater Good,' I said dryly, but she only nodded, either missing the sarcasm or choosing to ignore it.

'In a small way,' she agreed. 'But I was also curious to meet some of our kindred from beyond the empire. There are stories, of course, but you never really know how true they are.'

'Then I hope we lived up to your expectations,' I said, doing my best to hide my amusement.

'You certainly did,' she assured me, although for some reason she seemed to be looking at Jurgen as she spoke, then she ambled away down the corridor without so much as a backward glance.

'Heretic,' Jurgen muttered, the minute she was out of earshot, fingering the butt of his lasgun as though tempted to use it.

'Quite,' I agreed, envying him his uncomplicated response to things. The encounter had disconcerted me more than a little, and I still couldn't shake the conviction that that had been precisely the point. I took a deep breath, adjusting my face, and approached the door Au'lys had indicated. 'Come on. Let's find out what all this is about.'

Au'LYS HAD CALLED the room a conference suite, but it was like none I'd ever been in before. There were aspects of it I recognised, of course, like the softly glowing hololith display suspended in the air, but the image inside it was crystal sharp, instead of wavering like the

---

1. *A matter of some debate among the xenopsychologists of the Ordo Xenos, some of whom hold to Cain's opinion, while others assert that the upper echelons of the tau are perfectly aware of the vast disparity between our two powers, but remain convinced of their ultimate victory regardless. Quite why any would be so deluded as to think that is beyond me, but it's certainly true that most denizens of their empire have a faith in the Greater Good no less strong than our own in His Divine Majesty.*

ones I was used to, and the edges formed a perfect sphere, instead of hazing away in a diffuse blob. It took me a moment to pick out the projection unit from among the other mechanica ranged about the room, as there was no sign of the tangle of power cables and optical links I would have expected, nor of any tech-priests ministering to it. The hololiths I was used to needed constant adjustment, anointing, and the occasional devotional kick to remain focused. It also didn't help that everything looked the same: flat, glossy surfaces mounted at an angle in rounded lecterns, with glowing runes appearing and disappearing on them pretty much at random.

The biggest surprise was the absence of a table, which would have formed the focal point of any Imperial conference chamber. Instead, it seemed, we were expected to perch on round, padded seats, which were scattered around the carpet like fungus erupting from a lawn. About a dozen of these were occupied, by roughly equal numbers of humans and tau, with about half as many again left vacant. All the humans I could see, sitting or standing around the periphery, wore Imperial garb, so I assumed any other turncoats among the xenos contingent were being kept tactfully out of sight.

Leaving Jurgen to join Zyvan's bodyguard, and investigate the refreshment table on my behalf, I claimed a seat between Donali and the Lord General, who smiled at my attempt to perch on the blasted thing without slithering off.

'They're comfortable enough, once you get used to them,' Zyvan assured me, before wobbling a bit himself, and glancing sardonically at Donali. 'So I'm told.'

The diplomat, of course, looked perfectly at ease, but since he'd spent half his life liaising with the tau, he'd had plenty of time to get used to their peculiar taste in furnishings. He inclined his head in greeting. 'Commissar. We were beginning to think you'd got lost.'

'I had an excellent guide,' I assured him. 'Au'lys Devrae. I take it you've met?'

'Our paths have crossed,' Donali said blandly.

'And you never thought to mention there were human traitors among the invasion fleet?' I asked, perhaps a little more bluntly than was polite. This was evidently news to Zyvan, as his eyebrows rose quizzically, and he gazed at the diplomat in a fashion most men would have found intimidating to say the least.

'She isn't attached to the fleet,' Donali explained. 'I gather there are humans under arms among the empire's forces, just as there are vespid, kroot, and others, but they wouldn't be deployed against the Imperium[1]. They fear the resulting bad feeling would impede efforts to find a diplomatic solution here.'

'To say the least,' I agreed. The abhorrence most Guardsmen felt for traitors and heretics would make it almost impossible to rein them in.

'But there are humans here?' Zyvan persisted.

Donali nodded. 'They call themselves Facilitators. Not an exact translation of the tau phrase *ku'ten vos'kla*[2], but close enough. They move in after a world's been annexed, helping what's left of the local authorities to rebuild the infrastructure, and nudging everything towards promoting the idea of the Greater Good.'

'So if Devrae's already here, the tau must have thought Quadravidia was in the bag,' I concluded.

'Wrapped up, and ready to hand to the ethereals,' Donali confirmed.

'Which rather begs the question of why they changed their minds,' Zyvan said.

'Looks like we're about to find out,' I said, as a flurry of activity near the door caught my attention. A tau in an ornately decorated robe, its intricate intertwinings of multicoloured thread no doubt an indication of his status for those able to decode them, was just entering the room, surrounded by a retinue of lackeys thick enough to obscure most of him from view. Many of them clutched thin, flat devices I assumed to be data-slates, and all glanced in our direction with varying degrees of curiosity, apprehension, and disdain. None of them had anything which looked like a weapon, but I knew better than to take that at face value. 'Our host has arrived.'

Donali nodded. 'Someone senior from the water caste. Not sure

---

1. *Not entirely true, but such clashes are rare, and confined almost exclusively to Imperial invasions of tau worlds with a substantial human element among the population.*

2. *Literally 'those who guide wisely.'*

who, but a fast courier boat arrived in-system last night. I'm told they've brought the latest information with them.'

'But not, I presume, what that information is,' Zyvan said sourly.

Donali shook his head. 'The water caste like to keep the cards in their hands hidden for as long as they can,' he said.

I turned, leaning as far as I dared on my precarious seat, trying to get a better view of the half-hidden diplomat, but just as his face was about to emerge from the scrum the familiar figure and odour of Jurgen loomed up in front of me, blotting out what little I could see of the approaching delegation. 'They've got tanna[1], sir,' he said, in pleased surprise, handing me a delicately worked tea bowl brimming with the fragrant infusion. For want of anything better to do, I took it and sipped, savouring the delicate flavour[2] of the drink.

'I remembered your fondness for that particular beverage,' a tau voice told me, and I rose to my feet, extending a hand in greeting. If I'm honest, I hadn't recognised the sound of it, all tau vocal cords mangling Gothic in pretty much the same way to my ears, but I never forget a face that's nearly got me killed.

'El'hassai,' I said, the sixty years since I'd last seen the tau diplomat falling away like so many days the moment I got a clear sight of him. No doubt one of his own kind would have detected signs of aging, Throne knows I'd acquired more than my own share, but he looked pretty much the same to me. 'I'm pleased to see you so well.'

'And I you,' El'hassai responded politely, shaking the proffered hand just gingerly enough to let me know he hadn't forgotten the augmetic fingers lurking beneath my glove, before turning to Donali. 'Erasmus. It's been far too long a time.'

'It has indeed,' Donali said levelly, although I'd wager he was as surprised as I was to be greeted by our old sparring partner from Gravalax.

'Lord General,' El'hassai went on, not missing a beat. 'A great pleasure to meet you at last.'

---

1. *A Valhallan beverage, for which Cain had a particular and inexplicable liking.*

2. *Though many adjectives spring to mind concerning the flavour of tanna, 'delicate' is not one of them. It's like describing a Baneblade as 'dainty.'*

'No doubt.' Zyvan inclined his head courteously, his impatience manifest. 'I look forward to hearing what you have to say.' Like me, he'd spent many years cultivating a bluff, no-nonsense public face, which robbed his bluntness of any implied offence; or at least it would have to any Imperial citizen familiar with his reputation. No point in leaving anything to chance, so I stuck my oar in too, diverting the tau's attention as quickly as possible, in case that aspect of the Lord General's personality had somehow been omitted from the briefing slate[1].

'I must confess, I'm curious too,' I said, sipping the tanna again, with a fine show of appreciation for our host's thoughtfulness. 'Especially since you roped me in as your messenger boy.'

'Hardly that,' El'hassai assured me, although I wasn't fluent enough in tau body language to tell if I was being patronised or not. From what I remembered of him, his good opinion of me was genuine enough (I'd saved his life, so it damn well ought to have been), though, so I gave him the benefit of the doubt. 'But your presence was a fortuitous coincidence we were happy to take advantage of.'

'Any time,' I assured him blandly, adding 'but I still think they could just have picked up the bloody vox,' *sotto voce* to Zyvan and Donali as the tau diplomat wandered away towards the hololith. Neither had time to reply, although Donali made an interesting choking noise in the depths of his goblet.

'Thank you for your attendance,' El'hassai said, turning to face the room, his voice cutting easily across it. The murmur of conversation died away to an expectant silence, broken only by the faint humming of the recirculators, and the rather less faint sound of Jurgen's jaws making short shrift of the finger food on the side table. 'No doubt our offer of a truce has been cause of a fair amount of speculation,' at which point he glanced in the direction of the Imperial contingent in a manner which, in a human, I could only describe as arch, 'but I'm sure you'll agree our reasons for it are sound.'

---

1. *Most unlikely; the water caste making a habit of preparing detailed psychological appraisals of anyone their diplomats are liable to come into contact with as a matter of course. Then again, they appeared to believe Cain's reputation was entirely genuine, so were clearly capable of being misdirected on occasion.*

'I might, if you ever got round to telling us what they were,' Zyvan muttered. Then his expression changed, as an image appeared in the hololith. 'Emperor almighty!'

'And all His saints,' I added, feelingly. The image was crystal clear, almost as though the horror it depicted was present in the room with us, although if it had been the chamber would have needed to be bigger than the entire orbital. Leprous hide thicker than the armour of a battleship, pocked with ineffectual weapons fire, loomed up at us out of the depths of space, spinning below our vantage point like a biological moon. Beyond the horizon of chitin, other, massive creatures of the same monstrous ilk swam through the void, surrounded by clouds of lesser organisms too numerous to count.

'A tyranid fleet,' Zyvan said, raising his voice to address the room, although the sudden eruption of gasps, murmurs, and muttered prayers to the Emperor among the Imperial delegation made it abundantly clear that we'd all recognised it for what it was. He indicated the larger bioships. 'Kraken and escorts.'

'Mostly,' El'hassai said, in remarkably even tones. 'The large one in the foreground would appear to be a leviathan, although the image we have of it is only partial.'

I stared at it, trying to take in the full scale of the horror before me, like a mountain made flesh. Or, given its environment, an asteroid might be a more apposite comparison. My mind flashed back to the burning, dying thing I'd glimpsed in the midst of the eruption on Nusquam Fundumentibus, where we'd been forced to sacrifice an entire city to kill a crippled cousin of this monstrous thing; that had seemed huge enough, and I'd seen only a fraction of its mass.

'Where did this come from?' I asked, realising as soon as I'd spoken just how many ways so imprecise a question could be misinterpreted, but El'hassai seemed to grasp my meaning well enough.

'This is the last transmission from an exploration vessel, lost in the Coreward Marches[1] a little less than two cyr ago.'

---

1. *No area in or around the Damocles Gulf has this Imperial designation, so it seems El'hassai was translating the name from its tau equivalent. Since anywhere coreward of T'au would be on or near their border with the Imperium, this is hardly much help in fixing the location; if he was more precise, Cain doesn't mention it.*

'About eighteen months,' Donali murmured, for the benefit of those of us unfamiliar with the tau calendar. 'Twenty at the most.'

'And you've only just got it?' I asked, trying not to sound too sceptical.

El'hassai nodded, a gesture he seemed to have picked up from his prolonged contact with humans[1]; I remembered him doing the same thing on Gravalax. 'The vessel launched a courier drone[2] shortly before it was destroyed,' he said. 'The images you're seeing now were uploaded to it in real time.'

I watched with horrified fascination as innumerable tiny pustules swelled up on the body of the bloated horror beneath us, then burst, spewing clouds of spinning organisms into the void. Thousands upon thousands of them, their hardened carapaces protecting them from the cold and vacuum of space, fangs and talons and bioweapons poised for massacre. I'd faced innumerable horrors spawned from the tyranid hive fleets myself, but never anything so hideous as these: half warrior, half boarding pod, all implacable killing machine. Some were carrying creatures I recognised – genestealers, termagants and raveners for the most part, encysted behind semi-transparent membranes – while others seemed to be more than sufficiently lethal on their own accounts.

'Why don't they just fire the main engines?' I asked; if I'd been the tau captain I'd be halfway to the Ghoul Stars by now.

'According to the telemetry recovered, the engines were at full power by this point,' El'hassai said soberly. 'We conjecture that the vessel had been immobilised in some fashion; the stresses on the hull would be consistent with constricting tentacles or gripping claws.'

Zyvan nodded. 'Seen that a few times,' he agreed. 'They ram a ship, latch on, and send in the killers.'

The onrushing swarm was filling the hololith by now, each detail

---

1. *Or cultivated to put them at their ease during negotiations.*

2. *Not to be confused with the small drones commonly used by the fire caste and others, these are essentially self-guided torpedoes, just large enough to hold a databank, a gravitic drive, and a machine spirit to pilot it; lacking astropaths, this is the only way for exploration vessels to remain in contact with their home worlds, other than taking full-sized courier ships along for the ride.*

more ghastly than the last, and I must confess to a feeling of relief as the image finally disappeared in a burst of static.

'At this point,' El'hassai said evenly, 'we believe the main reactor overloaded, although there is no way to tell if this was deliberate, or how much damage the explosion inflicted on the leviathan. We may hope that it was sufficient to kill or cripple the hive ship, but in any event, many of the swarm will have survived.'

'And become aware of the presence of prey,' Zyvan said.

'Precisely,' El'hassai agreed. He did something to the projection controls and a fresh image appeared, a star map studded with familiar constellations. Little icons popped up, marking Imperial, tau, and unclaimed worlds; although it went without saying that their idea of these categories didn't entirely coincide with ours. This was hardly the time to reopen old quarrels, though, so I refrained from saying anything, although I was pretty sure I could hear Zyvan's teeth grinding. 'The message drone was recovered here,' a fresh icon appeared well within the boarders of the Tau Empire, 'last kai'rotaa–'

'About two months back,' Donali murmured quietly.

El'hassai continued speaking, as if unaware of the comment. '–and our preliminary analysis of its data places the encounter with the tyranid fleet somewhere around here,' he concluded.

Another icon appeared, and Zyvan shook his head in perplexity. 'That can't be right,' he said. 'The main tyranid incursions are coming in from the Rim[1].'

'They have done until now,' I said, my eye falling on the marker pinpointing Nusquam Fundumentibus. The dormant brood we'd discovered there had to have come from somewhere, and the fleet the tau had blundered into certainly seemed close enough to have sent out a scouting party several millennia ago. 'But it wouldn't be the first time an isolated splinter fleet popped up without warning.'

'Our experience also,' El'hassai agreed. 'In view of the evident risk, we sent scout vessels to backtrack the message drone, and found that the

---

1. *On the Eastern Fringe, at least, which would, naturally, be his main concern. Hive Fleet Leviathan's thrust up through the galactic plane would have little bearing on the immediate tactical situation in the Damocles Gulf.*

tyranids have indeed altered their course.' A line began to extend from the point where the luckless explorator crew had first encountered the hive fleet, towards the position of the drone's recovery.

'They followed it,' I said heavily, the coin dropping. Which was hardly surprising; the tau had done pretty much everything they could to attract the 'nids short of handing them a menu and a map.

'They did,' El'hassai confirmed. Another icon flared. 'The scout fleet encountered them here, and engaged a few of the outlying bioships before being forced to withdraw. If they continue to advance at the rate they have been, they'll be into the border region in a matter of weeks[1].' The line extended itself, cutting back and forth across the wavering one between the two powers.

'That puts over a dozen inhabited worlds at risk,' Zyvan said, in the tone of a man determined to get all the bad news out of the way in one go. 'If the fleet absorbs that much biomass, it'll become unstoppable.'

'Which is why we propose putting aside our present dispute,' El'hassai said, nodding gravely. 'The Greater Good demands it.'

Zyvan was nodding too, still trying to absorb the implications. 'I believe it does,' he agreed.

---

1. *It's unclear here whether he actually used the Imperial term, or Cain is simply translating with hindsight.*

FIVE

AFTER A BOMBSHELL like that, there wasn't much to do except return to Zyvan's flagship and work out our strategy, while the tau went into a huddle of their own to do the same. Although, as they'd already had a couple of months to think about it, I was sure they'd have most of their preparations well in hand by now.

'We can't just abandon Quadravidia,' General Braddick urged, leaning his weight on the arms of one of the reassuringly solid chairs around the main data display. He was evidently sufficiently unimpressed with the opulence of Zyvan's private quarters, and the presence of the most senior Guard officer in the Eastern Arm himself, to be inhibited from speaking his mind. We'd convened in the operations room of the Imperial flagship, a space apparently converted from a cargo bay or munitions store[1], judging by the amount of hastily-welded ducting and jury-rigged cables cluttering up the place. Just like home, in fact, to an old campaigner like me, who trusted utility over aesthetics, particularly where warfare was concerned. The corridors leading to it had been carpeted and paintings and holoprints strategically placed over the most unsightly blemishes in the paintwork, as befitted its

---

1. *As was his habit, Zyvan had simply taken passage on the largest warship in the flotilla, commandeering the space he needed; an arrangement the Navy seemed as happy with as possible under the circumstances, no doubt reflecting that at least that way they got to keep an eye on whatever he was up to.*

occupation by someone of Zyvan's exalted status, but he liked his workspace to be as uncluttered and free of distraction as possible.

'We won't,' the Lord General assured him, appreciating plain speaking as he always did. 'But you'll have to hold on here with no more than a token garrison.'

Braddick smiled, mirthlessly. 'No change there, then.'

'Except that the tau will be pulling out too,' I reminded him. The hololith in front of us was wavering in the reassuring manner I was used to, and I nodded my thanks as an enginseer muttered a benediction and thumped an already dented panel with a mechadendrite, bringing the starfield back into focus. 'They're transferring their assets to reinforce the defences of three of their systems along the edge of the Gulf.' As I gestured, they obligingly flared a rather bilious shade of green.

'The three closest to the projected line of the tyranid advance.' Braddick nodded, to show he was keeping up, although he had no need to demonstrate his tactical acumen; his record was more than sufficient to do that. 'Are they leaving a token garrison here too?'

'They say not,' I told him. 'They consider the risk of a misunderstanding escalating into a resumption of hostilities to be too great.'

'So they're just going to pack up and leave,' Braddick said, not bothering to hide his scepticism. 'After all the effort they've made to take the place?'

'The tau are nothing if not pragmatists,' Zyvan said. 'There's no point in them expending any more resources to hang on here, if doing so costs them three other worlds lost to the 'nids.'

'Who would then be strong enough to devour Quadravidia whoever holds on to it,' I pointed out. Braddick nodded again, clearly liking that idea no more than we did.

'Envoy El'hassai has assured us that their troops will complete the withdrawal long before we're ready to vacate the system,' Zyvan said. In fact they'd already begun to leave, with about half the strength of the besieging army on its way to defend the vulnerable outposts along the border by now. 'Another three days should see Quadravidia firmly back in Imperial hands.'

'Thank the Throne,' Braddick said feelingly, for which I could hardly blame him. A couple of weeks ago he'd been staring defeat in the face, and this unexpected deliverance certainly had a whiff of divine intervention about it; even for a die-hard cynic like me.

'One thing you might care to keep an eye on,' I said, keeping my voice as neutral as I could; but Braddick was no fool, and fixed a steely eye on me at once.

'What haven't I been told?' he asked, with an understandable touch of asperity.

'The tau have made an offer of reparations, which His Excellency the governor is minded to accept,' I said, in my most diplomatic tone.

'Because His Excellency the governor is a self-obsessed, inbred imbecile, who can't see the trap for the honey,' Zyvan added, not diplomatically at all.

'What sort of reparations?' Braddick asked, in tones which told me all too clearly that he shared the Lord General's opinion of the Emperor's anointed representative on Quadravidia.

'Assistance with the reconstruction effort,' I told him. 'Resources, expertise and civilian advisors to coordinate everything with the Administratum and the Adeptus Mechanicus.'

'Preaching subversion and heresy the whole time, no doubt,' Braddick snorted.

'No doubt,' I agreed, 'and I'd keep a particularly close eye on a bunch of human renegades calling themselves "Facilitators" if I were you.'

'You can count on it,' he assured me, before turning back to the hololith. 'What's the wider strategy?'

'The only one that makes sense,' Zyvan said. A world on the Imperial side of the border flared crimson, indicating the presence of an Adeptus Mechanicus holding[1]. 'Fecundia provides half the arms and ammunition in the sector[2].'

---

1. *A cartographic convention which has led to occasional confusion, given that most Imperial tactical displays use red to mark contact with the enemy; though few incidents were so embarrassing as the orbital bombardment of the Shrine of the Omnissiah on Kaftagrie, by an Imperial Navy flotilla under the erroneous impression that it had fallen to the Traitor Legion besieging it.*

2. *An exaggeration, but a pardonable one; it certainly manufactured a high proportion of the materiel used by Imperial Guard units in and around the Gulf, including lasguns, powercells, and most common variants of the Leman Russ.*

'If we lose it, we're frakked,' I agreed, contemplating the display. 'And it's the nearest Imperial world to the tyranids' line of advance.'

'Assuming the tau have extrapolated their course correctly,' Zyvan said, a note of caution entering his voice. Neither of us could see what the xenos would have to gain by feeding us false information, but that didn't mean they weren't being selective about what they passed on. Throne knew, I would be if I were in their shoes. He manipulated the controls, kicked the lectern, and the line of the hive fleet's projected course extended.

I nodded, in grim satisfaction, as it almost clipped one of the tau worlds highlighted in green. 'If they bypass Fecundia, then the tau will be next on the menu,' I said. 'Meaning we can fall back to the Sabine Cluster while they bear the brunt of the onslaught. That should give us more than enough time to dig in, in case any splinter fleets or stragglers drift coreward across the border.'

'Why not do that straight away?' Braddick asked, no doubt noticing that we'd be far closer to Quadravidia if we did. 'Let the Mechanicus defend the forge world themselves.'

'If they had anything there capable of it, we would,' Zyvan said. 'But they'd be overwhelmed in a matter of days by a fleet that size.'

'These are their assets,' I said, bringing up a fresh data display. 'One company of skitarii and that's about it. No Titans, no militia. Why would they waste resources on their own defence when they know the Guard need them so much they'll step in at the first sign of a threat?'

'How very efficient of them,' Braddick said sourly.

'Indeed,' I said. In truth, I felt a certain sneaking regard for the cogboys, who'd been astute enough to realise that the steady stream of Imperial Guard units putting in to resupply there already gave them all the protection they needed; at least under normal circumstances. Unfortunately, these were anything but.

'We can't take the risk of leaving them to fend for themselves,' Zyvan said firmly, and that was that; just one sentence, and we were committed.

All in all, I supposed, it could have been worse; at least no one was suggesting we went charging off to engage the hive fleet head on. With any luck it would bypass the forge world entirely, leaving the tau to blunt their advance while we sat on the sidelines, poised to render them all possible assistance short of actually doing anything, leaving us ready to mop up the survivors of both sides; we might even be able to annex a couple of their worlds for a change into the bargain (which would serve them right for trying to grab Quadravidia, if you asked me).

That was the theory, anyway, but of course it didn't work out like that.

DESPITE MY FOREBODINGS, the tau completed their withdrawal on schedule, leaving only a handful of so-called merchantmen orbiting the war-ravaged world. El'hassai, of course, insisted that they were only there to deliver humanitarian cargoes to help with the relief effort, and that their formidable armaments had been deactivated. For all I knew, he was right; the locals could certainly do with all the relief they could get. Of course, it was going to come with a heavy price tag if I was any judge; but nobody asked me, least of all the governor. On the mercifully few occasions I couldn't avoid talking to the puffed-up popinjay he seemed absurdly pleased with himself, apparently believing the whole thing to have been his idea all along, so I just kept my own counsel, and made sure I included a verbatim record of his most asinine remarks in my next dispatch to Amberley. We were due to leave orbit within days, and, after that, whatever happened to Quadravidia was going to be someone else's problem in any case.

Being mainly concerned by now with the upcoming defence of Fecundia, I was more than a little surprised when I wandered into Zyvan's command centre a few hours before our scheduled departure to find El'hassai already ensconced there, deep in earnest conversation with the Lord General.

'Commissar.' The tau diplomat glanced in my direction, smiling a welcome; although, as with so many other apparently human expressions, I wasn't entirely sure how much of that was genuine, and how much it was studied to put me at my ease. So I plastered an equally welcoming expression on my own face, and extended a courteous hand.

'Envoy. An unexpected pleasure,' I said. I glanced at Zyvan, whose face was a carefully studied mask of neutrality behind his immaculately trimmed beard. 'To what do we owe this visit?'

'The envoy has a proposal to make,' Zyvan told me, in his most non-committal tone, 'which he hopes will foster trust between us in the face of our mutual enemy.' Which sounded to me like a direct quotation.

El'hassai nodded his agreement. 'Indeed so,' he declaimed, glancing towards the Lord General, then back to me. 'An exchange of observers. To facilitate communication between the tau and the Imperial elements of our alliance.'

'In other words, some of our people tag along to…' Zyvan gestured to the green blob most likely to end up on the hive fleet's snack trolley, and hesitated. 'Dreth… thingy.'

'Dr'th'nyr,' El'hassai supplied helpfully, untroubled by the world's typical lack of vowels.

'Exactly,' Zyvan agreed, 'to report back on the tau deployment, and pass on any useful intelligence they can gather about the 'nids.' Not just the 'nids either, of course, but we all knew what was remaining unsaid, and no one was tactless enough to verbalise it.

'Pass it on how?' I asked. 'The tau don't have astropaths, do they[1]?'

'We do not,' El'hassai confirmed, 'although we are entirely agreeable to the Imperial delegation including one.'

'That could be arranged,' Zyvan agreed. 'It'd keep the two fleets coordinated more effectively than sending dispatches by courier boat.' Until the astropathic connection was severed by the shadow in the

---

1. *In fact, the tau appear to have no psykers of any kind among them, although there is much speculation among the Ordo Xenos as to whether or not the Ethereal caste's ability to inspire and lead might be an entirely natural phenomenon, or have something of the warp about it in a manner not yet evident or explained. Similar doubts exist about the other races associated with the tau, although the question remains a little less clear cut; and surely only the most optimistic could believe that the humans in the tau empire are entirely free of taint, those afflicted undoubtedly being encouraged to use their curses in the name of the 'Greater Good'.*

warp cast by the approaching tyranids, anyway. This in itself would be sufficient to let the other group know the attack had fallen elsewhere.

'And who did you have in mind to lead this delegation?' I asked, already perfectly aware of the answer to that, and determined to head it off. None of the forge worlds I'd seen before had been particularly inviting, but there was a fair chance that the 'nids would bypass Fecundia entirely, whereas joining the tau in the defence of Dr'th'nyr seemed tantamount to charging straight down the gullet of the nearest hive ship to me.

'Precisely the question we were debating,' El'hassai said smoothly. 'You have the confidence of both powers, and extensive experience of campaigning against the tyranids.'

Which, needless to say, I was hardly keen to extend any further. It wouldn't exactly be politic to say so, though, so I nodded thoughtfully, as if I was actually considering the implied proposal.

'I do indeed,' I said evenly. 'Although that may not be the most essential quality where this job's concerned.'

'Really?' Zyvan asked, raising an eyebrow. 'What do you think would be?'

'Familiarity with the tau way of doing things,' I replied promptly. 'If the tyranid attack is directed at Dr'th'nyr,' and I have to say I made a pretty good fist of the pronunciation all things considered, to no one's surprise greater than my own, 'it'll be vital to know precisely what's going on. One moment's hesitation or misunderstanding in the heat of battle could lead to catastrophe.' I shrugged, in my most artless, self-deprecating fashion. 'And, with the best will in the galaxy, I'm hardly *au fait* with the complexities of tau protocol.'

'Who would you suggest, then?' El'hassai asked and I put on my most decisive face.

'Donali, of course,' I said. 'He's spent so much time with the water caste he'll know exactly what to do in any situation without needing to be briefed. Leaving everyone free to prosecute the war with the greatest efficiency.'

'There's much merit in your analysis,' El'hassai said, after a moment, to my carefully concealed surprise, and even greater relief. 'You have a fine grasp of the principle of the Greater Good.'

'I just think it makes more sense to send a diplomat to do a diplomat's job,' I said, hardly able to believe I'd been able to palm the job off on someone else quite so easily, 'while I get on with the soldiering.'

Zyvan nodded in agreement. 'I'd rather have you with the fleet anyway,' he admitted, which promptly triggered a fresh flare of unease I hadn't bargained for, as I tried to work out what he knew that I didn't. 'We'll have to thrash things out with the cogboys, and you know what they're like.'

'They can be a bit difficult to work with,' I agreed. But at least they were human, more or less, and I'd find it a lot easier to keep them between me and the 'nids if the worst came to the worst. I shot a quick glance at the hololith again, just to make sure I was making the right choice, but it seemed I was. The tyranid advance still looked most likely to skirt the Fecundia system altogether, before driving in towards the tau outposts. 'They should follow our advice without arguing too much, though. It would be the most rational thing to do.'

'Well, you'd know,' Zyvan said, fortunately without either of us knowing just how wrong he was about that, 'you've had dealings with them often enough.'

'I have,' I agreed, tactfully refraining from the 'more than enough, actually,' which would have been rather more accurate. Members of the Adeptus Mechanicus were all very well in their way, and I'd even known a few whose company I'd quite enjoyed, but even the best of them could be irritatingly single-minded, particularly on the occasions we'd been forced to make a choice between some cherished piece of junk and my even more cherished hide. Luckily, in my experience, most acolytes of the Omnissiah could be convinced to follow the path of pragmatism by reducing the debate to a simple either-or choice, where the one I liked least involved certain annihilation for us all; or, if all else failed, pointing out which one of us was currently holding the gun. I shrugged. 'After all, they need us just as badly as we need them.'

'Quite so,' Zyvan said, clearly thinking that wasn't exactly the firmest of foundations for an alliance between two of the vast number of organisations and factions making up the Imperium, let alone ourselves and a bunch of land-grabbing xenos who'd turn their guns on us again the first chance they got, if we didn't manage to do it first.

'If that's settled, then, I'll leave you to it,' I said, preparing to withdraw. Ally or not, I'd rather postpone chatting about our tactics until El'hassai had joined the exodus of his compatriots.

'Everything but the designation of the tau representative among the Imperial fleet,' Zyvan said, with a faint inclination of the head which indicated he'd rather I stayed right where I was. And with good reason. Technically, the Commissariat would have to concur that any appointment he agreed to didn't constitute an unacceptable security risk, and having me sit in would short-circuit the ratification process nicely. Not that I'd be particularly happy with any candidate, but at least we'd be aware of who was spying on us, and able to keep them well away from anything really sensitive.

'I propose Au'lys Devrae,' El'hassai said, looking from one of us to the other, with a fine show of bafflement at our resulting expressions. 'She speaks fluent Gothic, and is of the same species, which should greatly facilitate understanding and communication.'

'Out of the question,' Zyvan said, and I nodded emphatically.

'She'd be lynched within days,' I explained. 'Most Imperial citizens would regard her as a heretic, pure and simple.'

'That complicates matters,' El'hassai said, evenly. 'We have few Gothic speakers left in the Quadravidia system, even fewer with appropriate diplomatic credentials. Since most of those are also human, they would hardly fare any better.'

'Hardly,' I agreed, straight-faced, waiting for the inevitable suggestion which, I strongly suspected, was what he'd actually intended all along.

'I will have to accompany you myself,' El'hassai said, to my complete lack of surprise.

'Of course,' Zyvan agreed, with a fine show of courtesy, and gestured to the nearest of his aides, who promptly tried to look as though he hadn't been eavesdropping on the entire conversation. 'Marlie will see to the allocation of your quarters.'

'Thank you.' El'hassai stood, and proffered a hand to the faintly baffled-looking young man. 'I will be accompanied only by a small retinue: half a dozen advisors, amanuenses and the like.'

'All tau?' I asked, trying not to picture the reaction of a typical Naval rating coming face to face with a kroot in the corridors, let alone a vespid. At least the slight humanoids looked reasonably unthreatening, unless they were stomping about in one of their battlesuits, and there didn't seem much prospect of that.

'All tau,' El'hassai assured me. 'Mainly from the water caste.'

'Mainly?' I asked, and the tau nodded. 'I believe that a fire warrior or two will assist my understanding of the tactical situation.'

'By all means,' Zyvan said, clearly not happy with the request, and equally clearly far from surprised. But then, if I were taking passage on a xenos vessel, I'd have wanted a squad of storm troopers with me at the very least.

'I shall then delay you no longer,' El'hassai replied, and wandered away, Captain Marlie trotting at his heels like an anxious party host wondering if they've ordered enough canapés.

'Are you sure that's wise?' I asked, as soon as the door had rumbled closed behind them, and Zyvan shook his head.

'No, but what choice have I got? Donali will want to take a bodyguard, so we can hardly refuse El'hassai the same courtesy.' He shrugged. 'And it's not as if they're going to take over the ship with just a couple of pulse rifles.'

'I suppose not,' I agreed, and we got down to the serious business of working out how best to protect a world apparently devoid of any defences.

Editorial Note:

Since there now follows another of Cain's characteristic elisions, picking up his narrative at the point of his arrival in the Fecundia system, this seems as good a place as any to insert some of the background he so conspicuously fails to provide.

Sekara's travelogue, which I've drawn on extensively while editing these volumes, is of little use in this case, his entry on Fecundia consisting of nothing more than the phrase 'Dreary beyond belief.' Accordingly, I've been forced to make use of less cosmopolitan material, in order to give an accurate impression of the world on which Cain was shortly to find himself fighting for his life.

WELCOME TO FECUNDIA!
A Tithe Worker's Survival Guide
Also available in auditory and direct inload formatting.

Blessings of the Omnissiah be upon you for choosing to dedicate
your life to the fabrication of His bounty.
(Please omit the preceding benediction if directed into such service
by the Magistratum of your home world.)

FECUNDIA IS A forge world, consecrated to the service of the Machine God, and every manufactory is a temple to His greatness. The manufactoria themselves cover approximately thirty-eight per cent of the total surface area, while ancillary facilities such as habitation clusters, protein synthesis units and atmospheric reclamators account for a further seventeen.

As a result, adequate nutrition and air sufficiently devoid of particulates to be barely carcinogenic are freely available in all work and leisure spaces, although augmetic upgrades to both digestive and respiratory systems are recommended for all long-term residents. (Your supervisor will be happy to explain the procedure for repaying the cost of such enhancements.)

Exposure to the unregulated environment is not recommended, and should be restricted to the briefest possible time, unless a full-body upgrade has been obtained. (Average redemption time for this enhancement 285,000 production hours.) Short-term exposure is survivable for the unmodified, provided full protective clothing is worn; in such a case it is essential to check joints and seals periodically for signs of corrosion.

The uninhabited areas are composed of ash desert, acid lakes, spoil ridges, and three mineralogical extraction plants. Since most indigenous resources have been consumed, recovery efforts are under way on the remaining planetary bodies and most large asteroids. Preliminary processing of extraplanetary resources is conducted in the orbital refineries, before the raw materials are delivered to the surface by direct ballistic insertion; the recovery of these payloads from the landing grounds is a job highly sought after, since every hour spent on the surface is considered to be three for the purposes of production hour computation, and many vacancies are currently available in this area.

If caught in the open, it is advisable to seek shelter immediately, particularly if the wind rises. Scourstorms are capable of abrading the hull armour of a heavy crawler, and can inflict severe injury on even augmetically enhanced humans in a matter of moments.

SIX

I HAD FEW expectations about the world awaiting us, and those that I did were swiftly lived down to. From orbit, Fecundia resembled nothing so much as a vast pustule, swollen and livid, choked with the detritus of its industry. Much of the surface was obscured by thick clouds the colour of diarrhoea, which swirled above the hive zones[1], each one of which sprawled for hundreds of kilometres in every direction. Around them was nothing but a wilderness of spoil and waste. The place had been an uninhabitable ruin before the Mechanicus moved in, and they'd hardly done much to improve it that I could see[2].

'Quite a spectacle, is it not?' El'hassai remarked at my elbow, in studiedly neutral tones, and I started, having been too lost in my own thoughts to have noticed his all but silent approach.

'If you like that sort of thing,' I conceded. The night side of the world below was glowing a dull, flickering red, the light of uncountable furnaces making it look as though the whole planet was on fire. I was reminded of the volcanic hellhole I'd so recently escaped from by

---

1. *He seems to be drawing no distinction between the manufactoria themselves and the adjoining habs; which, to be fair, were so intermingled it was hard to tell where the dividing lines were in any case.*

2. *Terraforming efforts had begun in M35, with the establishment of an atmosphere, which rapidly became all but unbreathable as the business of plundering the world's resources had begun in earnest.*

the skin of my teeth[1], and shuddered. 'Remind you of anywhere back home?'

'Our fabricatories are less… profligate with their usage of energy,' El'hassai said, a little prissily, I thought, but then with xenos it was often hard to tell what they were really thinking.

'Good for you,' I responded reflexively, letting him pick the sarcasm out of the remark if he liked.

'It hardly looks like a tempting target for the tyranids,' he went on, clearly choosing not to. 'Our encounters with them would tend to suggest that they prefer their planets more verdant.'

'There's about twenty billion people down there,' I corrected him. 'Even if half of them are mostly metal. And probably twice that number of servitors[2]. More than enough biomass to make an attack worth their while.'

'I sit corrected,' El'hassai said, raising his eyes from the cloacal world beneath us to the cold, clear void surrounding it. A few of the uncountable pinpricks of light bespattering the sable backdrop were moving against the luminescent smudge of the bulk of the galaxy, and he gestured towards them. 'The picket ships appear to be taking up their positions with commendable alacrity.'

'They do,' I agreed, although the fleet's deployment was nothing to do with me. The Naval contingent had their own commissars assigned to them, who would be sufficiently versed in three-dimensional tactics to understand what was going on. Nevertheless, I strongly suspected that most of the vessels we could see were actually cargo haulers, feeding the insatiable appetites of the furnaces below with raw materials or carrying away the spoils of their labour to half a hundred worlds[3]. Of

---

1. *Pyria, noted for its extreme geological instability, on which Cain had encountered an eldar raiding party the year before.*

2. *Actually three or four times would have been a more accurate guess.*

3. *Though Fecundia's strategic value to the Imperium was predicated on its prodigious output of munitions, it produced a great many non-military commodities too; hardly a world in the sector was without ground vehicles produced there, and the chemical fertilisers made alongside the military explosives (often utilising the same reaction chambers) were all that made food production possible on three neighbouring agri-worlds of otherwise marginal fertility.*

more immediate concern were the troop ships carrying the Imperial Guard contingent, which should have made orbit by now, and begun ferrying soldiers to the surface ready to begin fortifying the hives. Precisely how we were going to manage that was still proving a major headache, as we had barely enough manpower to protect even one of the population centres below, let alone all of them; but at least there was little prospect of us running out of ammunition.

Before the conversation, or my thoughts, could turn in a more pessimistic direction, a familiar odour heralded the arrival of my aide. 'Bit of a mess,' he remarked, glancing out of the viewport.

'Forge worlds generally are,' I reminded him, and he nodded, with a sniff of disapproval.

'Like that last one we went to,' he agreed. 'Cak everywhere.' Then he shrugged. 'I dare say it'll be better indoors.'

'We'll find out soon enough,' I said, hoping he was right. 'I take it the shuttle's ready?'

Jurgen nodded. 'Lord General's compliments, sir, and he'd like to see you aboard it at your earliest convenience.'

'Not his exact words, I'm sure,' I said.

Jurgen shuffled his feet. 'That was the gist of it,' he said doggedly. It would have been unkind to press him for further details, as he was evidently attempting to spare my feelings and, knowing Zyvan as well as I did, I was more than capable of filling in the blanks for myself in any case.

'Then we'd better not keep him waiting,' I said, turning to El'hassai, who still seemed mesmerised by the starfield beyond the armourglass. 'Will you be joining us, ambassador?' Truth to tell I was in two minds about asking, but protocol demanded that I did, and at least if he tagged along I'd be spared the necessity of regurgitating our discussions with the Mechanicus for his benefit at a later date. Not to mention feeling a lot more comfortable knowing where he was.

'That would be the most efficient course of action,' the tau agreed, turning away from the suppurating planet below and falling into step at my elbow as we made our way to the docking bay. The corridors were crowded with Guardsmen and Navy personnel, who stepped aside, with varying expressions of bemusement, hostility or repugnance at the sight of the xenos, but El'hassai ignored them all. For my own part, I barely noticed, commissars hardly being welcome anywhere they went, but Jurgen returned scowl for scowl, clearing a path for us as effectively as Zyvan's bodyguard of storm troopers would have done.

It seemed we were to travel aboard Zyvan's personal shuttle, which was fine by me: its deeply padded chairs and carpeting were a great deal more comfortable than the hard seats and metal decking of the more utilitarian transports I was used to taking to and from orbit, and I knew from experience that the drinks cabinet was well stocked.

'Forget your vox-bead?' the Lord General greeted me, as we walked up the ramp. Then his eye fell on El'hassai, a couple of paces behind, flanked by the bodyguards who'd joined him as we'd entered the hangar bay. 'Envoy. Good of you to join us.' If his demeanour was anything to go by, however, he would have been perfectly happy for the tau to have remained aboard the ship.

Sure enough, as I settled into my chair and accepted the amasec Jurgen poured out for me, Zyvan leaned closer, and lowered his voice. 'Are you sure that's a good idea?' he asked, *sotto voce*.

'We're meant to be in an alliance,' I reminded him, equally quietly. There was little chance of being overheard above the rising note of the engines, but you never knew with xenos[1], so I kept my voice low nevertheless. 'The cogboys know we've got a delegation aboard, so why not let him sit in on the initial meeting?'

'If you think they'll wear it,' Zyvan said, shrugging.

'Why wouldn't they?' I asked, in honest bemusement.

Zyvan shrugged again, and took an appreciative sip of his amasec. 'Why do the cogboys do anything?' he asked, reasonably enough.

OUR DESCENT WAS as smooth and untroubled as we could have hoped for, the buffeting as we entered the atmosphere mild enough even for Jurgen's sensitive stomach; but then Zyvan's personal pilot would

---

1. *In fact, tau and human hearing appear to be in a broadly similar range, although the average tau seem deaf to the higher frequencies, while capable of distinguishing sounds most humans would perceive merely as uncomfortable vibration. Which probably accounts for their lamentable taste in music.*

have been one of the finest in the fleet, so that was hardly surprising. The view of the world through the viewports hardly improved as we approached it, the thick clouds of corrosive smog I'd seen from orbit blanketing the ground until we'd almost reached the surface for which I could only be grateful, judging by the brief glimpses of what awaited us that I was able to catch through the occasional gap.

At length, bright, flashing luminators stabbed through the murk, guiding us towards the landing zone, and I began to discern the vast bulk of the primary manufacturing complex below and around our hurrying shuttle, looming out of the smog like a volcanic mountain range. The light of the beacons was joined by innumerable others, speckling the oppressive mass of artificial cliff faces surrounding us, or carried aboard the shoal of other air traffic among which we moved, like minnows skirting the ramparts of a reef. A not unapt comparison, I suppose, as, like a reef, the hive had accreted gradually, by the actions of uncountable individuals, over thousands of years. Eventually, it would wither and die, the resources it had been put here to plunder exhausted, and the Mechanicus would uproot themselves and begin again on some other lump of rock unfortunate enough to possess something they wanted[1].

'Aren't we heading for the main shuttle pads?' I asked, as, with a surge of acceleration which left Jurgen looking distinctly green around the gills even by his standards, our pilot lifted us out of the main traffic, to soar majestically over the rising peaks of the hive range.

'The magi running this place want to keep our meeting discreet,' Zyvan said, and I nodded, approving. Trying to work out an effective strategy was going to be hard enough as it was, without getting bogged down in official receptions and all that sort of thing. Especially as tech-priests weren't exactly renowned for throwing a good party.

---

1. *By this time their prospection fleet had, in fact, identified five other worlds in the sector suitable for exploitation, and begun preliminary work on two of them, estimating that they would become fully-functioning forge worlds by the end of the first century of M43. Of the other three, one was of equal interest to the tau, who had fortified it heavily against rival claims, the second was overrun by orks and not felt to be worth the trouble of cleansing, while the third lay directly in the path of Hive Fleet Kraken, and was therefore considered a poor long-term investment of resources.*

'Where, then?' I asked, and Zyvan gestured towards a spire, topped with a cogwheel icon big enough to have parked a Baneblade on each of the spurs[1].

'The Spire of Blessed Computation,' he said, squinting at the dataslate in his hand. It was a plain, military field model, incongruously drab against the garish dress uniform he'd put on for the occasion, but he was, as ever, more concerned with the practicalities. I'd often thought that he'd prefer to do without any of the ornamentation and ceremony which surrounded him if he could, but he was just as trammelled by the protocols of his position as I was by mine. I must have looked puzzled, because he added, 'it's where most of this miserable rock's run from.'

'Good choice, then,' I said. The closer we were to the cogboys' command centre, the easier it would be to liaise with them.

'I'm glad you approve,' Zyvan said, not entirely joking.

The spire was so close by now that it was blotting out much of the hive, its upper storeys becoming clearer as we glided towards it through the ocean of murk. The sun was barely visible, discernable only as a luminescent disc, dim enough to look at directly, glimmering wanly through the clotted brown clouds walling us off from the rest of the universe so that we were almost entirely reliant on the luminators to see where we were going. I thumbed my palm[2], and hoped the pilot had a reliable auspex. From this distance the sides which had seemed so smooth from a couple of kilometres away looked gnarled, like the bark of an impossibly tall tree, encrusted with thousands of protruding substructures, vents, antennae, and work platforms. Servitors and spirejacks, armoured against the hellish conditions of the open air, swarmed around it, doing Emperor knew what.

'That must be it,' Jurgen said, with a sigh of relief which gave me the full benefit of his halitosis, and prompted a brief, envious glance at the full face helmets sported by El'hassai's fire warrior escort. I

---

1. *Not the downward-sloping, ones, obviously.*

2. *A gesture common on several worlds in the sector, where the thumb is folded into the hand so that the fingers form a stylised aquila wing, meant to invoke good luck or ward off misfortune.*

followed the direction of his gaze, and found we were descending towards a small landing platform, jutting from the vertical face of the spire, one of many such lost among the myriad of excrescences.

'Looks that way,' I agreed, narrowing my eyes to peer through the curdled air. Landing lights were flashing, guiding our pilot in, and striking flickering highlights from the augmetic enhancements of the honour guard of scarlet-uniformed skitarii lining up beside the doorway leading inside the tower. A thought struck me, and I glanced at Zyvan in some consternation. 'They surely don't expect us to step outside, do they?'

'It won't be for long,' he assured me. 'Magos Dysen says short-term exposure to the atmosphere is quite harmless.'

'Quite,' I said, inflecting it like assent, while ruminating on just how much imprecision the simple little word might be reflecting. 'It's all right for him, he doesn't have lungs to frak up in any case[1].'

'Not biological ones, at any rate,' Zyvan said. But before we could debate the matter further, a faint tremor in the hull plating told us that the pilot had landed with just as much skill as I would have expected, and the time for conversation was past.

---

1. *From which we can infer that Cain had at least taken the time to familiarise himself with the datafiles on the most senior members of the Adeptus Mechanicus on Fecundia.*

SEVEN

THE FIRST THING to strike me as we strode down the ramp was the smell, a thick, sulphurous humidity which slapped me in the face like a flannel soaked in tepid swamp water. The heat boiled up around us through the stinking air, rising from the manufactoria below in urgent, foetid thermal gusts, as though the forges themselves were constantly breaking wind. Even forewarned as I was, I coughed, almost gagging, envying the tau warriors their respirators in earnest now.

'Smells a bit,' Jurgen observed, oblivious to the irony as ever, while I fell into place beside Zyvan and the small knot of aides who had accompanied him. Not trusting myself to reply, and breathing as shallowly as I could, I merely nodded.

The landing platform was smaller than I'd realised, barely large enough to hold the shuttle, and my already good opinion of our pilot was raised another notch. The craft's nose was only a handful of metres from the wall, close to where the inviting illuminated rectangle of the doorway gaped open, while the starboard landing skid was even closer to the vertiginous three-kilometre drop into the heart of the furnaces. With a shudder, I realised the outer edge was without a balustrade or even a handrail to check a careless misstep, and resolved to keep the bulk of the utility craft between me and oblivion. Clearly, the tech-priests who worked here regarded a sense of self-preservation as superfluous to requirements.

'Nicely done,' Zyvan congratulated our pilot over his vox-bead, and turned to me. 'He put us down where we can use the shuttle as a windbreak.'

'For which we should all thank the Throne,' I agreed, feeling my greatcoat flapping like a pennon in the gale-force gusts passing the hull. Without it, I'd have been hard-pressed to remain on my feet. An alarming vision of being picked up and flung into the void by the turbulent air flashed through my mind, and I suppressed it firmly.

'Welcome,' the officer in charge of the skitarii detachment said in the flat drone of a vox-coder, making the cogwheel gesture generally favoured by followers of the Machine God as he did so. 'Centurion Kyper, Primus Pilem, Cohort Fecundia.' Like most of the skitarii I'd come across in the course of my erratic progress around the galaxy, he looked more like a heavily-augmented ogryn than anything human, his musculature bulging with chemical enhancement and interlaced with bionics.

'At ease,' Zyvan said, not bothering to introduce himself; if Kyper didn't realise at once who he was, he had no business being there. He gestured in my direction. 'Commissar Cain is accompanying me, along with the tau envoy, and his escort.'

'Tau envoy?' Kyper echoed, sounding as surprised as his even mechanical buzz allowed. I could see little of his face inside the hood protecting it from the elements, and most of what I could was too metallic to allow any expression to register, but I didn't need to look him in the eye to realise he was rattled. He began chirruping rapidly in binaric to his two companions, both of whom were dwarfed by the hulking combat servitor at the end of the receiving line. 'We were not informed of this.'

'It was a last-minute decision,' I said, my voice rasping through the thin coating of ash, and no doubt other less savoury substances, obstructing my larynx.

'He must remain on the shuttle,' Kyper said firmly.

'That's not your decision to make,' Zyvan snapped, in the tone of a man to whom putting obstructive underlings in their place had long ago become second nature.

'Is there some difficulty?' El'hassai asked, appearing at the bottom of the boarding ramp, his words punctuated by small, precise coughs. He addressed the skitarii directly. 'My diplomatic credentials have been fully approved by–'

'Unsanctified presence,' the combat servitor cut in, lumbering into motion. 'Purge and reconsecrate.'

'Call that thing off!' I bellowed, in my best put-the-fear-of-the-Emperor-into-'em voice. But before Kyper could move an augmetically enhanced muscle, the construct had raised its autocannon arm, and rattled off a burst of heavy-calibre rounds which whined and ricocheted from the now badly dented boarding ramp. El'hassai scuttled back up it with commendable alacrity, and the servitor plodded forward, heading towards the shuttle with murder obviously in mind.

'Get back in the air!' Zyvan voxed the pilot, but he'd cut the engines as soon as we'd landed, no doubt anticipating a long and tedious wait for our preliminary discussions to be completed, and we all knew there was no way the shuttle could lift before the servitor got to it.

I retuned my vox-bead just in time to hear the pilot acknowledge the order. 'Powering up,' he said, and the main engines burst into life with a roar which rattled my teeth. 'Fifteen seconds to take-off thrust.'

'We don't have fifteen seconds!' I snapped. 'The damn thing will be aboard by then! Raise the ramp!'

'I'm already trying,' the pilot informed me, his voice ringing with the forced calm of an expert in a crisis. 'That autocannon burst disabled the servos.'

'Then take it out!' I ordered, with an eye on the chin-turreted multilaser beneath the cockpit.

'I can't target it,' the pilot told me, with the air of a man following bad news with worse. 'It's already inside the range.'

'Then we'll have to do it!' I turned to the skitarii. 'Open fire, or call it off. Your choice.'

They chirruped at one another in consternation for a moment.

'With regret, commissar, we can do neither,' Kyper told me. 'The unit is programmed to protect the spire from unauthorised entry, and damaging it would run counter to the tenets of the Omnissiah. I can request the appropriate termination codes from a higher authority, but…'

'Oh for frak's sake!' I expostulated, drawing my sidearm. Taking on a fully armoured combat servitor went against all my instincts of self-preservation, but if El'hassai died, I knew who'd get the blame; he wouldn't even have been there if I hadn't invited him. I cracked off a couple of shots at the construct's armour-plated back, with nothing more in mind than diverting its attention long enough for the pilot to get into the air, before bolting for the safety of the doorway. But even as I turned, the portal hissed shut, trapping us on the narrow landing stage. 'Now what?' I snapped, exasperated.

'The machine spirits are sealing the spire in response to the weapons fire.' Kyper said.

At which point the flaw in my plan became obvious. The servitor turned, ponderously, and brought its weapon arm around to point at me. 'Hostile action initiated,' it droned. 'Retaliate. Retaliate.'

I jumped for my life as a line of autocannon rounds chewed up the rockcrete towards me, Zyvan and his aides scattering away from the line of fire like startled waterfowl, and rolled to my feet, cracking off another shot, hoping to hit something vital. No such luck, of course, anything vulnerable was tucked well away behind the armour plate.

'Allow me, sir,' Jurgen said, opening up with a burst from his lasgun. Predictably, it had little effect, although it did check the thing's progress for a moment as it swung to let off a burst in his direction, which whined and ricocheted from the landing skid behind which he'd taken refuge. Then it turned back towards me, apparently intent on dealing with one thing at a time[1].

'Requesting shutdown codes, authorisation Alpha Beige Zero Zero Seven Six Eight Cantata,' Kyper said, apparently over some internal vox-link. 'Urgency utmost.' At least he was finally doing something, but unless he did it fast, it was going to be too late for me.

---

1. *Probably because, being out in the open, Cain was now the most visible target.*

I dived aside again, chips of rockcrete from the near miss stinging my face, and came up facing the shuttle, just as the pitch of its engines rose to a scream. Brown fog swirled around my ankles, made turbulent by the backwash, and I ran towards the jammed ramp as hard as I could. It was a desperate gamble, but at the moment it looked like being the best of a lot of bad options, most of which were liable to end up with me dead.

'Lifting now!' the pilot called, and I leapt desperately for the rising slab of metal, feeling the edge of it slamming into my midriff, driving the air from my lungs (which, considering its quality, was probably no bad thing). At which point I became all too aware of the pistol in my hand, which rather precluded grabbing hold of anything else.

I barely had time to swear before I felt myself slithering back towards the lip of the drop. Flailing desperately, I managed to get a grip on one of the retaining bolts with my free hand, which left me dangling like a half-landed fish, while the panorama of the hive wheeled vertiginously below me. Why I didn't simply let the laspistol go, I have no idea, but by that point I was probably too terrified to have opened my fingers if I'd tried.

'Hold on, sir!' Jurgen voxed, which struck me as the single most superfluous piece of advice I'd ever received. Then the servitor opened fire again, the heavy calibre rounds stitching a line of impact craters along the underside of the ramp, missing my wildly kicking legs by far too narrow a margin for comfort, and I divined the reason for his warning. Why it should have continued to take its spite out on the shuttle, instead of turning on my aide the minute it had a clear shot at him, I'll never know, but it continued to target us with the single-minded vindictiveness of an ork[1].

'Starboard engine hit,' the pilot said, his veneer of professional detachment sounding thinner than ever, and the shuttle lurched sickeningly, almost dislodging my precarious hold. My shoulder muscles were screaming in protest by now, my arm feeling as though

---

1. *Such constructs are usually programmed to concentrate their fire on the greatest perceived threat; in this case the shuttle's multilaser, and the presence aboard it of a xenos interloper, compared to which Jurgen and his lasgun would simply be a minor irritation.*

it was about to come free of its socket. A plume of thick black smoke, looking perfectly at home in what passed for an atmosphere around here, began seeping from the engine pod, whirling away to play with its friends rising from the furnaces so far below. If I fell, I'd probably be immolated before I hit the ground (or the roof of something, at any rate), which was hardly the most reassuring of thoughts. 'I'll have to set down again.'

Crushing me like a bug in the process. 'Stay airborne!' I yelled desperately, hoping to appeal to his sense of duty. My own predicament was hardly likely to give him pause, commissars hardly being the most popular of figures among the military[1]. 'If you land, that thing'll kill the ambassador!'

'It's land, or crash,' the pilot said stubbornly, 'and he certainly won't survive that!'

'Your concern for my welfare is most gratifying,' a familiar voice cut in, raised over the whine of our abused engine, the roar of air buffeting into the confined space above the ramp, and the metallic whine and clatter of another fusillade from below. 'But I believe I shall be adequately protected.' A slender, four-fingered hand[2] wrapped itself around my wrist and pulled, with surprising strength. He wasn't able to haul me onboard entirely by his own efforts, of course[3], but I got enough of a boost to shift my centre of mass firmly onto the wildly bucking ramp, and after that it was relatively easy to haul myself to safety.

'Thank you,' I said, making it to my feet with some difficulty, and shoving the laspistol back in its holster at last. There was no more time for conversation, though, as the landing platform was growing ever larger, the murderous servitor continuing to blaze away at us as we descended. It seemed our pilot was too busy trying to get us

---

1. *Typically, the high regard he was held in, admittedly in stark contrast to most of his colleagues, doesn't seem to have occurred to him.*

2. *Three and a thumb, for the pedantic among my readers.*

3. *Given their relatively slight stature it's no surprise that tau, on average, are somewhat weaker than humans, but, as in so many other respects, it's never wise to underestimate their resolve or tenacity in a crisis.*

down in one piece to retaliate with the multilaser.[1] I stumbled as the shuttle lurched again, and clutched reflexively at El'hassai for support, fortuitously dragging him aside as the stream of autocannon rounds chewed up the bulkhead where he'd been standing a moment before. 'I hope this protection of yours is ready when we hit.'

'It is,' El'hassai assured me, and, looking round, I saw that the pair of fire warriors had accompanied the tau diplomat onto the ramp. Each drew a thin line from somewhere in the recesses of their armour and clipped them firmly around stanchions at the top, freeing their hands to handle their weapons. A second later, twin plasma bolts streaked from their pulse rifles, impacting squarely on the rogue servitor.

'Good shooting!' I called, even though they probably didn't understand a word I said. Encouraging the troops had become an ingrained habit by now, particularly when I was in the firing line. 'That's put paid to it!'

My elation turned out to be somewhat premature, however, the Adeptus Mechanicus having done the job of building the thing rather too well. The construct staggered under the barrage – which, I noted with approval, Jurgen was adding to with the dogged determination I'd become so familiar with over the course of our long association – then recovered, attempting to raise the fused stump of its autocannon once again as it recovered its balance.

'That's drawn its teeth, at least,' Zyvan voxed, with clear approval. I caught a glimpse of his hand hovering over his sidearm, undoubtedly itching to draw it and take a crack at the thing himself, but it was going to be hard enough smoothing things over with our hosts already, without him blowing holes in one of their toys as well.

Then the deckplates beneath my feet rose up as the shuttle smacked into the landing stage with a bone-jarring impact, throwing El'hassai and myself to the floor. The tau just had time to shout something in his own tongue, though whether it was an urgent enquiry about how his compatriots were faring, or simple profanity of the sort I was giving voice to, I had no idea. The shuttle bounced, struck the pad again, and finally came to rest, the deckplates canted at an odd angle.

---

1. *Or, more likely, felt that the risk of hitting Zyvan by accident was too great to try it.*

'Good landing,' I voxed to the pilot, the palpable relief in my voice dispelling all possible suspicion of sarcasm.

'Better bail out while you can,' he responded, popping the emergency seals in the cockpit as he spoke and scrambling down a rope ladder to the deck. The shuttle shifted slightly as his weight dropped away from it, and with a thrill of horror I suddenly understood why the little craft was tilted at so sharp an angle. In his hurry to get us down, and with his control of the ship impaired by the damage the rogue servitor had inflicted, the pilot hadn't been able to land entirely on the platform. We were teetering on the edge, buffeted by the irregular gales rising from the depths below, and it only needed a particularly strong gust to overbalance us altogether.

'Acknowledged!' I snapped, then turned back to El'hassai, who was staggering to his feet alongside me. 'We need to get out now. This bag of bolts is going over the side at any moment!'

'Ra'sncr'ns and Gl'den'sn,' he replied, which flummoxed me for a moment, during which I examined him surreptitiously for any visible signs of head trauma, before I followed the direction of his eyes and realised he was talking about his bodyguards. 'Are they dead?'

'They're definitely not well,' I replied, hurrying to the nearest, whichever it was. He (or she, I've never found it that easy to tell, even without the body armour, and it only matters to another tau anyway) was hanging slackly from the cable they'd used to brace themselves with. Unable to work out how to detach it, I simply drew my chainsword and severed it with a single swipe, catching the comatose warrior as he fell. He stirred feebly as my arm closed to support him, which at least answered one question, although if I'm honest, under the circumstances, I'd have preferred to find a corpse I could abandon at once without losing face. Unwilling to waste any more time, I hefted him across my shoulder, and turned to see how El'hassai was doing with the other.

The second warrior seemed able to walk, thank the Throne, although he was leaning on El'hassai heavily enough to slow them both down, which meant I was three or four paces ahead of them as I jumped the metre or so to the smooth rockcrete of the landing deck.

With sixty-odd kilos of xenos[1] weighing me down, my landing was far from elegant, which was hardly surprising, all things considered. Just as well, too; as I stumbled, a whining chain blade slashed through the place where my head would have been. I recoiled reflexively, dropping the fire warrior in the process, and rolled under another swipe. The servitor turned to follow me, its left leg dragging a little, which let me open the distance between us nicely.

'I can't get a clear shot, sir!' Jurgen yelled, from the direction of the doorway. Everyone else was clustered around it, arguing and gesticulating, which was bad news from where I was standing. Even if they managed to get it open, I'd never reach safety through the crush. I'd just have to keep holding the construct off, and hope for the best.

'I have obtained the shutdown codes for the unit,' Kyper droned, not before time if you asked me. 'Transmitting them now.'

'Much obliged,' I told him, rejecting the pithier alternatives which had occurred to me in the interests of diplomacy, and took up a guard position with my chainsword. I might as well look suitably heroic now the worst of the danger was past, and there was no telling how long the shutdown order might take to kick in anyhow. Just as well I did, too. No sooner had I got the blade up than the blasted thing took another hack at me, which I parried purely by reflex. Sparks flew as the whirling blades clashed, and I stepped back again, ducking under the raised nose of the shuttle. 'Soon would be good.'

'Retrying,' Kyper said, the single word sending an understandable chill through me. 'The servitor's communication nodes appear to be compromised by battle damage.'

'No kidding,' I said, deflecting another lightning-swift blow, and hacking hopefully at the construct's exposed innards on the backstroke. The tau weapons might not have stopped it, but they'd cracked its shell like a cooked crustacean. I was rewarded with a foul-smelling spray of mingled ichor and lubricants, but the thing barely slowed, and I dodged another slash in the nick of time, ducking around the landing leg beneath the nose. As the servitor's blade slammed into it, the whole shuttle shifted, with an ominous grating sound, and I

---

1. *Not a bad estimate, if the combat armour is also taken into account.*

started back, only to find myself a mere three or four strides from the brink of the abyss.

There was little time to worry about that, though, as the servitor continued to close, ignoring the steady plinking of lasgun rounds against its back. Jurgen was losing no time in resuming the offensive now that the strut was affording me some cover from the occasional stray round which missed the target. The crackling, spark-spitting servitor and I became locked in a lethal waltz, hacking and slashing at one another around the thick metal obstruction, spinning this way and that in an attempt to find an opening in the other's defences, or parrying a sudden unexpected blow. A game in which I had the advantage in the short-term, instinct and intellect keeping me ahead of the construct's limited repertoire of pre-programmed moves, but an advantage which would be swiftly eroded as I tired in the face of its unrelenting onslaught.

As I continued to trade blow for blow with the mechanical killer, El'hassai finally jumped clear of the teetering shuttle, his floundering arrival on the landing deck accompanied by the other armoured warrior. The flurry of movement in the corner of my eye as they hit, staggered and fell snatched at my attention for a potentially fatal second. Only reflexes honed in uncountable practice drills and far too many encounters like this one preserved me from decapitation. As it was, I raised my own blade in the nick of time, without conscious awareness of the movement, to deflect what would have otherwise been a lethal outcome to the moment of distraction.

'Get out of the way!' I yelled, aware only that they were now blocking Jurgen's line of fire. The tau seemed to interpret this as concern for their welfare, however, as El'hassai turned to wave briefly in my direction before helping his companion back to his feet. As he did, I noticed the safety line still hanging from the fire warrior's equipment pouch, and a desperate idea began to form. 'Ambassador! The cable!'

'The cable?' El'hassai asked, his voice issuing from the comm-bead in my ear, and I blessed Zyvan's foresight in giving him limited access to our vox-net. 'What of it?'

'Can you get it off his armour?' I asked, the simple question punctuated with blows and parries to such an extent it felt diced into its component syllables. Quick on the uptake, El'hassai wasted no time in a verbal reply, merely fiddling with some kind of catch and holding up a small box, about a palm's width across, as it came free. 'Good! Chuck it over!'

Well, he did his best, but he was a diplomat, not an athlete. The little box arced through the air in my general direction, clanged from the underside of the ominously groaning shuttle, and clattered to the rockcrete terrace about three metres away, rather too close to the edge of the drop for my liking. 'My apologies,' he said, with a final glance over his shoulder at me and his comatose compatriot, before scuttling for the door as fast as his companion's stumbling gait would allow.

'Don't worry about it,' I said, certain that he wasn't exactly going to lose a lot of sleep anyway. I feinted to the right, as though about to break left, hoping the construct would react as predictably as I thought it would. Luckily it did, taking a ponderous step round to the left to intercept the real movement. Which I never took, carrying on the rightward lunge after only the most fractional of pauses, praying to the Emperor I wasn't about to take on a chainblade with my teeth.

Maybe He was listening for once, or maybe it's true what they say about fortune favouring the foolish, but by the time the servitor realised I wasn't where it thought I was going to be I'd hit the rockcrete hard, my outstretched hand scrabbling for the tau's cable reel. For a moment I thought it was sliding out of reach, but I batted it back with the edge of my chainsword, feeling the toes of my boots slipping out over the abyss for a heart-stopping moment; then the strangely-shaped lump of polymer was in my hand, and I scrambled back from the edge, breathing hard.

'Look out, sir!' Jurgen warned as I rose to my knees, and I turned to see the servitor plodding after me with relentless determination, shouldering the landing strut as it strode past. With an ominous grating sound, the precariously balanced shuttle shifted again, and I distinctly felt an answering shudder in the rockcrete. The servitor swept its blade down, spraying me with gravel and chippings as the whirling teeth ground through the rockcrete, and I scrabbled backwards. As I rose to my feet my head clanged painfully against the sloping metal belly of the stranded shuttle, only the padding of my cap preventing me from being stunned by the unexpected blow. This was bad. I was hemmed in, with no line of retreat.

'How do I work this thing?' I voxed, parrying yet another triphammer blow from the relentless machine, shuffling sideways in a crouch to retreat as far beneath the tilting hull as I could. The servitor was unable to stoop, and I hoped it wouldn't be able to reach me so easily there.

'Pull out as much line as you need, and lock off with the safety catch,' El'hassai told me, as though this was something everyone should know. I tugged at the end, experimentally, and found the reel inside the little box ran free, without a hint of snagging or friction. A small indented switch near the hole snicked into place as I prodded it, and the whole thing locked up solid. So far, so good. 'Releasing it again will rewind the cable automatically.'

'That won't be an issue,' I assured him, fumbling the box around in search of something else to press. 'How do I get it to stick?'

'The flat side of the casing will adhere by molecular bonding if you activate the upper control, the pad at the end of the cable adheres if you activate the lower,' El'hassai explained, with commendable brevity.

'Got it,' I said, parrying another mechanically predictable swipe from my lumbering opponent as I spoke, wondering how long my luck would continue to hold out. I slapped the flat side of the little box against the underside of the shuttle, convinced as I did so that I could feel the whole vessel shifting slightly under my hand[1], and squeezed the button El'hassai had indicated. To my vague surprise, it held[2].

Now for the difficult part. Pressing the second button, I swung the end of the cable, in an arc in front of me, whipping it back and forth in a figure of eight, using the cable to fend off the construct. As I'd hoped, it reacted at once, swinging the stump of its autocannon around to entangle the line, intending to reel me in to a messy encounter with

---

1. *Most unlikely; if it had been that critically balanced it would have toppled from the vibrations induced by Cain and El'hassai's disembarkation.*

2. *As it most certainly should; a molecular bond effectively makes both components a part of the same object.*

its chainblade. Timing the movement exactly, I swung up my own weapon to deflect the blow, and rolled out beneath it, coming to my feet behind its elbow. Despite the temptation to get in a parting blow, I dug my toes into the rockcrete and ran as hard as I could towards my companions.

'The shutdown procedure is still failing,' Kyper said, sounding as disgruntled as possible with a mechanically filtered voice.

'Then forget it. Just get the bloody door open!' I snarled. Finding the unconscious tau in my way, and all too aware of the audience clustered around the door, I resisted the temptation to hurdle him and keep going, opting instead to stoop as I passed and grab an arm. Dragging him with me hardly helped my progress, needless to say, and I turned, expecting to see the servitor bearing down on me again. To my relief, though, it was right where I'd left it, anchored to the downed shuttle, well out of chainblade reach. I began to relax.

'Be right with you, sir,' a familiar voice said, and I was joined by Jurgen's body odour, followed an instant later by the man himself. He took the tau's other arm, which speeded us up nicely.

'Thank you, Jurgen,' I said, as we reached the locked portal. I turned, just in time to see the shuttle shift, with a loud groaning of overstressed metal and the shriek of rending hull plates. Then, almost too quickly to register, it had gone, vanishing over the lip of the abyss, dragging the servitor with it.

'One thing I'll say for you, Ciaphas,' Zyvan said, after a moment of horrified silence, which was eventually broken by a reverberating boom from somewhere near the base of the spire. 'You really know how to make an entrance.'

EIGHT

NEEDLESS TO SAY, our spectacular arrival hadn't exactly made a favourable impression on our hosts. Our reception was decidedly frosty, even by the woeful standard of hospitality usually enjoyed by guests of the Adeptus Mechanicus.

Once we finally got inside the spire, and not before time if my aching lungs were anything to go by, the contrast with the outside world was stark, to say the least. I'd been in enough Mechanicus shrines over the years to find the chill, filtered air, with its pervasive scent of ozone, volatiles, and charring insulation familiar enough, as was the overabundance of polished steel surfaces and embossed cogwheels. The usual specimens of venerated mech-junk were scattered about the place, protected from the grubby fingers and mechadendrites of the curious onlooker by cases of meticulously-burnished glass, while the overly-bright luminators did their best to make the metal walls shine in an appropriately reverential manner.

Kyper and his skitarii hurried us through the labyrinth of corridors, which differed only in the arrangement of the technotheological knick-knacks littering the walls, as fast as they could, presumably in an attempt to prevent the xenos from seeing very much; although, given the condition of two of them, that wasn't particularly rapid, and only El'hassai was well enough to sightsee in any case. Not that he seemed the remotest bit interested in doing so, dividing his attention more or less equally between his limping companion, and the one being carried as gently as possible by the most junior pair of Zyvan's underlings.

'I've seen happier cogboys,' I muttered to the Lord General, heedless of the augmented hearing the skitarii probably possessed. None of them gave any sign of having heard me, they just went on chirruping agitatedly at one another in their teeth-aching private language, no doubt making sure that whatever blame might be going around for the debacle on the landing pad, it wouldn't be alighting on them.

'How could you tell?' he riposted, with a sour look at our escort. 'None of the ones I ever met could crack a smile without splitting their heads open.'

'Wait here,' Kyper told us, as we reached a pair of bronze doors roughly twice the height they needed to be for a normal man to enter, although I suppose those tended to be in short supply around here. He shoved the left-hand one open, just wide enough to slip through, and slammed it closed behind him with a boom which echoed uncomfortably around us, reminding me all too clearly of our shuttle's terminal impact among the forges so short a time before.

'I'll do no such thing,' Zyvan declared, his beard bristling, and strode forward to seize the handle. The skitarii moved to block him, and he glared at them, utterly affronted. 'I'm the Lord-bloody-General of the Rimward Sectors, and I don't wait for anyone. They wait for *me!*'

In the silence that followed, I distinctly heard the scuffle and click of sidearms being loosened in their holsters behind us, his aides having no option but to follow the Lord General's lead. Any exchange of fire with the skitarii would have been suicidal, of course, they were all augmented to the gills, and I had no doubt that the hellguns they carried were the least of the lethal surprises they kept about their persons. Moreover, they were hardwired for combat, and would probably open fire purely by reflex the moment they felt threatened. Of rather more concern to me, however, was the fact that

I was standing right between the two factions, in the perfect spot to be riddled by the crossfire. Definitely time to put a stop to this.

'Perhaps we should simply withdraw,' I said, stepping forwards to place a restraining hand on Zyvan's arm, before he could shoulder the door open. I was certain that if he did, trusting in the authority of his position to protect him, the skitarii's neural programming would interpret the movement as a hostile act, and they'd open fire as surely as heretics were damned. 'If the Adeptus Mechanicus doesn't want our help, we can use the resources we brought here in the defence of other systems.'

'Don't think I'm not tempted,' Zyvan snarled, turning to address me directly. No one else could have got away with grabbing his arm like that, but the red sash gives you a lot of leeway[1], and, to my relief, it seemed he was in the mood to listen. 'It's still more than likely that the 'nids'll just sail straight on past this pustule on the arse of the galaxy anyway.'

I tapped the comm-bead in my ear, through which I'd been monitoring our erstwhile pilot's conversation with flight control aboard the flagship. Under less fraught circumstances, I'd have found it quite entertaining, as they hadn't reacted entirely happily to the news that our shuttle had become an expensive pile of scrap, and we'd quite like another one as soon as they could manage it. 'Then I suggest we return to the landing platform,' I said. 'A replacement shuttle's on the way, and if we wait for it there, we can avoid any further unfortunate misunderstandings.'

At which point the door jerked open with quite unnecessary force, confirming my guess that at least one of the skitarii had been relaying our discussion to whoever was waiting inside. Kyper appeared in the gap, almost nose to olfactory sensor plate with Zyvan and myself, looking as agitated as possible with a face composed almost entirely of motionless ironmongery. 'Lord General,' he droned, standing aside and gesturing expansively with an arm which would have looked rather more inviting without

---

1. *Typically, it doesn't seem to have occurred to Cain that Zyvan was prompted to listen by his personal regard for him, rather than the authority of his office.*

quite so much serrated metal grafted along the edge of it, 'you are welcome.'

'Since when?' Zyvan muttered to me, but strode into the chamber beyond without further comment, or backward glance at the rest of us. I followed, with the semblance of a courteous nod at the centurion turned commissionaire, Jurgen falling into place at my shoulder as reliably as always. Zyvan's underlings surged forwards too, only to be checked by Kyper's upraised hand.

'The xenos may not set foot in the Sanctum of Ratiocination,' he insisted firmly. 'They are to be returned to your ship with all dispatch.'

'The tau delegation is here at my personal invitation,' I said, ignoring him, in favour of getting a good look at the chamber I'd just entered. It was high, vaulted in precious metals, and dominated by a huge icon of the Emperor in His aspect of the Machine God. A crescent of seats, each with a data lectern planted firmly in front of it, enclosed a raised dais, on which a venerable tech-priest, so heavily augmented he barely seemed to qualify as human any more, was attended by a gaggle of junior acolytes and a couple of hovering servo-skulls. The surrounding seats were full of other magi, most of them heavily enhanced as well, although one seemed to retain a fair amount of her original flesh: enough, at least, to show some semblance of an expression on her face, although, like a good little tech-priest, she was trying to look impassive, rather than agog at the drama unfolding in front of her. 'I appreciate that they're hardly natural allies, but we do have common cause against the tyranids.'

'That is not the issue,' the pile of machine parts on the dais grated, as though affronted at having to communicate with us by something as imprecise as Gothic[1]. 'They defile the domain of the Omnissiah with their unhallowed devices!' He glared through the door at the armoured fire warriors, the lenses of his optical filters seeming to flare red with wrath, although I suppose it was simply the reflection of his robe. Pretty much everyone in the room was wearing some shade

---

1. *Probably he was simply out of practice, after decades of communicating almost exclusively in binary.*

of the colour, apart from a couple in white[1], and I wondered briefly if the subtle variations in hue were signifiers of status in some way. Then again, it could equally well have reflected the number of times the garment had been to the laundry.

'Then the matter is easily remedied,' El'hassai said, apparently refusing to take offence, although Throne knows I would have done in his place. He removed something from his ear, then delved into his pockets, and handed the comm-bead and a few other items I didn't recognise to the limping warrior. 'All examples of tau technology will be returned to the landing pad forthwith, to await the arrival of the shuttle.'

'They'd be better destroyed,' the woman advised, and the presiding magos chirruped and hummed for a moment, apparently communing with his colleagues in the fashion of their kind.

'Removal will suffice,' he said at last, somewhat grudgingly if I was any judge. 'On the strict understanding that no xenos device pollutes the sanctity of Fecundia again.' It was clear that what he really meant was any bearer of such devices, but under the circumstances he could hardly say so in so many words. 'As it is, we must simply bear the intolerable affront of their presence for a short while longer.'

'Intolerable affront?' Zyvan roared, still in no mood for diplomacy himself. 'You opened fire on us, destroyed our shuttle, and damn near killed Commissar Cain! *That's* an affront, you self-righteous bag of bolts!' He turned on his heel, apparently on the point of marching out of the room. 'I wish you luck with the tyranids, because unless I hear an apology in the next five seconds, we're leaving orbit as soon as we dock!'

'Lord General,' the woman said, rising to her feet with a glare at her superior which didn't need the almost inaudible squeal of a binary exchange that accompanied it to transmit the message. Zyvan

---

1. *A tradition still stubbornly maintained by a handful of tech-priests, who claim it predates the russet generally favoured by the priesthood of Mars. It seems likely that this unconventional attire is meant to display the wearer's position on one or other of the countless doctrinal disputes continually raging among the disciples of the Omnissiah, although what these may be is utterly opaque to outsiders, and unlikely to matter to anyone but the participants.*

hesitated; if anyone else had spoken at that point, I truly believe he'd have made good on his threat, or at least given me a hard time arguing him out of it. His temper was not easily roused, but quite formidable when it was, and it hadn't taken me long to realise why having a commissar around when he was most liable to be irritated was a good idea. But the clear feminine voice had taken him by surprise, cutting though the fog of anger with which he'd surrounded himself. 'Magos Dysen may have chosen his words a little carelessly. Few of us, I'm afraid, are used to discoursing with those from outside our order.'

'Quite,' the magos grated, not happy to have his face saved by an underling (or the front of his head, anyway, since he no longer possessed anything which could fairly be described as facial features). 'Magos Kildhar is correct. No offence was intended. Had we been aware that the xenos would be accompanying you, the servitor's cortex would have been amended with appropriate updates to its instruction set.'

'Fine,' I said. 'It was all a bit dramatic, but no harm done in the end.' A disturbing thought belatedly crossed my mind. 'There wasn't anyone under that shuttle when it went over the edge, was there?'

'No one of any significance,' Kildhar assured me.

'Production of mattocks, trivets and flue dampers will be significantly disrupted, however,' one of the seated tech-priests put in, sounding distinctly affronted. 'Extensive repairs to the manufactory will be required.'

'We have, however, gained significant amounts of refined raw materials,' another cut in, equally determined to look on the bright side. He glanced at Zyvan. 'Unless you wish the component parts of the shuttle returned to you? I am assured it is beyond repair.'

'Help yourself,' Zyvan said gruffly, his anger beginning to dissipate. Like most tech-priests, these idiots were clearly in a world of their own, into which the real galaxy seldom intruded. Unfortunately, one of its least pleasant facets was about to descend on them in uncountable numbers unless we did something about it, and Zyvan's pique notwithstanding, we had little option other than doing our best to defend them. Though it still seemed as if the tau border worlds were more likely to be targeted, we couldn't take that for granted. Losing Fecundia, and the munitions produced there, could cost us half the sector, and as little as that only if we were lucky.

'Then perhaps we'd better get down to business,' I suggested, giving them something other than their real or imagined grievances to think about. There were, of course, no chairs for visitors anywhere in the chamber, but it didn't take long to remedy that deficiency once I'd tactfully pointed it out. Dysen tweedled grumpily at one of his servo-skulls, which scooted out of the chamber, returning a few minutes later at the head of a small comet tail of servitors bearing seats fashioned of bright polished steel, the backs filigreed into a representation of the Holy Cogwheel. Hideously uncomfortable, but the chairs our hosts were sitting in were almost identical so it would have been churlish to complain, although I'll wager the bloody things were a good deal better suited to their tin arses than to our natural ones. As the meeting wore on, I even began to feel a kind of wistful nostalgia for the tau mushrooms.

'The good news,' Zyvan said, taking full advantage of his status as the senior military member of the expedition to remain on his feet while he conducted the briefing, 'is that the main hive fleet is continuing on its course.' He gestured to the hololith display, fizzing and wobbling in the air above his head, while a covey of adepts prodded hopefully at the projection equipment. Not for the first time, I had the feeling that most of our audience resented the exchange of information proceeding at what must have seemed like a snail's pace to them.

'Then it seems we have little to fear,' Dysen said, gazing up at the image, which finally steadied. The projected line of the tyranids' advance passed the Fecundia system altogether and a palpable sense of relief swept across the room as the coin dropped for everyone else.

'With respect, magos,' I said, pouncing on the chance to stand up that the intervention offered, and pointing dramatically at the display as I did so, 'such a conclusion would not only be premature, but potentially fatal.' The last thing I needed right now was to be dragged back to the main battlefront, which would be all too likely if Zyvan made good on his threat to leave Fecundia to its own devices.

'How so?' Dysen asked, clearly out of his depth. At least he was honest enough to admit his own ignorance, instead of blustering it out, and I found my opinion of him rising a little in consequence.

'Because this is only our best guess at their course, based on the most recent intelligence we have,' I told him. 'The Navy and the tau have both sent scout squadrons to verify it, but until they do, we must work on the assumption that the 'nids could diverge from this trajectory at any time. The population of Fecundia is certainly large enough to tempt them here if they become aware of its presence.'

'And even if the main fleet holds its course,' Zyvan added, 'they can still send out scouts of their own in search of prey. We've observed that kind of thing many times before.'

'Then our ground forces should remain alert,' Kildhar put in, much to my surprise. 'If they become aware of us, we should expect infiltrating organisms to probe our defences.'

'We should,' I agreed. 'You seem remarkably well informed, magos.'

'I am a magos biologis,' she explained, 'and the ways of the tyranids are not entirely unknown to me.'

'Lucky for us,' I said, blissfully unaware of how wrong I was about that.

'I stand ready to render any assistance you may require,' she assured us.

'Good,' Zyvan said, evidently somewhat mollified by the display of co-operation. 'At least someone here's taking this seriously.'

'I think you'll find we all are,' Dysen droned. 'Even though our priorities may differ in some respects.'

'Our priority is to secure this world,' I said, stepping in quickly to stifle another potential outbreak of discord. 'On that we all agree.' I glanced sideways at El'hassai as I spoke, wondering if that was entirely true in his case. After all, if Fecundia fell, the tau would be able to rampage unopposed across half the Gulf, assuming there was anything left of it after the 'nids had finished. His face was impossible to read, however, although his head inclined in a barely perceptible nod.

'We do,' Dysen said, to my unspoken relief, 'and your advice in the matter will be heeded.'

Which was not the same as being accepted, of course, but it was the best we were going to get at the moment, and once we had thirty thousand heavily armed Guardsmen stationed on planet, I was pretty sure our view would prevail.

'Have you enough vessels to defend the system from invasion?' Kildhar asked, looking at the hololith with a calculating expression. 'If I read these icons correctly, only a third of them are warships.'

'That's true,' Zyvan admitted, 'the majority are troop carriers. They'll be returning to Coronus as soon as the Imperial Guard units have disembarked. But the Navy assures me that we have sufficient firepower among the warships to see off a hive ship or two.'

'Then let us hope the tyranids don't send any more than that,' Dysen said dryly.

Zyvan turned back to the hololith. 'Battlefleet Damocles is fully aware of the threat, and moving to meet it,' he said. 'Three flotillas and a battlegroup are on course to rendezvous at Quadravidia, ready to intercept the main tyranid advance in deep space as soon as its course is reliably determined.'

'Somewhat reassuring,' Kildhar said, in a tone which implied it was anything but. 'If I read the data correctly, however, this rendezvous will not take place until between five and thirty-seven days after the hive fleet's closest approach to Fecundia, depending on the vagaries of the warp currents.'

'Then, as Magos Dysen has so succinctly put it,' I said, shamelessly flattering the venerable tech-priest in the interests of making life easier, 'let us hope the tyranids are considerate enough to attack in manageable numbers.'

'The fleet defending Dr'th'nyr is considerably closer,' El'hassai pointed out, 'and could relieve this system if required.'

'I thought I made our position clear,' Dysen rumbled. 'Unhallowed technologies will not be tolerated in a system dedicated to the worship of the Machine God.'

Zyvan opened his mouth to say something, his face darkening again, and I stepped in hastily to forestall him.

'I'm sure that the Omnissiah would never allow sufficient harm to befall so devout a world as to make that necessary,' I said, entirely untruthfully. Most of the cogboys ranged around the room nodded smugly.

'Then the matter is unlikely to arise,' El'hassai agreed, his accent dissipating the sarcasm I was certain was there.

'To return to your own point, magos,' I said, addressing Kildhar directly, 'the greatest threat in the short term is likely to come from infiltration, rather than a mass assault. The Navy will, of course, be making continuous auspex sweeps, but tyranid spores are notoriously hard to detect in small numbers. Any advice you could give on enhancing the sensitivity of our instruments would be gratefully received.'

'Of course.' She inclined her head. 'I will make the appropriate arrangements.'

'The real problem's the number of other ships in the sky,' Zyvan said. 'Every auspex in the fleet is being clogged up with thousands of returns[1]. We need to close the system to civilian traffic for the duration of the emergency.'

'Out of the question,' Dysen said, quite predictably. 'We're completely reliant on imported foodstuffs. Our protein synthesis plants can only provide enough nutrients for forty-seven per cent of the population.'

'Then ration it,' Zyvan snapped.

'Not an option, I'm afraid,' Kildhar said, with a passable attempt at a regretful expression. 'Nutritional intake for the general populace is precisely calculated to maintain the maximum level of health with the minimum expenditure of resources. Even a five per cent reduction will have noticeably deleterious effects, and reducing daily allowances to a level commensurate with equal distribution would starve everyone to death within a month.'

---

1. *Like all forge worlds, Fecundia was continually surrounded by a swarm of freighters bringing in food and raw materials, and carrying away the products manufactured there. Zyvan may have been exaggerating the number of civilian vessels present, but not by much; shipping records for the time show an average of six to eight hundred arrivals and departures a day, while many more would be in orbit transferring cargo at the same time.*

'That couldn't happen,' I said, to her evident surprise. I smiled, without humour. 'The riots would have levelled the hives long before that.'

'A good point,' she agreed. 'The tithe workers would undoubtedly respond in an emotional manner.'

'So we can't reduce the level of shipping,' Zyvan said, reluctantly, although that was fine by me; the more ships in orbit, the better my chances of making a run for it if the 'nids really did overwhelm our defences.

'It would appear not,' I agreed. 'So we'll just have to make the best of it.' I glanced around the room. The undercurrent of unease and suppressed hostility still crackled in the air like distant lightning. 'And good luck with that,' I added quietly to myself, thumbing my palm for good measure.

NINE

Wɪᴛʜ ʀᴇʟᴀᴛɪᴏɴꜱ ᴀꜱ strained as they were between the expeditionary force and the Adeptus Mechanicus, it was hardly surprising that the bulk of the liaison work fell on me[1]. Zyvan wanted as little to do with the tech-priests as possible, while Dysen made it abundantly clear that the feeling was entirely mutual. I, on the other hand, was supposed by all parties to be a paragon of the Imperial virtues, so both were inclined to listen to me. More inclined than they were to listen to one another, anyway. Accordingly, I spent the next couple of weeks in a complex gavotte of half-truth and misdirection, intended to give the Lord General and Magos Senioris alike the impression that I considered their view of things the more reasonable, and that with a little more flexibility we'd be able to talk the other one round. No doubt Donali would have made a better fist of it, but he was parsecs away and at least I'd had plenty of practice at that sort of thing, after a lifetime of successfully deflecting blame and taking credit I didn't deserve.

The biggest disadvantage of all this, so far as I was concerned, was that I was forced to relocate from the comfort of the flagship to the relatively spartan conditions of the forge world, in order to discharge

---

1. *Or Jurgen, knowing Cain.*

my responsibilities most effectively. Apart from the full-time job of trying to talk some sense into Dysen, there was the small matter of an Imperial Guard army to deploy and get settled in, with all the friction between them and the local civilians which that normally entailed. Even more so in this case, as there were innumerable areas closed to us on the grounds of doctrine, safety, or sheer bloody-mindedness. At least the Death Korps seemed happy enough to rough it out in the wilderness, which would have killed more of the other regiments than the enemy, so they were out from underfoot, but the rest, a motley collection from over a dozen worlds[1], presented me with a constant stream of headaches. More than once I was tempted to pack the whole thing in and recommend our withdrawal, on the grounds that the 'nids were still bearing down on Dr'th'nyr like Jurgen catching sight of an all you can eat smorgasbord, and only the reflection that, if I did, Zyvan would undoubtedly take us off to confront them directly stayed my hand. Besides, we still couldn't be entirely sure that the world was out of danger yet, and going down in history as the man who lost the Gulf would hardly have been the finest of ends to my undeservedly glittering career.

Fortunately the Mechanicus maintained a number of comfortably furnished suites near their inner sanctum for the convenience of visiting Imperial dignitaries, which they seemed to consider me as, so I was less incommoded than I'd feared, but I certainly missed the artistry of Zyvan's personal chef, the bland diet of soylens viridians on which I was obliged to subsist for the most part wreaking predictable havoc on my digestion[2]. Jurgen managed to get hold of some spices from somewhere, which preserved my taste buds from terminal atrophy, but if it hadn't been for my periodic visits to the flagship to liaise with Zyvan in person I don't suppose I'd have had a decent meal my entire time on Fecundia.

---

1. *Mostly from within the sector, although regiments from Brimlock, Elyssia and Valhalla were also present; including the 12th Field Artillery, the unit with which Cain had commenced his career, although if he found time to make a social call on his old comrades-in-arms he doesn't bother to mention it.*

2. *Consisting as it does mainly of reconstituted pulses, the consequences of relying on it as a staple become all too evident remarkably quickly, particularly in a confined space.*

'How's the deployment going?' he asked, having the decency to wait until I'd finished chewing and swallowing. I hadn't been able to time things to take advantage of his hospitality on this visit, more's the pity, but Jurgen, reliable as ever, had trotted off to the nearest galley the moment we'd docked, returning with the welcome booty of hot salt grox baps and a steaming mug of recaff, which I'd seized with gratitude.

'No worse than we'd expected,' I replied, alternating bites at the food with the conversation as we made our way through the familiar bustle of the command centre. An image of Fecundia was rotating gently in the hololith, looking more like a giant canker than ever, speckled with icons showing our current state of readiness. Far too few were accompanied by the fully operational rune than I liked, and I made no bones about saying so, certain that Zyvan would share that opinion. 'But I'd be a lot happier if we had more units in position by now.'

'So would I,' the Lord General agreed. He looked at the faintly translucent image with a grimace of distaste. 'At least we've got the main habs fortified.'

'Now I've managed to persuade Dysen to go along with it,' I said, seeing no harm in reminding him of how hard I'd been working down there. 'He wanted to secure the production facilities first.'

'No doubt,' Zyvan said, accepting the mug of recaff Jurgen had procured for him as well with a nod of thanks, and the most barely perceptible of flinches. 'How did you persuade him?'

'By pointing out that he wouldn't be able to produce anything at all if the 'nids ate his workforce,' I said. In fact it had been Kildhar who'd first seen the logic of that, and helped to talk him round, but as she wasn't here to dispute the point I didn't think it was worth confusing matters by saying so.

'Quite.' Zyvan took a quick slurp of the warm, bitter drink, and turned back to the hololith. 'Not that we need his permission to do anything we damn well like.' Which was technically true now most of our guns were planetside, if you believed force of arms could win any argument. But if it came to that, the machine spirits of Fecundia would be certain to take the side of the affronted tech-priests, which would hardly make our job any easier.

'Nevertheless, it's probably better to keep the cogboys happy for as long as we can,' I said. If war really came, hard choices would have to be made about who and what could be saved, and I knew in my bones that our differing priorities would make that all the harder, particularly if old grievances were still simmering away.

Zyvan sighed. 'You're right. Glad that's your problem, though.'

'I thought you would be,' I said, and he smiled for the first time since my arrival.

'Our main weak spot's the wilderness,' he said, studying the slowly rotating globe. 'We can dig in to defend the hives, but nothing can last out in the open for long. For all we know the 'nids could have a beachhead out there already, and we'd never even know it.'

'Until they massed for an attack,' I agreed, liking the idea no more than he did. The hellish conditions on the surface wouldn't worry the tyranids at all, the ones who couldn't burrow under it simply growing thicker armour to protect themselves. 'Trouble is, we don't have much that can operate effectively in those conditions, so any long-range recon is right out.' I indicated the few icons outside the fortress-like walls of the hives. 'The Death Korps are forming an extended picket line, backed up by whatever armour we can get out there, but our tanks and carriers can only run for a few hours before coming in again.'

'Why?' Zyvan asked, and I shrugged.

'Ash. Keeps getting in to the tracks and engines, whatever the cogboys rig up to try and filter it. Every time one of our vehicles goes out, it needs stripping down completely as soon as it gets back, or it'll seize up solid.'

'I can see why you want to keep Dysen sweet,' Zyvan conceded. 'What about the skitarii?'

'Patrolling too,' I said, indicating their icons. The Mechanicus troopers were augmented enough to survive out there too, if not exactly thrive, and were mounting periodic sorties from the hive, although I strongly suspected that was as much to keep an eye on the Death Korps as it was to keep a lookout for tyranids. 'They're meant to be liaising, but so far they've stuck to their zones and we've stuck to ours, so we haven't had a major conflict of interest. If the 'nids attack, though, they're just as likely to go their own way. Best not to formulate any strategy which relies on their co-operation.'

Zyvan snorted, and took another slug of recaff. 'I'd worked that out for myself,' he told me, to my complete lack of surprise. 'It's worse than having a Sororitas contingent to work around[1].'

'But with fewer hymns,' I said, eliciting the second smile of the day, before returning to the topic at hand. I studied the necrotic globe as dispassionately as I could. Despite our best efforts, there were still huge swathes of it across which we were all but blind. 'It seems to me that we're pretty much reliant on orbital reconnaissance.'

'We are,' Zyvan confirmed. 'The Navy's scanning the surface for tyranid biosigns, so far as they can through the dust storms, as well as keeping a watch for any incoming spores. Nothing so far, but it doesn't mean they're not there.'

'I thought Kildhar was supposed to be tweaking the auspexes,' I said. 'Any luck with that?'

'A little,' a new voice put in, and the magos biologis herself crawled out from behind a sensorium suite cluttering up the far corner of the room. Zyvan had evidently forgotten her presence there, judging by his expression, mentally running back through our conversation in the hope that neither of us had said anything too indiscreet. If she had overheard us, she showed no sign of irritation or embarrassment, but then tech-priests seldom did, so it was hard to be sure. No point worrying about it that I could see, though, so I simply shrugged. 'We've installed some new filters,' she went on, 'which should refine the data, and help eliminate false positives. We don't want to go to high alert and turn out the skitarii only to find ourselves chasing an ambull colony when they get there, do we?'

'There are ambull down there?' I asked, astonished at the idea that

---

1. *Since the Adepta Sororitas believe they take their orders from the Emperor Himself, by way of the Ecclesiarchy, they have little time for the instructions of any mere generals or Chapter Masters they may find themselves fighting alongside. Or inquisitors, for that matter, although members of the Ordo Hereticus tend to make a little more headway with them than the others.*

the polluted wasteland could sustain any life at all, let alone the huge, aggressive burrowers.

Kildhar nodded. 'An entire ecosystem, in fact. My title is far from honorary, I can assure you.'

'I'm sure it's not,' I said. 'I was just wondering if there's any chance of a steak when we get back.'

'It's possible, I suppose,' Kildhar said, looking faintly puzzled. 'Some of the surface workers hunt them if the opportunity arises, but the consumption of animal tissue is a singularly inefficient way of ingesting nutrient.' She looked disparagingly at the remains of the bap in my hand. 'Soylens viridiens is far more convenient, and provides everything necessary for continuing good health.'

'Except flavour,' I said feelingly. 'And texture.' My mouth flooded with saliva at the thought of a sizzling chunk of dead flesh.

'Oh.' Kildhar looked more baffled than ever. 'Those.'

'I'll see what I can do, sir,' Jurgen said, with quiet confidence, and my spirits rose at the prospect of a proper meal at last. My aide's talent for scrounging bordered on the preternatural, and I was certain that if ambull steak was to be had anywhere in the hive, he'd find it, even if it meant bagging the brute himself.

Then another, more disquieting thought struck, and I turned back to the tech-priest. 'If there's an ecosystem, that means the 'nids can find prey if they get through. They'll be able to build up their strength far quicker than we bargained for.'

'That would be the case,' Kildhar admitted. '*If* they get through. We'll just have to make certain they don't.'

Easier said than done, if you asked me, but verbalising the thought wouldn't get us very far, so I just trotted out some platitudes about us all working together to ensure that, and left her to it, moving further out of earshot as I resumed my conversation with the Lord General. 'Any news from the scout squadrons?' I asked, and Zyvan shook his head, his expression grave.

'Nothing yet,' he said, 'but the closer they are to the hive fleet, the deeper in its warp shadow they are. Their astropaths won't be able to send anything until they clear it.'

'If they ever do,' I said, the image of the tau explorators' last moments rising up vividly in my mind's eye.

Zyvan nodded, clearly thinking the same thing. 'If they do swing this way, we'll get very little warning. If any.'

'Then we'd better hope she knows what she's doing,' I said, with a glance at Kildhar, who was back at work by now, poking hopefully at something in the sensorium with her mechadendrites. It responded with a loud pop and the flash of an electrical discharge.

'Indeed,' Zyvan agreed, making the sign of the aquila as he spoke.

THE REST OF my business with Zyvan took some time, as you'd expect with the collated reports of an entire army to summarise, and, by the time I'd finished, my estimable aide had returned to the galley more than once. At last, though, we said our farewells, and plodded back to the hangar bay, where an unpleasant surprise awaited us.

'What do you mean, there are no shuttles?' I demanded, more in astonishment than in anger. The Naval non-com[1] who'd broken the news stepped back a pace, and swallowed nervously.

'The one you came in on's been reassigned, sir. Medevac. Priority one.'

I felt a chill run down my spine. 'I was unaware that any of our units were in combat,' I said, wondering if the 'nids had managed to sneak in under our noses, in spite of Kildhar's best efforts with soldering irons, coding patches, and incense burners. Then another, more ominous thought struck: a friendly fire incident between the Guardsmen and skitarii would complicate things hideously, if I could even begin to smooth matters over at all...

'They aren't, sir,' the matelot made haste to assure me, much to my relief. 'It was an industrial accident, in the Rusthill munition works. The Lord General felt it would be good for morale if we were seen to be helping out.'

'It would,' I agreed. The injured workers and their colleagues would

---

1. *If Cain is a little vague about Naval ranks that's hardly surprising, given that he spent his entire career attached to the Imperial Guard, and would be far less familiar with their insignia and rank structure.*

appreciate the efforts made on their behalf and want to repay the debt by keeping us well supplied, the Mechanicus would get their precious plant working again that little bit faster, and the experience of working together would help to overcome the lingering animosity which was continuing to make my job more difficult than it needed to be. It was a good call, and one I'd probably have made myself in Zyvan's shoes. On the other hand... 'How long until a shuttle becomes available?'

'I couldn't say, sir,' the sailor told me, visibly relieved not to be shot on the spot for giving me the bad news. 'Some time, though, be my guess. Sounds like a real mess down there.'

'What about that one?' Jurgen asked, pointing a grubby finger in the vague direction of a crimson Aquila, picked out in gold around the feather plates, and bearing a silver cogwheel on its fuselage.

'That would be mine,' Kildhar said, striding through the airlock. 'For the exclusive use of the Adeptus Mechanicus.' She favoured us with a friendly nod as she spoke, the stiffness of her neck mute testament to the unfamiliarity of the gesture. She could have used some lessons from El'hassai in mimicking normal human responses, but at least she made the effort. 'I'm surprised to find you still aboard, commissar.'

'And I you,' I replied, already wondering if I could turn this to my advantage. There would surely be room for a couple of extra passengers aboard the shuttle, since she seemed to be alone. 'My consultations with the Lord General took a good deal of time.'

'As did my adjustments to the sensoria.' If she was surprised to find Jurgen and I falling into step with her, she gave no sign of it. 'But I believe they will prove adequate to the task.'

'I'm pleased to hear it,' I said. 'Some excellent news to pass on to the Magos Senioris when I see him.' I glanced at my chronograph, exaggerating the movement just sufficiently to make sure it was noticed. 'Which was supposed to be within the hour.'

'I am sure you will be able to obtain transportation soon,' Kildhar said, pausing at the foot of the boarding ramp, and pointedly refusing to take the hint.

'We could come with you,' Jurgen said, with characteristic bluntness. Subtlety was just something that happened to other people so far as he was concerned. 'If that would be convenient, miss,' he added, with a belated attempt at politeness.

'I'm afraid that would be impossible,' Kildhar said, doing her best to sound as though she meant it. 'My pilot servitor has pre-programmed flight instructions, which cannot be overridden. Otherwise this vessel would also be assisting in the current crisis.'

'A simple hop to the surface will do us fine,' I persisted. 'We can return to the spire from any of the pads in the hive.'

'Regrettably, I will not be landing within the hive itself,' Kildhar said, with the air of a regicide player successfully assassinating my king. 'And my destination is closed to outsiders.'

'I see,' I said, my curiosity piqued, although if I'd known what that was going to lead to, I'd have told it to sit down and shut up. At the time, though, I just felt that anything the Mechanicus didn't want us to know about was probably something we needed to, and the chance to uncover it was too good to miss. It was bad enough trying to defend this miserable clinker as it was, without our allies springing any unpleasant surprises at the worst possible moment. 'I'm sure Magos Dysen will appreciate you weren't able to help us keep our appointment with him. And the Lord General certainly won't object to him being kept out of the loop for a while longer.'

A faint frown of uncertainty began lapping around the immobile, metallic parts of Kildhar's face, while she worked it out. 'Wait here a moment,' she said at last, disappearing inside the shuttle. A few seconds later she appeared in the unoccupied upper cupola, partially obscured by the bands of metal holding the armourglass panels in place, and busied herself with a vox-unit. Whether by accident or design, she kept her back to us, so I wasn't able to glean the substance of the conversation by attempting to lip read, although at that distance I probably wouldn't have been able to make out much in any case[1].

After a few moments of discussion, accompanied by a good deal

---

1. *Almost certainly, as tech-priests conversing among themselves are unlikely to confine themselves to Gothic.*

of emphatic arm waving, she returned, and beckoned us aboard the Aquila. 'Under the circumstances,' she said, 'and since it's you, a majority of the senior magi are prepared to allow you limited access to the facility.'

'Jolly good of them,' I said, following her up the ramp. Although, had I known what awaited us on the surface, I would have walked back to Fecundia, rather than set foot on the blasted shuttle.

TEN

OUR DESCENT WAS uneventful, and as uncomfortable as I'd anticipated. True to form, the Mechanicus had apparently decided that refinements like seat padding were unnecessary, and probably inefficient to boot, so we found ourselves perching on a welded metal bench, above which safety harnesses had been fastened at what seemed to me to be the most inconvenient height rational analysis could have determined.

There was little attempt at conversation from any of us. Our voices would have had to be raised to be heard over the shriek of the engines in any case, soundproofing being another refinement the tech-priests apparently considered redundant[1]. Jurgen had lapsed into his usual airsickness-induced torpor as soon as we hit the atmosphere, while Kildhar maintained a thoughtful silence, her eyes unfocused[2], and I was as preoccupied as ever, wondering if I was doing the right thing. Something about the tech-priest's words in the hangar bay disturbed me, and I replayed them in my mind obsessively.

---

1. *Most of them would have found the noise inspiring in fact, considering it the shuttle's hymn of praise to the Omnissiah.*

2. *Probably processing data, or interfacing directly with the on-board systems.*

'Since it's you,' she'd said. At the time I'd taken that purely as a reference to my reputation, and the toehold in the Mechanicus camp my position as Dysen and Zyven's go-between had afforded me, but on reflection there had been something about the cadence of her voice which had hinted at something else. And she seemed to have arranged clearance for me to visit this shrine remarkably quickly, given how hidebound the disciples of the Omnissiah generally were by tradition and precedent, and how jealously they guarded their secrets.

'Where are we going, exactly?' I asked, as her eyes finally focused again. By this time we were skimming across one of the ash wastes, a patch of blight downwind from the furnaces of the south-western manufactory zone, which seemed to stretch halfway to the horizon. Bilious brown and yellow clouds scudded across its surface, whorled into phantom shapes by the slipstream of our passage: noxious effusions from the heart of the slowly cooling embers of industry, whose toxic touch would suffocate or burn the unwary to death in a matter of moments. Offhand, I could think of few places I'd ever been which looked so singularly uninviting.

'Regio Quinquaginta Unus,' she replied. 'One of our most sacred shrines. Few outside our order are even aware of its existence.'

'Then I'm honoured to be made an exception,' I said, in my most diplomatic tone.

'What's so special about it?' Jurgen asked, roused from his silent suffering by the prospect of being back on the ground before long, and cutting directly to the heart of the matter as he so often did.

Kildhar seemed taken aback by the directness of the question, and pondered a moment before making a reply. 'It's a repository,' she said at last. 'Of knowledge so ancient its origins are lost to us. And a sanctuary, for those dedicated to its recovery and application.'

'You're talking about archeotech, aren't you?' I said, and the tech-priest nodded. She seemed to be getting better at it, I noted absently, unless it was just that she meant it this time.

'Recovered from a dozen places across the sector,' she told me reverently, 'and brought here for preservation and study.'

'I can appreciate why you would want to keep that confidential,' I said, suppressing a shudder. I'd come across a few revenant artefacts myself over the decades, and the consequences had never been good. Memories of dodging genestealers in the bowels of a space hulk jostled with those of the lunatic fervour in Killian's eyes as he tried to convince me that dragging the galaxy into damnation was the best way to save it, and of the relentless advance of the gleaming metal killers in the labyrinth of tunnels beneath Interitus Prime. 'That kind of knowledge can attract the wrong kind of attention.'

'Then we must rely on your discretion,' she said.

'I'm honoured that you think you can,' I said, truthfully enough, already beginning to compose an urgently worded dispatch to Amberley in my head as I spoke[1]. For all I knew the Inquisition was already perfectly aware of this stockpile of primordial junk, but it never hurt to spread the word a little further, especially if one of the inquisitors in the know happened to be a dangerous loon[2], like the late and unlamented Killian.

There was little time for further conversation after that, as the Aquila banked sharply and the shrine itself came into view. A hexagonal block of rockcrete rose up out of the dark grey drifts beneath us, looking not unlike one of the thousands of defensive bunkers I'd observed, cowered in, or tried to avoid assaulting in the course of my long and inglorious career, until the profusion of vox antennae, heat sinks, and substructures encrusting its surface allowed me to get some sense of scale. It was at least two hundred metres high, and twice that across. As we rose above it, the outline of a blessed cogwheel became visible, inlaid into the roof, and encircling the centre of it, running just inside the narrowest portions of the hexagon. In the very centre the motif was repeated, enclosing a raised landing pad, which at the moment appeared to be unoccupied.

'I can't see any guards,' Jurgen said, turning in his seat to get a better view, and almost throttling himself with the misaligned crash webbing.

---

1. *Which was, indeed, compelling.*
2. *Practically a requirement for service with the Ordo Malleus.*

'I'm sure there must be some,' I said, with a quizzical glance at our hostess. 'Skitarii?'

'Three contubernia are stationed here at all times,' she told me, in a faintly evasive manner.

'Three squads,' I said thoughtfully, translating the term into its Imperial Guard equivalent[1]. 'Should be enough for an installation this size.'

'It's proved adequate so far,' Kildhar assured me. The Aquila was on its final approach now, its landing jets flaring, and I felt the sudden surge of acceleration against my spine as it rose a little to position itself above the centre of the pad. Then the engines powered down, and the landing skids ground against the rockcrete. 'And, of course, we take other precautions.' There was a hint of a smile hovering round her lips, despite her best efforts to retain the expressionless face expected of a tech-priest; clearly she was expecting me to ask what.

'I'd expect nothing less,' I said, as the whine of our engines died away, refusing to play the game. If I did ask, she'd just tell me I didn't have the right clearance, subtly underlining who was really in charge here, whereas if I affected complete indifference there was every chance she might let something slip in an attempt to needle me into a response. Before she had the chance to try, though, the Aquila lurched again, prompting a questioning look from my aide.

'We're not about to take off again, are we?' he asked, in tones of resigned dread.

I shook my head. 'The engines have powered down,' I pointed out, beginning to wonder why the pilot hadn't dropped the ramp already. But even as I spoke, the whole shuttle shuddered for a second time, and began to descend slowly through the surface of the roof. The thick raft of rockcrete, and the supporting girderwork, rose smoothly past the viewport, and I found myself looking down into a hangar not dissimilar to the one from which we'd so recently departed. Being part of a Mechanicus shrine rather than a warship, however, the metal

---

1. *A near enough approximation, although the actual numbers might vary: combat servitors like the one Cain encountered on his initial arrival would sometimes be attached directly to the formation in place of a regular trooper, as would specialists with other useful skills.*

walls were bright and reflective instead of drab and stained, and the ground crews scurrying towards us wore the red robes of enginseers instead of void suits.

'I would recommend remaining seated,' Kildhar said, a trifle smugly, as I half rose to catch a glimpse of a thick roof sliding closed above us. Clearly, since it was showing so openly, she was finding our surprise a source of considerable amusement. The elevator platform stopped moving, with a faint jerk, and I wavered a moment before regaining my balance.

'A neat trick,' I allowed, as a small tractor scuttled across the hangar to attach itself to our shuttle's nose, and began dragging us away into a corner[1] next to a refuelling point.

'We have plenty more,' Kildhar assured me, as the Aquila stopped moving at last, and the boarding ramp began to descend.

JURGEN AND I walked down the ramp cautiously, getting our first good look at our surroundings as we did so, Kildhar following a pace or two behind. The air in the cavernous hangar was tainted with the sulphurous stench of the outside atmosphere, but it seemed perfectly breathable. Indeed, within a matter of moments I barely noticed the residual smell at all[2]. 'That was a good deal more comfortable than our first arrival,' I remarked, with rather less tact than I might have employed, but Kildhar took the intended meaning without offence.

'Direct exposure to the environment this far from the hive can be severely deleterious, even to the augmented,' she said. 'And, of course, many of the artefacts arrive here in an extremely fragile state. It's far better to offload them where they can be properly protected.'

'Quite right too,' I agreed. 'And from the hangar, they go where?'

'That depends.' Kildhar was leading the way towards a wide, high portal, following the marks made on the floor by innumerable trolley wheels. Clearly some of the specimens they dealt with were of a

---

1. *Which implies that the landing skids had been mounted on wheels or gravitic repellers, probably somewhere out of Cain's line of sight.*

2. *Probably because the contaminated air which had entered along with the shuttle was quickly dissipated by the air currents from the recirculators.*

considerable size, judging by the dimensions of the tunnel beyond. 'We have a wide range of analyticae here, capable of all kinds of measurement and experimentation.'

'Just so long as they know what they're doing,' Jurgen muttered to me, in a voice he fondly imagined was inaudible.

'We do,' Kildhar assured us, the breeziness of her manner enough to show that she believed that, even if I didn't. She led the way deeper into the massive building at a brisk pace, changing direction so often that I was forced to conclude she was deliberately trying to confuse us. My innate affinity for complex tunnel systems was proving as reliable as ever, though, and I was sure I'd be able to find my way back to the hangar if I had to. 'It's not much further now.'

'I'm pleased to hear it,' I said, with another ostentatious glance at my chronograph. 'But I'm afraid I'm already late for my meeting with Magos Dysen. Perhaps if you could take us to a vox?'

'That won't be necessary,' Kildhar said, a trifle smugly. 'Alternative arrangements have been made.' She paused, in front of a doorway which seemed rather larger than it needed to be. 'We don't have guest quarters as such, but we do have occasional visitors. If you care to wait in here, the Magos Senioris will be with you within the hour.'

'Thank you,' I said, completely wrong-footed, and determined not to show it. Kildhar tapped out a complicated access code on a keypad near the door, which obligingly slid open, with a faint squeal of unlubricated runners.

The room beyond was as spartan as I'd come to expect of our hosts' tastes, containing little beyond an array of data lecterns, a polished steel conference table with devotional icons of machine parts chased in bronze, and an array of those hideously uncomfortable seats. Several of them seemed far larger, and more robust, than the others, and I gave them a curious glance. Come to that, a few of the lecterns seemed set unusually high as well, so much so that I wouldn't have been able to use the keyboards without standing on tiptoe. That reminded me of something, but, as is always the way when you try to bring an elusive memory into focus, the harder I tried, the further it slipped from my conscious mind.

'Any idea what this is, sir?' Jurgen asked, peering at one of the curiously-shaped pieces of metallic detritus scattered around the room on finely-wrought display stands.

'None whatsoever,' I shrugged, ambling over to take a look at it. A few corroded wires protruded from the casing, their bright ends showing where power feeds or instrumentation had been clipped to them during the examination process. 'But if it's stuck in a case in here, it's either been wrung dry or written off.' I glanced at Kildhar, who looked faintly reproving.

'Neither,' she said, a little primly. 'The Omnissiah's works can never be fully apprehended, nor casually discarded.' Then her expression softened a little. 'But you are substantially correct. This artefact has been thoroughly examined, and no lines of enquiry remain open at this time which seem likely to yield further knowledge.'

Intrigued, I leaned a little closer, and began to read the inscription engraved on the miniscule metal plate riveted to the stand, in letters so small I could barely make them out. 'Atmospheric sampler, M28...' At which I broke off, impressed in spite of myself by the staggering antiquity of the thing. 'M28,' I resumed, trying to ignore Kildhar's expression, which on a face less threaded with metal I would only have been able to describe as smug, 'recovered 854935. M41, Serendipita system...' Then the penny dropped, and I turned back to the tech-priest, reeling with shock. 'This is from the *Spawn of Damnation*!'

'Quite so,' she agreed, as if that was the most natural thing in the galaxy. 'Most of the artefacts recovered from the hulk have been brought here for safekeeping.' Which made a bizarre kind of sense, if you thought about it. Fecundia was the nearest forge world to Serendipita, stuffed to the gills with tech-priests, and with the right facilities to analyse the loot properly.

Which also explained why I'd been granted access to the place. If it hadn't been for me, setting the orks and genestealers aboard the derelict at one another's throats, they'd never have got half so much from it before it disappeared back into the warp. Assuming it had, for you never could tell with space hulks, whose movements were as capricious as the warp currents they drifted on. 'Is it still there?' I asked, unable to resist the question.

'No.' Kildhar sounded truly regretful at this, the first real emotion I'd heard seeping into her voice. 'It disappeared back into the warp in 948, and hasn't been sighted since. Efforts were initially made to track it, but were unsuccessful. In recent years, the Reclaimers have had other calls on their attention.'

'Haven't we all,' I said feelingly. Between the tau and the tyranids, the Imperium was coming under greater pressure in the Eastern Arm than it had done in over a millennium, and none of its other foes had been particularly quiet either. I had no doubt that the Space Marine Chapter I'd been foolish enough to board the derelict alongside would find plenty to keep them amused, even without a vast, three-dimensional labyrinth stuffed with lethal creatures to loot.

'Indeed so.' Kildhar hovered for a moment on the threshold. 'And a great deal is currently demanding mine. I trust your consultation with the Magos Senioris will prove productive.' And with that she withdrew, the door grinding closed behind her.

'Typical,' Jurgen said, collapsing onto the nearest chair, and pulling a porno slate from his pocket to help pass the time. 'Not even the offer of a mug of recaff.'

'She's probably already eaten this month,' I said sourly, strolling along the length of the room. There were about half a dozen other exhibits ranged about it, all but one from the *Spawn of Damnation*, and all equally incomprehensible to me as to their age and purpose.

Jurgen suspended his perusal of anatomically improbable artistic engravings, and glanced in my direction. 'Lucky I brought a flask of tanna along, then. If you feel you could do with one.'

'Most definitely,' I agreed, accepting the warm drink gratefully. But before I could taste more than a mouthful, a strident alarm began to blare. 'Emperor's bowels, now what!'

Abandoning the steaming flask, I hurried towards the door, anticipating the worst, which in my experience is always the way to bet. I tugged at the handle, but it refused to slide open, and I looked at the keypad in consternation. Kildhar had punched in the number so rapidly it would have been impossible to follow the blur of her augmetic fingers, even if I'd been paying attention, which, I'm bound to admit, I hadn't.

'Allow me, sir,' Jurgen said, raising his lasgun and firing a couple of quick rounds into the mechanism before I could stop him. Too late to worry about how our hosts would react to that now, so I simply seized the handle, and tugged again. 'Oh, nads'.

'Couldn't have put it better myself,' I agreed, with rather more asperity than I'd intended. With the locking mechanism destroyed, we were trapped, unable even to discover what had so stirred up the tech-priests. I strained my ears, trying to discern anything which might give us a clue, and hoping to the Throne it wasn't going to be the premonitory rumblings of some titanic explosion that was about to immolate us all. But the walls were thick, lined in metal, and all I could hear was the humming of the circulators. Which sparked another idea. 'Can you see anything that looks like an air vent?' With our only exit immovably jammed, I was damned if I was going to just sit around waiting for the bang.

'Over here, sir,' Jurgen called, after a moment of searching, his voice raised to be heard over the harsh bleating of the alarm. He pointed helpfully to a grille near the floor, about twenty centimetres by ten.

'Well done,' I encouraged him, feeling I owed him that much for my earlier moment of pettishness, 'but I was hoping for something a bit larger.'

Jurgen shook his head. 'They're all the same, I'm afraid, sir.'

'Then we'll just have to improvise,' I said, drawing my chainsword, thumbing the speed selector up to maximum. It wouldn't be the first time I'd carved my way through a wall or a door with it, although I'd seldom had to use it on anything as robust as the ones here looked. 'Watch out for sparks.'

But before I could make my first attack, the slab of metal bulged as something struck it hard from the other side, jarring it free of its runners. Jurgen and I exchanged an uneasy glance, and then stepped back, raising our weapons. My free hand fell to the laspistol holstered at my side, but before I could draw it, another blow shivered the door, and a quartet of incredibly sharp talons punctured their way through. As I watched, momentarily paralysed in disbelieving horror, the hand behind them clenched into a fist, ripping a hole the size of my head in the thick steel plate.

Jurgen opened fire at once, directing a burst of las-bolts through the aperture, and the creature beyond recoiled for a moment before pressing its attack. Then a second set of talons punctured the metal as though it were cardboard, slashing down to open a jagged rent, while the first ripped a diagonal tear across to join it. I drew my laspistol as a second pair of hands, tipped with smaller claws and bearing an extra finger apiece, took a firm hold of the ragged barrier, before yanking it free of the runners and tossing it aside.

From the moment the first set of talons had burst through the door I'd had a queasy feeling that I knew what manner of beast was on the other side, and now I knew I was right. I just had the merest fraction of a second to register the fact, before Jurgen's and my fingers tightened on our triggers, and a purestrain genestealer, its jaws agape, charged straight down the barrels of our guns.

ELEVEN

Our first volley checked the hideous creature's rush and it faltered, staggering under the multiple impacts of Jurgen's burst of automatic fire, to which my brief flurry of additional las-bolts added very little if I'm honest. Cauterised craters exploded across its thorax, raising a fine spray of ichor and pulverised chitin, which we were close enough to see wafting around its body like mist rising from an early morning swamp. It recovered fast though, jaws snapping, and leapt forwards again leaking rancid fluids through its cracked carapace, but Jurgen and I were no longer there, having jumped aside in opposite directions. It turned to follow me, both of the arms on its left side reaching out, in the apparent hope of snaring me in its lower hand while it dissected me with the scalpel-sharp talons of the upper.

I was ready for it, however, having faced genestealers before, and ducked under the grabbing hand, slashing upwards with the chainsword. Its teeth whined for a moment as they bit into the creature's tough outer shell, then came free, lopping off the extended limb like a diseased tree branch before slicing through its underbelly. A gush of offal erupted from it, making a ghastly mess of my greatcoat, and splattered on the floor at our feet. Tough and tenacious as the creature was, it couldn't last long in that condition, and it lunged forwards, apparently intent on making one last attack on Jurgen as a final act of revenge. Before it could reach him it slipped in its own entrails and crashed into the table, denting it and sending several of the hideously uncomfortable chairs surrounding it flying with a clatter which resonated loudly in the metal-lined room. Incredibly, despite the battering it had taken, the monstrosity still stirred feebly, trying to rise, and I swung my chainsword, decapitating it though if I was any judge, it had expired altogether an instant before the blade actually hit.

'Well, that got the door open,' Jurgen said, determined to look on the bright side, and I nodded grimly.

'We know what all the fuss is about, too,' I agreed, raising my voice above the blaring of the alarms, which echoed twice as loudly now they were no longer muffled by the intervening door. 'The 'nids have arrived.' I tapped the comm-bead in my ear, hoping for a tactical update, but I could hear nothing on any of the Imperial Guard channels; none of the vox-units in the vicinity were tuned to them, and all I could raise was incomprehensible gibberish. We'd just have to hope that it was an isolated incursion, rather than the full-scale invasion my panicked imagination persisted in picturing. 'Come on. We need to find out what the hell's going on.'

Which turned out to be blind panic, so far as I could see, the corridor outside choked with red-robed acolytes scurrying in every direction, warbling at one another in their incomprehensible dialect. The sight of Jurgen and me, armed and spattered with chunks of diced genestealer, didn't exactly help their equanimity, and I soon gave up trying to stop one and ask for information. Most just gibbered for a moment, pointing back the way they'd come, and scuttled off again, as fast as their legs (or in some cases wheels, grav plates, or springs) would carry them. As they seemed to be passing down the corridor in both directions, I couldn't even follow my instinctive response at times like this, and get as far away from wherever the greatest danger seemed to be as quickly as possible.

'Back to the hangar, sir?' Jurgen asked, as the crowd cleared a little, and I nodded. I didn't have a clue where anything else was in this labyrinth, and if we struck out at random we could wander around it indefinitely, or at least until the tyranids caught up with us. We might be able to commandeer a shuttle there, or at least find a parked one with a vox I could use to get back in touch with Zyvan and find out just how much trouble we were in.

'Seems like our best option,' I agreed, turning to lead the way, but before I could take more than a handful of steps in that direction, a flurry of motion at the end of the corridor checked my stride. Three more 'stealers had loped into view, slashing and tearing at any tech-priests still laggardly enough to be in the way. A welter of blood and lubricants marked their progress, sullying the floor beneath their talons and bespattering the walls in their wake. Few of their victims moved after they passed by, although a couple continued to twitch in a flurry of electrical sparks, their internal power cells earthing through the metallic surface they were sprawled across.

There was no need to verbalise my sudden change of plan, Jurgen and I had fought side by side far too long and often for that. Pausing only to unleash a flurry of las-bolts in the vain hope of slowing them a little, we turned and ran, hoping desperately that something would present itself in the handful of seconds we had before the creatures caught up with us.

'Knew I should have brought the melta,' Jurgen grumbled, as the sinister rattle of talon on metal became audible even over the shrilling of the alarm. If they were close enough to hear in spite of all that racket they must have been more or less on top of us already, and I didn't dare to look back. Turning to glance over my shoulder would cost only a fraction of a second's lead, but even that was liable to prove fatal. Besides, I didn't want the last thing I saw to be a genestealer's gullet.

'Would have been handy,' I agreed, although he could hardly be blamed for having left his favourite toy behind. The bulky weapon wasn't exactly ideal for lugging around the corridors of a starship, and we'd had no warning of the tyranid attack, so there'd been no reason to think we'd need it. Then another thought struck me. 'Got any grenades?' He generally kept a couple about his person, even when we were some distance from the front, a habit I'd been grateful for on several occasions in the past.

'Can't use 'em,' he said regretfully. 'Too many civilians about.' There were indeed a number of tech-priests still cluttering up the corridor, although their fondness for augmetics had enabled the majority to open up an impressive lead, and, judging by the noises behind me, the ones who hadn't were getting fewer by the second.

'Krak then,' I said, rather less concerned about collateral damage to cogboys than the realisation that a frag charge going off close enough to incommode the 'stealers would probably shred Jurgen and I into the bargain.

'Got one of those,' my aide confirmed, rummaging in one of his collection of equipment pouches, and priming the grenade he produced deftly with his teeth. He lobbed it back over his shoulder without breaking stride. 'Can't see what good it'll do, though.'

'Neither can I,' I admitted, 'but it can hardly hurt now.' The floor shook as the anti-armour charge went off, and something small, sharp and metallic pinged off the wall next to my ear. We must have damaged an electrical circuit somewhere, because the shrieking siren suddenly went quiet, leaving my ears ringing with the absence of noise. The scuttling behind us seemed to have diminished too, and I decided to risk a glance back after all.

The desperate stratagem seemed to have bought us a little time, at least. The high-explosive charge had blown a hole in the metal floor, exposing a tangle of pipework and cabling from which some kind of vapour was rising in a cloud. The 'stealers seemed dazed by the explosion, but I couldn't count on that happy circumstance continuing for long.

'That gave 'em something to think about,' Jurgen said, sending another hail of las-bolts down the corridor as he spoke. Given the choice I'd simply have put as much distance between the hideous creatures and myself as possible, but we did have an audience of cowed tech-priests to think about, most of whom looked even more dazed than the genestealers. They were milling around and chirruping to one another, as if they couldn't believe the mess we'd just made of their nice clean corridor, but under the circumstances felt it best not to object and I had no doubt that at least a few of them had pictcorders built into their augmetic eyes. The last thing I needed was images of Cain the Hero acting like the poltroon I actually am making the rounds, especially if I needed my undeserved reputation to help me make a run for it later. So I cracked off a couple of shots myself and flourished the chainsword, taking up a defensive stance as if I meant to protect the survivors from a renewed charge.

'Get to safety,' I told them, with the best show of concern I could feign, glancing back over my shoulder. I was about to add a couple of rote platitudes, in the interests of hurrying them up, when the vapour cloud ignited, engulfing the 'stealers in a fireball and sending a pressure wave down the passageway which knocked me sprawling to the chill metal floor.

I staggered back to my feet, still trying to grasp this unexpected turn of events. Clearly, whatever was in the pipe had been flammable, although whether it had been ignited by one of our las-rounds or a spark from the damaged wiring was impossible to guess. I had little time to ponder the matter, however, as at that point a blazing genestealer burst from the inferno and plunged blindly towards me, although whether it was impelled by the brood mind, or simply crazed with agony, I couldn't tell. I fired at it by reflex, leaping aside at the last possible minute and getting a lucky strike in with the chainsword, which severed the ligaments in its legs. Crippled, it crashed to the floor, where it rolled around, flailing and giving me an anxious few moments avoiding its teeth and claws, before finally accepting the fact that it was dead.

'The other two have had it as well,' Jurgen told me, trotting back from a quick trip to check. 'Lucky that pipe exploded, or it could have been nasty.'

'It could indeed,' I said, giving up trying to count the number of slaughtered tech-priests in the corridor beyond the pall of smoke. Throne knows I had little enough in common with cogboys, and even less patience on occasion, but I still found the sight depressing, probably because it could so easily have been me lying there with my innards on display.

'The Omnissiah truly processes your data,' an awestruck tech-priest of indeterminate gender[1] told me, making the sign of the cogwheel.

'Jolly decent of Him,' I said, not quite sure how to respond to that. I was still getting nothing intelligible though my comm-bead, but maybe my interlocutor had access to other sources of information. 'Any idea how many more of those things are loose around here?' Genestealer broods were usually a lot bigger than the quartet we'd already seen and accounted for.

The cowled head shook, the fire behind us reflecting in the metal face, making it flicker disturbingly in the depths of the robe.

'Any other infiltrating organisms? Lictors, maybe?' I don't mind admitting I quailed inwardly at the prospect, although I kept my feelings from showing on my face with the ease of long practice. Genestealers were bad enough, but the idea of hunting, or, more likely, being hunted by, organisms perfectly adapted to stealth and ambush was far more disturbing.

'I regret I have no current information,' metal-face said, making the cogwheel gesture again for no reason that I could see, presumably because they didn't know what else to do with their fingers. 'Xenobiological queries should be directed to Magos Kildhar.'

Of course. 'And do you have any idea where she is?' I asked, already sure I knew the answer I was going to get.

'I have no current information in that regard either,' the tech-priest said, sounding genuinely regretful. 'Her analyticum is located on level twenty-eight, section three, however. Should you wish to consult her, that would be the most likely place to effect an encounter.'

'Thank you,' I said, 'but my duty now is to report to the Magos Senioris and the Lord General.' Who ought to know what the hell was going on, if anyone did.

'The Magos Senioris is due to arrive imminently,' the tech-priest said, clearly determined to be as helpful as possible. 'Indeed, he may already have landed.'

---

1. *After a certain level of augmentation, the difference is purely academic in any case.*

'Then we need to get back to the hangar as quickly as possible,' I said, seizing the opportunity the Emperor had just dropped in my lap. 'His protection must be our highest priority.' And that would be best achieved by getting him back on the shuttle and away from here as quickly as possible, preferably accompanied by me. I glanced back at the fire behind us, still blocking the corridor. 'If you could suggest an alternative route?'

'Down that way, first right, second left...' the tech-priest began, reeling off a list of directions that threatened to go on almost indefinitely. After the first few, I realised that we'd be heading back the way we'd come, or at least close enough to it to rely on my knack of remaining orientated in places like this, and cut them off in full flow.

'We'll find it,' I said confidently, and began double-timing it, Jurgen and his lasgun a reassuring presence at my heels. Now the wretched alarm wasn't drowning everything else out, I was able to use my ears as well as my eyes. The clatter of our boot soles on the metal floor raised distracting echoes, compounded by the ones created by the number of confused and frightened cogboys scattering out of the way as we ran, but I was pretty sure I couldn't hear the sinister scrabbling of genestealer claws anywhere behind us. Nevertheless, I kept a sharp look out, darting quick, apprehensive glances into every nook and crevice we passed, paying particular attention to the pipework and ducting depending from the ceiling; the cursed creatures could cling to the sheerest of surfaces, and I'd seen too many of the Reclaimers brought down by ambush from above on our ill-fated foray aboard the *Spawn of Damnation* not to be paranoid about the possibility of falling victim to a similar attack.

'I thought there were supposed to be skitarii stationed here,' Jurgen said sourly, hurdling a stray CAT[1] as he did so. 'What's keeping them?'

'I think they're busy,' I told him, disentangling the distinctive heavy *crack* of hellgun fire from the overlapping echoes that pursued us. It

---

1. *Cyber-Altered Task unit, a mobile mechanism built to carry out simple tasks; like a basic servitor, although their lack of organic components makes them far less versatile, and incapable of being programmed for anything other than their original purpose.*

seemed to be coming from more than one direction, although more than that I couldn't distinguish, nor, if I'm honest, was I concerned enough to make the effort of doing so. The firing was all sufficiently distant for me to be confident that we weren't about to stumble into the middle of a skirmish, and that was all I cared about at the moment.

We pelted round the last of the corners on the tech-priest's itinerary, dodging a servitor still plodding about whatever errand it had last been sent on, oblivious to the commotion surrounding it, and I found myself in a corridor I recognised at last.

'This way,' I told Jurgen, my spirits rising, only to have them dashed a moment later. The sound of gunfire was up ahead too, echoing from the direction of the hangar.

TWELVE

I'D BE LYING if I told you I didn't hesitate at that moment, but in truth I had no option but to charge ahead regardless. There were too many cogboys cluttering up the corridor for any sign of faltering resolve on my part to go unnoticed and, to compound the issue, I'd said in so many words that I meant to protect Dysen from the genestealers. Whether or not the tech-priest had recorded or transmitted the conversation, it was out there among them, no doubt being passed from one to another in excited snatches. So yet again I was committed to a course of action that ran directly counter to all my instincts, as a glib excuse intended to keep me out of trouble rebounded to bite me on the arse. Besides, getting to the hangar, and through it to safety, meant facing whatever awaited us ahead whether I liked it or not, and at least it sounded as though I'd have some skitarii to hide behind this time, instead of playing 'nid bait on my own.

The wide, high doorway to the hangar was open, and once again my nostrils were assaulted by the sulphurous reek of the outer air, so strong that it even overpowered Jurgen's distinctive odour. That meant Dysen's shuttle must already have arrived, descending on the lift from the landing pad and admitting a tranche of the all but unbreathable outer air along with it.

We'd almost reached the gaping entranceway when a crimson-uniformed skitarii cannoned through it, propelled by the genestealer which was trying to gnaw his face off. Blood and less identifiable fluids were seeping through wide gashes in his body armour from wounds which would have felled a normal man, but he was still fighting fiercely, his heavily augmented body soaking up the kind of punishment only a Space Marine could normally have withstood. The pair of them rebounded from the opposite wall, leaving a dent in the polished metal surface, and waltzed towards Jurgen and I, so engrossed in their private struggle that they were probably equally oblivious to our presence.

Reacting instinctively, my duellist's reflexes cutting in without conscious thought, I pivoted to avoid the intertwined antagonists and struck at the genestealer's back with my chainsword. The whirling blade cut deep, spraying the damaged wall with fragments of chitin and viscera. Taken completely by surprise, the abominable creature turned and snapped at me, its razor-edged fangs clashing together close enough to have taken my arm off, if I hadn't stepped back to open the distance a little. The beleaguered skitarii rallied, taking advantage of the 'stealer's moment of distraction to smash his forearm into the side of its head, laying it open with the serrated blade inlaid along its length. Partially stunned, the hideous creature loosened its grip on him, raising its neck to strike with its fangs, like a serpent. Seeing my chance I stepped in again, severing its spinal column with a precise horizontal swipe.

Roaring with rage, the fleshly parts of his face engorged and almost as red as his uniform, the skitarii seized both sides of the purestrain's head between his hands and twisted. With a hideous ripping, crunching sound, remarkably similar to that produced by Jurgen and a plate of seafood, the 'stealer's head came clean away from its body.

After regarding his grisly trophy for a moment, the skitarii threw it aside and strode towards me, trampling the body of his fallen foe underfoot as he came. His face was still contorted, even more marginally human than a soldier of the Adeptus Mechanicus normally looked, and I began to feel concerned for my own safety. He was out of his head on 'zerk[1], or something very like it, and probably in no fit state to distinguish friend from foe, or even care. Then, almost at the last minute, I recognised the patchwork of augmetics encrusting his face.

'Centurion Kyper, report,' I rapped out, in my most commanding manner, pleased to note out of the corner of my eye that Jurgen's lasgun was levelled at him. I hoped he wouldn't have to use it, but if it meant me staying in one piece, I'd let him gun down the skitarii officer in a heartbeat, and worry about the political implications later.

But, to my relief, Kyper's eyes began to clear, a vestige of understanding returning to them almost at once.

'Commissar Cain,' he grated out. 'You are welcome. Plenty of 'stealers still to kill.' The fires of drug-induced frenzy began to blaze up in him again and he turned back towards the fray, evidently determined to make a start on the job as quickly as possible, completely undeterred by the fact that he was leaking vital fluids like a corroding tap.

'Is the Magos Senioris safe?' I asked urgently, before the tidal wave of bloodlust could sweep him too far away for rational discourse.

'He is,' Kyper confirmed, then leapt back into the fray, apparently intent on ripping the next 'stealer unfortunate enough to cross his path limb from limb[2]. That was something, anyway; if Dysen was still in the hangar, his shuttle must be too, and there was still a chance I could use both to get my own miserable carcass to safety. An optimistic thought which lasted all of the next two or three seconds, at which point I got my first clear sight of the battle raging within the landing bay.

---

1. *A combat drug designed to enhance strength and aggression, most commonly used by the penal legions; the long-term effects on unaugmented physiologies are deleterious in the extreme, but this isn't considered a disadvantage where the troopers aren't expected to survive more than a battle or two anyway.*

2. *From which we can infer that, to Cain's eyes at least, the centurion appeared unarmed; an impression which may not have been entirely accurate, as Mechanicus skitarii tend to have a number of implanted weapon systems designed to enhance their lethality at close quarters.*

'Hybrids!' Jurgen said with loathing, directing a stream of lasgun fire at a hunched, three-armed monstrosity hefting the hellgun it had just taken from a dying skitarii, with every sign of being able to use it, an impression it confirmed a moment later by turning it on us. The hail of high energy las-bolts went wide, however, and before it could rectify its mistake, my aide's superior marksmanship took it down with a clean shot to the head.

'Several,' I agreed, spotting more of the semi-human abominations, with a growing sense of puzzlement. Genestealers were common enough in the front ranks of a tyranid invasion, but I'd never heard of them being accompanied by their cross-species offspring before. They only appeared after implanted victims of the brood mind had been embedded in a world's population for at least a generation. But there had been no reports of the kind of social turmoil which would point to a genestealer cult being active on Fecundia, and in any case, among so heavily augmented a population, I'd have expected them to find slim pickings indeed.

Then another bounding purestrain tried to take my head off with a swipe from its fearsome talons, and I had no more time to mull the matter over. Diving aside in the nick of time, I cut at its neck, being rewarded with a gout of noxious fluid before Jurgen brought it down with another burst of lasgun fire.

'Over there, sir,' my aide called, and through the maelstrom of running, shooting, slashing figures, all of them inhumanly fast and lithe, whether augmented human or xenos abomination, I caught sight of Dysen and his bodyguards at last. They seemed to have had the same idea as I'd had, attempting to punch through the melee to the shuttle which had brought them here, but they weren't getting very far. The majority of the 'stealers and their progeny were clustered under the spread wings of the great transport vessel, still resting on the lift which had brought it below, like a brood of chicks seeking the protection of its parent. The sheer press of their numbers was effectively cutting the tech-priest and his party off from it, which meant there wasn't much chance of me getting aboard unshredded either.

'What's going on?' I yelled, as our hacking, slashing, and las-bolt-punctuated progress brought us within earshot of the Magos Senioris at last. 'Kildhar had only just told us you were coming, then all hell broke loose!' I'd made for him as soon as my aide pointed him out, of course, partly to look as if I was trying to make good on my ill-advised boast, but mainly because putting a party of heavily-armed skitarii between me and the 'stealers seemed like my best chance of getting out of here with a full complement of limbs.

'Then you know as much as I do,' Dysen said, remarkably testily for a man who was supposed to be above such petty human traits as an emotional reaction to stress. But then I don't imagine his ordered, rational world had ever been rocked quite so much before.

I shot a purestrain which had just counted out another of the skitarii, clambering over the corpse of its victim in its eagerness to get to Dysen, taking it in the throat as it hinged its jaws impossibly wide in the disconcerting way such creatures do. It collapsed across the body of its final victim, twitching and gurgling its last, although I'm bound to admit the kill had been a lucky one, and probably wouldn't have taken place at all if it hadn't taken a battering from the skitarii before my turn came around. 'Persistent, aren't they?' I said, feeling a show of insouciance would go down well if anyone was recording this scrap for posterity[1].

'My gratitude, commissar,' Dysen said, ducking behind what was left of his escort with prudent alacrity. 'I was informed you were on your way, but feared you'd perished.'

'I was thinking the same thing about you,' I riposted. Apparently my conversation downstairs[2] had indeed been passed on by whatever arcane means the cogboys used to keep in touch with one another. I indicated the shuttle. 'We need to get you back aboard, and out of here. Is there a safe haven the tyranids haven't landed near yet?'

'There's been no landing,' Dysen said, sounding as confused as his

---

1. *As a matter of fact Dysen was; his internal pict recordings show the action did indeed take place much as Cain describes it, although with rather more audible profanity.*

2. *The first time he mentions a change of level, although, given that the hangar was just below the roof, that's hardly a surprise.*

implanted vox-coder would allow. 'Not so much as a single spore.'

'Then where the hell have all the 'stealers come from?' I demanded. The xenos began to pull back, towards the shuttle on the lift platform where so many of them had already taken refuge. The skitarii rallied, harrying them from all sides with hellgun fire. Most of the hybrids had managed to scavenge weapons of their own by now, and replied with alacrity, but with far less accuracy or effect.

'I have no idea,' Dysen said, his even mechanical tone somehow managing to convey that this was a state of affairs he was far from happy with, intended to rectify at the earliest opportunity, and that if anyone was responsible for the creatures being able to infiltrate the shrine they were in for a far from merry time. 'They attacked the hangar as soon as we disembarked.'

'I see,' I said, sending a couple of las-bolts after the disengaging brood, the palms of my hands tingling as they always did when my subconscious started jumping up and down, yelling, in an effort to get my forebrain to recognise looming catastrophe when it saw it. Something really wasn't right about the 'stealers' tactics.

'We've got 'em on the run, at least,' Jurgen said, snapping a fresh powercell into his lasgun. He glanced at me. 'Last one, sir. Then I'm down to the bayonet.'

'That won't be necessary,' Kyper interrupted, trotting across to join us, looking more like a carcass stapled together with augmetics than ever; when he finally ran out of combat drugs, he was going to drop like a puppet whose strings had been cut. But at least he was in the right place to be put back together, I supposed. 'They're going to ground in the shuttle. If we send in the heavy flamers, we'll get the lot.'

'Oh, Throne,' I said, the coin dropping at last. Retreating 'stealers never congregated in the middle of an open space, they always ran for cover in the shadows, from where they could mount another ambush. 'They're not going to ground!' I pointed to a couple of perfectly human-looking figures in the middle of the pack, one wearing a torn and ragged flight suit. 'They're planning to fly out of here!'

'That's ridiculous,' Dysen said. 'Genestealers aren't capable of operating complex mechanica. Piloting a shuttle requires dexterity and intellect.'

'Which their hybrids possess!' I practically screamed at him. I'm no expert on the subject, but I'd encountered enough nests of the pernicious creatures to know that, after a few generations, some of their offspring are all but indistinguishable from humans[1]. 'Besides, they've implanted the pilot!'

'How can you tell?' Kyper asked, in what seemed like honest confusion.

'Because he looks like he's bladdered,' Jurgen supplied helpfully, 'and cogboys don't drink.' As if to underline his words, the pilot stumbled, clutched at the arm of the nearest multi-limbed horror to steady himself, and staggered on, leaning against it for support, looking remarkably like a couple of Guardsmen determined to sample every bar in town before their two day pass expires.

'The brood mind is still trying to integrate him,' I explained, rather more diplomatically, 'which is why he seems so disorientated. In a short while, even his closest friends won't notice anything out of the ordinary.'

'He hardly seems in a fit state to fly,' Kyper said, undeterred. 'And our heavy combat servitors will have scoured the vessel long before he is.'

'He doesn't have to be,' I explained, as though to a child. As if to underline the urgency of the situation, a thin wisp of sulphurous vapour drifted in though the open hangar roof, and I watched it coil around the supporting girderwork with distant fascination, as though seeing the future of this world in microcosm. If the brood escaped from here, they'd go to ground, spreading their taint until everything was enmeshed in their toxic grip, waiting for the day they grew strong enough to challenge humanity for the mastery of Fecundia. 'The brood mind has access to all his knowledge. One of the hybrids can fly the ship.'

'It seems you're right,' Dysen said, to my surprise. 'One of them is

---

1. *While the others of that generation revert to purestrain genestealers, ready to continue spreading their taint.*

now seating itself on the flight deck.' Emperor alone knows how he could tell that[1], but I was happy to take his word for it. Any doubts I might have had about his veracity were rapidly dispelled by the rising scream of the shuttle's engines as they powered up for take-off.

'Then there's no time to lose,' Kyper said decisively, rallying what was left of his men with a rapidly modulated squeal of high-pitched gibberish which made my teeth ache. 'We must assault before they leave the ground.' He turned to me, and for a heart-stopping instant I thought I was going to be invited to lead this suicidal charge down the maw of the enemy. 'Commissar, I must ask you to ensure the safety of the Magos Senioris.'

'I'm gratified by your confidence,' I said gravely, careful not to say anything that sounded like a guarantee. For once I wasn't going to have to work at extricating myself from the sharp end, and I took a moment to savour the novelty.

In another moment they'd gone, charging towards the shuttle with all the finesse of a mob of orks, but I couldn't deny they looked well nigh unstoppable. The brood mind clearly disagreed, though, as a flood of enraged chitin boiled out of the open boarding ramp, meeting them head-on in a clash which seemed to shake the very walls.

'Why don't they just take off?' Jurgen wondered aloud as battle was joined anew, with inhuman ferocity on both sides. Talon against chainblade, las-bolt against fang, the eventual winner anybody's guess. Watching the intricate dance of that lethal melee, I could only be thankful that this time I'd been left on the sidelines. 'They were all aboard and ready to go.'

'A good question,' I mused, my palms tingling again. We were missing something, I was sure of it. Then a flash of movement caught my eye, and I whirled to face the door. 'And one with a bloody bad answer!' Which I should have expected. After all, I'd heard firing elsewhere in the building on my way up here. If I'd thought about it at all, other than simply trying to avoid it, I would have assumed

---

1. *Either by magnifying the images provided by his augmetic eyes, or by interfacing directly with the shuttle's telemetry in some fashion, probably.*

it was just a handful of stray 'stealers like the ones Jurgen and I had encountered being tidied up by the skitarii, but this was something far worse.

'That's the broodlord,' Jurgen supplied helpfully, as if I hadn't recognised the terrifying apparition at once. I'd faced another just like it in the catacombs beneath Gravalax, and it would have been the end of me if Jurgen hadn't barbequed it with the melta, which was currently tucked away somewhere in the nest of clutter that constituted his quarters aboard the flagship. No point bemoaning its absence though, I might as well wish for a Leman Russ or Space Marine Dreadnought to hide behind. We'd just have to make do with what we had, and, if all else failed, make sure it got to Dysen before it reached me.

'Explains what they were waiting for,' I agreed, making the best show I could of readying my weapons. The monstrous creature prowled into the hangar, looming over its progeny and the beleaguered defenders alike, half again as tall as any of them. Like the purestrains, all six of its limbs were tipped with talons capable of ripping through ceramite, and its tail was barbed, scything deep gouges in the floor and walls as it lashed to and fro. Its head turned slowly from side to side as it advanced, as if sniffing the air, although that seemed like a quick route to asphyxiation so far as I could see. Then it broke into a loping run, bounding towards the shuttle, seemingly indifferent to the fate of its broodmates.

'Stop it!' Dysen bellowed, his usual flat monotone boosted by some kind of implanted amplivox, which I presume he'd activated so I could hear him clearly over the din of the battle taking place around the boarding ramp[1]. Unfortunately the broodlord heard him too, and turned aside, bearing down on us like death itself coming to claim my very soul. Why it would have bothered with us, instead of making directly for the shuttle and safety, I have no idea: perhaps it just feared a flank attack, and was intending to take us out of the equation first, or perhaps the last few moments of the purestrains

---

1. *A reasonable assumption, since he would have been able to exchange data with the skitarii directly.*

we'd killed in the corridor were still echoing round the brood mind, prompting it to take posthumous revenge on their behalf[1].

I tried to move as the hideous thing charged straight at me, its jaws agape, affording me far too good a view of the teeth poised to bite off my head with a single snap, but my limbs refused to obey. I'd been transfixed by terror before, of course, so often that the sensation had almost come to feel comfortably familiar, but it had always been momentary. My sense of self-preservation had kicked in again within an instant, reflex and the instinct to survive urging me into motion. This time, however, I remained paralysed, my eyes locked on those of the creature before me, overwhelmed by the utter futility of attempting to oppose it.

'Nice big target, anyway, sir,' Jurgen said cheerfully, opening fire on full auto, seemingly unworried by his rapidly-draining powerclip. And why would he be? If we didn't bring the hideous killing machine down in the next few seconds, we'd be too dead to care about conserving ammo, and any we had saved would be of no further use to us anyway.

Something about his voice snapped me out of my stupor, and I rattled off a series of shots from my laspistol, wondering what in the name of the Throne had got into me[2]. We might just as well have been shooting at a Baneblade for all the good our las-bolts did this time, however, succeeding in nothing more than adding to the already impressive collection of cauterised craters pocking the surface of its thick natural armour. (If anything about so vile a piece of tyranid selective breeding could ever be described as 'natural'.) I threw myself aside as it took a swipe at me with its abdominal scything claws, and parried the blow with my chainsword, which was almost swept out of my hand as a consequence. I rode the blow, rolling desperately clear

---

1. *A fanciful suggestion, but there is still much we don't fully understand about the nature of genestealer brood telepathy, so perhaps we shouldn't dismiss the notion completely out of hand. More likely, however, is that it was hanging back until the skitarii had been driven from the boarding ramp, and only noticed Cain and the others when Dysen attracted its attention.*

2. *In all probability the genestealer patriarch was using the power of the brood mind to launch a psychic attack, which Jurgen, being a blank, was able to nullify.*

as the patriarch turned to follow me, which, perhaps fortunately, took it away from Dysen. Right at that moment I'd have had no objection at all to the ghastly creature chewing a few lumps out of him, but in retrospect the consequences for the already shaky alliance I was supposed to be holding together would not have been good.

'Krak grenade!' I called, hoping Jurgen had more than the one he'd already used, but my aide shook his head regretfully.

'None left,' he called back. 'Got a couple of frags though.' Which would do as much harm to me as the scuttling horror I was fighting for my life against, and we both knew it. He shook his head ruefully. 'Never thought we'd need armour-piercing.'

I looked desperately around for help. The skitarii had troubles of their own, and weren't about to come to my aid, that much was clear. There were noticeably fewer of them in the melee round the shuttle ramp than there had been a moment ago, although there was a gratifying number of genestealer cadavers there too. The fight for the landing pad had developed into a grim game of attrition, with too much at stake for either side to stop short of complete victory or annihilation. I parried another pair of swipes from the broodlord's scything claws, one after the other, backing desperately away from the implacable killing machine.

Then a familiar odour materialised at my shoulder, followed by the welcome sight of Jurgen raising his lasgun to spit another stream of fire in its hideous face. Hardly had he squeezed the trigger, however, doing little more than making our monstrous adversary flinch, than the powercell ran dry. 'Duck!' I yelled, in the nick of time, and he did so, evading the clashing jaws by what seemed no more than a handful of centimetres.

I looked round desperately for some way out, or, failing that, some means of distracting the creature, and my eye fell on the Magos Senioris, doing his utmost to look as inconspicuous as possible for someone swathed in a gold-embroidered, vivid crimson robe. He'd gone to ground behind a bank of switches and dials, from which thick, insulated cables ran towards the lift, and the germ of an idea began to form. 'Dysen!' I yelled. 'Can you close the roof from there?'

If something happened to prevent the lift from rising, the 'stealers would be forced to break off, either piling aboard the shuttle before it was too late, or diverting their attention to deal with the new problem; which would be hard luck on Dysen, I suppose, but at least the skitarii would be able to give watching his back their full attention again.

'That would mean overriding the blessed safety protocols,' Dysen protested, his expression resembling an ecclesiarch who'd just overheard someone suggesting that perhaps Horus had been a bit misunderstood. 'Without proper tools, incense or unguents!'

'Does this seem particularly safe to you?' I called back, hacking desperately at the thorax of the broodlord, doing little more than scratching a gouge in the thick chitin which protected it, and the tech-priest nodded briskly.

'Your logic appears sound,' he conceded, exuding a tangle of mechadendrites from somewhere under his robe and plugging himself into the controls. Short as the conversation had been, it had distracted me at a crucial moment. I just had time to register Jurgen's warning shout, when a huge, taloned hand shot out and made a grab for me. I evaded frantically, almost making it, but the clutching fingers grabbed the hem of my greatcoat, yanking me upwards with an audible ripping of cloth.

I hung there for a moment, kicking and wriggling and making random swipes with my chainsword, hoping to at least fend off a strike from the huge claws which I knew for certain would disembowel me. Then the overstressed stitching gave way. I plummeted a couple of metres to the metal floor, landing hard despite instinctively exhaling and going limp to cushion the blow, and looked up, half dazed, to see a huge mouth ringed with razor-sharp teeth descending far too fast to have even the faintest hope of avoiding. Nevertheless, I tried, scrabbling frantically backwards, raising my chainsword instinctively.

'Commissar! Stay down!' a new voice called, deep and resonant, and loud enough to echo around the vast chamber. Before I could even think of mustering a reply, let alone raise my head to see who had spoken, the unmistakable roar of a bolter deafened me. The broodlord's thorax erupted into a swamp of offal as a hail of explosive bolts tore into it, ripping its left-hand scything claw clean off, and it leapt back, away from me.

I sometimes feel as though my entire life has been nothing but a succession of mostly unpleasant surprises, but even as inured as I was to the unexpected, I must confess to having been taken aback by the sight of my deliverer. A Space Marine in Terminator armour was plodding into the hangar, the storm bolter in his right hand still smoking from the discharge which had so discouraged the genestealer patriarch. Twin rocket pods were mounted above his shoulders, and he turned towards the melee with calm deliberation. 'Skitarii, disengage!' he called, his voice carrying easily over the din.

'That's one of the Reclaimers,' Jurgen said, as though the Adeptus Astartes' sudden appearance was in no way remarkable.

I nodded, having recognised the yellow and white heraldry with which I'd become so familiar on our ill-starred voyage in pursuit of the *Spawn of Damnation* as soon as I'd seen it. 'I should have realised,' I said. 'We saw the artefacts from the space hulk downstairs. Who else could have brought them here?'

'Who else indeed?' the Space Marine said, casually reminding me of their preternatural hearing, and discharged a rocket towards the greatest concentration of genestealers, while the surviving skitarii scattered in response to his order. It detonated in the centre of the group, scything down a handful of the loathsome creatures in a burst of shrapnel, and he began to follow up, dropping the survivors with quick, precise bursts of bolter fire.

'Interface engaged,' Dysen said, reminding me of his presence, which, under the circumstances, had rather slipped my mind for a moment or two. With a loud *clunk* the roof above our heads began to grind, painfully slowly, closed.

'Excellent work,' I encouraged him, wondering if the gap would close fast enough. 'Can they still raise the platform?'

'Of course not,' Dysen assured me, still basking in the flattery if I was any judge. For all their prattle about being above mere human reactions, the average tech-priest has always been remarkably susceptible to it in my experience. 'They'll never be able to get off the ground now.'

Which was tempting fate, if ever I heard it. With a banshee howl almost loud enough to drown out the screaming engines, the wounded broodlord charged forward like a Khornate berserker, scattering the reforming skitarii, who, to my relief, were once again screening the Magos Senioris and myself from any further harm. It thundered up the ramp, pursued by another burst of bolter fire from the Terminator, which made a satisfactory mess of the genestealer stragglers, but failed to inconvenience its primary target any further. The shriek of the engines rose another octave in pitch, and, to my horror, I saw the shuttle begin to rise from the surface of the pad.

'They'll never make it,' Jurgen observed, as though offering an opinion on the outcome of a finely-poised scrumball match, his eyes flickering between the slowly ascending shuttle and the incrementally narrowing gap in the ceiling.

'If that thing crashes in here, neither will we!' I said, gesturing urgently towards the door. 'Magos, can you disengage from the controls?' Not that I cared particularly, but it looked good to ask.

'The process is now irreversible,' he assured me, the mechadendrites disappearing back into the recesses of his robe as he spoke.

'Then let's move!' I said, suiting the action to the word, and running for the doorway as fast as I could, trying to look as though I was taking point in case there were any laggardly genestealers still about who might have missed the bus. The others were hard on my heels, the skitarii forming up around Dysen again, who showed a remarkable turn of speed for someone so weighed down with all the scrap embedded in him.

By the time we'd made it to the corridor, the gap in the roof was noticeably smaller than the length of the shuttle, which seemed to be fluttering around the hangar like a bird trapped inside a room.

'We have them,' Kyper said, with what sounded like vindictive satisfaction, despite the lack of inflection in his artificially generated voice. He and the skitarii levelled their weapons[1], clearly anticipating a stampede from the shuttle as soon as it grounded, and determined

---

1. *So either Cain was mistaken about him being unarmed before, or he'd picked up a fallen one during the melee.*

not to let any of the 'stealers find their way back inside the shrine.

'I don't think so,' I said, as the pilot pulled the shuttle's nose up, and triggered the main engine. A backwash of heat roiled across the floor, knocking the skitarii who'd been incautious enough to take up position opposite the gap in the wall from their feet, and charbroiling the scattered cadavers around the empty landing pad. The solitary figure of the Reclaimers Terminator remained standing, however, the searing wind appearing not to inconvenience him in the slightest, detritus and body parts swirling about his impassive form. 'It's just going to make it.' And, indeed, it looked for a moment as though the almost suicidal gamble was about to pay off. The shuttle was practically standing on its tail, accelerating upwards through the narrowing aperture, but there still seemed to be a metre or so of clearance around its reduced profile.

The Terminator thought otherwise, however. The missile pods above his shoulders elevated to track the fleeing target, and a flurry of rockets streaked through the air, impacting on the main engine and the fuselage around it.

'Take cover!' I yelled, quite unnecessarily under the circumstances, and threw myself flat behind the comforting solidity of the wall. The rear half of the shuttle exploded, a sheet of vivid flame boiling like an incandescent thunderhead across the hangar, and the entire vast building seemed to shudder around me. Searing heat and a hurricane force wind blasted down the corridor, whirling loose equipment, wall panels, and a couple of stray servitors away with it, then the blazing fuselage crashed back to the hangar floor, shaking the walls once again with the impact.

Klaxons began to blare, and fire retardant foam began to issue from concealed nozzles, drizzling down on the inferno below like a thick, sticky snowfall. Specialised servitors activated, sallying forth from their niches to battle the flames, directing jets of the stuff into the hottest patches.

'That's put paid to 'em,' Jurgen said, with mordant satisfaction. I began to nod my agreement then froze, the gesture half-completed. Unbelievably, something was moving in the heart of the blaze, half-concealed by the leaping tongues of fire, the dense clouds of smoke, and the blizzard of foam. Something moving towards us with evident purpose.

My hand fell to the laspistol I'd just shoved back in its holster – although what good it could do against something capable of surviving a crash like that was beyond me – but before I could draw it, and make an utter fool of myself in the process, the smoke cleared a little and I realised it was the Terminator, plodding clear of the catastrophe he'd caused, parting the flames like a curtain before him. I craned my neck upwards, fixing my eyes on his helmet, nestled below the raised, hunched shoulders of the bulky armour. A moment later the faceplate hinged open, revealing its occupant, who extended a huge armoured gauntlet, large enough to have crushed my ribs with a single squeeze.

'Commissar Cain,' he rumbled, in the deep, resonant tones of a typical Adeptus Astartes. 'An honour to meet so staunch a friend of our Chapter.'

'The honour is mine, to have served alongside it,' I lied shamelessly. 'Though I must confess to finding your presence here something of a surprise.'

Before he could reply to that, another voice broke in, which, in its own way, took me equally aback.

'Brother-Sergeant Yail,' Kildhar said, trotting down the corridor towards us, her red robe flapping with the agitation she was failing so dismally to conceal. 'Have the specimens been successfully reacquired?' She glanced at the furnace beyond the door, and her shoulders slumped. 'I see not.'

'Specimens?' I looked at her, then back to the hulking Space Marine, who wasn't exactly looking shifty, but rather gave the impression that he would have been if the ability to do so hadn't been genetically engineered out of him. 'I think you've got some explaining to do, magos.'

THIRTEEN

'You've been *breeding* the damn things?' Zyvan expostulated, with a glare across the conference chamber at the Adeptus Mechanicus side of the polished steel table fit to freeze helium. El'hassai, seated next to him, looked equally grim, if I was able to interpret his expression with any degree of accuracy. Kildhar, still chastened from a long and uncomfortable tête-à-tête with Dysen while we'd waited for the Lord General and his retinue to arrive, quailed visibly, and the Magos Senioris emitted a burst of static from his vox-unit which sounded uncannily like an irritable clearing of the throat he probably no longer had. 'And why were we not informed of the presence of an Adeptus Astartes unit on Fecundia?'

Yail, who had divested himself of his Terminator suit in favour of the lighter and more comfortable tactical armour worn by the majority of his brethren[1], smiled sardonically. He alone remained standing, partly because none of the chairs in the typically spartan conference room

---

1. *Cain's superficial familiarity with Space Marine terminology appears to have been acquired during his secondment to the Reclaimers as their Imperial Guard liaison in 928: his experiences at the time have already been disseminated, and need not detain us any further at this point.*

Dysen had put at our disposal could have taken his weight without buckling, but mainly, I suspected, because that way he loomed over everyone else even more impressively than usual. Besides which, as I'd observed before, Adeptus Astartes seldom seemed to sit anyway. 'We are not, properly speaking, a combat unit,' he said.

'I'm sure the genestealers you incinerated would be delighted to hear that,' I replied, feeling the need to lighten the mood a little.

Yail's smile became a little more good-humoured. 'Forgive my imprecision. Every battle-brother is ready to fight, of course, whenever that becomes necessary. But that isn't the reason we're here.'

'Then what is?' Zyvan asked, curbing his temper with an effort probably only I knew him well enough to appreciate. He was never going to be particularly pleased about being dragged down to the surface from the flagship to begin with, particularly after the rocky start we'd had, but to discover that our hosts had been keeping secrets from us despite their promises of co-operation had been disconcerting in the extreme. However forthcoming they were from now on, there would always be a nagging little voice in the backs of our heads, wondering *what else haven't they told us?*

'Observers,' Yail said. He hesitated, no doubt balancing our need to know against the traditions of his Chapter which, from what I recalled, tended to be long on keeping their own counsel, and short on being forthcoming with outsiders. No wonder they got on so well with the cogboys. 'For some centuries, the Reclaimers and the Adeptus Mechanicus have been working in concert. We seek out archeotech, when and where we can, for them to analyse, in return for knowledge we can use to fight the Emperor's enemies more effectively.'

'And you're here, now, because?' Zyvan prompted, making it clear he wasn't going to be impressed, intimidated, or fobbed off.

Yail looked surprised for a moment, then carried on, acknowledging the interjection with a courteous nod of the head. 'One of our Apothecaries has been exchanging information with Magos Kildhar. He is accompanied by several Techmarines, keen to further their studies of the Omnissiah in this most hallowed of places, and an escort of battle-brothers, which I have the honour to command.'

'Wait just a minute,' I cut in, an instant before the Lord General could explode. Zyvan's high rank notwithstanding, the Reclaimers still seemed to have a better opinion of me than anyone else in the Guard contingent, and my interrupting would be a lot less likely to put the brother sergeant's back up. 'You mean you knew about Kildhar's pet 'stealers?'

'Of course they did,' Kildhar said. 'They supplied us with our first specimens.'

'That is correct,' Yail agreed. 'A working party of Chapter serfs was ambushed by genestealers about sixty years ago, aboard the *Spawn of Damnation*. By the time they were recovered, most of the survivors had been implanted.' Precisely what the Serendipitans and I had most feared, of course, but by that time it was far too late to say 'I told you so'.

'Before they could be cleansed, one of the Adeptus Mechanicus delegation assisting the cataloguing of the finds requested permission to study them.'

'And that would be you, I suppose,' I said, with a glance at Kildhar, hardly less warm than the one she'd received from Zyvan a few moments before.

'It was,' she confirmed, her voice not quite as even as a tech-priest normally strove to achieve. 'The opportunity to study the breeding cycle of these creatures in secure conditions was almost unprecedented.'

'Excuse me,' El'hassai put in quietly from our corner of the table, 'but all our information indicates that a tainted individual must mate with a normal member of their own species to pass on the altered genes. Is that not so?'

His intervention led to an audible intake of breath from among the Mechanicus contingent, or at least from those members of it who still had their own lungs. The tau diplomat's presence in the most secure and secret shrine on the planet must have galled them intolerably, but we needed the xenos support against the tyranids, and that was the end of it. Any attempt to exclude him after so momentous a revelation would have undermined the entire alliance, so the seething cogboys just had to lump it.

'It is,' Kildhar said, after an uncomfortable pause, during which it became clear that no one else was going to talk to the xenos, and, if the amount of chirruping in binaric was anything to go by, all the other tech-priests were of the opinion that it was her fault he was here in any case. 'Fortunately, we were able to source sufficient felons scheduled for harvesting for servitor components, and use those.'

El'hassai went a peculiar shade of grey. 'A difficult decision,' he said evenly. 'But the Greater Good sometimes demands hard choices.'

Kildhar nodded stiffly, apparently appreciating someone speaking civilly to her, even if it was a xenos heretic she'd probably rather see burned. 'Some debate about the appropriate use of resources was involved,' she allowed, 'although the acquisition of knowledge inevitably takes priority over mere utility.'

'I would appreciate a copy of your findings,' El'hassai said at last, after a pause during which he took several deep breaths for some reason.

'I have made it clear to Magos Kildhar that I expect complete disclosure,' Dysen said, his even mechanical drone not quite managing to conceal his reluctance. 'And full reports on every other line of research she is currently conducting.' Needless to say, I felt a distinct shiver of foreboding at those words.

'What other research?' Zyvan asked, getting in just ahead of me this time and evening the score.

Kildhar smiled, in a fashion I found far from reassuring. 'I suggest Commissar Cain conducts the initial inspection,' she said. 'After all, he made the work possible in the first place.'

I APPROACHED KILDHAR'S analyticum with mounting trepidation, the tech-priest having been remarkably unforthcoming since her disquieting remark in the conference chamber, but I concealed it well. I was damned if I'd give her the satisfaction of appearing intrigued or disconcerted by it. Instead, I passed the long walk through echoing corridors, many of which still bore the mark of the genestealers' rampage, in small talk with Yail, asking about my former acquaintances among his Chapter, most of whom it turned out he'd never met[1].

'Bit of a mess,' Jurgen remarked, as we skirted a section of floor marred by scorch marks, bolter holes, and some disquieting stains.

I nodded in agreement. 'Any idea how the 'stealers got out?' I asked pointedly, and Kildhar shook her head.

'That has still to be determined,' she said, probably trying to think of an underling she could plausibly pass the blame on to. 'Many of the data recorders were damaged in the breakout, so it isn't clear how they managed to circumvent the security protocols.'

'I doubt they had to try very hard,' I said dryly, 'given that they can claw holes in ceramite.'

The parts of Kildhar's face that were still fleshy enough to do so flushed, but whether in embarrassment or anger I couldn't tell Before she had a chance to speak and settle the question, Yail's baritone chuckle echoed around us like someone lobbing boulders down a well, drowning out any riposte she may have made. 'You have a point, commissar. But perhaps the question we should be asking isn't how they got out, but why now?'

'I see what you mean,' I agreed. With their formidable combination of the purestrains' brute force and the hybrids' intellect, the whole brood could probably have broken out any time they liked. 'They must have sensed the approach of the hive fleet.'

'That would be my conclusion too,' Yail agreed.

'Every precaution was taken,' Kildhar insisted. 'The containment pens were surrounded by energy barriers as well as physical ones.'

'To which the power supply was interrupted,' Yail added, 'by means as yet unknown, thus providing a salutary lesson in the perils of underestimating a foe.'

'Not a mistake I'd imagine your Chapter would be in the habit of making,' I said, giving in to the childish impulse to tease Kildhar a little more, but I couldn't help feeling she deserved it, if her hubris had indeed been responsible for costing so many innocent lives.

---

1. *Which was hardly surprising: like most Adeptus Astartes Chapters, the Reclaimers numbered around a thousand warriors, operating in company or smaller sized units, often isolated from the others for decades, or even centuries, at a time.*

People in the Guard had been shot for much less, some of them by me.

'They wouldn't,' the sergeant agreed, handily overlooking the leading role they'd taken in delivering the xenos abominations to Fecundia in the first place.

At which point we reached our destination: a thick metal door, like many of the others we'd passed, and at first sight equally unremarkable, unless you counted the number of biohazard warnings pasted to it. None of the others had had a genecode reader welded to the locking plate, however, nor a pair of Space Marines in full tactical armour standing guard outside. Both had their helmets on, their sinister yellow beaks[1] turning to watch us as we approached. Yail stopped to exchange a few words with them, confirming that the last of the stray 'stealers had been tracked down and eliminated, much to my relief, while Kildhar got her genes scanned.

The door clicked open, proving that she was definitely her, and she gave me a tight smile as she passed through. 'This way,' she said, unnecessarily.

After all that build-up, the chamber inside seemed remarkably prosaic, so far as I could tell. I'd been in enough Mechanicus shrines to recognise the general layout, even if I had no idea what most of the humming, clicking, and flashing devices were supposed to be doing. The usual bright metal cogwheel was welded to the wall, and various liquids slurped and bubbled their way through labyrinths of glassware on a couple of workbenches. A handful of red-robed acolytes were trotting about poking things and staring at pict-screens, while a servitor or two took care of the tedious stuff. The only thing to strike me as a little unusual was a pervading scent of counterseptics and biological decay, pungent enough even to eclipse Jurgen's body odour until I got used to it, forcing me to glance back over my shoulder to make sure he was still with me.

'I take it the 'stealers didn't get out this way,' I said, and Kildhar shook her head.

---

1. *Evidently the older Corvus-pattern, which the Reclaimers generally awarded to those showing particular bravery or initiative on the battlefield.*

'Their pens are... were on the level above,' she told me.

I nodded; we'd descended rapidly in a clanking, rattling lift, but my instinct for remaining orientated in enclosed spaces was working as well as ever, and I already felt certain that we were now far below the shrine's foundations. Behind the stark metal panelling surrounding us, and which acolytes of the Machine God were so unaccountably fond of, would be nothing but bedrock. Unless you counted the warren of air ducts, power conduits, and service shafts that the 'stealers had used to effect their escape, of course. 'So this is your mysterious line of research,' I said, trying not to look totally flummoxed.

'This is just routine tissue analysis,' Kildhar corrected me, allowing herself a most unmagos-like *moue* of scorn. 'The research is through here.' She conducted Jurgen and I through the bustling analyticum towards an unprepossessing doorway which, on first entering, I'd assumed led to a storeroom or the necessarium[1]. As we passed through it, however, I found my pace faltering, while a barely suppressed gasp of astonishment dribbled though my lips, rendered visible by a sudden onslaught of bone-chilling cold.

We were on a high metal bridge over a deep natural cavern, every surface of which was rimed with frost. Since whoever had built it apparently shared most Fecundian tech-priests' distaste for handrails, I determined to watch my step carefully. One slip and I'd plunge to a messy and painful death. Jurgen, of course, was completely unconcerned, as sure-footed on the thin coating of ice as he would have been at home on Valhalla.

'Nice to see your breath again,' he commented, as though this was a good thing. 'Why's it so cold?'

'That, I'd imagine,' I said, pointing at the huge, humming tangle of pipes and metalwork at the other end of the gallery. 'It looks like a refrigeration unit.'

'It is,' Kildhar said, apparently miffed that a mere unmodified human could spot the obvious. 'The specimens here have to be kept frozen.' She kept walking as she spoke, as blasé about the slippery surface underfoot as my aide.

---

1. *Hardly a facility most tech-priests were likely to need, I'd have thought.*

'At least they won't be walking out of here,' I said, although the shiver I felt down my spine at her words wasn't entirely due to the cold.

Kildhar apparently didn't feel that that particular sally merited a reply, merely leading the way towards an open elevator platform at the end of the bridge.

I took my place as close to the centre of it as I could, while the tech-priest engaged the controls and, with a lurch which nearly took my feet out from under me, we descended some fifteen or twenty metres to the floor of the cavern. This proved to consist entirely of ice, which crunched beneath my boot soles as I stepped out on to it, thin crystals of the stuff spraying away from my tread like flakes of finely drifted snow. The top of the ice was encrusted with hoar frost where the moisture in the air was continually freezing, although, beneath this thin layer, the rest was as transparent as glass. It was hard to estimate its depth, as the ceiling-mounted luminators overhead reflected back in dazzling patterns, but at a guess the bedrock floor of the cavern was at least as far again beneath our feet as the depth we'd descended from the bridge above.

'Commissar,' a new voice greeted us, unquestionably another Space Marine by its timbre, and I turned, to find an armour-clad giant emerging from a modular hab unit that had been set up within the shadow of the walkway above. This one was unhelmeted, as indifferent to the bitter cold as my aide, and, to my astonishment, bore a face I recognised. 'It has been a long time since our paths last crossed.' Six and a half decades, in fact.

'Sholer,' I said, extending a hand in greeting. 'The years have treated you well.'

'You too, evidently,' the Reclaimer said, engulfing my proffered glove in his own gargantuan grip. 'I trust the fingers are still satisfactory.'

'Eminently,' I assured him. The augmetic digits on my right hand had been grafted on by him, in the apothecarion aboard the strike cruiser *Revenant*, after my fortuitous deliverance from the necrons of Interitus Prime. 'I've a good deal to thank you and Drumon[1] for. I trust he is well.'

'As do I,' Sholer agreed, in a manner which made it clear that this was more of a pious hope than a realistic expectation. 'No doubt we shall receive news when the *Spawn of Damnation* is relocated.'

'He was still aboard when it returned to the warp?' I asked, unable to keep the incredulous horror I felt at the prospect entirely out of my voice.

Sholer nodded. 'When it became clear that transition was imminent, an expeditionary force was landed aboard in the hope of keeping the hulk in Imperial hands at its next emergence point. Contact has yet to be re-established.' And wasn't likely to be either, after all this time. Chances were it had emerged in the path of the oncoming hive fleets, or in the heart of an orkhold, or, just possibly, was still drifting among the warp currents.

'The Emperor protects,' I recited, to fill the awkward silence, and found myself hoping that in this case, at least, it would turn out to be true. Then the reason for his presence began to percolate through my surprise at finding him here at all. '*You're* the Apothecary that Kildhar's been working with?'

'He is indeed,' Kildhar told me. 'Which is why you were given permission to visit Regio Quinquaginta Unus in the first place, despite the reservations of the Adeptus Mechanicus. The advice of a Space Marine is never to be taken lightly.'

'I'm gratified to hear so,' Sholer said, turning away. I fell into step beside him, trotting a little awkwardly on the slippery surface to keep up with his greater than human stride. 'Although, it seems, we are to explain our work here to non-specialists despite my reservations.'

'And mine,' Kildhar added. 'The Magos Senioris, however, is most insistent.'

'As is the Lord General,' I reminded them. 'If we're to defend this world against a hive fleet, we need every scrap of information which might have a bearing on that.'

---

1. *The Techmarine who crafted the fingers, and who subsequently became the closest thing to a friend Cain had among the Reclaimers.*

'Our research here is purely theoretical,' Kildhar said, a trifle tetchily. 'We're attempting to refine our understanding of the tyranids' genetic mutability, but that won't make them any easier to shoot at.'

'Unless they break free and go on the rampage,' I pointed out, a little irritably myself if I'm honest. The bitter cold was giving me a headache, and the steady succession of surprises wasn't exactly helping my mood.

'There's no fear of that with these specimens,' Sholer assured me, with a gesture towards the ice at our feet.

I glanced down, and recoiled instantly in shock. A huge, gaping mouth lay less than a metre beneath my boot soles, large enough to have swallowed me whole, and I flinched aside instinctively. The huge, serpentine form of a tyranid trygon lay embedded in the transparent ice, inert and unfeeling, apparently dead. But then we'd thought that about the frozen army of such creatures we'd found on Nusquam Fundumentibus. I had no doubt that if this one thawed out, it would be burrowing its way to the surface in search of a snack as fast as its cilia could carry it.

'Where the hell did that come from?' I asked, relinquishing my instinctive grip on my half-drawn weapons. 'Dysen said there hadn't been any tyranid landings.' The little voice in the back of my mind began chanting *What else haven't they told us?*, just as it had in the conference room, but with a harder, more insistent edge.

'There haven't,' Sholer assured me, no doubt divining that I'd be more inclined to take his word for it than Kildhar's. 'These specimens have all been acquired from offworld, and were brought here in a completely dormant state.'

'Hence the construction of this facility,' Kildhar put in, determined to have her two coins' worth, 'to ensure they remained that way.'

'What happens if the power cuts out?' Jurgen asked, clearly sharing my reservations. 'We've seen frozen 'nids before, and they were up and at us the minute the ice melted.'

'It can't,' Kildhar assured us. 'The refrigeration plant is equipped with multiple redundant backup systems. The power supply could only be interrupted by an accident catastrophic enough to level the whole shrine.'

'Like an exploding power plant?' Jurgen suggested, and the tech-priest nodded, clearly wondering if he was mocking her, or simply getting the matter straight in his head.

'Which is hardly likely,' she said.

'Quite,' Sholer agreed, leading the way across the ice again, pointing out one specimen after another like an elderly dowager fussing over her collection of tea bowls. 'Over here we have the most basic bioforms, hormagaunts, termagants, and the like. The synapse creatures are in the far corner, and the burrowers you've already seen...' And, indeed, other serpentine creatures, some as large as the trygon I'd trampled on, others small enough to infiltrate a line of fortifications and fall on the defenders from behind, were still underfoot as we trudged through the thin scattering of frost.

'Where did you find them all?' I asked, no more enthused by the discovery that an entire army of the hideous creatures was right beneath our feet than you might expect. I was already sure I knew the answer to that, Kildhar's words upstairs taking on a new kind of clarity, but it wouldn't hurt to be sure.

'Nusquam Fundumentibus, of course,' Sholer confirmed. The two systems weren't exactly neighbours, but were close enough to make the journey through the warp as straightforward as such things ever were. 'There were a great many organisms which never revived, and the Adeptus Mechanicus there showed no inclination to study them *in situ.*'

'Hardly surprising, under the circumstances,' I put in dryly, 'given how many of their colleagues got eaten.'

'The analyticae of Fecundia are unsurpassed anywhere in the sector,' Kildhar said, sounding affronted, 'which the Nusquan Mechanicus are well aware of. They were more than happy to cede the study of these creatures to us.'

Jurgen muttered something which sounded suspiciously like 'I bet they were.'

'So what's the main line of your enquiries?' I asked, hoping I'd been in time to drown him out, but doubting that I had. Sholer, at least, had the preternatural hearing common to a member of the Adeptus

Astartes, and Kildhar probably had some augmetic enhancement which worked just as well. 'In simple terms, so I can convey it to the Lord General and his staff in language we can all understand.'

This time it was Kildhar's turn to subvocalise, but since she was much better at it than my aide, all I was able to catch was something to do with blunt crayons.

'Our primary focus is on the mechanism by which the hive mind is able to maintain control of the swarm,' Sholer said. 'If we were able to disrupt that, depriving it of the ability to coordinate across a wide area, it would give us a significantly enhanced tactical advantage.'

'It certainly would,' I agreed, momentarily dazzled by the prospect. 'And are you able to?'

Sholer shook his head. 'Our work is at a very early stage,' he said. 'But we believe we can identify some of the neural pathways involved.'

'Oh,' I said, trying and failing to conceal my disappointment.

'Thanks to you,' Kildhar said, a curious half-smile on her face, which left me feeling distinctly uneasy. She pointed downwards, right where she was standing, and, despite a sense of foreboding which grew stronger with every step, I plodded over to join her. 'We have all the high-grade neural tissue we could wish for.'

I stared down at a seared and blackened piece of meat, about the size of a Baneblade. Raw flesh was livid around the necrotic patch, still seeming fresh despite the damage done to the far side, and I was incongruously reminded of a rare steak, charred on the outside while all but untouched within. 'What the hell is it?' I started to ask, but then fell silent as a memory intruded. Something huge and living, on the verge of taking flight, falling back into the volcanic eruption Jurgen and I had triggered at the near cost of our lives. 'Holy Throne, that's a piece of the bioship!'

Kildhar nodded. 'One of its cortical nodes. Most of it was too badly burned to salvage, but some fragments of it fell on the ice fields and were frozen quickly enough to preserve the tissue. This was the largest and most cohesive piece.'

I tried to speak, to verbalise my utter horror and abhorrence, to ask how they could possibly have been so staggeringly stupid, but the words just wouldn't come. All I could do was stare at the hideous mound of flesh, which had the potential to destroy us all.

FOURTEEN

'THEY MUST ALL be destroyed at once,' Zyvan said firmly. This time we'd managed to call our council of war aboard the flagship, and he seemed much more at his ease, clearly feeling more in control of the situation on his home ground although his reaction the previous evening, when I'd relayed the news of what I'd found in the depths below the Mechanicus shrine, had all but melted the bulkheads. 'The potential damage if they revive is incalculable.'

- To my well-concealed relief, his voice held no hint of his initial impulse to turn the battleship's lance batteries on the shrine from orbit, despite his insistence for most of our long and somewhat fraught conversation that it was the only way to be sure. That may well have been true, but would hardly have improved relations with the cogboys, not to mention the Reclaimers, who would certainly have taken a dim view of a clutch of their battle-brothers being vaporised along with everything else. Besides which, the shrine was a large and solid structure, which would probably take several volleys to level. We were just as likely to melt the ice with our first shot, and let the damn things loose ourselves. All factors which I'd striven hard to convince him of. (I could just have pulled my gun on him, of course, but that would have rendered things distinctly less cordial between us, and I'd wanted to avoid that if possible. We'd worked together well for over sixty years by that point and I'd grown used to the benefits of his hospitality.)

Luckily, he'd calmed down enough to see sense in the end[1], and we'd worked out what we hoped would be a more diplomatic approach. After all, the lance batteries weren't going anywhere, and would always be available as a last resort.

'And how do you suggest we do that?' Dysen droned, from the far side of the conference table. If he was at all angered at being dragged up here, he concealed it well, although since Zyvan had travelled to meet him to discuss the genestealer debacle, he could hardly complain about returning the favour. No doubt he would have preferred to be consulted over a vox-link, but on a world where information was constantly being exchanged at a bewildering rate, the only way to keep anything confidential was to discuss it face to face, preferably in a sealed room, and even then your chances were only marginally on the side of success.

Accordingly, we were a small and select gathering. Apart from myself, Zyvan, and Dysen, only El'hassai and Sholer were in the room, although Jurgen lurked just outside it, his lasgun and dubious personal hygiene equally ready to repel attempts at intrusion. Kildhar had protested at her exclusion, of course, but since the Magos Senioris outranked her, and Sholer could answer questions about the research they'd conducted together just as well as she could, her presence was hardly necessary. The Space Marine, on the other hand, was essential. If we were ever going to defend Fecundia successfully, then the Reclaimers had to be kept in the loop. Once again, I seemed to be the only one they were willing to even pretend to listen to, so that meant asking their advice at every opportunity, to keep them engaged in the conversation at all.

The same thing applied to the tau envoy, and I shuddered to think what might be in the reports he was preparing to send home. The

---

1. *Typically, it doesn't seem to have occurred to Cain that the good opinion Zyvan had of him almost certainly played a large part in his willingness to listen.*

only mercy was that, lacking astropaths, the other tau would still be in blissful ignorance of the utter shambles we were making of our end of the arrangement. Zyvan had, of course, offered the use of one of our own choir, through which he could contact the astropath accompanying Donali directly, and El'hassai had, just as politely, refused the offer, knowing full well that he might just as well drop a copy of everything he sent on Zyvan's desk if he did.

'It would be quite a task,' Sholer agreed. 'Every organism would have to be individually disinterred from the ice, and incinerated, or otherwise rendered incapable of revival. Hardly something which could be done at once; I'd estimate at least a month. And let us not forget we have an unprecedented opportunity to gain a decisive tactical advantage over the tyranids, one I would be loath to throw away.'

'Quite so,' Dysen agreed. 'The genestealer breakout was unfortunate, but the organisms we have frozen are hardly in a position to emulate them.'

'The commissar and I disagree,' Zyvan said, his tone remarkably even under the circumstances.

I nodded. 'I've seen how quickly these creatures can revive from hibernation,' I said. 'They almost overran Nusquam Fundumentibus after only a handful were thawed out to begin with. The last thing we need is to provide the hive fleet with an army of infiltrators before they've even got a spore on the ground.' I might just as well have saved my breath, of course. Sholer looked as obdurate as only a Space Marine could, Dysen whirred and clicked quietly to himself, equally unmoved, and Zyvan glowered at the pair of them, his choler rising. Seeing that this could only end badly, I turned to the tau, more to divert everyone's attention than because I expected it to do any good. 'Envoy, do you have a comment to make?'

To my surprise, El'hassai nodded, doing a good job of looking thoughtful, unless a cogitating tau always looked that much like a ruminative human in private[1]. 'Both arguments are compelling,' he

---

1. *Having had the opportunity to interact over a prolonged period with members of the species, becoming a familiar enough presence to catch them in the occasional unguarded moment, I can confirm that they do indeed look just as gormless as the average human while lost in thought.*

said, ever the diplomat, 'but on balance I'm inclined to agree that disposing of the specimens prematurely would be unwise. If the Apothecary's research does indeed reveal a weakness in the tyranids, the Greater Good can best be served by allowing him to continue unhindered for as long as possible.'

Tech-priest and Adeptus Astartes alike looked dumbfounded for a moment, then relaxed as this unexpected declaration of support sank in. Zyvan looked equally shocked, then took several deep breaths, a primed grenade willing itself not to explode. I, on the other hand, having spent as much time as I had around diplomats, homed in immediately on the thinly veiled get-out clause.

'What exactly do you mean by "as long as possible"?' I asked, making everyone else sit up as they began to digest the implications of the phrase.

El'hassai steepled his fingers, a gesture I had no doubt at all was a practised affectation for the benefit of the *gue'la*[1] in the room. 'The dictates of the Greater Good notwithstanding,' he said, 'I also share the reservations you and the Lord General have expressed. I would suggest that while Apothecary Sholer and Magos Kildhar continue their endeavours, preparations are made to expunge the specimens quickly should that become necessary.'

'Sounds reasonable to me,' Zyvan agreed, seizing on the prospect of a face-saving compromise, to my unspoken relief. Against all the odds, it seemed, the tau was holding this ramshackle alliance together, rather than being the wedge that drove it apart, as I would have expected. He turned to Dysen. 'Could something like that be rigged up?'

'It would be a considerable challenge to ensure the physical destruction of so many all at once,' the Magos Senioris said thoughtfully, 'but the Omnissiah will undoubtedly guide us to a satisfactory solution. Perhaps venting the fusion reactor into the storage chamber would suffice.'

---

1. *The tau word for humans, one of a handful of simple phrases Cain apparently picked up during his occasional contacts with members of the race which didn't involve physical violence.*

'Then we'll leave that in your capable hands,' Zyvan said, avoiding any hint of sarcastic inflection by a miracle. 'Please keep us informed of your progress.'

'On both endeavours,' I added, not wanting them to be able to claim they thought we only wanted to know about one or the other. As I've remarked before, the seeds of distrust they'd planted by trying to keep us in the dark about Kildhar's research were germinating nicely, *what else haven't they told us* becoming an almost constant refrain in the back of my head. I don't mind admitting, the sooner we were out of there, and able to leave this benighted rock to its own devices, the better I'd like it.

Now we had at least the appearance of a consensus, the meeting wound down as quickly as possible in a flurry of broad generalisations and non-specific promises of action, everyone eager to be out of there before the others had a chance to change their minds or come up with further reasons to object. Sholer and Dysen departed in the direction of the docking bay as soon as they decently could, followed shortly by El'hassai, no doubt hurrying back to his quarters to compose an appropriately trenchant missive to his superiors, although how he intended to deliver it, I had no idea[1].

'I want that facility completely surrounded,' Zyvan said, as soon as the door clicked shut behind the tau. 'If the 'nids get free, they'll have to be contained.'

'That'll take a lot of manpower,' I pointed out. 'Even a full company would be stretched pretty thin, if you deployed them in a wide enough cordon to avoid an orbital bombardment.'

The Lord General smiled. 'If I didn't know better, I'd swear you were a psyker.'

'I ought to know how your mind works after all this time,' I said. 'Besides, it's what I'd do.' Which was true enough.

Zyvan nodded. 'We'll keep the lance batteries targeted, at least for now. We won't need them for anything else, unless the hive fleet shows up.'

---

1. *No doubt a number of messenger drones had come aboard the Imperial flagship with him.*

'Which, Emperor willing, it won't,' I said, tempting fate as usual. I called up the area around Regio Quinquaginta Unus on the tactical display, and considered it carefully. 'You'll have to use the Death Korps. None of the other units will stand a chance, being deployed in the open like that.'

'I hadn't considered anyone else,' Zyvan agreed, and shrugged. 'The problem's going to be keeping them concealed, though. They're good at what they do, but that doesn't generally involve much sneaking about.'

'I wouldn't bother trying,' I said. 'The cogboys'll know they're there anyway. If they squark about it, just tell them you've decided to give the shrine some extra protection now you know how vital it is. They won't believe you, but they won't risk calling you on it.'

Zyvan chuckled. 'They won't have the nads,' he agreed, which was literally true of most tech-priests, given their penchant for excessive augmentation.

At which point, our amusement was abruptly curtailed, as Jurgen knocked on the door. Even before the booming echo of knuckle against metal had time to die away, let alone either of us call out for him to enter, his aroma burst into the room, followed an instant later by his grime-encrusted face.

'Sorry to interrupt, sir,' he said, 'but we've just heard from the scout fleet.' He sucked his teeth, in the way he always did while trying to find the best way of putting something he knew I wouldn't want to hear. 'It doesn't sound good,' he added, after a pregnant pause.

I'VE NEVER YET met an astropath I'd describe as sociable, which I suppose is hardly surprising given that at least part of their attention is constantly on the whispering of the warp in their minds, waiting for a message to form. I'm not easily spooked[1], but I can't deny they make me uneasy. Perhaps it's the tattoos of warding, a visible reminder that they might be possessed by a daemon at any moment, or perhaps it's the way their blind, sunken eyes stare at you wherever you are in the room, as though they're looking directly into your soul.

---

1. *Ha!*

Madrigel, the most senior astropath on Zyvan's staff, epitomised most of these traits: gaunt and skeletal, only his head and hands emerging from the shroud of his robe, he lurked inside his chamber like one of the tunnel ghouls said to haunt the lowest depths of the underhive in which I spent the first few years of my life[1]. There was no question of us receiving a message so sensitive in the middle of the command centre, surrounded by witnesses, even if he could have been prised out of his den, so I found myself hunched in the claustrophobic cell in which he lived and worked[2], trying to make him out as best I could through the all-pervading gloom. Having no need of light himself, he hadn't bothered to kindle one, leaving Zyvan and I to make do with the flickering illumination of the candles beneath the incense burner, which, judging purely by the smell, seemed to contain a smouldering pair of Jurgen's socks. (My aide, of course, I'd dispatched back to my quarters, having no wish for his secret to be revealed by Madrigel suffering a seizure in front of the Lord General.)

'What have you got?' I asked, a little more brusquely than I'd intended, keeping my eyes fixed on the astropath by a considerable effort of will.

His thin lips parted to allow his tongue to dart out, licking them in a faintly reptilian fashion which made my flesh creep. 'A good deal,' he replied, in a voice which put me uncomfortably in mind of the wind rustling through the flayed skins hanging from the ramparts of the eldar reaver citadel on Sanguia, 'very little of which has been rendered in a manner comprehensible to you.'

Which, coming from most people, I'd have considered an outrageous and deliberate insult, but given Madrigel's vocation it was probably no more than the literal truth. When I'd first been spat out by the schola progenium I'd assumed, like most of the line troopers I was serving alongside (or behind, if the enemy were

---

1. *Despite my best efforts, I have thus far been unable to determine the world on which this stood; or, equally likely, was burrowed into.*

2. *Actually a fair-sized suite, although, to be fair to Cain, he probably remained unaware of the existence of the rest of the rooms.*

about), that astropaths were little more than living vox-sets, capable of parroting anything dictated or shown to them. Only much later in my career, as I blundered my way into the upper echelons of the Imperial military, did I begin to apprehend the truth, that the crisply-worded dispatches and grainy pict feeds from outside whichever stellar system I happened to be desperate to vacate at the time had arrived in the form of fragmentary images and sensations in the mind of a sanctioned psyker, probably only marginally sane to begin with. Only after long and arduous processing could the original meaning be disentangled from whatever the astropath had first tried to transcribe, an undertaking which often involved the use of other sanctionites as filters, and which typically took far more time than the fluid situation in an active war zone could easily afford.

'Then just tell us what we need to know,' Zyvan said. 'What have you heard from the scout fleet?'

'Heard?' The darting tongue tasted the air again. 'Nothing. Babble. Still being worked on. But we all felt it. The whole choir.'

'Felt what?' I asked, already sure I wouldn't like the answer. I was right, I didn't.

'Fear,' Madrigel said, his dry whisper hanging in the air for several heartbeats. 'The astropaths on the scout ships were all terrified.'

'Doesn't mean much,' Zyvan said bluntly, trying to sound as though he meant it. 'They'd been inside the warp shadow, cut off from the rest of the universe. Hardly surprising they would have found it upsetting.'

'More of a blessed relief,' Madrigel croaked, with absolute sincerity. 'If there's anywhere in the galaxy a psyker would feel at peace, it's inside the shadow around a hive fleet.'

'Apart from the tyranids coming after them,' I added, feeling it was about time somebody in the room paid attention to the real issue. To my surprise, the astropath nodded.

'Exactly,' he pronounced sibilantly. 'Which they did. There are many echoes of pain and fear, the smell of blood and burning. We don't have the details, but the fleet has been in combat.'

'That's not good,' I said, with considerable understatement. Their orders had been simply to observe and report, avoiding contact if at all possible. 'Any idea how much of a mauling they took?'

'A bad one,' Madrigel said, and the last faint hope I'd clung to flickered and died. 'Ships were lost.'

'How many?' Zyvan asked, his voice grim.

'That will not be known until the processing is complete,' Madrigel replied, his tongue flickering again. It was almost hypnotic, and I forced myself to concentrate on the rest of his face, which was hardly an improvement, all things considered. 'But more than one.'

'How about the survivors?' I asked. 'They must have got away if they're back outside the shadow.'

'Damaged,' the astropath said. 'Wounded. Traumatised.' It was hard to tell if he was talking about the ships, their crews, or both; members of his order tended to talk in metaphor half the time anyway, worse than ecclesiarchs. 'Limping home to lick their wounds.'

Zyvan and I exchanged troubled glances, the same thing occurring to both of us. There was only one world within reach where the battered fleet might hope to find the facilities they needed to repair any significant combat damage, and we were currently in orbit around it.

'They're heading here,' I said, and Madrigel nodded.

'They are. We can feel the connection with the minds of our brethren growing stronger with each passing hour.'

'Then the 'nids will be right behind them,' Zyvan said. That much was a given. Engaging with the hive fleet would have alerted it to the presence of prey, and, at the very least, a portion of it would be detached to follow the survivors, to see how much else was on the snack trolley. If we were really unlucky, the whole damn pack of them would be heading in our direction by now.

'I'll warn the cogboys,' I said, my mouth dry, keeping my voice steady with a supreme effort. Our worst fears had just come to pass. All I could hope now was that the warning we'd been given would be enough to prepare for their arrival.

Editorial Note:

Unsurprisingly, Cain devotes no more of his attention to the fate of the scouting expedition. Accordingly, I've appended the following extracts, in order to place his account of events into a somewhat wider context.

Transcript of evidence given by Captain Nansi Blakit of the frigate *Amazon* to the board of enquiry into the loss of the vessels *Egregious, Cleansing Flame, Emperor's Hammer* and *Xenovore*, 485992.M41.

Captain Blakit: We made all speed to the estimated position of the hive fleet, based on the information the tau had given us. In the light of the danger our orders put us in, I commanded the crew to charge weapons, and to prepare for incoming fire before making the transition back into the materium.

Admiral Jaymstea Flynt (Chairman): A precaution also taken by the captains of the other vessels in the flotilla?

Captain Blakit: I believe so. None of them being blithering idiots with a death wish.

Codifier Mallum (Administratum observer, recorder of minutes): May I remind the captain that speculation and personal opinion are not evidence?

Admiral Flynt: You may not. Captain Blakit's record speaks for itself, and any observations an officer of her experience sees fit to make are pertinent to this enquiry.

Captain Blakit: That's telling her, Uncle Jym.

Admiral Flynt: Strike that last remark from the record. Carry on, Nansi.

Captain Blakit: There was nothing on the auspex, although we knew we must be close. None of the astropaths could get through to the main fleet, so we must have emerged inside the warp shadow cast by the tyranids.

Codifier Mallum: Speculation…

Admiral Flynt: Quiet, Mallum. You're not the only drone around here who can push a quill.

Captain Blakit: So Commodore Stocker dispersed the fleet. Not much, but with a mean separation of about fifty million kilometres. I told him it was a bad idea, but he wouldn't listen.

Inquisitor Vail (Ordo Xenos observer): Why so?

Captain Blakit: He was in command. He had every right to disagree with the opinion of a more junior officer.

Inquisitor Vail: I mean, why was it a bad idea?

Captain Blakit: I thought it would be more prudent to keep the fleet close enough for the ships to be able to support one another with overlapping fire arcs. Captain Warka of the *Hirundin* agreed with me.

Admiral Flynt: But the commodore didn't?

Captain Blakit: He felt we'd stand a better chance of returning an auspex echo with the fleet dispersed. As soon as one vessel got a contact it was supposed to vox the others, and we'd all rendezvous around it.

Inquisitor Vail: Tyranid bioships are notoriously difficult to detect at a distance.

Captain Blakit: That was the problem. By the time the *Xenovore* was close enough to be sure she had a hard return, the tyranids had detected her as well. Probably from a lot further away. She was jumped by a swarm of the smaller drones, backed up by a couple of things the size of cruisers. We all responded to her mayday, but we were so widely dispersed that even the closest ship didn't pick it up until over two minutes after it was transmitted.

Admiral Flynt: That was the *Egregious*?

Captain Blakit: It was, the only cruiser in the squadron. Commodore Stocker's flagship. The *Emperor's Hammer* and *Cleansing Flame* arrived about three minutes after she did, just as the *Xenovore* blew up. The tyranids were already aboard and overrunning her. Detonating the plasma core was the only option the poor bastards had left.

Codifier Mallum: More speculation? Or do you have hard evidence that the *Xenovore* was scuttled deliberately?

Captain Blakit: I can show you the pict feed of their chief engineer overloading the reactors just before he was ripped apart by hormagaunts, if you like. You might find it educational.

Admiral Flynt: You were receiving datafeeds from the *Xenovore* at this point?

Captain Blakit: From all four vessels engaged with the enemy. Commodore Stocker ordered the rest of us to withdraw, and get the intelligence we'd gathered back to the main fleet. Captain Warka and I protested, but he threatened both of us with a court martial if we attempted to intervene.

Inquisitor Vail: Very wise. If you'd tried, you'd be dead too, and we wouldn't have a clue what killed you. I take it the tyranids were reinforcing the whole time?

Captain Blakit: They were. We held station as long as we could, in case any survivors got off, but it was hopeless. The *Emperor's Hammer* got some saviour pods away, but they were grabbed or swallowed by the drones. The screaming on the vox…

Admiral Flynt: Were any of the surviving ships attacked?

Captain Blakit: We all were. The void was full of them. Captain Warka took overall command of what was left of the squadron, as he had seniority, but we were still so widely dispersed it was impossible to coordinate a defensive strategy. We hung on as long as possible, to get as much of the datafeeds as we could record, but one by one we were forced to retreat back into the warp or be destroyed ourselves.

Admiral Flynt: And after you'd made the transit?

Captain Blakit: We rendezvoused in open space, outside the shadow, where our astropaths could make contact again. Assessed the damage, and ran for Fecundia, hoping we could get patched up enough to fight before the tyranids made planetfall.

Inquisitor Vail: You seem very certain that that would be their next target.

Captain Blakit: We were. The astropaths told us. The boundary of the shadow had shifted. Only one thing I know could account for that: the tyranids had changed direction to follow us.

From *The Crusade and After: A Military History of the Damocles Gulf*, by Vargo Royz, 058.M42.

THE DIRE NEWS brought by the battered survivors of the Imperial Navy scout squadron was soon in the hands of Battlefleet Damocles, and preparations for its deployment were made accordingly. From all over the sector, ships began to converge on the forge world Fecundia, determined to preserve it, for if it fell, the Imperium's ability to fight on against these ghastly creatures would be dealt a crippling blow. The majority, of course, were to pass through the Quadravidia system, which itself had remained in Imperial hands only by a near miracle so short a time before.

The tau, meanwhile, had turned their attention to fortifying a handful of worlds across the recently contested border between the two powers, seemingly unaware that at least some elements of the oncoming hive fleet had changed course away from them or, if they were, still fearing that these remained the most likely targets for the full fury of the tyranid invaders. In either event, they showed no inclination to divert any of their assets to the direct defence of an Imperial world, nor did the Imperium feel inclined to ask the xenos for their assistance.

So it was that both partners in the uneasy alliance looked first to their own, and awaited the onslaught.

FIFTEEN

THE NEWS THAT the tyranids were on their way swept Fecundia like one of the bone-scouring winds continually ravaging the surface, and did about as much damage in the process. Most of the Guard units held steady, of course, largely due to the fact that the majority of regiments on planet had never encountered the scuttling horrors before, and I spent several days inspecting outposts and garrisons to spout encouraging platitudes, assuring them that if they could face down orks, eldar, and the dupes of the Ruinous Powers they could certainly send the hive fleet packing. The Death Korps were the exception, as in so many things, having lost scores of their number to a splinter fleet the year before, but, typically, were too heavily dosed up on combat drugs to care. As usual, the only thing that seemed to bother them was the prospect of not taking enough of the enemy with them when they fell[1]. Needless to say, this was an attitude I found hard to understand, but quite comforting, given that I fully intended to keep them between me and the onrushing horde.

---

1. *For a Death Korps trooper, dying in action is a given; although the majority do try to put it off as long as possible, to be of the greatest service to the Emperor in the interim.*

The real damage the news did was among the civilian population, of course. I must admit the cogboys managed to hold up surprisingly well, most of them making a reasonable fist of hiding their apprehension, but the foundry workers had no such inhibitions about expressing their emotions, and Kyper and his skitarii spent as much time suppressing riots as they did preparing the planet's defences. Most of the thralls who weren't out causing trouble preferred to spend their time in the temples of the Omnissiah praying for deliverance, although I gather they drifted back to the production lines quickly enough once the tech-priests started telling them He'd find the job a lot easier if they built up a good stockpile of arms and ammunition first.

The only good news was the arrival of the battered remnants of the scout fleet, which reinforced our orbital defences a little, followed in short order by a steady stream of warships from all across the sector. Within a month Fecundia was surrounded by a hundred vessels[1], which went some way towards easing my mind. If Kildhar's enhancements to the sensoria really worked as well as she seemed to think, it would take a very determined assault to land anything on the planet capable of hurting us.

Of course determination was practically synonymous with the 'nids, so I didn't rest entirely easily, not least because she and Sholer still had their collection of deep-frozen death and destruction stashed away beneath the foundations of Regio Quinquaginta Unus, and, despite their reassurances, I was far less sanguine about it not thawing out at the worst possible moment than they seemed to be.

A concern I'm bound to say that Zyvan shared, and voiced aloud the morning I wandered into the operations centre aboard the flagship to find him staring at the hololith in a thoughtful manner. The festering globe of Fecundia was surrounded by glittering fireflies, colour coded to differentiate the warships from the cargo

---

1. *Considerably more, if the defensive armament of the armada of merchant ships continually arriving and departing from the forge world is taken into account; although this would be so feeble against the might of a hive fleet Cain can be forgiven for apparently discounting it altogether.*

haulers, and I nodded in an approving manner. The net seemed as tight as we could make it, and anything attempting to land would have a hard time getting down unvaporised.

'Heard anything from Madrigel?' I greeted him, still clinging to the hope that the 'nids would realise the pickings were better among the tau, despite the improbability of such a development, and he shook his head.

'Nothing good,' he said. 'None of our astropaths can detect a thing.'

'Then we're inside the shadow,' I said, while a prickle of apprehension danced across my scalp.

'We are.' Zyvan nodded grimly. 'There might be a few more ships on the way in, but we can't count on that. And, bar any news they bring if they do turn up, the next thing we'll know is the arrival of the 'nids.'

'Then we'll just have to hope Kildhar knows what she was doing to the auspexes,' I said, feeling an almost irresistible urge to thumb my palm as I spoke.

'I just hope she knows what she's doing in that bloody meat locker,' Zyvan rejoined. 'They still haven't worked out how the genestealers escaped, and that was bad enough.'

'Sholer should be keeping an eye on her,' I said, trying to sound less apprehensive than I felt. I hadn't known the Apothecary all that well aboard the *Revenant*, having been unconscious for most of our time together[1], but he seemed to take his duty as seriously as any other Space Marine, which was about as reliable as you could get. 'And the other Adeptus Astartes have got the analyticum pretty well locked down.'

'Well, you'd know, I suppose,' Zyvan said, sounding far from convinced. 'You've served with them.'

And seen them torn to shreds by the genestealers infesting the *Spawn of Damnation*; not the most comforting of thoughts, so I suppressed it firmly. Even more firmly than the associated idea

---

1. *In the apothecarion, recovering from his ordeal on Interitus Prime.*

that it would take a lot more than Yail and his combat squad[1] to keep a swarm that size bottled up if it decided it would rather be somewhere else.

'How are the Navy contingent?' I asked, looking again at the cloud of contact icons surrounding the leprous image of the forge world beneath us. A few warships were accompanied by runes indicating that they were still under repair, which was hardly surprising. Pretty much the first thing most of the captains had done was take advantage of the orbital docks to bring their vessels up to peak fighting efficiency, which was fine by me. The vast majority were registering as fully armed, crewed[2], and ready to get stuck in, which was something of a relief, but only a partial one. I've never been all that keen on being aboard a spaceship under fire, particularly since my mercifully short attempt to breathe vacuum aboard the *Hand of Vengeance*, and the pict images of the horrors which had overwhelmed the tau explorators were still far too fresh in my mind for comfort as well. The thought of playing tag with those things around the corridors of the battleship[3] was far from inviting, and I couldn't help wondering if, formidable as it seemed, the fleet would be enough to check the advance of the tyranid hive.

Zyvan shrugged. 'Impatient,' he said, which didn't surprise me either. Most of the admirals I'd met were firm believers in carrying the fight to the enemy, an ethos the Navy as a whole subscribed to wholeheartedly, and I didn't imagine twiddling their thumbs in orbit waiting to be shot at would sit at all well with the majority of the fleet.

'Have the analysts got anywhere with the intelligence the scouts

---

1. *An informal Adeptus Astartes designation for a squad of about five Space Marines, typically a full-strength tactical squad split into two teams for mutual fire support. Nowhere in Cain's account does he give the actual number of Reclaimers on Fecundia, if he even knew, but, given his familiarity with Space Marine nomenclature, it would be safe to assume about half a dozen, plus Sholer and the neophyte Techmarines referred to in passing.*

2. *No doubt the press gangs had been busily making up for any combat losses.*

3. *The first time Cain mentions the class of ship Zyvan had set up his command centre aboard. If he's being literal, rather than using 'battleship' as a colloquial term for an Imperial Navy vessel, it was probably the Retribution-class* Throne Eternal, *the only ship of its size involved in the defence of Fecundia.*

brought back?' I asked, which was as close as I felt like coming to asking the real question on my mind: was the hive fleet big enough to give the matelots a bloody nose, or would the first assault be pushed back in short order?

'Still chewing through it,' Zyvan said, a remarkably tactless choice of words under the circumstances. 'But we know there's at least a couple of leviathans among them. Possibly more, judging by the number of smaller bioships the imagifers recorded.'

Which was far from good news. Our only chance of killing one of the void-swimming giants would be to swarm it, and that would mean clearing a path through its screening escorts first. Large as the fleet around Fecundia was, it would be a very closely fought engagement indeed if it came down to that.

'We need an edge,' I said, uneasily aware that I was echoing Sholer's words of justification for keeping his precious specimens intact. Maybe it was time to press him and Kildhar for some results.

'We do,' Zyvan said, unenthusiastically, coming to the same conclusion. 'Think you can get some simple answers out of your Apothecary friend?'

'Not if he doesn't want to give us any,' I said. My good standing with the Reclaimers had already won us more concessions than anyone else would have got out of a member of the Adeptus Astartes determined to mind his own business, but I was under no illusion that I could push that any further than I already had. 'But it wouldn't hurt to ask.' It was beginning to dawn on me that a diplomatic errand to consult Sholer in person would be just the thing to get me out of the firing line when the fleets engaged.

'Then ask, by all means,' Zyvan said, his enthusiasm for the proposal probably having as much to do with being able to get on with the war without having a scarlet-sashed backseat driver querying his every move[1] as with any expectation of a satisfactory answer.

---

1. *Probably intended as a piece of self-deprecating humour, since, as previously noted, the relationship between the two men was far warmer than would normally be the case between a senior officer and the member of the Commissariat attached to his command; a happy knack Cain seems to have had throughout his career (cf his accounts of his service with the Valhallan 597th.)*

'I'll get right on it,' I said, in blissful ignorance of the consequences to come.

TO MY RELIEF, commandeering an Aquila was simple enough this time around, the locals having been considerate enough not to disrupt my travel plans with any more destructive mishaps. The atmosphere in the hangar bay was markedly different from our last flight, however, the tiny utility craft awaiting us dwarfed by the Furies and Starhawks[1] being fuelled and armed all around it. Jurgen and I walked towards our transport through a maelstrom of frantic activity: deckhands lugging armoured cables as thick as an ork's forearm, small trains of warheads trundling past on wheeled trolleys and the stomping bulk of Sentinel power lifters, all reducing our progress to an erratic waltz, as we changed direction with every step to avoid a fresh obstruction. Servitors were everywhere too, of course, carrying loads too bulky or dangerous to be handled by the unaugmented, and there seemed to be an inordinate number of red-robed Mechanicus adepts about the place, chanting litanies, burning incense and sanctifying the systems of the spaceborne weapon platforms on which our very survival was so shortly to depend.

'What kept you?' our pilot greeted us, with a cheery wave through the armourglass cockpit canopy, his voice crackling a little through the comm-bead in my ear.

'Sightseeing,' I replied briefly, in no mood for banter, but well aware that distracting him with a visible show of annoyance was hardly the best way to ensure our safe and speedy delivery to our destination. The pilot nodded, taking the hint, and went back to checking his instrumentation, while my aide and I strode aboard and took our seats.

Our departure was as straightforward as these things ever are,

---

1. *Spaceborne interceptors and anti-ship attack boats respectively; both unlikely to be found aboard a Retribution-class battleship, so Zyvan's flagship may have been one of the many cruiser class vessels among the fleet rather than the* Throne Eternal *after all. A ship so equipped may also have carried a complement of Shark-class assault boats, but, since attempting to board a tyranid vessel would be the action of a madman, no attempt appears to have been made to deploy them if present.*

the deckplates on which the small vessel was parked falling away gently beneath us, seemingly in concert with the rising pitch of the engines. Slowly we began to move towards the gaping maw of the inner lock gates, the metre-thick slabs of metal grinding closed as we passed through them. As usual, it took several minutes to extract the air before their outer counterparts started moving apart, gradually revealing a speckling of pin-sharp stars, most of which were promptly occluded by the cankerous face of the forge world below. During this enforced wait the pilot kept us hovering, balanced in place on the manoeuvring thrusters, which greatly raised my opinion of his skills. It would have been no easy task in the cross-currents created by the air pumps, and most shuttle jockeys would have set down on the deck to make life a little easier.

We drifted out into the void at last, surrounded by a faint puff of ice crystals from the residue of air the pumps had been unable to extract, and I looked about us, noting the visible signs of readiness to face the oncoming storm. A squadron of Furies coasted past with flaring engines, one of the groups screening the flagship from enemy drones, and, glancing back, I could see a score or more others clamped to the hull, awaiting the call to action[1].

Everywhere I looked in the sky, it seemed, a loose star was drifting, its motion obvious against the fixed backdrop of the galaxy: the unmistakable spoor of a spacecraft, too far away to make out, but betrayed to the naked eye by the light reflecting from its hull.

'There's a lot of them,' Jurgen remarked, although whether this was intended as reassurance or simply an observation I had no idea.

'Good,' I said, turning my attention to the world towards which we were descending. It looked no more inviting than it had on any of the previous occasions I'd done so, the portions of the surface visible between the thick clouds of airborne waste resembling nothing so much as rotting offal. Even the lights of the hives had little chance of punching through the murk, which was being stirred up across half the

---

1. *Which implies that the vessel, whatever it was, had no dedicated fighter hangars, and that the docking bay being used to arm those Cain saw inside may well have been used only for utility craft in the normal course of events: which in turn means that the flagship may have been the* Throne Eternal *after all. I give up.*

southern hemisphere by one of the periodic storms capable of laying waste to entire continents (assuming the vast midden had anything so clearly identifiable as a continent to lay waste to, of course). Nevertheless, I couldn't help trying to pick out our destination, or, at least, its general location.

Occupied as I was in this futile endeavour, it took me a moment to realise that our pilot was throwing us around in a rather more violent manner than usual. Fortunately the Aquila's internal gravity field was remaining steady, or Jurgen and I would have been flung against the bulkheads hard enough to have broken bones. As it was, the rapid oscillation of the planet across the viewport was my first clue that things were beginning to go as wrong as they usually did.

'What's happening?' I voxed the pilot, trying to keep an edge of testiness from my voice. It seemed as though he had his hands full, and none of the reasons that I could think of for that made distracting him now a particularly good idea.

'We've got incoming,' he told me, in a voice which didn't have to add *so shut up and let me get on with my job* to append that particular message. Leaving him to it seemed like the best idea, so I switched channels and spoke to Zyvan instead.

'Kildhar's modified auspexes are picking something up,' the Lord General told me, in tones of some surprise. 'They started returning echoes about thirty seconds ago, and the Navy scrambled everything they've got to intercept.' Which explained the violent manoeuvring, at least; our pilot must have been jumping around to get out of the way of the fighter squadrons.

'I can't see anything,' I said, inanely I suppose in retrospect, as my chances of picking anything up with the naked eye would have been miniscule. 'Have you mobilised the ground forces?'

'They're as ready as they'll ever be,' Zyvan said. The trouble was, we'd both fought tyranids before, and were under no illusions about what that actually meant. I realised then that he must have been simmering with frustration, an unwilling spectator to a spaceborne clash of arms he couldn't influence or participate in: perhaps the most galling position possible for a warrior of his prowess and tactical acumen.

'Any sign of–' I began, then broke off as something from a nightmare howled past the viewport[1]. 'Holy Throne!'

It was hard to focus on, seeming to consist mainly of spines and talons, each larger than our shuttle. The one thing I could say for sure was that it dwarfed the pack of fighters snarling and yapping at its heels, still peppering its back and flanks with lascannon and missile strikes as it passed out of sight.

Then, without any warning at all, the void lit up, the main batteries of the warships all firing at once. And they had plenty of targets to choose from. The flickers of a thousand impacts, as energy beams and torpedo volleys struck home against steel-hard chitin, dazzled my eyes, and our pilot's voice was in our ears again. 'Hang on back there,' he counselled. 'It's going to get rough.'

I bit down hard on the sarcastic rejoinder which had almost escaped my lips, and did as I was bid, cinching the seat restraints a little tighter. Jurgen did the same, his face paling slightly beneath its usual carapace of flaking skin, no doubt fearing for his delicate stomach, not something which usually troubled him until we were well within a planetary atmosphere. His knuckles were white around the melta he carried across his lap, and I found myself hoping he'd remembered to leave the safety on: the last thing we needed at this stage was to vaporise a chunk of the fuselage by accident.

'Sounds as if they've arrived,' he said, craning his neck for a better view of the carnage beyond the viewport. The tyranid bioships were retaliating in kind, lashing out with tentacles to ensnare the smaller vessels, and spitting gobbets of something corrosive which burned and melted hulls from a safer distance. The Navy seemed to know what they were doing, though, I had to give them that. I caught a brief glimpse of the lance batteries of a cruiser slicing through the tendrils holding a destroyer in place, but before I could see the smaller vessel turn vengefully on its tormentor our Aquila lurched vertiginously, and began plunging towards the surface of the planet.

'What was that?' I asked, my sudden flare of alarm overriding my

---

1. *A clear figure of speech, as sound doesn't travel in a vacuum; something the producers of pict shows seem curiously unwilling to admit.*

resolve not to bother the pilot unduly before we were once again standing on a solid surface.

'Haven't a clue, but it nearly got us,' he snapped, and the starfield beyond the sheet of armourglass began to do somersaults. 'We need to get into the atmosphere fast.'

Well he wasn't getting any argument on that score, I can assure you. The tyranids were in space, and anywhere they weren't was fine by me. The view outside began to steady once again, as the pilot angled the Aquila for atmospheric entry, and I took my last look at what I gather is now commonly referred to as the first battle of the Siege of Fecundia. I'd be the first to admit I'm no expert on the complexities of fighting in three dimensions, but I'd been involved in a fair few ship-to-ship actions over the years, and it seemed to me that we were more than holding our own. Most of the tyranid ships seemed relatively small, about the size of our destroyers or light cruisers, although I had no doubt that they had far worse in reserve; this was a scouting raid, meant to size up our defences in preparation for a stronger assault, a tactic I'd seen the swarms on the ground use innumerable times. Just my luck to be caught in the middle of it, in a light utility craft, liable to be swept from the sky with a single volley.

'They're launching fighters,' Jurgen said, with an apprehensive glance at the nearest drone ship. I twisted in my seat, impeded by the crash harness I'd tightened a few moments before, and felt the breath catch in my chest.

'Those aren't fighters,' I said, 'they're mycetic spores.' I tapped my comm-bead, using my commissarial override code to cut in on whatever vox-traffic might be going on among the Imperial Guard units on the surface; bad manners to interrupt, of course, but under the circumstances I didn't think anyone would object. 'All ground units stand to,' I broadcast, trying to sound appropriately calm and dignified, instead of frightened out of my wits. 'Spores incoming. The tyranids are on their way.'

SIXTEEN

I HAD LITTLE enough time to concern myself with conditions on the ground, however, as it soon became clear that our chances of reaching it intact were diminishing with every passing second. I could see only two or three of the spiky bioships[1] from where I sat, although I had no doubt that many more were uncomfortably close. All were taking fire from every ship that could get a clear shot at them, and probably a few that couldn't, judging by the frequency and violence of the evasive manoeuvres our pilot was making. By now the first faint tendrils of the upper atmosphere were reaching up to claw at our hull, so even the internal gravitic compensators weren't enough to prevent us from being shaken about. Jurgen groaned audibly as we corkscrewed through what felt like a complete barrel roll, a spread of torpedoes passing all around us to impact on the closest of the spaceborne monstrosities, but fortunately for both of us managed to retain control of his breakfast.

'It's breaking up!' he gasped, no doubt happy to have something to

---

1. *Probably the subspecies of vanguard drone classified by the Navy as 'stalkers,' although his description is sketchy enough to have applied to innumerable other variants; tyranids not being all that big on uniformity.*

take his mind off the miseries of motion sickness, even if it was the prospect of imminent death. For a panic-stricken moment I thought his hypersensitivity to our hurtling progress had allowed him to spot some flaw in the fabric of the shuttle that was about to doom us all, then my eyes followed his, and I realised he meant the tyranid ship the torpedoes had just gutted. Fragments of flesh and ichor, already flash-frozen into deadly missiles hard enough to penetrate our hull if they struck at this velocity, fountained out into space from the site of the wound, and the dying drone lurched, plummeting into the atmosphere less than a kilometre away, still spitting out spores as it went. Then it began to charbroil from the friction of the air, its chitinous exoskeleton sizzling and crisping as it spiralled in towards the ground.

'Brace yourselves!' Our pilot just had time to shout a warning before the atmospheric shockwave hit, sending our Aquila tumbling like a ration can kicked by a careless boot. How Jurgen remained outside his last meal was beyond me. The effort must have been truly heroic, and I have to admit to relieving my feelings with a volley of profanity which would have made a courtesan blush. In my defence, I can only say that it seemed to me at the time that it was either then or in front of the Emperor, and I already had more than enough ground to make up in that regard without letting rip at the occupant of the Golden Throne as soon as I arrived. Sparks flew from overstressed electrical circuits, and stress fractures cracked open around welded joints, but the enginseers had evidently done a good job of consecrating the circuit breakers of the gallant little craft, as, despite my fears, nothing burst into flame. Just as well too, as we'd never have made it to the extinguishers without breaking our necks.

After a subjective eternity of noise and random motion our course steadied a bit, and I became aware of Zyvan's voice in my earpiece, demanding to know what was going on in tones of quite gratifying concern.

'We're all right,' I assured him, hoping to convince myself of that at least as much as the Lord General. 'Just crashing a bit.' Which, given the number of times I'd marked my arrival on a new world by making a dent in it, was perhaps a little more sanguine than it sounds. I'd managed to walk away from all the previous occasions, after all (or, to be more accurate, limped, crawled, or run like frak, depending on how likely the impact was to be followed by an explosion), and our pilot seemed to know his business. He still had some measure of control, and our engines appeared to be functioning as well as could be expected under the circumstances. All in all, it seemed to me, we were most likely to get away with nothing worse than a hard landing; certainly nothing to compare with our concussive arrival on Perlia, or almost literally world-shattering one on Nusquam Fundumentibus.

'Glad to hear it,' Zyvan said, after a short bark of what sounded suspiciously like hastily stifled relieved laughter. Once again, it seemed, my baseless reputation for sangfroid in the face of danger was getting another fillip.

'We're being sucked into the slipstream of the bioship,' our pilot cut in, either unaware of, or indifferent to, the fact that I was already voxing on another channel. 'I haven't enough power left to break away clean.'

'Why not?' I asked, a renewed shiver of apprehension breaking through my carefully constructed optimism.

'Diverting most of it to the on-board gravitics,' he explained, which was more than good enough for me. If he hadn't been, Jurgen and I would have been little more than a stain on the bulkhead by this time.

'Probably best to follow it down anyway,' I said, trying to sound as though it was a sound tactical choice rather than putting the best face on something that couldn't be avoided. Never let it be said that Ciaphas Cain ever shirked the call of duty, at least when a Lord General was listening in. 'Some organisms might survive the impact,' (something I'd put money on, knowing the 'nids) 'and the ones from the spores will probably rally there.' Also a pretty safe bet, based on my previous encounters with tyranid swarms. The synapse creatures would be attempting to coordinate the rest into a cohesive horde, while the others would be impelled by instinct to seek out their guidance. A little bit of aerial reconnaissance should be safe enough, enhancing my spurious reputation for leading from the front without actually having to put myself in any physical danger for a change, especially if we could pot a few with the Aquila's autocannon[1] into the bargain.

'Might be best to let them congregate,' Zyvan said, 'then take the lot out from orbit.'

'If the Navy's got time,' I said. 'They seemed a bit busy the last I saw.'

'They still are.' Zyvan sighed regretfully. 'But relay the coordinates anyway, you never know. It'll help get some ground units there, if nothing else.'

'Will do,' I assured him, then settled down to enjoy the rest of the flight as best I could. (Which I'm bound to admit wasn't all that much.) At least the buffeting was beginning to die down a little, as the pilot broke through the maelstrom of turbulence into the pocket of dead air behind the plummeting bioship. It was crisping up nicely, so far as I could see through the heat-hazed air, smoke and steam billowing around it while greasy flames licked greedily at its leading edge. Fragments the size of a Chimera kept breaking off it, each more than capable of swatting us from the skies if it hit, and our pilot was forced to evade several times as these lethal pieces of scurf came rather too close for comfort.

Between the heat haze, which tinted the horizon the colour of ackenberry preserve, and the cloacal palette of the landscape below, it was hard to tell where the sky ended and the ground began, so I was taken by surprise when the incinerating corpse beneath us suddenly disappeared in a cloud of ejecta. 'Impact!' I voxed, to show I was paying attention, while fist-sized nuggets of the Fecundian surface began to rattle against our hull. Not that they were the worst of it by any means. We were flying though a plume of particulates, among which they were the largest chunks, the vast majority of it being made up of gravel and dust, admixed with a generous dollop of pulverised

---

1. *An odd choice of weapon for a spacecraft, where the recoil would have to be compensated for by bursts from the manoeuvering thrusters with every shot: for which reason lascannon are more common on Navy craft. Presumably this particular one was generally employed on ship to surface runs, making defence within an atmosphere a higher priority, or had been dispatched by the Adeptus Mechanicus as a courtesy to Cain.*

flesh. 'It's down!' More or less, anyway; most of it was still bouncing, and breaking up into ever smaller portions as it did so.

At which point I began to detect a worrying change in the note of our engine, which began to waver alarmingly in pitch. 'That doesn't sound good,' Jurgen said, displaying his gift for understatement to its fullest, and I felt a sickening lurch in the pit of my stomach as the Aquila dropped like a stone. A second or so later it rallied, clawing its way back towards the sky for a moment, only to falter a second time.

'Brace for impact!' our pilot called, quite unnecessarily, as I'd already been in similar positions far too often for comfort, and knew an impending catastrophe when I saw one. I was already strapped in about as securely as I could be, so I simply held on and hoped for the best, nudging the barrel of Jurgen's melta a little further away from my chest with the toe of my boot. I'd just seen a shipload of 'nids being barbequed, and had no desire to share their fate at this stage.

The Aquila struck the ground hard, driving the breath from my lungs in a single explosive oath, lurched, slithered, and came to rest in an oddly anticlimactic lack of fire, flood, or rending metal. I inhaled deeply, and instantly regretted it; quite aside from Jurgen's proximity, the cabin was evidently no longer airtight, admitting eye-watering amounts of what passed for an atmosphere around here. I tapped the vox-bead in my ear, but could raise nothing but static. Evidently the Aquila's vox system was down, or at least unable to relay transmissions. Which, coupled with the lack of sound or movement from the cockpit, was disquieting to say the least.

'Door's jammed, sir,' Jurgen said, to my complete lack of surprise, giving the thick metal panel separating us from the flight deck an ill-tempered kick. It would be hopeless attempting to hack through it with the chainsword, and using the melta in such a confined space would probably incinerate us with the backwash, not to mention the pilot, so I gave it up as a bad job and turned my attention to the rear access ramp[1]. Reaching it entailed scrambling up the steep slope the floor had become, canted a little to starboard, but the ridging in the

---

1. *A common configuration with Aquilae, although, given their numbers and ubiquity, nothing so straightforward as a standard design could truly be said to exist.*

deckplates gave us a firm enough foothold for the purpose.

'This is stuck too,' I said, leaning my full weight on the emergency release handle. Jurgen joined me, and, after a moment or two of concerted effort, and a few heavy blows with the butt of his lasgun, we managed to loosen it enough to crank the hatch open a centimetre or two. Immediately the passenger compartment became full of thin, powdery dust, suffocatingly thick, and the stench seeping in from outside redoubled. Choking, I fumbled my sash from my waist and tied it around my nose and mouth, obtaining a measure of relief thereby, although my lungs continued to ache and there seemed nothing I could do for my stinging, streaming eyes.

Jurgen followed my lead, rapidly wrapping his head in a towel he produced from somewhere within his comprehensive collection of webbing pouches, rather to my surprise I must confess, as that was hardly an item I would have associated with him in the normal course of events. 'Getting it now, sir,' he assured me, leaning into the handle with renewed confidence, and being rewarded almost at once with a slightly wider gap and a fresh influx of sand.

My aide's optimism notwithstanding, it took us an appreciable time to widen the aperture sufficiently to wriggle through, which I did with all dispatch, having entirely lost patience with the choking tomb we'd been confined to for so long[1]. My eyes were met by a vista of complete and utter desolation: Throne knows I've seen some Emperor-forsaken hellholes in my time, but this was up there with the worst of them. A desert of rust-coloured sand[2] undulated away in every direction, unrelieved by anything save the glowering clouds of distant sandstorms, none of which, I was relieved to note, appeared to be moving in our direction. On the far horizon the looming mesa of a hive, its upper slopes shrouded in the smoke from its forges, was the only thing appearing to offer any hope of rescue or relief, although I didn't put our chances of reaching it much higher than

---

1. *Possibly not as long as Cain appears to believe, his perception of time almost certainly having been distorted by the unpleasant and claustrophobic nature of his surroundings.*

2. *Probably quite literally, given the amount of mineral waste released into the environment over several millennia of energetic exploitation of the system's natural resources.*

non-existent. It must have been a hundred kilometres away at least, across terrain so lethal even the Death Korps treated it with respect.

I extended a hand to help Jurgen up, and he passed me his lasgun and melta, leaving himself free to scramble out of the crippled Aquila relatively unencumbered. Instead of doing so, however, he vanished again, with a brief 'Hang on a moment, sir,' and began rummaging energetically through the equipment lockers. Leaving him to his scavenging I returned my attention to the horizon, reminded all too strongly of the ork which had attacked me during a similar moment of inattention after our precipitous arrival on Perlia, and having no intention of being taken by surprise on this occasion.

It might have been my imagination, but I was sure I could see movement in the distance. I blinked my stinging eyes as clear as I could, and shaded them with a hand. A thick pall of dust still shrouded a large portion of the landscape, marking the site of the tyranid ship's demise, and I stared at it suspiciously, unable to make out anything more inimical than wind-driven sand and yet I couldn't discount the knowledge of what that cloak of dust concealed.

'Found a few things,' Jurgen said, scrambling up beside me. 'Might be useful.'

'They might,' I agreed, taking a quick look at the collection of survival gear he'd found. A collapsed habitent, awkward to carry, but essential if we decided to strike out from the crash site; attempting to sleep in the open here would be all but suicidal. A handful of ration packs, enough to keep us going for a couple of days, longer if we were careful, and about five litres of water. At the sight of the cool, clear liquid, I was immediately seized by a raging thirst, which I knew better than to slake; we'd need every drop before we were done, and my sand-abraded throat would just have to wait for relief for as long as I could stand it. The only other item I could see any immediate use for was a primary aid pack, which reminded me... 'Better check on the pilot, I suppose.'

Jurgen nodded, clearly thinking precisely what I was: if he was in any condition to have joined us, he definitely would have done by now. He certainly hadn't been fixing the vox, the bead in my ear remaining as silent as ever, despite me having cycled through every frequency I could reach.

On the verge of clambering down from my perch on top of the Aquila, I hesitated. I still couldn't be certain that I'd imagined the movement I thought I saw, and I didn't need the persistent itching of my palms to tell me I needed to be positive one way or the other before we moved off. I asked Jurgen for the amplivisor he usually carried, and raised it to my eyes.

The first direction I looked in was the crash site, of course, but if there were any 'nid survivors there, they were remaining under the cover of the debris cloud raised by the impact of their arrival. After a few minutes of intense scrutiny, I'd still seen nothing moving but dust eddies. I was almost beginning to breathe easier, despite the bitter experience of decades, and the almost literal unbreathability of the air, when I decided to sweep the horizon just to make sure.

'Frak,' I said, feelingly. Something was definitely moving, between us and the looming ramparts of the hive – not close enough to make out yet, but definitely in large enough numbers to raise a visible plume of dust in their wake, whatever they were. Heading in our direction, too. I swept the lenses to left and right, and this time, far closer, was able to make out the unmistakable six-armed silhouettes of a small brood of genestealers, then, about a kilometre beyond them, the larger profile of a lictor, flickering like a badly-tuned pict-caster as its chameleonic skin attempted to mimic the constantly-changing clouds of dust blowing about it. 'We need to move.'

'Right you are, sir,' Jurgen acknowledged, as matter-of-fact as if I'd just asked for a fresh bowl of tanna. Slinging the bulky melta behind him, and holding his lasgun ready for use, he slithered down the tilting hull of the crippled Aquila, taking the bulk of our supplies with him. A moment later I followed, after a last, apprehensive look at the moving dots in the distance.

SEVENTEEN

My boots landed in deep sand, which almost immediately began to work its way inside my socks, the sharp-edged granules making my feet itch abominably. Within a few hours they'd be rubbed raw, and I'd be slogging through the dunes on a mass of blisters. No point worrying about that now though, and the way things were going, sore feet would probably turn out to be the least of my worries. So I put the matter out of my mind as best I could, and slithered through the drift towards the downward-tilted nose of the battered utility craft, following the furrow left by Jurgen.

Emperor knows I'm no enginseer, but even I could see it wouldn't be flying again without some serious benediction from the tech-priests. The wings were flexed in a fashion the designers would never have envisioned, its landing gear was badly buckled, and several inspection panels had been jarred loose by the impact, revealing partial glimpses of the mechanica inside. The nose was deeply buried in the sand, which reached halfway up the armourglass surrounding the pilot's seat. Though the panes had been cracked and crazed with the force of our landing, none had shattered completely, effectively hiding the cockpit from view. My pessimistic assessment of our pilot's chances of survival dropped even further, if that were possible.

Then the distinctive *crack* of a lasgun echoed flatly around the dunes, and I broke into a floundering run, drawing my weapons and barking my shin painfully on the sheared-off stub of the chin-mounted autocannon. As I caught my first glimpse of Jurgen's target, a reflex of revulsion stilled the breath in my chest which, given the quality of the air, was probably no bad thing.

A trio of scavenging hormagaunts had ripped the cockpit asunder, and begun feeding on the body of the pilot. There was no telling by this point precisely how or when he had died, but I found myself hoping it had been during the crash. One of the gaunts lay twitching on the sand, part of its head ripped away by Jurgen's las-bolt, but the other two were already moving, bounding towards my aide with murderous intent.

'Take the left!' I called, cracking off a shot with my laspistol at the one on the right as I spoke. Jurgen complied, chewing up its thorax with a quick burst of automatic fire, and the hideous thing stumbled and fell, leaving him well beyond the reach of its scything claws. I wasn't so lucky, the hasty pistol shot at the target I'd selected missing its head entirely. Before I could adjust my aim it was on me, with a vicious swipe calculated to rip me in two.

I'd anticipated the move, though, knowing such creatures only had a limited repertoire of responses, and swung up my chainsword to block it. The whirling teeth bit deep, severing the tip of a razor-sharp talon as long as my arm, and I pivoted, bringing the screaming blade round to deflect the follow-up strike from the other claw I knew had to be coming. Gaunts always struck in the same scissoring pattern, hoping to catch their prey between the two keen edges of their primary weapons. Unfortunately for this one, it was now off-balance, and I was able to evade it neatly, slicing off the secondary arm which was reaching out towards me with its smaller, hook-like talon in the process. Undaunted, it came on, mouth agape, and stuffed with far too many fangs for my peace of mind, but I'd anticipated this too, and squeezed the trigger again, putting a las-bolt through the back of its throat and into what passed for its brain.

Too stupid to realise it was dead, the foul thing rallied, then leapt into the attack again, only to fall heavily to the sand as it finally got the message and expired.

'Sorry, sir,' Jurgen said, with an apologetic shrug, 'they took me by surprise.' He poked the one he'd downed cautiously with the barrel of his lasgun, and it twitched feebly for a second before vomiting up a rancid mess of bile and masticated pilot. Ignoring the mess on his boots, my aide put another round through its skull to make sure it wouldn't be getting up again, although, if I was any judge, it only sped things up by a second or two.

'Me too,' I said, conscious of the irony. All the time I'd been scanning the horizon, the vile creatures had been right under our noses. 'What worries me is how many more of them there are.' There must have been dozens of spore pods ejected by the drone we'd followed down, and the others left in orbit, and they'd all have been directed towards the same area[1]. That meant there were hundreds of the ghastly things roaming the desert, if not thousands[2], which was hardly going to make it any easier tramping across a lethal wilderness in an attempt to find help.

I glanced round apprehensively, conscious of how badly hemmed in we were by the whispering sands. The faint hissing of the grains as they were blown over one another by the wind would mask the sounds of any more approaching, and we couldn't see beyond the next dune. All we could do was keep a sharp lookout every time we crested one, hope the conditions here made us equally hard to detect, and pray to the Emperor that none of the swarm were burrowers.

'Better get moving,' I said at last, conscious that if we delayed much more I'd lose my nerve entirely. Staying where we were wasn't an

1. *A reasonable assumption, since tyranid tactics tend to depend on overwhelming numbers. Typically, vanguard swarms are deployed in only a few locations, in an attempt to establish beachheads from which they can expand their depredations, while solitary scout organisms, most often lictors, are scattered more widely, in search of more potential targets for the following wave.*

2. *Each spore pod typically contains around twenty of the smaller organisms, although the number can be less, particularly in the case of larger creatures: lictors are generally deployed singly, for instance, as befits their role of solitary pathfinder, and carnifexes invariably so, given their bulk.*

option, as the hive mind would be aware of the loss of its meat puppets, and would surely send more to investigate[1]. Picking up the survival gear we'd dropped in the melee meant putting my weapons away, which gave me a moment's disquiet, but there was no help for it. Our chances were slender enough as they were, without leaving our food, water and shelter behind. Reluctantly I scabbarded my chainsword, holstered the laspistol, and shouldered the habitent. It was just as unwieldy as I'd expected, but, with the melta slung across his back, Jurgen would have found it even more awkward.

Slogging through the dune field was every bit as gruelling as I'd anticipated. We soon discovered that scrambling up them was more effort than it was worth, every step sliding back almost to its starting point in the loose grains and raising clouds of the stuff which made breathing even more difficult. So, despite my apprehension about being ambushed, we remained at the bottom of the gullies between the sand drifts, trying as best we could to keep moving in the direction of the hive, although the haphazard arrangements of the dunes meant that we seemed to spend as much time moving parallel to it as towards our destination. My initial estimate of how long it would take us to get there revised itself depressingly upwards with practically every step, until it was so far in excess of the maximum time we could possibly survive out here that I gave up thinking about it in sheer self-defence.

We'd entirely lost sight of the downed Aquila within moments of leaving it, which I couldn't help thinking was something of a mixed blessing; although we were now hidden from any further tyranid organisms drawn to feed on the carrion we'd left scattered about it, it would have been a useful marker point in this wilderness of sand. My sense of direction, so reliable in enclosed spaces, was far less helpful in this accursed wilderness, and I was soon completely disorientated. Even the sun was no help, obscured as it was by the huge pall of debris flung up by the crash of the bioship. All about us was the same dust-hazed twilight, casting no shadows, merely deepening inexorably as the day wore on.

---

1. *Probably not, in fact, as the gaunts Cain describes seem to be acting from instinct rather than direction; but with tyranids it's never safe to assume anything.*

After what my chronograph assured me had been no more than a couple of hours of fruitless plodding, but which felt like a day and a night, I called a rest stop, and luxuriated in a mouthful of water. The parched tissue of my mouth seemed to absorb it directly, like a sponge, but enough of it trickled down my throat to clear the worst of the dust still settled there, and I followed it with a second swallow before passing the bottle to Jurgen. He drank as abstemiously as I, and resealed it, the lessons learned in our arduous journey across the desert region of Perlia needing no reminder or reinforcement.

'We need to know where we are,' I said, eyeing the side of the nearest dune with scant enthusiasm. But we couldn't keep plodding on blindly forever, and the short break and some fresh water had perked me up as much as possible under the circumstances. Taking the amplivisor again, I began to make my way up the sand pile. I'm not embarrassed to admit I used my hands as much as my feet, another lesson learned the hard way on Perlia, and probably a wise precaution anyway, since I had no wish to announce my presence by skylining myself.

From the top, the landscape looked just as bleak as ever, and I swept the amplivisor across it, finding little to raise the spirits. The far distant line of the hive, like a thundercloud on the horizon, seemed no nearer than before; hardly a surprise given the tiny fraction of the intervening distance we would have walked, but it lay more on my right hand than I'd expected, and I resolved to adjust our course accordingly. The dust plume I'd spotted before was far closer now, enough for the amplivisor to pick out individual dots among it, but the intervening haze prevented me from discerning any further detail. Another good reason to go wide, though; the organisms looked unusually large, and there were at least a dozen that I could see.

I continued scanning the panorama before me, picking out several groups of gaunts wandering in the middle distance, and, far away, what looked like the leprous bulk of the pod which had brought them, but there was no sign of the genestealer brood or the lictor I'd spotted before, which suited me fine. Then, much closer at hand, I saw a gleam of reflected light, so bright it could only have come from a metal surface.

My spirits soared. Out here, amid so much desolation, the only possible explanation for that would be a human presence. Probably a vehicle of some kind, or, at the very least, an Adeptus Mechanicus altar, set there to monitor something, and through which we could attract attention and rescue.

'Jurgen!' I slithered down the dune in a flurry of sliding grains, which all but buried me as I came to a precipitous halt at the bottom. 'There's something metallic out there!' I floundered to my feet, creating a miniature sandstorm as I did so. 'I can't tell what it is from here, but it means humans. We can get a ride back, or call for help.'

'If the 'nids haven't eaten 'em already,' my aide added, and, recalled to the grim realities of our predicament, I nodded.

'We'll move in cautiously.' I'd taken careful note of the position of the object, whatever it was, and was sure I could find it without too much difficulty, in spite of the open nature of our surroundings. From here we'd just have to skirt two further dunes, and our objective ought to be in sight.

Before moving off, I drew my laspistol. Jurgen's point had been a good one, and any humans out here would surely become bait for the tyranids before long, including ourselves.

My aide readied his lasgun too, and we began to advance cautiously along the gully between the dunes, watching for any sign of movement. Despite an almost overwhelming impulse to break into a run, I kept my eagerness in check, all too aware of the consequences of letting our guard down, even for a moment. Tyranids excelled at attacking from ambush, and this environment seemed purpose-made to conceal a lethal surprise.

Sure enough, a surprise was waiting for us round the final corner, although under the circumstances I would almost have preferred more 'nids. 'Frak,' I said feelingly, followed by a few more choice expletives.

'That's the shuttle,' Jugen said, in his customary matter of fact tone. 'How did it get here?'

'It never moved,' I said, kicking the half-buried cadaver of the hormagaunt he'd first shot. Like the others, and the rather more widely-distributed remains of our luckless pilot, it had already acquired a tenuous shroud of wind-driven sand; another few hours and it would have been completely buried. Come to that, the entire Aquila would probably disappear in another day or two. 'We got turned around in the dune field somewhere.'

I might have said a great deal more, but before I got the chance something inhumanly fast and at least twice my height burst from the sand no more than a handful of metres away, and charged at me, its talons and reverse-jointed forelimbs straining in my direction, the feeding tendrils around its jaw writhing like a nest of snakes. The lictor had found us.

EIGHTEEN

I REACTED INSTINCTIVELY, cracking off a couple of shots from the laspistol in my hand which struck the ghastly thing squarely in the middle of its armoured chest, leaving cauterised craters of vaporised chitin as visible evidence of my marksmanship, but either the thick plates protecting its thorax were holding, or I'd failed to hit anything vital behind them. Jurgen began shooting too, with scarcely any greater success, but at least the burst of automatic fire managed to check its rush sufficiently for me to reach for my chainsword. Not that I expected to hold my own against something so monstrously fast and agile, and with so great an advantage in reach, for long, but it was clear I wasn't going to bring it down with the laspistol.

At which point I found the habitent, which I'd slung from my shoulder on that side, was impeding my ability to draw the close combat weapon. Without even thinking about it, I grabbed the bundle and threw it at the lictor, an impulse which undoubtedly saved my life. At that instant, a volley of viciously-edged barbs erupted from somewhere in the centre of its las-bolt-pocked thorax, hissing through the air towards me. By great good fortune my fumbling throw had caused the packed survival shelter to erect itself, the thin dome of weatherproofed fabric popping out of its cover in mid-air, and the flesh hooks snared it, ripping it to shreds as the thin ropes of sinew they were attached to attempted to drag it into the reach of the lictor's writhing feeding tendrils.

'The melta!' I shouted, knowing that was the only weapon we possessed capable of bringing the hideous creature down reliably.

'Right you are, sir,' Jurgen responded, leaving off trying to find a weak spot with his lasgun in favour of unslinging the heavy weapon from its awkward position across his back. Even for a marksman of his exceptional skill, the chances of felling a lictor with the small-arm alone were miniscule; we'd have needed a whole squad concentrating their fire to be certain of bringing something that size down with las-weapons. All I had to do was buy him the few seconds he needed to ready a shot, and try not to get ripped to shreds in the meantime.

Which was a lot easier said than done. I took advantage of the lictor's confusion to get in closer, behind the tattered remains of the habitent, which it seemed to be having some difficulty disentangling from its flesh hooks: a fortuitous development for me, because until it managed to do so it wouldn't be capable of winding them in again for another go, and while the fabric and memory polymer frame were still flapping about in front of its face its vision was partially obscured. Something else I could make good use of.

I leaped aside, just in time to evade a strike from the inner edge of one of its wickedly serrated scything claws, which, had it succeeded, would have snapped closed along the surface of its upper arm, cutting me in half. As it was, the deadly limb passed harmlessly over my back, close enough for the breeze of its passing to stir my greatcoat, raising a cloud of dust as it did so. I lunged with the whirling blade of my chainsword, driving in for a thrust to the pit of its middle arm, only to realise that the hand at the end of it was lashing out to grab me. Changing direction at the last moment, I narrowly evaded a grip tipped with talons capable of puncturing ceramite, and although it cost me the chance to plunge my blade deep into one of the towering creature's few vulnerable spots, my hasty deflection robbed it of three of its fingers, leaving only a solitary thumb behind.

Surprised and hurt, the lictor roared, giving me the benefit of a blast of halitosis compared to which Jurgen's exhalations carried the sweetness of a spring breeze, and charged in again, but this time I got the distinct impression that its attack was more cautious. The tyranids breed their scout organisms to remain hidden, attacking from ambush only when they're certain of success, and when they don't manage to make a quick kill it disconcerts them. This one seemed to be thinking[1] that it might have made a mistake in picking on me, and I was keen to reinforce that impression. If I could throw enough of a scare into it, its instinct to run and hide might cut in, preferably before it dealt me a mortal wound.

So, in spite of all my own instincts urging me to turn and flee, I did the one thing it would never expect prey to do, and charged in, bellowing like a berserk ork, swinging the chainsword in the loose horizontal figure of eight old Myamoto de Bergerac[2] used to refer to as the floating leaf (although in my case, he used to say, it was more like a plummeting brick[3].) At worst, the flickering blade would create a barrier between me and the lictor, across which it would be unable to strike without the risk of further pruning, and at best it would allow me another chance to do some serious damage. I didn't expect to be able to kill it, of course, but I could certainly make it decide that this particular meal wasn't worth the effort of trying to eat.

I seemed to succeed beyond my wildest dreams. As I bore in, the ghastly creature actually flinched, rearing back as I slashed at its belly, the tendrils around its mouth thrashing as its head rose up, then, to my horror, began to descend. I'd overreached myself, something my old schola tutor had chided me for on more than one occasion, and now I was about to suffer the consequences. If I raised the blade

---

1. *In so far as it was capable of thinking at all.*

2. *Cain's duelling instructor at the schola progenium.*

3. *Either Cain's standard of swordsmanship had improved considerably since his days as a progenii, or, as seems more likely, this was a rare case of a schola tutor unbending enough to share a joke with a particularly favoured pupil. As I've had occasion to remark elsewhere in my editing of his memoirs, Cain's academic record is undistinguished in most respects, apart from a precocious talent for combat skills, in which he appears to have shown considerable aptitude.*

to protect my head from the descending feeding tendrils, the lictor would disembowel me with its talons. With nowhere else to go I threw myself flat, buying a couple more seconds...

Then the landscape vanished in a vivid glare of light, and the stench of charred flesh. Jurgen had fired the melta, in the nick of time. I looked up to see the hideous creature toppling to the sand, a hole big enough to punch my fist through seared deep into its gut.

'Look out, sir!' my aide warned, and I rolled aside as the thrashing, kicking monstrosity slammed into the ground exactly where I'd been a moment before, its death throes raising a pall of dust which uncannily echoed the slowly-dissipating shroud around the last remaining remnants of the bioship which had sired it[1]. I rose to my feet, skirting it as widely as I could, and went to join him.

'Thank you, Jurgen,' I said. 'Impeccable timing, as always.'

'Looks like the tent's had it,' he said, with a venomous glare at the now still cadaver.

'It does indeed,' I agreed, allowing the full realisation of just how badly we were frakked to settle over me. Without some kind of shelter, we couldn't hope to survive a night in the toxic wasteland which surrounded us. Which left only one option, particularly as the gathering twilight was now definitely shading into night. 'We'll have to bunk down in the Aquila tonight, and make a fresh start in the morning.'

'Right you are, sir,' Jurgen agreed, as though our chances of actually making it to the safety of the hive were no worse now than they had been when we first set out. 'At least we'll have something solid between us and the 'nids if any come calling.'

'There is that,' I agreed. 'We'll take two-hour watches, turn and turn about.' Of course we were both so exhausted we needed far more sleep than that, but right now I didn't give much for my chances of staying awake any longer than a couple of hours in any case, and if we both fell asleep at the same time, neither of us were likely to wake. Ever.

---

1. *Or not. The mycetic spore which delivered it to the surface could have been dispatched by any of the tyranid ships in orbit.*

'I'll take the first watch,' Jurgen volunteered, as we scrambled up the slope we'd both slithered down a few hours before. At least we had the bent and rent metal of the fuselage to provide hand and footholds, so it wasn't so tortuous a process as clambering up the side of the dune had been, but the effort still left us gasping in the foetid air. The wind was beginning to rise as the ground cooled with the onset of night, and the hissing, slithering sound of the sand grains drifting had intensified, rather more so than I would have expected, given my experience of nightfall in the deserts of Perlia. Right on cue, the palms of my hands began to itch.

And with good reason. From the elevated perspective of the Aquila's half-buried rump, the desert beyond seemed to be moving, with clear, malign purpose. A score or more hormagaunts were scuttling over the crest of the adjacent dune, to join easily as many again already milling around the corpse of the lictor, and I belatedly remembered something else the camouflaged killers were known for. Leading the swarm to fresh prey.

'It laid a trail,' I said, hoping Jurgen would attribute the huskiness of my voice to the dehydration of my throat. 'We have to get out of here now.' But a single glance at our surroundings was enough to demonstrate the sheer futility of that hope. We were already surrounded, a tiny island of life amidst a sea of tyranids, and that, I knew, could only end one way.

AT FIRST, THE ghastly horde seemed not to notice us, being completely absorbed in the feeding frenzy which rapidly removed all traces of the deceased lictor, not to mention that of the trio of gaunts we'd killed before setting off on our futile circular stroll. They probably devoured the last mortal remains of our late pilot, too, although I tried not to look too hard in that direction.

'At least they can't shoot at us,' Jurgen murmured, hunkering down in the lee of the wedged-open cargo ramp, which had already acquired a thin coating of gritty sand, but not yet nearly enough to soften the edge of the metal beneath it. He braced the melta against a convenient stanchion, steadying the bulky weapon as best he could, and carefully laid his lasgun down next to it. Continuing to work methodically, he replaced the partially discharged power packs of both weapons with fresh ones – keeping the weaker for later, as we'd certainly need every single shot we could get before long – and opened the flap of the pouch in which he kept his grenades. 'Lucky I stocked up again on these.'

'How many?' I asked, keeping my voice as low as possible. I didn't know how acute the gaunts' hearing was, and I had no desire to find out the hard way[1].

'Three frag, two krak,' Jurgen said, equally quietly, pushing the two anti-armour charges to the bottom of the pouch, and laying the others out ready for instant use. I could hardly blame him for bringing the krak ones along, we'd been more than glad of their extra punch often enough before now, but I'd cheerfully have traded them for another couple of the anti-personnel devices given the chance. Come to that, I might just as well wish the Aquila intact and the pilot back from the dead, ready to fly us out of here, into the bargain. But since none of these were about to happen, we'd just have to make the best use of the few grenades we had.

'Let's hope it's enough,' I said, knowing it wouldn't be, and followed my aide's lead, snapping a fresh powercell into the butt of my laspistol, stowing the used one in a convenient pocket in the faint hope of ever getting a chance to reload. Not wanting to find myself unexpectedly running dry, I made sure it went into a different one from the fully charged clips. I'd scabbarded my chainsword to make scrambling up the side of the Aquila a little easier, and drew it stealthily now, careful to make sure it didn't betray our whereabouts by clinking against any of the metal surrounding us. After some internal debate I started the teeth spinning, on the lowest setting, partly so the characteristic keening wouldn't be too loud, and partly to conserve the power, as I

---

1. *As so often with tyranid organisms, it's almost impossible to draw any general conclusions about such matters, as the characteristics of individual members of a subspecies can vary greatly from brood to brood. But since gaunts are primarily hunting predators, he was probably right to be cautious.*

had no means of recharging it, nor time enough to do so[1].

Despite my obvious fears, it was the wind rather than any noise we made which was to be our undoing. It continued to freshen as the temperature plummeted to levels which made me glad I hadn't discarded my greatcoat during the heat of the day (which the constant flurrying of abrasive sand would have made most unwise in any case), and which left Jurgen looking a good deal more comfortable. Not that he'd be really happy unless there was a dusting of frost on the ground, but, as he'd remarked in the storage facility where so many of these hideous creatures were being kept dormant, being able to see his breath was always a considerable fillip to his spirits. Unfortunately for both of us, the direction of the breeze was slowly changing, so that after a quarter of an hour or so, during which time the twilight deepened so much it became almost impossible to distinguish the gaunts as anything other than an inchoate mass, it was unquestionably blowing past us in their direction.

Dimly, in the gathering gloom, I saw first one brutally elongated head rise, sniffing the air, then another, and another, each turning in our direction as they caught our scent. As the first few to detect us began bounding in our direction, with the fast, loping stride of their kind, others turned to follow, until the whole pack of the monstrous, misshapen creatures was swarming towards us.

'Wait till you have a good target,' I counselled, all too aware that every shot would have to count if we were to stand even the slightest chance of keeping that solid mass of chitin-armoured death from rolling over us.

'This one's good enough,' Jurgen said, squeezing the trigger of the melta and sending a roiling mass of superheated air into the heart of the swarm. It punched a hole clean through the onrushing mass, felling several of the brutes, and crippling others, which fell,

---

1. *Chainswords vary as much as any other device common throughout the Imperium: the model Cain favoured was a military design, built for ruggedness rather than aesthetics, with a powercell capable of being recharged in the field in the same manner as those of a lasgun. In an emergency it could be replaced by a fresh unit, but doing so would be both time consuming and require specialised tools; hardly an option under the circumstances.*

disrupting the charge. Jurgen followed up with another three shots in rapid succession, but for every one which fell another handful leapt over the resulting carnage, powering up the dunes towards our fragile refuge. The main advantage the melta had given us was flash-burning a handful of 'nids just outside the cone of destruction it wrought, setting fire to their spasming corpses instead of simply vaporising them. Now the scene was dimly lit by the flickering flames of their immolation, which allowed us the dubious privilege of being able to see what was about to kill us.

I cracked off a few laspistol shots, which must have hit something in so tightly-packed a swarm, but the gaunts continued galloping towards us, utterly heedless of whatever damage I may have been able to inflict. Catching a flash of movement out of the corner of my eye, I turned, to find that a second group had flanked us, and was now bounding up the slope in a haze of scattered sand, barely slowed by the treacherous footing. Thrusting the pistol back in its holster, I picked up the frag grenades from Jurgen's pitifully small pile of ordnance, and lobbed one into the middle of the pack. It detonated loudly, its payload of shrapnel scything through the chittering host and felling a gratifying number, but still the rest came on, and I was forced to follow up with the other two before the charge was broken. Meanwhile, Jurgen continued to squeeze the trigger of the melta almost without respite, the actinic flash of the successive discharges even more blinding than usual in the deepening darkness, adding lightning to the thundercrack of the grenades' detonation.

With nothing else to do, I drew my laspistol again, and flourished the chainsword, using it to drive back one of our would-be flankers, which had persisted in trying to scale the dune despite the reduction of so many of its companions into their component parts. It met blade with scything claw, just as I'd expected, and I was forced to dispatch it in a flurry of blows.

'That's it,' Jurgen said, dropping the melta and seizing his lasgun.'I'm dry.' No point in even considering reloading, by the time he'd grabbed a fresh powercell from the storage pouch the survivors would have rolled right over us. Even before he'd finished speaking, the crackle of his lasgun was echoing round the dunes, firing short, precise bursts designed to save as much ammunition as possible. What would happen when that ran out, I didn't dare think.

Engaged as I was in fighting for my life, I had little opportunity or inclination to pause and admire the havoc he'd wrought among the first wave of the swarm, but he'd undoubtedly bought us a handful of precious moments and I felt a few words of appreciation wouldn't come amiss, particularly as I was unlikely to be able to defer them until later.

'Good shooting, Jurgen,' I said, lacking the time for anything more effusive; besides which, we'd fought together for over seventy years by that point, and I wouldn't want his last emotion to be embarrassment.

'You're welcome, sir,' he replied, as phlegmatic as ever, continuing to fell tyranids as he spoke. Then the lasgun went silent, and he ejected the powerpack in one fluid movement, his hand already swooping towards the pouch in which he'd cached the reloads.

He was never going to make it, that much was clear, the leading gaunt was already leaping into the attack, and my chainsword was stuck in the belly of the one I'd just dispatched. I desperately yanked the weapon clear of its toppling corpse, and turned, expecting to see the top of the downed Aquila liberally decorated with my aide's intestines, and his assassin already turning its attention to me, but instead a blizzard of lasgun fire echoed across the dune field, and the leading gaunt was falling, almost cut in half by the hail of las-bolts. Huge, multi-limbed creatures were cresting the surrounding dunes, and, for a second, I quailed, wondering what new horrors were about to be unleashed on us, then realisation dawned. They were horses, protected like their riders from the hellish environment by respirators, and thick barding in lieu of the greatcoats worn by their masters.

'It's the Death Korps!' I called, exultantly, as the column of riders wheeled and began to advance down the side of the dunes towards the milling mass of the surviving gaunts; quite a hazardous undertaking, it looked to me, but the horses seemed to know what they were doing, keeping their footing well enough on the treacherous sliding surface, and leaving their riders free to get on with the important business of potting 'nids.

'So it is,' Jurgen agreed, as though I'd pointed out a casual acquaintance in a crowded mess room. Not all our rescuers were armed with lasguns[1], a fact which became clear when launched grenades and gouts of blazing promethium from a flamer began to fall among the milling hormagaunts, along with the withering barrage of las-fire which continued unabated.

After that, the battle became a massacre, the Death Korps mopping up the last few 'nids in pretty short order, displaying the fine disregard for their own survival which so characterised the Guardsmen from that regiment as they did so. Indeed, they got so close that more than one of the gaunts finally expired under the hooves of their mounts, after first being brought down by close-range weapons fire, and, in at least one case, an explosive-tipped lance through the chest[2]. Feeling it politic to show willing, now that someone else was getting chewed up on our behalf, I took a few laspistol shots at likely targets, although, truth to tell, I doubt that they added much to the general sum of hurt being dished out to the scuttling horrors. Jurgen had much better luck with the melta, as soon as he'd changed the power pack.

At length, the field was ours, the only 'nids in view were dead or dying, and the sergeant in charge of the detachment spurred his horse up the side of the dune to stand next to the crashed Aquila. Bloodshot eyes regarded me through the round lenses of his full-face breathing mask, the pachyderm snout of the air tube snaking up over his shoulder to the filter pack on his back, his head almost on a level with my own, since I was still perched on top of the crumpled fuselage.

'Commissar Cain?' he asked, in the flat voice of someone knowing

---

1. *Cain may be misremembering here, as most cavalry in the Imperial Guard carry laspistols as sidearms, but it's also quite possible, given the harshness of conditions on the surface of Fecundia, and the difficulties of operating vehicles there which he's already alluded to, that this squadron were acting as dragoons rather than cavalry per se, and were accordingly equipped like an infantry squad.*

2. *A common piece of equipment among these mounted units, so, even if acting as mounted infantry on this occasion, this was almost certainly their usual role.*

it was a bloody stupid question, but determined to go through the formalities in any case.

'That's me,' I agreed, unable to think of anything else to say that didn't sound equally inane. I tilted my head in Jurgen's direction. 'And that's my aide, Gunner Jurgen[1]. We had a pilot, too, but the 'nids ate him. Never caught his name.'

'Ridemaster Tyrie.' The death rider sergeant nodded a perfunctory greeting, clearly a man of few words. 'Lost our vox-man a couple of days back, or we'd have told you we were coming.'

'I'm just glad you got here when you did,' I told him, truthfully enough.

The eyes behind the lenses regarded me for a moment, and blinked, as if registering my dilapidated condition for the first time. 'Least you had the sense to stay put and wait,' he said.

---

1. *Prior to his secondment to Cain, Jurgen had served in an artillery regiment.*

NINETEEN

WE SET OFF at first light, since there seemed no point in adding to the danger of the journey by trying to dodge tyranids in the dark. There were no synapse creatures among the vanguard swarm so far as we could tell[1], which meant that the rest of the broods roaming the desert would be unaware of the fate of their compatriots. It was still possible that some might stumble across the pheromone trail left by the deceased lictor, but Tyrie's men had set sentries, so we would have some warning of their approach and sufficient firepower to prevail against all but the largest of swarms. I can't claim that I slept easily that night, but I certainly managed a good deal better than I'd expected, despite sharing a habitent with Jurgen, whose snores dislodged constant minor sandfalls from the surrounding dunes[2]. The filtered air within went a long way towards restoring my spirits too. Even adulterated as it was by the presence of my aide, it was a big improvement over the muck I'd been forced to breathe outside, and

---

1. *Usually the case; so as safe an assumption as possible where creatures as notoriously unpredictable as the tyranids are concerned.*

2. *Probably exaggeration for effect, although, having had my own slumbers disturbed by him through several intervening walls, I wouldn't swear to it.*

the dull ache in my chest receded for the first time since our overly heavy landing.

Accordingly, having breakfasted on a couple of ration bars and enough tepid water to slake my thirst, I re-tied the much-abused sash around my face with some reluctance, and crawled outside to face the tainted air.

'Better take this,' Tyrie greeted me, holding out one of the breather masks he and his men were equipped with. I took it at once, despite the knowledge that it had come from one of the casualties of the skirmish the night before[1], slipped the straps over my head, and inhaled gratefully. The filtered air was overlaid with the smell of rubber and stale sweat, but that was a small price to pay for being able to breathe without pain, and I restored what was left of my sash to its customary position around my waist.

'Thank you,' I said, my voice sounding muffled in my ears, and did my best to shrug the filter unit into place across my shoulders. After watching me squirming ineffectually for a moment, Tyrie stepped in and adjusted it, without a word. 'Much obliged.'

The ridemaster shrugged. 'Orders are to get you there in one piece,' he told me, already turning aside.

'And where's "there", exactly?' I asked, falling into step beside him, and cocking my head at an odd angle to keep him centred in the breather's limited field of view. For someone as paranoid as I am, being deprived of my peripheral vision was distinctly unnerving.

'Where you were going in the first place,' Tyrie told me, as though it should have been obvious. 'Mechanicus shrine.'

Which was mixed news indeed. Now that the first assault on our fleet in orbit had been beaten off[2], a swift return to the flagship, getting as far away as possible from the tyranids still polluting the planet's surface, was looking distinctly attractive. On the other hand,

---

1. *Typically, Cain is vague both about the number of men in the unit to begin with, and how many were left; since they'd lost at least one casualty before their arrival (the vox-man Tyrie mentioned), but appear from the rest of his account to still be close to full strength, we can infer no more than two losses, perhaps three at a stretch.*

2. *It's unclear here whether Tyrie had already told him this, or he's writing with hindsight.*

Sholer and Kildhar were expecting me, and there was still the little matter of their menagerie to deal with. Probably my best option would be to find out what they were up to as quickly as possible, while Jurgen went looking for whatever orbit-capable vessels might be sitting around on the pad, and requisitioned one. I could plausibly claim an urgent need to report back to the Lord General, and the state of my uniform would speak for itself. I'd seen more savoury-looking Nurgle cultists than the apparition which stared back at me from every reflective surface.

'How soon can we get there?' I asked, practically salivating at the prospect of the hot meal and mug of recaff waiting for me at our destination. Even soylens viridiens seemed palatable right about now.

Tyrie shrugged, and reached up to pat the neck of a horse, which was gazing into the middle distance with an air of patient boredom, which at least reassured me there weren't any more 'nids in the immediate vicinity. 'That depends,' he said, glancing at me sideways through the lenses of his breather. 'How fast can you ride?'

BY AND LARGE, my attitude to riding animals can best be described as distantly cordial. I've never had an active antipathy to the brutes, but I've always inclined to the view that if the Emperor intended us to get around in such a manner He'd never have given us the AFV[1]. The number of occasions on which I've been forced to rely on so archaic a form of transport have been few and far between, and it took me some time to get used to the curious rocking sensation of the horse beneath me, uncannily reminiscent of a small boat in a gentle swell. After the first hour or so I was beginning to feel some considerable discomfort in the posterior, but I was damned if I was going to admit the fact. I had no doubt my tight grip on the reins, and continual swaying as I tried to retain my balance, was affording the experienced horsemen around me enough amusement as it was. Fortunately the

---

1. *A typical example of the Imperial Guard mania for three letter abbreviations (or TLAs, as Cain insisted on calling them), in this instance referring to Armoured Fighting Vehicles such as the ubiquitous Chimera and its bewildering array of variants, whose primary purpose is to transport troops in relative security on the battlefield while carrying sufficient heavy weaponry to provide effective fire support for them when they disembark.*

full-face masks they wore were enough to conceal their expressions, so we could all pretend to be dignified, but the contrast with their own relaxed postures was telling.

To add to my discomfiture, Jurgen seemed hardly less at ease in the saddle than they were, guiding his own mount with faint nudges of the knees as easily as if he rode a horse every day. He moved up to flank me, taking me by surprise, since the breathers we were wearing not only restricted my field of vision, but robbed me of my usual olfactory warning of his approach. 'Making good time,' he said.

'I suppose so,' I responded. The truth was, the monotonous landscape was so dulling my senses that I had no idea how far we'd come, or how far we had still to go. We'd left the crash site shortly after sun-up, following a set of coordinates in Tyrie's map slate which I hoped would soon bring the blocky mass of Regio Quinquaginta Unus into sight, but so far all I'd seen was the endless undulating sand, and the looming rockcrete ramparts of the distant hive. The pall of dust above the impact site where the bioship had met its end had dissipated overnight in the endless desert wind, but I could see nothing of its fate from this distance, and wasn't about to suggest diverting to take a closer look; Throne alone knew what horrors awaited us there. Besides, the sooner we got to the Mechanicus shrine, the sooner I'd be able to find out what was going on. I'd already been out of contact for nearly twenty-four hours[1], and a day's a long time in a war zone. Practically anything could have happened, none of it good, and I tried not to dwell on the worst-case scenarios.

'These are a lot easier to ride than those sloth things,' Jurgen remarked, and I nodded; hanging on to the saddles strapped to their stomachs for dear life while our panicked mounts clambered, dangling, from the boughs of one kilometre-high tree to another, was not one of my happier memories[2].

'Definitely,' I agreed, not really in the mood for conversation, but

---

1. *A little less than a full Fecundian day, which lasted for twenty-six hours standard.*

2. *Possibly a reference to the Mantican Heresy, or the eldar invasion of Mythago, both campaigns in which Cain found himself on predominantly arboreal worlds.*

happy to seize on any distraction from the physical discomfort of my throbbing fundament. Before we could lose ourselves in happy reminiscences of bowel-clenching terror long past, however, Tyrie held up his pennant-tipped lance to halt the column.

'Something's out there,' he said, raising a hand to shade his eyes; a possibly futile gesture, as the lenses of his breather had polarised, like mine and everyone else's, converting them into small, round mirrors, in which I could see myself and the rest of our column reflected.

'Amplivisor, sir?' Jurgen offered, leaning at what seemed to me a reckless angle to proffer them. Trying not to look like a complete bluefoot[1], and praying to the Throne that I didn't topple off the nag's back in the process, I took them, a little unsteadily, and raised them to my eyes, only to find that the breather's lenses kept them too distant to focus.

Tyrie glanced back at me, in manifest disbelief, probably grateful that I couldn't see his expression. 'Magnification's built in,' he said.

'Right,' I said, stuffing the amplivisor in a convenient pocket. After a few moments fumbling, I worked out how to manipulate the lenses of the breather, and the dune field in the middle distance suddenly expanded to fill my vision.

'Better adjust it back when you're done,' Tyrie counselled, 'or you'll be falling over your own feet when you dismount.'

'What is it?' I asked, trying to make sense of what we were looking at. Something was definitely there, half-buried in the drifting sand, and what I could see of it was ridged and rounded, like plates of tyranid chitin. Not a creature, though, it was too still for that. 'A dead spore?'

'Looks like,' Tyrie agreed. 'It's close to our route, so we can check it out as we pass.'

'I'm more worried about what it delivered,' I told him. 'We've already seen a lictor, and 'stealers, as well as the gaunts.'

---

1. *A Valhallan colloquialism, meaning someone too naive and inexperienced to avoid frostbite; another of the many he acquired during his time with regiments from that world.*

'Whatever it is, we'll kill it,' Tyrie said. 'Unless we already did.' He gestured with his lance again. 'Move out.'

TYRIE'S CONFIDENCE NOTWITHSTANDING, I kept a sharp lookout as our mounts plodded onwards, paying particular attention to the downed mycetic spore in the distance every time we crested another dune and it came back into view. I had no doubt that its baleful cargo would have long since scattered in search of prey, perhaps even becoming part of the swarm which had attacked us the previous night, but that didn't stop me from dialling the lenses to their greatest magnification and sweeping the area around it in search of movement. Something about that dark and silent bulk struck me as ominous, although I couldn't have put my finger on what. Perhaps it was simply that the desolate emptiness all around us was making me feel uncomfortably exposed, which concentrated my attention on the only visible evidence of an enemy presence.

'Any sign of movement?' I asked, and Tyrie glanced at his portable auspex, before shaking his head.

'Not a thing,' he told me. Which might be good news, or it might not; tyranids weren't that easy to detect at the best of times, and I doubted that Kildhar's adjustments would have filtered their way down to individual pieces of field kit. So far as I knew, the handful of tech-priests capable of understanding and duplicating them were still working flat out on the sensoria suites of the warships in orbit[1]. If another lictor was lying in ambush beneath the sand, we'd have no more than a second or two's warning before it struck.

'Good,' I said, grateful for the ease with which the breather hid my disquiet. By now we were close enough to make the thing out without the aid of the magnifiers, although that didn't stop me from taking full advantage of the vision enhancement in any case. The spore was half-buried, inevitably, given the constant drift of the wind-driven sand, but that didn't make it any the less repugnant. If anything, it

---

1. *By this time the job was more or less completed, and a few were turning their attention from the Navy to the Imperial Guard, but the auspex arrays of command posts and air defence units were being accorded the highest priority.*

simply reinforced the impression of some malignant cancer erupting from the body of the planet.

'It's definitely split,' Jurgen said, studying the thing as carefully as I was. 'But not all the way.'

'Perhaps it was damaged on the way down,' I said, noting the telltale signs of cauterisation on the fleshier parts, and calcification of its outer armour. For whatever reason it had tumbled on the way down[1], being more or less evenly toasted, instead of bearing the brunt of the atmospheric friction on the ablative sheets of chitin intended to protect its soft tissue and whatever ghastly creatures it contained.

'We'd best check it out,' Tyrie said, changing direction slightly to take us directly towards it. I could have overruled him, of course, citing the urgency of my errand, but, despite my misgivings, I was reluctant to. I had a reputation to maintain, however little I actually deserved it, and had no doubt that my ineptitude astride the horse had already afforded the death riders a fair amount of amusement at my expense. It wouldn't hurt to remind them that I was supposed to be a Hero of the Imperium, despite my subjectively scorching saddle, and any apparent reluctance to put myself in harm's way would hardly help with that. Besides, the thing was bound to be dead by now.

'Better had,' I agreed, the ridemaster's laconic conversational style proving surprisingly contagious[2], surreptitiously taking advantage of my widely-perceived ineptitude in the saddle to fall a little behind the others. Dormant or not, there was no point in being the first to get near the spore when I had a troop of riders to hide behind.

As we got within a score or so metres of it, I began to appreciate the scale of the thing for the first time, all the previous examples I'd seen having been from a far safer distance. (Which was hardly surprising, as they'd been vomiting out swarms of malevolent creatures hell-bent on killing me, for the most part, and getting this close would have entailed hacking my way through them instead of following my natural

---

1. *Probably ejected by the crashing bioship too late to correct its attitude before entering the atmosphere, or even inside it.*

2. *Or Cain was more exhausted than he realised, which wouldn't be surprising under the circumstances.*

inclination to move rapidly in the general direction of away.) Even on horseback, it still towered at least twice my height, an obscene outcrop of necrotising flesh, only the breather protecting me from the charnel stench of its decomposition.

'Looks deserted,' Jurgen said, unslinging the melta from his back anyway, a precaution I heartily approved of. I found myself straining my ears over the muffled plodding of my mount's hooves in the sand, alert for any signs of ambush, but the horde of gaunts I expected to erupt from it failed to materialise. Perhaps Tyrie was right, and they were long gone, or they'd failed to survive the fiery descent from the upper atmosphere.

Spurred by that thought, I adjusted the breather's inbuilt optics to maximum magnification, and examined as much as I could see of the organism's interior through the slits in its carapace intended to let the occupants disembark. Fortunately the sun was perfectly angled to allow a shaft of light within, so I was spared the frustration of attempting to come to grips with whatever image enhancers might also have been installed in the mask's eyepieces. Sure enough, I could make out the slumped forms of several gaunts, the congealed remains of bodily fluids seeping from joints in their carapaces, baked and swollen tongues lolling from their distended jaws.

'There are gaunts inside,' I called[1], feeling it was time to make a show of actively participating in this fool's errand. Another few minutes, and we could resume our progress towards a shower and a mug of recaff with a gratifying sense of duty done. 'Definitely dead.'

'Best sort,' Jurgen added, sentiments with which I was in complete agreement.

I began fumbling with the optic control, trying to restore normal vision, but the wretched thing seemed to be stuck, probably due to a

---

1. *Which implies that none of the Death Korps had personal vox-beads. Though widely used, they're far from ubiquitous among the Imperial Guard; the constant logistical challenge of keeping supplies flowing to the many areas of conflict around the Imperium often mean that there simply aren't enough available to equip every line trooper, or even the commanders of every unit, while some regiments deliberately restrict their use to officers as part of their doctrine. In either event, riders would be a low priority for such items, as most of the time their long-range scouting role would keep them out of range of the other units in their regiment in any case.*

few grains of sand embedded in something vital. I banged it with the heel of my hand, in the fashion I'd seen tech-priests use with recalcitrant devices, and muttered a few half-remembered phrases from the Litany of Percussive Maintenance which they generally employed on such occasions. The Omnissiah obviously felt I deserved a few marks for effort, because my vision abruptly snapped back to the way it should be. A moment before it did, though, the shaking, magnified image had swept across the surface of the spore, and I was certain I'd seen a quiver of movement somewhere among the half-melted cluster spines protruding from its back.

'Incoming!' I shouted, heedless of the possibility of making a fool of myself. If the thing hadn't quite expired yet, and registered our presence, it would respond instinctively, and even damaged as they were, the spines would be enough to shred us. As I spoke I turned the horse's head, and kicked it in the ribs, not far from where the thick tubes pumping nutrients and whatever else enabled it to survive out here into its bloodstream entered the skin. It broke into a trot, which nearly unseated me, Jurgen's mount cantering a few paces to catch up before he slowed it enough to ride abreast.

With a crackle like a brushfire incinerating a bush, the spines arced through the air, bursting among the riders and fragmenting into a thousand razor-edged fragments which lacerated man and mount alike. A couple of horses fell, shrieking behind their breathing masks, until the chemical regulators shot them full of analgesics, and they stopped caring about the speckling of open wounds through which their lifeblood was leaking out into the thirsty sand. Most of the men were scarcely better off, but, true to the traditions of the Death Korps, paid no attention to their injuries, going to ground instead, their weapons levelled. In any other terrain, and if the spore hadn't been in such a bad way itself, able to launch no more than a tithe of its bristling armament, they'd probably have been wiped out to a man[1] on the instant. As it was, the drifted sand absorbed the larger part of the chitinous flechettes.

'Thanks for the heads-up,' Tyrie said, without any noticeable sarcasm

---

1. And horse.

that I could detect, his voice carrying easily in the quiet desert air. Belated as my warning had been, it had probably saved a few lives, as the riders had responded instantly to it by beginning to dismount. Had they not done so, they would have been above the majority of the sand ridges, unprotected from the cluster spine barrage. Hanging back had saved Jurgen and I from the worst of it, too, the pair of us, ironically, being the only two still mounted.

'Mind your eyes, sir,' Jurgen said, turning in the saddle to heave the bulk of his melta around. A second or so later the familiar eye-stabbing flash, muted by the polarised lenses of the breather, sparked, reducing the remaining spines to a charred ruin. My horse flinched, and I braced myself, expecting it to shy or rear in panic, but it calmed itself at once, by virtue of its training and the cocktail of chemicals sluicing through its system. 'Don't want it having another go.'

'Indeed we don't,' I agreed, turning myself to take a look back at the scene of confusion around the spore. The distinctive sound of las-fire was crackling in the air by now, although for the life of me I couldn't see what there was left for the Death Korps troopers to shoot at: the gaunts inside were all dead anyway, and lasguns would be completely ineffective against the vast slabs of chitin protecting them.

Almost at once I had my answer, as the sand beneath my mount's hooves churned, like wavelets in a choppy sea, making it stumble. This time it did rear, or tried to, throwing me from its back. I landed heavily and rolled clear, fearful of being trampled, but its front feet were being held by something sinuous and sinister, thrashing back and forth as the whinnying horse bucked frantically, trying to pull itself free. Then another tentacle burst from the sand, wrapping almost instantly around the desperate equine, the barbs along its length tearing jagged wounds in the horse's flanks as it constricted. With a loud *crack*, the charger's spine snapped, and its ribcage imploded. Still flailing in its death throes, my mount was dragged beneath the sand.

'It's trying to feed!' I shouted, glancing frantically around for any more telltale movement in the grains beneath my feet. Whether it was attempting to garner enough biomass to grow more cluster spines, or simply lashing out with its tentacles because it had detected our presence[1] I had no idea, nor, at that moment, did I care.

'Hang on, sir, I'm coming!' Jurgen called back, trying to regain control of his understandably skittish mount. My skin crawling, anticipating the strike of another subterranean tentacle at any moment, I drew my chainsword, thumbing the speed control up to maximum. The full-throated roar of a flamer, and the *crump* of exploding grenades behind me provided a little welcome reassurance that the Death Korps were still in the fight, but given their fondness for glorious last stands I couldn't count on their aid any time soon. 'Behind you!' my aide added, and I whipped round, to find one of the serpentine forms already lashing out at me.

Cursing the restricted field of vision left by the breather, I brought my blade up to meet it, slicing through the sinuous limb in a single fluid movement. All that seemed to do was confirm the presence of more prey within reach, however, as another three or four metres of it immediately extruded from the sand, spraying ichor from its tip like promethium from a flamer as it came. Foul, sticky fluid slathered my much-abused greatcoat, and caught me full in the face. Blessing the Emperor for the protection of the breather, I wiped the goggles as best I could with the fingers of my empty hand, restoring a measure of blurry vision and imparting an ineradicable stain to my glove just in time to see another couple of tentacles attempting to coil around me from opposite directions while the original struck from above. I lopped through the left-hand one, opening up enough space to evade the other two in a renewed welter of repulsive fluid, and turned to cut them all into a selection of chunks longer than my leg with a flurry of multiple blows.

'Stay back!' I called to Jurgen, who had his horse back under control now, and seemed on the point of charging down the slope they were perched on in an almost certainly doomed attempt to pluck me to safety. Not that I had any objection to being rescued, you understand, quite the reverse, but the fact that they hadn't yet suffered the fate of my own mount could only mean they were beyond the reach of the

---

1. *Probably both.*

spore's tentacles. If my aide attempted to move any closer, though, he and the horse would become fuel for its bioweapon, and I'd lose the best chance I had of getting out of this alive. 'Use the melta on any movement you see!'

'Right you are, sir,' Jurgen responded, with his usual brisk cheerfulness, and set to with a will, creating patches of steaming glass wherever the melta beam hit. Rather too many of them were close at hand for my liking, but after the first few shots I was pretty confident I could gauge the maximum reach of the ghastly thing, and was heartened to discover I was no more than a short sprint from safety.

To think was to act, and I ran for the sandbank atop which Jurgen was perched as though Abaddon himself was after me, laying about with the chainsword at every foul appendage which dared to break the surface too close at hand for my aide to risk a shot. Within seconds, although it seemed far longer at the time, I was trying to scramble up the slope without letting go of the weapon, while Jurgen called encouragement from the crest. 'Keep it up, sir!' he urged. 'You're almost there!' His words were punctuated by the flash and sizzle of the melta.

At which point something snagged my ankle and tugged hard, only the robust construction of my Guard-issue boot protecting the flesh beneath from serious injury. It seemed the spore had learned to keep its tentacles hidden beneath the surface[1], and was making a last-ditch attempt to take its revenge. I slashed down with the chainsword, but only managed to raise a fountain of sand, the snaring tentacle armoured from retaliation by the depth of the dune. Another tug, and my leg disappeared to the knee, with a wrench which almost dislocated it.

'Hold on, sir!' Jurgen called again, leaping from his saddle and slithering down the dune in a spray of fine powder. Without thought or hesitation he grabbed my free hand, and leaned back, pulling with all his might. 'I've got you!'

'So's the bloody spore!' I snarled, as, between them, both leg and arm felt ready to detach from their sockets. Brute force was never going

---

1. *Extremely unlikely, as no specimen has ever been recovered which showed the slightest sign of even the most rudimentary cognitive ability. More likely, Cain and Jurgen had simply incapacitated every appendage on or near the surface by this time.*

to overcome the hideous thing, although my aide's painful and well-intentioned intervention might have bought me a few more seconds, the pair of us were never going to break its grip on my foot. If I was to avoid the fate of my ill-starred steed, there was only one option left open to me. I took a deep breath, and angled the chainsword for what I hoped was going to be a swift, clean cut. 'Have you still got the medipack?'

'Of course.' Jurgen nodded, not really understanding the question.

'Good.' I took a deep breath, wondering if I could really go through with this, then decided I most definitely could, given the alternative. I already had a couple of augmetic fingers, after all; a new leg shouldn't be that hard to get used to. 'I'd be obliged if you could get it out ready.'

'Of course, sir,' he responded, the coin dropping, and letting go of my arm to start rummaging in his collection of pouches. 'Would you like a local analgesic?'

Very much, as it happened, but I shook my head. 'No time,' I told him, and raised the spinning blade.

TWENTY

BEFORE I COULD bring the blade down, though, the ground shook beneath me, staying my hand. I'd like to say I hesitated because I had no wish to botch the cut, making the chirurgeon's job any more difficult than it needed to be, but in truth it was simply because I was taken completely by surprise. A fast-moving shadow suddenly swept across us, trailed by the banshee keening of powerful turbines, and I glanced up to see the silhouette of a Space Marine Land Speeder stark against the sky. Before I could make out any more than the distinctive yellow and white livery favoured by the Reclaimers, however, the wind of its passage struck, shrouding Jurgen, his horse and I in a small but very determined sandstorm.

By the time our vision cleared, its pilot had banked round, impossibly fast and tight, in a turn which would have rendered a normal man unconscious or worse, and was howling in again on a second attack run. This time I saw a flurry of warheads streak from the missile pod bolted to its side[1], to impact squarely on the looming bulk of the spore, the armour of which was already shattered from

---

1. *Presumably a fragmentation warhead, spreading in flight, as normally a Land Speeder would only fire one missile at a time.*

the explosion I'd felt reverberating through the ground. At the same time, the gunner kept up a steady stream of fire from his heavy bolter, chewing up the exposed flesh within, an astonishing display of accuracy given the speed at which they were moving.

Suddenly, the obscene pile of engineered flesh collapsed in on itself like a fire-gutted building, and, at the same time, I felt the vice-like grip around my ankle slacken its hold. Dropping the chainsword, I took hold of my calf in both hands, and pulled, as hard as I could. To my relief, my foot came free, with an abruptness which dumped me suddenly on the burning hot sand[1].

'That was lucky,' Jurgen remarked, in his usual phlegmatic manner, extending a hand to help me to my feet as he spoke.

'It was,' I agreed, for want of anything else to say, and bent to retrieve my fallen weapon. There seemed little doubt that the spore was finally dead after a mauling like that, but I'd had enough unpleasant surprises for one day, and had no intention of taking any more chances. My aide clearly felt the same, because he kept his melta cradled ready for use, and his lasgun slung where he could take hold of that instead if he needed it in a hurry. Then the obvious question occurred to me. 'But what are they doing here?'

'Looking for us?' Jurgen suggested, unable, as ever, to recognise a rhetorical question when he heard one, and endeavouring to answer it to the best of his ability.

'That hardly seems likely,' I said, fiddling with the comm-bead in my ear, and scanning rapidly through the frequencies in an attempt to find out. The Adeptus Astartes were the finest warriors the Imperium possessed, and, irrespective of any residual goodwill I might have retained from our previous association, were hardly likely to be frittering their time away supporting a search and rescue operation which the Guard already had well in hand. Which, in turn, reminded me... 'We'd better go and find out if there are any of the Death Korps left.'

Which there were, Tyrie greeting us with a somewhat weary wave

---

1. *Possibly a subjective impression of its temperature, given his earlier remarks about the effects of spending so long in the saddle.*

as we hobbled over the crest of the dune concealing them from view; between the ravages of the tentacle and the saddle I could barely walk at all. The ridemaster and his squad seemed as chipper as possible under the circumstances, going about the business of tending to their wounds and recapturing their mounts with brisk efficiency, although I counted fewer heads than I remembered, and even fewer of the horses, but then his regiment wasn't exactly renowned for excessive displays of emotion. 'Thought we'd lost you,' he said.

'So did I,' I replied, determined to seem equally stoic. 'And you would have done, if it hadn't been for them.' I gestured up at the Land Speeder, which was still circling dementedly above us like a raptor on stimms, albeit at a far more sedate pace than hitherto. Then I broke off, as I finally heard a voice in the comm-bead, as deep and resonant as only a Space Marine could be.

'Two more survivors joining the others now. One of them looks like a commissar.'

'Could it be Cain?' a new voice cut in, taking me completely by surprise. It was unusual enough to hear a normal human on an Adeptus Astartes commnet at all, let alone a woman.

'It could,' I said, joining the conversation. 'I'm sorry to be a little late for our meeting, magos, but I was unexpectedly detained.' In truth, the voice might have belonged to anyone, but I knew the Reclaimers only had male Chapter serfs[1], and there couldn't be many among their Mechanicus hosts the Space Marines had taken that far into their confidence. Given how closely Sholer and Kildhar had been collaborating on their research, it hadn't been all that hard to guess precisely who I'd been listening to.

'Commissar,' Kildhar replied, failing dismally to prevent her astonishment from colouring her voice, however hard she was trying to keep it free of any emotional overtones. 'I must confess we'd feared the worst. The Lord General will be gratified. He remained confident of your survival, even though I assured him the odds were considerably weighted against it.'

---

1. *Drawn, like those of many others, from aspirants to initiation who failed the rigorous selection criteria, but were nevertheless judged worthy to serve in a support capacity.*

'Probably because he knows more about me than the odds do,' I said. Then, conscious that I had a reputation for understated modesty to maintain, I belatedly added, 'but it was a narrow enough squeak, I have to say.' I looked around at the handful of death riders, and the inadequate supply of mounts they now seemed to have brought under control. 'I'm afraid it looks as though I still won't be joining you for quite a while yet.' If anything, it seemed, the rest of our journey was going to be even more arduous than it had been up to this point.

'Don't worry,' Kildhar assured me. 'We'll pick you up on our way back.'

'Way back from where?' I asked, feeling the familiar premonitory tingling in the palms of my hands. I could think of only one place in this hideous wilderness liable to tempt the magos biologis out of the comfortable fastness of Regio Quinquaginta Unus, and that would certainly require an escort of Space Marines to venture near, but surely even Kildhar couldn't be as imbecilic as all that.

'The bioship crash site, of course,' she said, at once confirming that she could. 'We recovered some excellent specimens. Apothecary Sholer and I are eager to examine them as soon as we return.'

'Good luck with that,' I said, beginning to think sharing the back end of a horse with Jurgen for the next day or two might not be so bad after all.

'I'm sure the Omnissiah will guide our understanding,' she replied, as immune to sarcasm as most of her kind. Finding nothing else to say, I trotted out a few of the rote-learned platitudes that had come in handy so often in my line of work, and prepared to break contact. 'Stay where you are,' she added, just before I did so. 'The Land Speeder can see you clearly, and will guide us in.' Easy for her to say, of course, she'd probably appreciate the view of the now definitely deceased spore, but I must confess I found the idea of remaining so close to something which had almost killed me to be rather less appealing.

On the other hand, having a pair of heavily armed Adeptus Astartes keeping an eye on me from an altitude sufficient to spot an approaching threat from at least ten kilometres away was distinctly appealing, so, 'I'll be waiting,' I assured her, only realising that I should have asked for an ETA a second or two after I'd broken contact.

IN THE EVENT, I had less time to wait than I'd expected. Barely an hour had gone by, during which Jurgen and I endured the foul air as briefly as possible to fortify ourselves with another ration bar and a swallow or two of water apiece, before I once again felt a faint tremor in the sand, and saw a few loose grains begin to slip down the steepest slopes. After my encounters with the tentacles, and the buried lictor, this hardly seemed encouraging, and my hands fell automatically to the weapons at my belt. Jurgen, too, seemed a little nervous, and reached for his lasgun, eschewing the greater firepower of the melta for now. I didn't draw my pistol or chainsword this time, however; the Land Speeder would surely have spotted any obvious threat, and the hive fleet didn't seem to have dispatched any burrowing organisms in the first wave[1] which they might have missed.

Gradually, the vibration increased, the sandfalls growing both in number and intensity, while the horses shifted and pawed the ground uneasily. Tyrie and his death riders seemed unconcerned, their resolve being both bone deep and pharmacologically enhanced, but I noticed they kept their weapons to hand all the same. After a few moments I began to hear a new sound, the growl of a powerful engine and the creak and rattle of vehicle tracks, and my spirits rose. Despite the problems the Guard had found getting Chimeras to work in this unforgiving terrain, the Fecundians had doubtless found ways to resolve them, the locally built vehicles being a lot more reliable. So thinking, I envisaged something like an APC or a Trojan cargo hauler, perhaps with broader treads for better traction on the shifting sand, but essentially something akin to the transports I was familiar with.

The sound, however, continued to build, the horses becoming ever more spooked, and, I must confess, I could hardly blame them. I

---

1. *Hardly surprising, as these are generally held in reserve until the later stages of a tyranid invasion, when the hive mind has pinpointed fixed defences which need to be circumvented.*

could feel the vibration in my bones now, and the noise of the engine was getting so loud that I had to raise my voice to converse with Jurgen. If it increased much more, I'd have to rely on the comm-bead instead.

'That must be it,' he said, pointing towards a dark mass which had appeared above the dunes, growing steadily larger as it approached us almost head on.

I nodded. 'Seems roomy enough,' I said. Its upper hull had the familiar blocky silhouette I generally associated with Imperial vehicles, although something about its proportions seemed wrong, in a manner I couldn't quite put my finger on. Then it struck me. A vehicle large enough to be visible above the dune should be tilting by now, as it climbed the far slope, but it was still rumbling inexorably towards us, straight and level. 'Just how big is that thing?' I voxed.

'Big enough,' Kildhar assured me, a faint trace of amusement entering her voice in spite of her best efforts. 'We adapted one of the dust harvesters[1], to make sure we had enough room for an adequate cross section of samples.'

'You certainly seem to have that,' I agreed, as the scale of the gargantuan vehicle gradually became clearer. It wasn't anything like the size of a Titan, but it certainly seemed that way, looming over us like a hab block on multiple tracks which, as I'd surmised, were broad enough to spread its colossal weight enough to prevent it from sinking deep into the sand. I was reminded of the snowliner I'd travelled on, and taken refuge beneath, on Nusquam Fundumentibus, although this leviathan dwarfed even that, eclipsing the sun overhead as it rolled to a stop beside us. Somewhere far overhead a cargo hatch popped open, extruding a derrick, and a working party dressed from head to foot in environmental suits appeared from somewhere to begin hoisting whatever bits they could find of the spore which had almost killed us up to the open port.

'We made the best of what we had,' Kildhar agreed, her voice taking

---

1. *Mobile reclamation platforms, which sift the sand for trace minerals left by earlier generations of environmental pollution, or too scarce to have been worth the effort of mining conventionally in previous millennia.*

on a curious echoing quality, as the real thing caught up with the facsimile in my comm-bead after taking the scenic route through the intervening air. She was standing in a doorway above one of the tread units, about four metres from the ground, from which a boarding ramp was descending towards us.

'Can we drop you somewhere?' I asked Tyrie, feeling it was the least we could do after all the trouble we'd caused him, and the ridemaster shook his head.

'We'd rather ride,' he said, which didn't surprise me. He swung into the saddle and led his men over the crest of the dunes without another word. Just before disappearing, he turned and raised a hand in farewell, then the desert swallowed him, as though he'd never been. Only the tracks of the horses remained to attest to his presence, and they were already being smoothed by the wind. A few more minutes, and even those last tenuous traces would be gone.

'Odd fellow,' Kildhar said, strolling down the ramp to join us. 'But evidently blessed by the Machine God nonetheless.' After a moment's puzzlement, I realised her augmented vision must have revealed the network of chemical injectors and other subcutaneous alterations common to a member of the Death Korps.

'The Emperor certainly sent him our way in the nick of time,' Jurgen agreed. 'And those Adeptus Astartes.' He bestowed a baleful look on the thoroughly macerated spore, which by now was dangling from a heavy duty cargo sling, preparatory to being swung aboard. 'That thing would have killed the commissar if they hadn't bombed it.'

I didn't want to think too hard about that, so I smiled at Kildhar, not that much of an effort, given the circumstances of her arrival. 'I'm surprised you want it,' I said, flippantly. 'I'd expect you to be after a live one.'

'We've already got one of those,' she said, completely serious so far as I could tell, and, once again, I found myself questioning her sanity. 'But this specimen will be more convenient for chemical rendering.'

'If you say so,' I agreed, feeling it best to humour her, at least until I'd had a decent meal and a bath. My uniform was probably beyond salvage, but I could always get one sent down from my quarters aboard the flagship, and one for my aide while I was about it, although it would take more than a change of attire to improve Jurgen's appearance to any noticeable degree. 'I take it your examination of the crash site was fruitful?'

'Very,' Kildhar assured me, turning to lead the way aboard the huge crawler. The feel of hard metal underfoot, after slogging through shifting sand for so long, was an immense relief, although my thigh and calf muscles burned as we climbed the ramp, beginning to match the discomfort higher up. 'We obtained a great many tissue samples from the remains of the bioship, and a respectable number of motile specimens too.'

I had no need to ask what she meant by motile specimens, as that became obvious the moment we came aboard. Almost the entire lower deck of the growling leviathan had been converted into stout cages, high and wide enough to have confined a carnifex if anyone had been foolish enough to try, and a pack of hormagaunts flung themselves at the bars the moment we appeared. Remembering how easily they'd torn open the Aquila's cockpit to get at the pilot, I flinched and reached for my weapons, but they fell back at once, amid a crackle of energetic discharge.

'Are you sure that's enough to keep them confined?' I asked, and Kildhar nodded, in the slightly stiff fashion of most tech-priests making the effort to resurrect half-remembered body language.

'It should be,' she assured me. 'If they were being directed by the hive mind they'd keep attacking the barrier until they'd made a breach in it, but alone they're driven by instinct, not reason. Their self-preservation cuts in, and they break off.'

'What about the deck?' I asked. 'You can't keep that electrified. They'd just fry.' Which, come to think of it, sounded fine to me.

'Precisely what we are doing,' Kildhar said. 'The cages have a false floor, made of non-conductive material. If they break through that, they get a jolt from the charged one underneath. The ceiling carries a current too, although I don't see how they could reach it.'

'Very thorough,' I said, wishing I found that thoroughness reassuring. The digestion pools of the hive fleets were full of people who'd been equally confident of their precautions against the tyranids, and I had no wish to join them. But, for the moment at least, the creatures seemed confined, so I'd just have to suppress my misgivings as best I could. 'Is Sholer aboard too?'

'No.' Kildhar shook her head, with a little more confidence this time. 'Our research is at a crucial stage, and he felt it best to remain in the analyticum with the offworld specimens.'

'At least those aren't trying to bite anyone's face off,' I said, following her up an echoing metal staircase at the end of the chamber. Once on the upper decks, to my unspoken relief, she turned towards the crew quarters, instead of suggesting we take a look at the still living spore she'd alluded to, as I half feared she might.

'They hadn't when I left,' she said, which was hardly encouraging, although I supposed if anything from the freezer got out of hand the Apothecary would be more than capable of taking care of it. 'But then hardly any of them had revived.'

I felt a sudden lurch in the pit of my stomach, which might have been due to the vast vehicle getting under way again, although somehow I doubted that. 'How many were you trying to revive?' I asked, trying to keep my voice level.

'Only a handful of the less dangerous ones,' Kildhar said, as though there was any such thing where tyranids were concerned. 'As we had the opportunity to acquire some live specimens of this generation, I felt it might be instructive to have some of the historical ones active to run some comparative tests on.'

'And Sholer went along with this?' I asked, scarcely able to keep the shock and horror from my voice.

Kildhar was definitely improving at the nodding thing, probably due to the practice she was getting. 'He took a little persuading,' she said, 'but I was able to convince him the risk was slight.' Maybe she really did think that, but this was a woman who'd been keeping genestealers as house pets for the last sixty years, so I could hardly be blamed for finding her advice on safety matters a little less than reliable.

'I hope they're more secure than your 'stealers were,' I said, a little more waspishly than I'd intended[1], but the magos didn't seem to take offence at the remark.

'All possible precautions are being taken,' she said, leading us into the lounge area where the harvester crew could rest between shifts. I have no idea how many would normally be on board[2], but there were a couple of good-sized dining tables at one end, next to a galley from which appetising aromas seeped, displacing the rather more earthy one of my aide[3]. Come to that, I probably didn't smell all that fresh myself. Luckily the only other people in sight were cogboys, who'd probably had their sense of smell removed as surplus to requirements, or labourers so used to working on the surface that Jurgen and I were no more olfactorily offensive than everything else in their daily routines. All of them gave us a wide berth, which was fine by me[4]; right then I was in no mood for idle conversation, and remained so until I'd got outside a plate of something hot and steaming, and enough recaff to float a small battleship.

Kildhar disappeared as soon as Jurgen and I were ensconced with our rations, no doubt eager to resume poking hormagaunts with sticks, or whatever else it was she got up to with them, leaving us to eat in peace. I can't pretend either of us felt particularly deprived of her company, but once I was feeling reasonably human again I tapped the comm-bead and asked where she was, partly because I was feeling robust enough for a proper briefing now, and partly because I didn't entirely trust her out of my sight for too long.

'I'm on the control deck,' she informed me, much to my surprise, as I'd have wagered pretty heavily that she wouldn't be parted from her precious specimens under any circumstances. She then compounded my astonishment by giving me quick, concise directions to the location, which my aide and I lost no further time in following.

---

1. *Hardly surprising, given the ordeal he'd just been through.*

2. *Between two and three hundred, depending on the type of harvester, area of operation, and the expected yield of usable minerals.*

3. *Which indicates that, by this time, he'd discarded the breather, although the point at which he did so isn't clear.*

4. *And hardly surprising, given their visible weapons.*

TWENTY-ONE

THE CONTROL DECK was on the highest level of the great machine, and was fronted by an armourglass window taller than I was, allowing its captain a panoramic view of the landscape across which it was travelling. I can't deny that the sight was a spectacular one, the barren desert undulating beneath us like an ocean of sand so far below that we might almost have been flying, like the Reclaimers' Land Speeder, which kept circling us at about the same height[1]. From up here, I could see clear to the distant hive, or back the other way to the curve of the horizon, where the low-lying haze of a far-off sandstorm echoed the slabbed ramparts of the habs and manufactoria like a phantom mirror.

'Hard to believe something that size and so solid could ever fall,' Yail said, as I gazed thoughtfully at the looming ranges of serried rockrete. He was back in his Terminator armour, which showed several new gouges in the ceramite, and towered over everyone else in the echoing chamber as he strode majestically through the quincunx of control lecterns between us, the thralls manning them scuttling

---

1. *Presumably because its pilot had some difficulty travelling as slowly as the lumbering harvester.*

out of his way like nervous sump rats; and who, in all honesty, could blame them?

'We both know it will, if the 'nids get enough organisms on the ground,' I told him, and he nodded.

'True,' he rumbled. 'With tyranids, it's always about the numbers.' For a moment my imagination filled the sand below us with teeming horrors, and I shuddered at the idea, before Yail went on with quiet confidence. 'With us, however, it's strategy, and our faith in the Golden Throne. I know which I'd rather rely on.'

'Well said,' I agreed, because it's always wise to concur with over two metres of genetically enhanced super-warrior encased in the toughest power armour known to man.

'I prefer to rely on the power of the intellect,' Kildhar said, ambling over after concluding her conversation with the landship's captain. Whatever the substance of it, he seemed far from happy. 'Surely the most powerful weapon with which the Omnissiah has seen fit to gift us.'

'One you're clearly better fitted to wield than I,' I told her, since it probably wouldn't help to express my true opinion at this juncture. 'How are your researches progressing?' As soon as I finished speaking, I realised my mistake. I've never yet met a tech-priest who didn't take a generalised enquiry of that nature as an excuse to launch into a detailed exposition of their particular obsession. If they've got augmetic lungs or a vox-coder they don't even need to pause for breath, and can drone on for hours[1], but fortunately Kildhar had neither, and I was able to get a word in after only a couple of minutes. If my eyes glazed over in the interim, I was at least able to plead fatigue from our trek across the desert, although I doubted she'd even noticed. 'In terms a layman can understand,' I added, at the first opportunity.

The qualification seemed to take her completely aback, and she stopped babbling to stare at me blankly, like a servitor faced with a problem not covered by its programming. 'We're following up several promising lines of enquiry,' she told me after a prolonged pause.

'Such as?' I prompted.

---

1. *Quite literally.*

'The sub-molecular re-alignment of neurotransmitters in the brain tissue of organisms under the direction of the hive mind offers some intriguing possibilities,' she offered at last. 'Of course it's difficult to reproduce these conditions in the analyticum, without thawing out the hive node recovered from Nusquam Fundumentibus, but Apothecary Sholer is adamant that we should not attempt to do so.' This last in a faintly pettish tone, which made me strongly suspect that she'd been advocating just this course of action, and been overruled in no uncertain terms. Clearly Sholer was by far the less reckless of the two, and, despite my considerable doubts about the wisdom of their research in the first place, my opinion of him grew markedly warmer. 'We have had some success with cogitator simulations, however, which lead us to believe it might be possible to interfere with the control mechanism.'

'You could jam the influence of the hive mind?' I asked in astonishment, with a sudden flare of hope. If that were possible, it would hand humanity an enormous tactical advantage, turning the vast, unstoppable armies of the tyranids into mere swarms of mindless, instinct-driven beasts. Still hellishly dangerous, of course, but far easier to oppose and overcome than a cohesive whole driven by a malign intelligence.

'In theory,' Kildhar said, 'although finding an effective method of doing so would take a great deal more study.'

'Which we don't have time for,' I concluded.

'Regrettably, that is the case,' she agreed. 'Barring an unexpected breakthrough, I would estimate the necessary research to take a further two to three decades.' By which time Fecundia would either have been long since saved by conventional means, or reduced to a barren cinder lost in the wake of a reinvigorated hive fleet large enough to consume the entire Gulf region.

'Our best course of action would be to maintain the blockade,' Yail said firmly. 'If the Navy can inflict enough losses, the tyranids will be forced to withdraw in search of easier prey.' He plodded to a hololith tank in the corner, which I strongly suspected had been set up with the intention of briefing me, as the familiar image of Fecudia and the starships in orbit about it appeared as soon as he activated the device. 'Until they establish a beachhead on the surface, they'll be unable to replenish the biomass they're losing. It's simply a matter of holding on, until the tipping point is reached.'

'If we can,' I said, studying the tactical display carefully. 'They've a lot of ships in reserve, and every one of ours they cripple opens up a gap in our orbital defences. Once they've poked enough holes, they can start landing in force.'

'We saw off their first assault,' Kildhar said, as though she'd been manning an air defence turret personally. Yail and I exchanged a look.

'That wasn't an assault,' I explained, as carefully as I could. 'They were simply probing our defences. Getting some scout creatures down was just a bonus.'

'Lucky so many of 'em came down in the desert,' Jurgen said. 'If they'd hit the hives, there'd have been a real mess to clear up.'

'Some of them did,' Yail replied. If he was startled by my aide's sudden interjection, he hid it well. He manipulated the hololith again, and a rash of contact icons appeared across the face of the planet. 'Luckily, the Lord General had anticipated the contingency, and the Imperial Guard contained the incursion.'

'He's good at that,' I said absently, studying the display with a growing sense of disquiet. As I'd have expected, the majority of tyranid icons were in or near the main population centres, homing in on the greatest concentrations of biomass, but there was a small cluster in the desert, right about where we were.

The palms of my hands prickled again. I couldn't have said why, but something about that little group of contacts struck me as sinister. It wasn't unusual for tyranids to go to ground in the wilderness areas of prey worlds, of course, biding their time until they'd built up their strength by hit-and-run raids – I'd observed the tactic at first-hand on far too many occasions – but off-hand I couldn't recall a single instance in which they'd done so while simultaneously striking at far more tempting targets. The landing sites in the desert were definitely too close to one another to be purely random, which meant that the hive mind; which sent them must have had an objective in mind.

And there was only one possible target out here which made any sense. 'Regio Quinquaginta Unus,' I said, only half aware that I'd spoken the thought aloud.

'It's over there,' Kildhar said, with a faint air of puzzlement, gesturing in the direction of the huge slab of armourglass surrounding the bridge. 'You should be able to see it by now.' And indeed I could, the blocky six-sided structure rising out of the sand in the distance, almost as I remembered it on our first approach. Except that this time I was looking up at it, even from this tremendous height. It loomed over the harvester, a man-made mesa, so imposing in its solidity that, for a moment, I began to wonder if it could possibly really be under threat, despite my previous encounters with the ravening hordes of the hive mind, then reason reasserted itself. I'd seen far more formidable fortifications than this breached by the endless tide of malevolent chitin, and complacency in the face of the tyranids never ended well.

'There's something here the hive mind wants,' I said, setting out my reasoning as swiftly and concisely as I could.

Yail nodded thoughtfully. 'I concur,' he said, after a swift glance at the hololith, digesting the tactical information at once. We both looked at Kildhar, who stared back at us blankly.

'I have no idea what,' she said. 'I study their physiology, not their mental processes.'

'In pursuit of which, you've collected a small army of the things,' I said, scarcely able to credit that someone so intelligent could be so dense.

'But they're inert,' Kildhar protested.

'For now,' I said, remembering how readily the ghastly creatures had revived from their frozen tomb on Nusquam Fundumentibus.

'Whatever their objective,' Yail said, 'taking live specimens inside the shrine would be extremely inadvisable. We would simply be doing the hive mind's work for it.'

'That goes without saying,' I agreed, and Kildhar's face hardened (apart from the metallic parts, which were hard enough to begin with).

'The whole purpose of gathering them was to run tests, in the hope of finding a weakness we can exploit. Unless we take them to the analyticum, that would be impossible. I must insist they be delivered as intended.'

'And I must insist we refrain from doing anything so completely frak-witted!' I snapped, turning away. 'You can run it by Dysen if you want, but I can tell you right now what he'll say. And so will the Lord General.' Actually, knowing Zyvan, what he'd say would almost certainly require a little discreet redacting before being laid before a wider audience, but there was no point in going into that now.

'I will consult Apothecary Sholer at the earliest opportunity,' Yail said, and there, to the satisfaction of no one, the matter rested until we reached the shrine.

'YOUR ANALYSIS OF the tactical situation seems perfectly sound,' Sholer said. It had taken him some time to finish up whatever he was doing in the lower depths of the installation, and I'd taken the opportunity to have a hot bath and send what was left of my uniform to be laundered. Despite my preference for a complete change of clothes, there wouldn't be time to arrange it, and I fully intended to depart aboard the first shuttle to make it down here in any case. Despite a lingering dampness about both my hair and greatcoat, neither of which had had time to dry fully, simply having both free of the majority of the sand they'd acquired over the last couple of days made me feel a good deal more comfortable and optimistic.

'I'm glad you agree,' I said, taking an appreciative sip at the mug of recaff Jurgen had handed me before departing in search of some food to go with it. The steel-walled meeting room was a trifle chilly, and the lingering dampness hanging about me intensified it. We must have been close to the refrigerated vault where the creatures transplanted from Nusquam Fundumentibus remained entombed.

It was a small gathering, just the Apothecary, Yail, Kildhar and myself. Dysen had sent a vox message to convey that whatever we decided was fine by him, but carefully worded so that if it all went ploin-shaped no one could claim that he'd actively supported it, and Zyvan was too busy to be contacted at all, not entirely by coincidence I strongly suspected.

'The magos, however, also has a point,' Sholer went on, almost making me choke on the bitter liquid, 'and makes a persuasive case.' He paused, glancing across the room at Kildhar, who was seated rigidly on one of the metal chairs around the central table, trying to pretend she was interested in the data scrolling across the pict screen in front of her. She was the only one sitting; as I'd observed before, the Adeptus Astartes seldom did so, while I'd found the blasted chairs uncomfortable enough before, let alone now, while the memory of hours in the saddle was still so fresh in my mind, and elsewhere. She looked up, meeting Sholer's gaze, with an expression of pleased surprise. 'Although on balance, I'm bound to agree with Commissar Cain and the brother-sergeant. The risk of allowing infiltrating organisms within the sanctuary is too great to take.'

I disagree,' Kildhar said, keeping her voice tech-priest neutral with an obvious effort. If I was any judge, she'd rather shy the data-slate she'd been reading at his head. 'The specimens you revived remain secure. The same precautions should be sufficient to keep the fresh ones confined.'

I felt a fresh prickle of unease. 'Just how many 'nids did you thaw out?' I asked, doing a rather better job of hiding my feelings than Kildhar had managed. 'Just out of interest.'

'Eleven hormagaunts,' Sholer replied at once, in a manner I felt to be excessively casual, given how lethal the creatures were. 'They were clustered close together in the ice, so I inferred that they were part of the same brood.'

'A reasonable deduction,' Kildhar said, with clear approval, 'which should help us to compare like with like.'

'And where are they now?' Yail asked, with a glance at the door as though he expected a swarm of gaunts to start ripping their way through it at any moment. When a Space Marine in power armour[1] starts looking uneasy it's never a good sign, and I had to suppress the impulse to reach for my weapons.

'The holding pens on the lowest level,' Sholer said. 'They are perfectly secure, I can assure you.'

---

1. *It's not entirely clear whether, as before, Yail had discarded his Terminator suit in favour of the lighter tactical armour by this point, but it seems likely.*

'Like the genestealers were?' I asked, perhaps a little less than politely, but under the circumstances I was prepared to forego the niceties.

'The two aren't remotely comparable,' Kildhar said, a trifle testily for someone who was supposed to be beyond obvious displays of emotion. 'Genestealers are capable of abstract reasoning, particularly the hybrids. They could have planned their escape, overcome the security precautions by using their intelligence. Hormagaunts are just instinct-driven beasts.'

'Unless the hive mind is directing their actions,' Yail pointed out.

'That can't be the case, there were no synapse creatures accompanying them,' Kildhar said impatiently, as if that should have been obvious to everyone.

'Could they have been pre-programmed, though?' I asked. 'Like servitors?'

'An intriguing notion,' Sholer said, cutting across her indignant denial. 'There's no record of any previous instances of such a case, but that doesn't mean it's not possible.'

'You're all just jumping at shadows!' Kildhar declaimed, giving up any pretence of remaining calm. 'If we're ever going to stand a chance of overcoming the hive fleets, not just here but across the rest of the galaxy, we need to stay shortout dispassionate!' She took a deep breath. 'I apologise for the unnecessary vehemence of my remarks.'

'We've all been under a good deal of strain,' I said diplomatically, although privately I doubted that the Space Marines considered anything untoward about the situation. They spent their whole lives facing the enemies of the Emperor, and were hardly likely to get excited about the latest ones to be wandering across the sights of their bolters.

'Perhaps you would care to inspect the pens?' Sholer asked, addressing his remarks to me, although a brief inclination of his head included Yail in the invitation. 'Perhaps that would go some way towards alleviating your concern.'

'Perhaps it would,' I said, although I doubted it very much.

* * *

THE PENS WERE located a few levels beneath the meeting room, and, as I'd anticipated, the temperature of the air there was noticeably lower. I shivered, grateful for the recaff I still clutched, and the warm salt-grox bap Jurgen had managed to procure from somewhere on my behalf.

'You see?' Kildhar said, with the air of someone pointing out a self-evident truth. 'The specimens are totally secure.'

'They certainly seem to be,' I conceded. We were looking down into a sheer-sided square shaft lined with ceramite, too slick for the scuttling mass of gaunts to get a foot or claw-hold on, from behind the reassuring screen of a slab of armourglass thick enough to have shielded the driver's viewing slit of a Leman Russ. Below us and above them a steel mesh roofed the chamber, crackling every now and then as a portion of the charge it carried leaked across in the cool, damp air, in case they managed to find a way up regardless. 'Stealers would have been up and through it in no time, of course, but the gaunts were less well adapted to climbing.

'I felt it prudent to restrict our researches to hormagaunts, for the time being,' Sholer said, 'given the relative ease of being able to confine them.'

'Prudent indeed,' I concurred tactfully, which I suppose it was if you were really bound and determined to go ahead with this courting of disaster. Termagants were able to shoot at you, genestealers had already proved more than adequate to the challenge of freeing themselves, and most of the other creatures on ice were either able to burrow their way to freedom, strong enough to break straight through the walls, or could channel the will of the hive mind, none of which were particularly tempting prospects right at the moment.

'Then I see no reason not to put the newly acquired ones in the adjacent chamber,' Kildhar said, returning to her theme with a vengeance. Yail and I turned to Sholer, hoping he'd be able to convince her to finally drop the matter, but to our mutual surprise he seemed to be wavering.

'The hormagaunts, perhaps,' he said thoughtfully, while Yail and I looked at one another in mingled consternation and disbelief.

'You said yourself the risk was unacceptable,' I expostulated, and the Apothecary nodded pensively in reply.

'I did,' he said slowly, 'but, on reflection, Magos Kildhar still presents a compelling argument. Time is unquestionably of the essence, and our work would proceed more quickly and effectively with the facilities of the analyticum to hand.'

'What about the other specimens?' Yail asked, an instant before I could. 'Should they be purged?'

'Absolutely not!' Kildhar said. 'We can leave them aboard the harvester for the time being, and study them there as best we can.'

'Ready to be absorbed into the swarm the moment the second wave hits,' I said, making no effort at all to hide how I felt about that.

'We can take appropriate precautions,' Kildhar said, 'like we've done with the specimens in storage. I've already instructed the harvester captain to remove the dampers from the motivator power core. If it becomes necessary we'll be able to detonate it, and sterilise the entire load.'

'That might work,' I conceded, reluctantly. No wonder the captain had looked so fed up.

'It will,' she assured me, probably mistaking agreement for acquiescence.

I turned to Sholer. 'Does that mean you've got the freezer rigged too?'

'In a manner of speaking,' he told me. 'Magos Dysen's suggestion was essentially sound. The reactors have been reconfigured to vent raw plasma directly into the chamber, vaporising everything within it almost instantly. The only time-consuming part of the process was digging pressure vents to the surface, to give the expanding steam somewhere to go.' He permitted himself a thin smile, not an expression I normally associated with a member of the Adeptus Astartes. 'It would be somewhat ironic to destroy the shrine in order to save it.'

'Quite so,' I said, less reassured than I would have liked. 'These vents. Not large enough for anything to crawl up, are they?'

'Credit us with a little imagination, commissar,' Kildhar said. 'Of course they're not.' She hesitated. 'Well, some of the smaller ones might fit, I suppose, but we've put grilles on the ends of the shafts. And it's not as if anything's going to be moving around down there anyway, they're all frozen solid.'

'That's true,' I said. 'But I'm just as worried about things getting in from outside.'

'If they do, they'll be vaporised along with the others,' Yail pointed out. 'But I'll make sure combat servitors are posted to cover the tops of the shafts anyway.'

'Then I believe we're in agreement,' Sholer said, although he seemed to be the only one. 'We'll move the hormagaunts Magos Kildhar collected into the adjacent holding pen, and continue our researches for as long as we can.' He turned to Yail, who still seemed to me to be torn between loyalty to his Chapter and plain common sense. Unfortunately, as it always will for a Space Marine, loyalty won.

'I will see to the security arrangements,' he said, plainly not liking it.

'Then we have little to worry about,' Sholer said, inaccurately. He turned back to Kildhar. 'I wish it understood that, although I may have been swayed by your arguments for the moment, I will sterilise every last specimen the instant I see even a hint of a danger to this shrine and the people within it.'

Kildhar nodded, tightly. 'I would expect nothing less,' she said.

TWENTY-TWO

'THEY'RE COMPLETELY OUT of their minds,' I told Zyvan over the vox-link, heedless of whether the transmission was being monitored or not. 'Now we've made sure of that, I need a shuttle here as quickly as possible.' Before the inevitable happened, the shrine was over-run, and everyone got eaten, including me. No point in sounding as though I was making a panic-stricken run for it, though, even if I was, so I added 'I've wasted enough time away from the real war as it is.'

'Don't worry, Ciaphas,' Zyvan assured me, a trace of amusement in his voice, 'you'll be back here before the next wave hits. You've fought the 'nids more often than anyone else I can think of, and I'll need your insights in the command centre when we take them on again.' Which came as a relief. Despite my misgivings about being aboard a spacecraft with a tyranid fleet incoming, it would still be preferable to being stuck on the ground once the full force of the invasion was unleashed. If the worst came to the worst, and the fleet was forced to cut and run, I'd escape along with it instead of being marooned on a world doomed to be devoured. Unless the scuttling horrors I'd glimpsed on the tau explorators' pict-cast got to me first...

Torn between two terrors, I vacillated indecisively for a moment, before reason reasserted itself. I was definitely in danger here, now, from Kildhar's reckless insistence on bringing the creatures she'd rounded up inside, and it was pointless worrying about anything which only might happen in the future.

'I'll be waiting on the pad,' I said, and Zyvan chuckled, clearly believing me eager to get back in the fray.

'You'll get pretty bored,' he said. 'The Navy won't have a shuttle free for a while yet. Everything's on rearming and resupply runs, before the 'nids hit us again. A personnel pick-up's pretty low priority, even if it's for you.'

Nads, I thought. It sounded as though I was going to be stuck here for several hours at least. No point in sounding petulant about it, though, Cain the Hero was supposed to put duty first at all times, so I just put my cheerfully resigned voice on instead. 'Goes without saying,' I said breezily. 'Just try not to get stuck in without me this time.'

'We'll do our best,' Zyvan assured me, 'and we'll let you know as soon as your ride's on the way.' Which was all I could reasonably hope for, I supposed.

'Sorry to bother you, sir,' Jurgen said, his characteristic odour wandering into the room which had been made available to me a second or two before his corporeal presence. Like most Adeptus Mechanicus guest quarters I'd been obliged to avail myself of over the years, it was clean, ergonomically laid out, and curiously dispiriting, the closest thing to a human touch being the devotional cogwheel icon in a niche in the corner. 'Apothecary Sholer thought you might want to look in on the gaunts in the pen.'

'I suppose we should,' I said, somewhat heartened by the observation that he was still lugging the melta around, instead of leaving it in the adjoining room, which had been put at his disposal. Zyvan and the admiral[1] would want as full an account as I could give them of

---

1. *The first direct mention of the Naval officer in overall charge of the fleet, Admiral Boume, a much decorated and highly regarded commander. He would have been copied in on the intelligence reports Cain was preparing for Lord General Zyvan, but he and Cain don't appear ever to have met face to face; quite naturally, as Cain was attached to the Imperial Guard throughout his service, and the Navy has its own commissars assigned to oversee it.*

whatever the Mechanicus and the Reclaimers were getting up to, and observing the safety precautions they'd put in place to contain the newly-arrived specimens might put their minds at rest, although, in all honesty, I doubted that it would do the same for mine. This whole undertaking had *Catastrophe* written all over it, and the best I could hope for was to be long gone before everything fell apart.

I can't deny that with my aide and his melta at my shoulder I felt a little happier than I otherwise would have done given our destination, even going so far as to nod an affable greeting to a few of the skitarii patrolling the corridors in tense-looking pairs. They'd clearly been briefed to be ready for trouble, which was something of a comfort, knowing I wouldn't be left to face the worst alone if (or more likely when) it happened, although I still clung obstinately to the hope that I'd be gone before it did.

Kildhar and Sholer were waiting for us in the observation gallery, and I glanced into the pen below us as I entered, expecting to see the same milling mass of hormagaunts I'd looked down on the last time I was here. Instead of pacing, or sitting randomly about the floor, though, all were clustered in one corner, their heads raised, as if testing the wind.

'What's the matter with them?' I asked.

'Just what we were discussing,' Sholer said. 'We have not observed this behaviour on any previous occasion.'

'They're sensing the presence of the new specimens,' Kildhar said, the effort of modulating her voice all too plain; she was positively skipping with excitement[1] at the prospect of putting her theories to the test.

'And speaking of which,' I said, 'they would be where?' The adjacent pen was empty, so far as I could see, unless they had a particularly well-camouflaged lictor stashed in it.

'On their way,' Kildhar assured me, and moved over to a control lectern set in the wall beneath the slab of armourglass. She poked a couple of switches, and a panel in the wall of the empty pen slid

---

1. *Almost certainly a bit of dramatic licence on Cain's part, as a tech-priest of her age and seniority would be a little better practised at concealing her emotions than this.*

aside, to reveal a dark tunnel beyond. A moment later a torrent of hormagaunts bounded into the chamber, and the hatch slid quietly closed behind them. 'They'll be disorientated for a few minutes,' the magos biologis went on, 'exploring the boundaries, and searching for a way out.'

'They don't look disorientated to me,' I said, as the whole pack of them swarmed across the pen, throwing themselves against the wall separating them from the gaunts in the adjacent one. Those too had perked up the minute the newcomers had arrived, and begun attacking the barrier with their scything claws, seemingly undeterred by their compete lack of success in getting through.

'Fascinating,' Kildhar said. 'They're trying to join up, creating a larger group.'

'Which would be a really bad idea,' I reminded everyone, just in case they'd forgotten that somewhat basic fact.

'Indeed it would,' Sholer agreed, his attention almost entirely on some incomprehensible stream of icons and text, rushing across the pict screen in front of him too fast to be read. He glanced briefly at Kildhar, who seemed even more engrossed if that were possible, her eyes fixed unblinkingly on the blizzarding data in front of her. 'I'm picking up enhanced activity in the basal ganglia of all the monitored subjects.'

'As am I,' the magos responded, 'although since there was only time to attach external instrumentation, results from the fresh specimens will be less comprehensive and possibly less reliable.'

'Would one of you mind explaining what's going on here?' I asked, adding 'in layman's terms,' a trifle hastily as Kildhar opened her mouth to respond.

'We are attempting to monitor the brain activity of the creatures, which has changed significantly since the two groups became aware of their proximity to one another,' she told me. 'A task of considerable complexity,' she added after a moment's pause, meaning *so shut up and let us get on with it.*

I looked down, catching a glimpse of small metal boxes about the size of data-slates riveted to the carapaces of several of the new batch. The ones from the freezer weren't so adorned, although I thought I could detect some damage to the chitin of their heads, as if minor puncture wounds had been recently inflicted, and only partially healed[1]. 'They seem pretty agitated,' I said. Both groups were still attacking the wall between them with single-minded diligence, fortunately failing to make much of an impression on the thick slab of ceramite.

'As I predicted,' Kildhar said, 'they feel compelled to join together. If they do, their brain activity should synchronise.'

'Just as well they're not going to,' I said, just as she flicked another switch. The wall between the two cages began to sink into the floor, and both sets of gaunts grew even more frantic, if that were possible, leaping and scrambling over one another in their efforts to be the first over the top. 'What the hell do you think you're doing?'

'Gathering data!' Kildhar snapped. 'We could be on the verge of saving the galaxy!'

'And you could be on the verge of killing us all!' I riposted, lunging towards the controls, but Sholer was faster, stabbing the switch with his ceramite-encased finger. In his haste he overdid it a little, denting the lectern, and eliciting a shower of sparks from the abused array of controls. The descending wall ground to a halt, rose a few centimetres, and stuck, still low enough for both sets of creatures to surmount easily.

'This was not agreed to!' he rumbled, his voice deepening even more than usual.

'It's the obvious next step!' Kildhar riposted. 'We need reliable data on the blending of consciousness within the swarm!'

The two of them glared at one another, while I hovered indecisively, wondering how best to intervene without becoming the lightning rod for the heightened emotions of both. Kildhar would be relatively harmless, despite the augmetics she was no doubt stuffed with, but an angry Space Marine would be a force to be reckoned with, preferably

---

1. *Possible, though implausible; more likely, his imagination was filling in the gap, in response to Kildhar's implication that more sophisticated monitoring equipment had been surgically implanted in the older group.*

from a considerable distance. On the other hand, this was all being recorded for later analysis, and it wouldn't look good for me to be caught flat-footed, instead of doing something decisive to bring them back to their senses.

'Are they supposed to be killing each other?' Jurgen asked, snatching everyone's attention.

Relieved at the fortuitous interruption, I turned to look. My aide was right – the creatures in the newly-combined pen were tearing into one another with all the ferocity at their command, and, as they were hormagaunts in a feeding frenzy, that was a lot. Ichor and viscera sprayed everywhere, as the scuttling nightmares snapped and slashed at one another in what looked to me like an indiscriminate orgy of bloodletting.

'They should not,' Sholer said, looking down thoughtfully at the carnage below, his anger replaced by curiosity as quickly as flicking a switch.

'I don't understand it,' Kildhar said, a note of bewilderment entering her voice. 'All the data we've gathered suggested their minds should have meshed as soon as they came together.'

'Perhaps they require the mediation of a synapse organism to facilitate the melding,' Sholer suggested.

'Maybe they just don't like each other,' Jurgen said, cutting to the essentials as always.

'Maybe they don't,' Sholer agreed, to my considerable surprise. 'We've always thought of the tyranids as a single, unified threat, but there are some magos biologis who theorise that the different hive fleets compete for prey[1]. A contention I find myself far less sceptical of now than hitherto.'

'Because these are definitely from different fleets,' I said, the coin dropping. Looking down at the ichor-flecked melee, I found myself able to distinguish the combatants easily enough by sight: the gaunts from the freezer had the same speckled patterning on their thoraxes

---

1. *A view with many adherents among the Ordo Xenos, although far from universally accepted. Some even argue that if the tyranids were ever to succeed in devouring all other life in the galaxy, the hive fleets would fall just as readily on one another, until the ultimate survivor succeeded in absorbing all the available biomass into itself.*

I recalled so well from Nusquam Fundumentibus, while the new arrivals had darker banding on their carapaces, and the edges of their scything claws. Something about that combination of markings seemed vaguely familiar too, come to think of it, although I couldn't put my finger on where I'd seen it before. By that time I'd encountered tyranids on a dozen occasions at least, and the bewildering variety of colour and shading I'd seen exhibited by the creatures had become thoroughly mixed up in my mind.'

'Quite so,' Sholer said.

'We have to stop them!' Kildhar expostulated, staring downwards at the charnel pit beneath our feet. 'Before we lose the lot!'

'Good luck with that,' I said, having no inclination to try separating the combatants. In fact, the more of each other they killed, the better I liked it. The newcomers were definitely getting the best of it, although that was hardly surprising, given that they outnumbered the others by almost two to one. As I watched in horrified fascination, the last of the thawed-out gaunts fell, its head wrenched from its body, while a second assailant slashed its torso open from gushing neck to the root of its tail. 'Perhaps they'll calm down a bit now while they feed.'

'They don't look very hungry,' Jurgen said with a faint note of surprise, which I could hardly blame him for. In our experience hormagaunts were little more than voracious appetites on legs, and I expected them to begin gorging themselves on the cadavers of the fallen at once. The half-dozen or so survivors of the short and vicious melee in the holding pens seemed to have other ideas, however, ignoring the bounty of carrion their efforts had won in favour of flinging themselves against the wall opposite the partially-retracted barrier which had separated them from their recently-thawed adversaries.

'They don't,' I agreed, as they began attacking the wall, as single-mindedly and fruitlessly as before, so far as I could tell. 'Now what are they up to?' Something about the location they'd chosen made me uneasy, although I couldn't have said why. So far as I could see it was a blank panel, no different from those on any of the other walls, but something had attracted them straight to it.

'They're trying to get the access tunnel open,' Kildhar said, sounding completely bewildered. 'But they should be acting purely on instinct, not showing signs of reasoning ability!'

'Perhaps they don't know that,' I said, dryly. Then a more alarming thought struck me. 'The panel will hold, won't it?'

'Of course,' she assured me, with complete confidence. 'The locks can only be opened from up here.' She gestured towards the lectern, bearing the scar of Sholer's gauntlet, from which a thin wisp of smoke was still rising. Her expression wavered. 'Oh.'

'Brother-Sergeant Yail, meet me in the cryogenitorium,' Sholer rapped out, assessing the situation at once, and already on his way to the door. I glanced downwards, my worst fears realised: even as we spoke the gaunts had managed to get the sliding panel partially open, and a ridged and sinuous tail disappeared through the gap as I watched. 'Commissar, will you join us?'

'Right behind you,' I said, unable to think of an excuse to refuse on the spur of the moment that wouldn't have sounded feeble, even to me. I hurried out after him, Jurgen a reassuring presence at my heels, leaving Kildhar staring dumbly down at the mess below, clearly still wondering what could possibly have gone wrong.

THE CAVERN BENEATH the shrine was just as cold as I remembered it, and the surfaces underfoot just as treacherous. Fortunately, the route Sholer took to get us there terminated on the surface of the ice, instead of forcing us to take our lives in our hands at the top of the narrow and slippery bridge, bringing us out through the structure from which he'd emerged the first time we'd spoken on this world.

'Over there,' Jurgen said, pulling ahead of us on the frozen surface, as sure-footed as only a Valhallan could be in sub-zero temperatures. The gaggle of gaunts were clustered together a hundred metres or so away, flailing at the ice with their scything claws. 'Looks like they're digging.'

'Trying to revive something,' I said, remembering the gaunts we'd seen on Nusquam Fundumentibus doing precisely the same thing. On that occasion they'd released a particularly large and unpleasant bioform, which had tried to make a meal of me, the squad I was with and our transport vehicle, and would almost certainly have done so but for the intervention of a passing Valkyrie pilot with a warhead or two to spare. The thought was not a pleasant one.

'Or kill it,' Sholer said, putting on a burst of speed to keep up with Jurgen, something his power armour made look ridiculously easy. I floundered in their wake, not entirely unhappy to have a Space Marine standing between me and the murderous beasts, but reluctant to fall too far behind in case we were flanked. If I got cut off from the others I'd become easy meat, torn apart before my companions had a chance to intervene.

Not that the hideous creatures looked about to charge, still utterly intent on using their grotesquely elongated forelimbs as pickaxes, but it never paid to be complacent about 'nids, as I'd already had occasion to reflect. I drew my weapons, both fully recharged and ready for use, feeling a good deal more comfortable as soon as I felt their familiar weight in my hands. Jurgen had the melta on aim, and let fly at the nearest. The shot went wide, which was hardly surprising given that he was firing on the run, but it caught one of the others a glancing blow, raising a cloud of steam as the ice around it flashed into vapour. The mist hung for a moment, blanketing everything, reducing the brood to an inchoate mass of barely-seen movement.

'Here they come!' Sholer warned, drawing his bolt pistol in a single smooth motion, and planting a couple of explosive-tipped rounds in the middle of the thorax of the first gaunt to burst from the shrouding fog. Jurgen dropped to one knee, steadying his bulky weapon, and took down another, renewing the fog in a fresh burst of steam as he did so.

'Use the lasgun!' I told him, cracking off a couple of shots of my own at the nearest dimly-seen shadow, which had no effect at all that I could see. 'The melta's giving them too much cover!' Not to mention the risk of a near miss thawing out even more of the hideous creatures. Having caught up with my companions, I stood back to back with Sholer's reassuringly impregnable-seeming bulk, swinging the chainsword in a defensive pattern designed to protect me from anything rushing suddenly out of the murk.

'Right you are, sir,' Jurgen agreed, imperturbable as ever, dropping the melta as he spoke. The emitter hissed as it touched the ice, creating another, small patch of mist, which began to disperse quickly. I just had to hope the cover he'd inadvertently created for our assailants would do the same before they could take full advantage of it. A moment later the crackle of his Guard-issue small-arm, firing short, precise bursts, echoed across the artificial ice field.

As the mist lifted, we began to see our targets more clearly. Unfortunately, that meant they could see us equally well, which was far less encouraging. The whole pack of them began to bound forwards, thick drool slithering from their gaping jaws, flecks of it freezing around their muzzles alongside the blood and viscera deposited there during their brief scrimmage in the holding pens.

I braced myself to meet the charge, hoping my duellist's reflexes would be enough to prevent my head from being lopped off by a swipe from the first gaunt to get within reach, but the bone-chilling cold was getting to me in earnest now, stabbing through my torn and tattered greatcoat and slowing my movements as it leached the warmth from my blood. I cracked off a couple of shots from my laspistol, more in the hope of making them flinch than of actually dropping one, although in my experience once a gaunt got the scent of prey in its nostrils it would take a lot more than a las-bolt flicking past its ear to distract it. Jurgen managed to down one of the scuttling horrors with a sustained burst from his lasgun, which must have drained the powerpack faster than he liked, as he let it fall to the ice and snapped in a fresh one in a single fluid movement, never taking his eyes from the rich selection of targets bearing down on us as he did so. Sholer's bolt pistol barked again, and an elongated head exploded, the body it was attached to continuing to bound forwards a couple of paces before crashing to the ice in a spray of dislodged crystals and rapidly-congealing ichor.

'There are too many of them!' I gasped out, raising my chainsword to parry a slash from the leading gaunt. They'd split up as they charged, sweeping round to flank us, just as I'd feared a few moments before, but now all three of us were encircled, not just me. Somehow, being about to die in the company of friends didn't seem much of an improvement, although I supposed it would afford me the chance for a few last words. Not that anyone would survive to remember them, and the best I seemed able to come up with at the moment was a heartfelt 'Frak off!' at the one trying to close its jaws in my throat as I ran it through with the whirling blade, ripping the weapon free in a spray of viscera as I spun to meet the next attack. Just as I feared, my reflexes seemed painfully slow, and I'd have been an instant too late, losing my head for my pains, if I hadn't slipped on the frozen surface and stumbled at the last possible minute. The scything claw I'd meant to parry passed over my head instead, and I made to rise, striking up into the gaunt's momentarily-exposed underbelly.

'Stay down!' a new voice called, boosted by a helmet-mounted amplivox, and I did as it suggested, getting a mouthful of ice crystals as I tried to present as low a profile as possible. The distinctive *hisss-crack* of bolters being discharged, overlapping in short bursts, assaulted my eardrums, and I rolled clear as the shredded remains of the gaunt I'd been about to strike at dropped to the ice right on the spot I'd been a second before.

I rolled to my feet, to find Yail and a couple of his brother Adeptus Astartes double-timing it towards us, the muzzles of their bolters still smoking from the barrage which had taken down the whole pack, missing my companions and I by what would have seemed a miracle to anyone less familiar than I with the phenomenal standard of their marksmanship. Jurgen was getting back up too, brushing the ice crystals from his uniform, and bending to retrieve his precious melta, which I could hardly fault him for, as it was far more effective against the 'nids than his lasgun. (Anywhere it wasn't going to help them hide from us, anyway.)

'Sergeant Yail,' I said. 'Pleased to see you.' Which barely began to cover it, of course, but I had a reputation for sangfroid to maintain, and now the danger was past there seemed little point in being overly effusive.

'As am I,' Sholer said. 'I expected your response to be a little less tardy.'

'My apology for any inconvenience, Apothecary,' Yail said, his tone devoid of any trace of sarcasm which I could detect. 'It took us a moment to get through the security systems.'

'I thought you were supposed to have complete access?' I said, surprised, and Yail nodded.

'We are. However, Magos Kildhar ordered a complete lockdown of the lower levels, and that impeded our progress.'

'Well, I can't fault her caution,' I said, 'although her timing leaves a lot to be desired.' Something started nagging at me as I spoke. Given her recklessness in bringing the gaunts into the shrine in the first place, not to mention the genestealers she'd been breeding, this sudden rush of common sense to the head seemed uncharacteristic to say the least. But perhaps the shock of what had happened had made her sit up and smell the recaff (a mug of which I could really have done with about then).

'Any idea what the gaunts were trying to dig up?' Jurgen asked, passing me a flask from which steam rose invitingly into the frigid air. If I hadn't been aware of his remarkable psi-damping abilities, I'd sometimes swear the man was a mind-reader.

'Not yet,' I said, edging cautiously towards the cracked and pitted ice they'd been attacking so single-mindedly. They hadn't had time to get very deep, thank the Throne, barely scratching the surface in fact, but it was pretty clear what they'd been after. I tilted my neck to get a clearer look. 'Throne on Earth, it's the bioship fragment!'

TWENTY-THREE

'WHAT DID THEY want with that?' Jurgen asked, furrowing his brow in puzzlement.

'To kill it, I would imagine,' I said. 'You saw what they did to the gaunts from the other swarm.'

'But how did they know it was there?' my aide persisted.

'A good question,' Sholer said. Jurgen looked faintly surprised, then pleased with himself, praise from a Space Marine being rare enough at the best of times, let alone aimed in his direction. 'But it seems the hive fleet must be aware of its existence somehow, even though dormant[1].'

'Then the gaunts were still operating on instinct when they swarmed in here after all,' I said, happy to at least be able to discount the presence of a lurking synapse creature somewhere on the premises.

Sholer nodded. 'It appears so,' he said, turning to lead the way back to the exit. 'But the implications are disturbing.'

'Most definitely,' I agreed, my mind rather more focused on regaining

---

1. *Precisely how has still to be determined, despite the best efforts of hundreds of the magos biologis currently working for the Ordo Xenos; but then we still have only the most rudimentary understanding of how the hive mind perceives anything around it.*

the warmth of the upper levels than the implications of what we'd discovered. Time enough to discuss those once we'd thawed out, if you asked me. I reached for the handle of the thick metal door, and tugged at it. It refused to budge.

'Allow me,' Sholer said, with a hint of amusement. He reached out a hand, and slapped the plate of the genecode reader. Instead of registering his presence, however, the machine spirit remained obdurate, and the door securely locked. 'Override,' he said, 'in the name of Sholer, Apothecary to the Reclaimers.'

'Lockdown in progress,' the machine spirit responded, in a vox-coder drone uncannily like Dysen's[1]. 'Voiceprint recognition suspended. Genecode recognition suspended.'

'How did you get through?' I asked Yail, and he shrugged, quite a sight for a Space Marine in full armour.

'Forced it,' he said, to my complete lack of surprise. 'But it was easier from the other side.'

'It would be,' I agreed. Pushing, he and his comrades would have been able to put their whole weight behind it, whereas on this side the handle provided the only point of purchase. Only one of the Adeptus Astartes would be able to pull at a time, and with his superhuman musculature, supplemented by the power of his armour, the chances were he'd only succeed in yanking the thing clean off.

'I can get it open,' Jurgen offered, steadying his melta, and Sholer nodded his approval.

'Quicker than taking the bolters to it,' he agreed.

'Won't that give the specimens the run of the shrine if any revive?' I asked.

Sholer inclined his head again. 'In theory,' he agreed. 'But they can't thaw out while the refrigeration plant remains operative. And doors can always be replaced.'

'True,' I said, my desire to be out of the bone-numbing cold as quickly as possible overwhelming any other objections I might have had. 'Whenever you're ready, Jurgen.' I closed my eyes against the anticipated flash, which punched through my eyelids as brightly as it

---

1. *Not to mention billions of other tech-priests scattered around the galaxy.*

always did when he fired his favourite weapon this close to where I was standing, and felt the backwash of heat flow over me, restoring a semblance of feeling to my numb extremities at last.

'That's got it,' he said, which was hardly surprising given that he'd hit it from point-blank range, and I blinked my vision clear of the dancing after-images. The thick metal slab half-melted, slumping against its hinges, and without another word[1] the two Reclaimers accompanying Vail stepped forwards. Ceramite gauntlets reached out to grasp it, their fingers sinking into the softened metal, and with a groan like something alive and suffering the door gave way at last.

'Where to?' I asked, jogging gratefully through the gap into the relative warmth of the corridor beyond, doing my best to keep up with the superhumanly long strides of the Space Marines.

'To the power plant control chapel,' Sholer said, scattering red-robed tech-priests ahead of him like autumn leaves in a squall as he made his way through the maze of passageways on the lower levels. 'Sub-level three.' Which confirmed my tunnel rat's instinct that we were still a fair distance below the surface. As I trotted along in the wake of the Adeptus Astartes I filled Zyvan in on what was going on, somewhat breathlessly I must admit, as I had less wind than usual left for talking.

'You were right, they are insane,' the Lord General commented. 'The sooner you're back up here the better.'

'My sentiments exactly,' I agreed, trying not to pant too audibly. By this time we were approaching the control chapel, and I picked up my pace a little more, reluctant to fall too far behind the reassuring bulk of the Space Marines. The heads of the acolytes manning the genetorium snapped round in our direction as we burst through the door in a flurry of weapons and armour, visibly shocked by our sudden unmannerly intrusion into so sacred a space. Like many of their shrines, it was long on polished steel and blinking lights, with innumerable dials and switches set into lecterns and wall displays. Pict screens were flashing up icons and images which meant nothing to me, which was probably just as well for my peace of mind.

---

1. *Except, perhaps, over their helmet voxes.*

'Thank the circuits you're here,' Kildhar said, looking up as we shuffled around, trying to find somewhere to stand. The chapel was large enough, as such places go, but a quartet of Space Marines take up a lot of room, particularly when they're waving bolters around, and Jurgen's melta wasn't exactly compact either. 'This corruptfile imbecile won't vent the reactors into the cryogenitorium.'

'Good for him,' I said curtly. 'Considering we were locked in there.'

'Were you?' Kildhar looked confused for a moment, and then returned to her argument with the senior tech-priest present, which our arrival seemed to have interrupted. 'Well, you're not now, so let's get the static things vaporised before they eat us all.'

'That's a bit of a turnaround,' I muttered to Jurgen. The palms of my hands were itching again, a sign I'd learned to trust. Something really wasn't right about this. 'She's the one who was hell-bent on preserving them.' Sholer was looking puzzled too, in so far as I could read his expression at all.

'With respect to your exalted position, magos,' the tech-priest buzzed, the insect-like harmonics added to his voice by a loose wire somewhere in his vox-coder growing increasingly irritating with every syllable, 'our understanding is that the reactor is to be vented only if the specimens currently in cryogenic storage present a clear and present danger to the shrine.' Had he a jaw still capable of movement, doubtless he would have set it at this point. When a mid-ranking functionary begins any sentence with 'with respect', you know he'd rather take a swim in an open sewer than budge a millimetre from his stated position.

'It's my opinion that they do,' Kildhar said. 'And if you haven't the throughput to get the job done, I have.' Shouldering past the incredulous tech-priest, she stabbed at a bank of switches with the tips of her fingers. At once, a row of lights turned red, and a warning klaxon began to sound somewhere in the depths of the building.

'This course of action is premature,' Sholer said, as a clockface appeared on one of the pict screens, counting down seconds with what seemed to me to be unnecessary eagerness. He turned to the tech-priest. 'Abort the venting.' With a relieved nod, the red-robed minion took a step towards the lectern.

'Stop right there,' Kildhar said, cold and determined. 'I'll decommission anyone who goes near the vent controls.' She drew a bolt pistol from the depths of her robe, a master crafted one if the finely wrought chasing of the devotional iconography was anything to go by, and the tech-priest stopped moving as abruptly as if she'd already pulled the trigger. At this range she stood a fair chance of penetrating the Space Marines' armour, let alone my tender hide, and I hoped she knew enough about the weapon to avoid discharging it by accident.

Of course, you don't point a gun at a group of Adeptus Astartes and expect them to just stand there making idle conversation. In a heartbeat, three bolters and a bolt pistol were pointing right back at her, while the genetorium acolytes scurried for whatever cover they could find. Jurgen began to raise the melta too, but I forestalled him with a gesture. If anyone so much as hiccoughed, Kildhar would be reduced to shredded scrap and offal in a heartbeat, and I didn't see any point in barbecuing the remains into the bargain. Besides, there was a lot of delicate equipment scattered around the place, all of which probably needed to be kept in one piece if the almost inconceivable energies of the fusion reactor were to remain confined. I hadn't the slightest objection to the 'nids being vaporised, but the notion of sharing their fate was considerably less attractive.'

'Magos,' I said, trying to keep my voice pitched to a conversational level, 'this hardly seems necessary.'

She turned a glance of withering scorn in my direction. 'Haven't you worked it out yet?' she demanded. 'It all fits!'

'Of course,' I said, the pieces clicking into place at last, leaving me wondering how I could have been so blind. 'You were on the *Spawn of Damnation* too. No wonder you seemed so keen to preserve the implanted serfs, and bring them back here.'

'I'm not sure I follow, sir,' Jurgen said, his brow furrowing and dislodging a few flakes of skin in the process.

'The serfs weren't the only ones brought into the brood mind,' I said. 'They let themselves be brought to Fecundia, knowing the most senior of the people ostensibly studying them was a part of it as well.

And the so-called research was just an excuse to allow them to build up their numbers.'

'Exactly,' Kildhar said, the muzzle of her bolt pistol rock steady. 'Far more quickly than they could ever have done while trying to remain concealed among the general populace.'

'That's how they got out, too, isn't it?' I asked, almost blinded by the obvious. 'The genecode readers around the secure area were set up to recognise the print of someone whose genes had already been subverted. Every genestealer and hybrid in the shrine could simply walk through the door whenever they liked.'

'Then why didn't they?' Yail asked, looking ready to pull the trigger at any second. Not something I wanted him to do until I was sure I had all the answers; our alliance against the tyranids was shaky enough as it was, and if it turned out I was wrong, then its collapse could doom us all.

'Because they were waiting for the hive fleet to arrive,' I said. Now I was thinking about it in a wider context, it was no wonder the carapace markings of the gaunts Kildhar had brought in seemed familiar – they were the same as the ones on the genestealers that had done so much damage on the upper levels, and that I'd fled in terror from in the darkened labyrinth of the *Spawn of Damnation*.

'That's right,' Kildhar said, chipping in at just the right moment. 'They must have hoped to make it to the hives, and disrupt the defence effort.'

'Didn't they tell you?' Sholer asked, sarcastically.

'I'm not the corruptfile traitor!' Kildhar shouted, all attempts at tech-priestly detachment long past. 'Why would I have upgraded the fleet auspexes if I wanted the tyranids to invade?'

'Because that's what implanted genestealer victims do,' I said wearily. 'I've seen it before. They fight alongside you as hard as anyone, until the brood mind exerts its influence. Most of the time they don't even know what they are. But the brood mind's still in there, nudging them now and again.' I turned to Sholer for confirmation. 'Who was it who kept arguing in favour of bringing the gaunts inside?'

'Magos Kildhar,' he said, in tones of deadening finality.

'Precisely.' I turned back to the distraught tech-priest. 'You have to admit, you did precisely what the hive mind wanted you to do. Bring its meat puppets into the shrine, so it could try to neutralise the one thing on the planet it's afraid of.'

'But I'm me!' The hand holding the bolt pistol was trembling now, Sholer square in its sights. 'He's the one who damaged the locking mechanism and let them into the cryogenitorium!'

'An accident,' Sholer said dismissively.

'Of course you'd say that!' Kildhar laughed, a short, ragged bark, with an edge of hysteria. 'You're the one who approved my request to study the implanted serfs in the first place. Covering your tracks!'

'A ridiculous assertion,' Sholer said. 'I was accompanied by my battle-brothers on every occasion I boarded the hulk. Or are you asserting that entire squads of us have been implanted?' I glanced sidelong at Yail, trying to judge how he was taking all this, but I didn't know him well enough to pick up any subtle cues he might be trying to suppress.

'You've certainly given us a lot to think about,' I said levelly, maintaining eye contact with Kildhar as I spoke. Truth to tell, I didn't know what to believe by now, other than that the vital thing was to keep all her attention on me. Jurgen and I were half-concealed by the towering bulk of the Adeptus Astartes in their power armour, and I took advantage of that to signal to him with my hand. Out of the corner of my eye I saw him nod, almost imperceptibly, and begin to move away, after propping his melta against a convenient lectern. 'But then, you're the one hell-bent on killing the bioship fragment. If anyone's doing what the hive fleet wants, right now, it's you.'

'Precisely,' Sholer said. 'We have to continue our researches to the last possible moment.'

'The risk is too great,' Kildhar insisted, with a quick glance to the rapidly diminishing numerals. 'And if you've been implanted, that's the hive mind talking.' On the verge of making a dive for the control panel, Jurgen hesitated, and drew back. For a second, I must admit, it crossed my mind to simply shoot her, but if a stray round destroyed the lectern, there was no telling what might happen. For all I knew the reactor might run completely out of control, levelling the entire shrine, instead of simply belching the tyranids to vapour[1]. If my aide was going to seize his chance, I had to get her full attention, and keep it for a few vital seconds.

'I could say the same,' the Apothecary rejoined, accurately, but unhelpfully given our current circumstances.

'When did you last have an augmetic upgrade?' I asked, and a flicker of confusion appeared in the tech-priest's eyes. Clearly, whatever she'd been expecting me to ask, this wasn't it.

'I don't know. A while back. What does it matter?'

'A magos of your seniority usually has far more visible enhancements,' I said. If I'm honest, I was more or less guessing, although that certainly seemed true of the cogboys I'd encountered before.

'I've been busy,' she snapped.

'For how long?' I asked. 'Since your time on the *Spawn*?'

'I don't know.' Confusion was being replaced by doubt, now. 'Upgrades... system log...' Her eyes unfocused for a moment. As they did so, Jurgen grabbed his chance, leaping for the control lectern behind her, and pushing as many switches as he could reach back the way they'd been before. The lights went back to green, the clock on the pict screen vanished, and the siren stopped howling in the bowels of the building.

'Stop it!' Kildhar turned on him in a fury, bringing up the bolt pistol to fire. Before she could, I took her square in the middle of the chest with a laspistol round. Reckless, you may say, with the panel still behind her, but with Jurgen's life in the balance I simply took the shot, and worried about the possible consequences later. She staggered, and stared at me in outraged astonishment, charred wiring sparking and popping inside her ribcage. 'You couldn't... you shouldn't... last upgrade...' The bolt pistol fell from her nerveless fingers. Jurgen swooped, like a raptor on a vole, scooping the weapon up, and stuffing it into one of his collection of pouches for safe

---

1. *Presumably the same thought had occurred to the Space Marines. Using weapons as destructive as bolters surrounded by so much vital and delicate equipment would have been an act of desperation.*

keeping[1]. Then Kildhar's eyes cleared for a moment. 'You were right. Sixty-three years ago.'

'Because the screening prior to the augmentation process would have revealed the genetic contamination,' Sholer said, handing his own bolt pistol to Yail. Faint scuffling sounds behind the lecterns indicated that the tech-priests were getting their courage back, or were more worried about the consequences of leaving the machine spirits to fend for themselves for much longer than they were of emerging from cover, and a few nervous heads began to appear above and around the serried ranks of instrumentation. 'I should be confined until it's determined whether I too have been polluted.'

'If you think it's necessary,' I said, 'but I don't think there's much chance of that.' Space Marines had their health checked down to the molecular level on a regular basis. 'And the magos?'

I turned back to Kildhar, bringing my laspistol into line for a clean headshot. I'd granted the Emperor's Peace[2] more times than I cared to recall, but still I hesitated. The tech-priest met my eyes.

'Wait,' she husked. 'Valuable specimen. Study me…' Then her eyes rolled up in their sockets, blood loss and trauma from the chest wound taking the matter out of my hands. Perhaps fortunately; to this day, I couldn't tell you what decision I would have made.

'Preserve the body for dissection,' Sholer said, as he left the room, accompanied by one of the helmeted Reclaimers.

'I'll take care of it,' I assured him, relieved to note that Jurgen had retrieved his melta, and was covering my back once again. Right now, he was the only other person on the planet I felt I could trust.

---

1. *Cain appears with this weapon, or one very like it, in many of the propaganda prints bearing his likeness, although to the best of my knowledge he never used it in the field, preferring the laspistol he was used to. He eventually presented it to me, and it continues to serve the Emperor well as part of the armoury available to my entourage.*

2. *An Imperial Guard euphemism for mercy killing.*

TWENTY-FOUR

By the time I'd finished bringing Zyvan up to date, the sun was beginning to wester, painting the metallic walls of the conference room a shade uncomfortably reminiscent of blood. The revelation that Kildhar's pet genestealers had effectively been given the run of the place for the past sixty years had had a predictably seismic effect on everyone, from the Lord General on down. There was no telling how often one of the beasts had sneaked out of the holding pens to pass on the taint to an unwary cogboy, and everyone going about their business in the corridors seemed to be eyeing one another with thinly-veiled suspicion. Fortunately Regio Quinquaginta Unus was about as isolated as anywhere could be on this benighted ball of slag, but an awful lot of people had passed through it in the last six decades, and tracking them all down was proving to be an interesting challenge for the local Arbitrator's office[1].

'They've started mass genetic screening in the main population centres,' a hololithic facsimile of the Lord General told me, flickering a little, apparently seated in the middle of the table which occupied

---

1. *It's unclear here whether he means the actual local representative of the Adeptus Arbites, or the Fecundian law enforcers they would be overseeing. Probably both.*

the centre of the room. Fortunately, he was only about a third of his actual size, so he fitted quite comfortably. 'Starting with the most strategically vital institutions.'

'Have they found any hybrids or implants yet?' I asked, and Zyvan shrugged his insubstantial shoulders.

'Not yet. Twelve thousand down, twenty billion to go.'

'Not good odds,' I said, but that was the whole point of the tyranids sending their genestealers out ahead of the hive fleet. Quite apart from the damage their puppets could do directly, if they became numerous enough to thoroughly infiltrate a planet's population, the diversion of resources required to track them down would put a serious dent in the overall defence effort.

'What about the shrine?' Zyvan asked.

'Some good news there,' I told him, knowing he could use some. 'We've already screened half the cogboys, and they've all been clear so far. One or two of the others are still unaccounted for, so the skitarii are running a level by level search in case they've gone to ground somewhere.'

'Our most probable hypothesis, however, is that they were assisting the mass breakout,' Sholer put in, 'and were all killed along with the ones on the shuttle.' He'd been the first to be screened, of course, and, as I'd expected, turned out to be free of taint. For all I knew, his modified genes would simply have eaten any 'stealer attempt to subvert them in any case[1].

'That's something, anyway,' Zyvan said, not bothering to ask if we'd had the skitarii scanned. They'd been the first through the gene lab, after Sholer and his brother Adeptus Astartes, that went without saying. He coughed, a little delicately. 'And Magos Kildhar?'

'Was definitely tainted,' I said. 'I don't suppose we'll ever know how or when she was implanted herself, but it was probably some time before the serfs were.'

'Brother-Sergeant Yail is reviewing the mission logs for that period,' Sholer added, 'but our chances of success are not high.'

---

1. *The enhanced immune systems of Space Marines are indeed remarkable, but not that good.*

'Then let's concentrate on the present,' Zyvan said, bringing us back to the business at hand. 'Have you secured the bioship fragment?'

'It's still in the cryogenitorium,' I told him. 'Something that size, there's not a lot else you can do with it.'

'I've given instructions for it to be dug out and revived,' Sholer put in, earning a scowl from Zyvan, before adding 'subject to the agreement of Magos Dysen and yourselves, of course.'

'I have to say I'm not sure about that,' Zyvan said, and I nodded my agreement.

'Neither am I,' I admitted. Sholer and I had already discussed the matter, and, not for the first time, expediency was pushing me in a direction I'd rather not go. 'But we have to face facts. The hive fleet was desperate to destroy the node, and that's the first time we've seen one running scared of anything. We need to know why.'

'I agree,' El'hassai said, appearing next to the Lord General by increments, as he edged his way into range of the hololith projector. Sholer and I exchanged concerned glances, wondering how long he'd been lurking there, and how much of the preceding conversation he'd overheard. All of it probably, as Zyvan didn't look at all surprised to see him. Come to that, there didn't seem much point in trying to exclude the tau from our deliberations anyway, as we were supposed to be allies, and any tactical advantage we were able to come up with here would probably work just as well for them in the defence of Dr'th'nyr (although, since the warp shadow around the tyranid fleet was blocking our astropaths from passing on the information to the one accompanying Donali, whether they found out about it in time would depend entirely on how fast El'hassai's own channels of communication were). 'This is an unprecedented development, and understanding it could not help but advance the Greater Good.' He was standing behind Zyvan now, so his image no longer flared into insubstantiality around the sleeves of his robe, but the top of his head was losing focus instead, wavering in a fashion which made him look uncannily like an ornamental candle with a smoking wick.

'Your support is greatly appreciated,' I assured him, keeping a straight face with something of an effort.

'And your recommendation will be taken into account,' Zyvan added, stopping noticeably short of anything which smacked of 'and acted upon.'

'If we are to begin investigating the bioship fragment,' Sholer reminded us, 'then the sooner we begin, the better. Time is most definitely of the essence.'

'Absolutely,' I agreed. The sky beyond the armourglass window was beginning to turn purple, the colour of a fresh bruise, mottled with the first few stars to come out, most of which were probably orbiting warships, reflecting the light of the disappearing sun like a constellation of small but deadly moons. The onset of night intensified my apprehension; although the chances of an unsuspected tyranid horde scuttling out of the darkness were miniscule, and the shrine was protected from the approach of anything inimical by auspex arrays of quite staggering sensitivity, my primal hindbrain was preparing to huddle round the campfire with a nice sharp rock close to hand. 'So far as I'm concerned, the sooner you get on with it the better.'

'I concur,' El'hassai said, from the relative security of a couple of hundred vertical kilometres away.

'And Dysen tells me he trusts your judgement,' Zyvan said to Sholer, in the tone of a man who knows a passed buck when he hears one. He sighed, heavily. 'I still have my doubts about the wisdom of this. But under the circumstances, I don't see that we have any choice. Do the best you can.' He smiled, bleakly. 'I suppose we can always sterilise the site from orbit if it all goes to the warp.'

Which, considering I was still standing there, was hardly the most cheering thing he could have said.

'Any news of that shuttle?' I asked, hoping the association of ideas wouldn't be too obvious. 'There's nothing I can do here, apart from get under the Apothecary's feet, and we've still got a war to fight.'

'Last I heard, the Navy had some flight time freeing up,' Zyvan said. 'We can probably get a shuttle away to pick you up in the next couple of hours.'

'Best news I've had all day,' I told him accurately, still gazing out of the window across the darkening landscape. Night was falling in earnest now, and I traced the faint trail of a shooting star somewhere out over the desert. There would be plenty more over the next few nights, as the debris from the battle in orbit spiralled in, incinerating as it plummeted through the atmosphere towards the ground.

Then I stiffened, my eyes narrowing. The first bright streak across the sky was followed by another, and another, falling as thick and fast as rain in a thunderstorm. I turned back to the hololith, my panicked questions dying on my lips. Zyvan was standing, talking to someone outside the range of the projection field, while the insubstantial figure of the tau diplomat hovered on its fringes, flickering in and out of existence like a warp wraith trying to cling to its handhold in reality.

'Something's wrong,' Sholer said, his eyes still fixed on the miniature drama being enacted on the tabletop.

'Very,' I agreed. 'Take a look outside.'

'Holy Throne!' he said, succinctly. 'That looks like–'

'The second wave's just hit,' Zyvan informed us. 'Far heavier than the last one.'

'Of course,' I said, recognising the typical tyranid tactic. This time round they'd try to get enough organisms on the ground to really stretch our dirtside defences, gathering the information they needed to completely overwhelm us on the next try, or the one after that, or the one after that. In the meantime they'd be creating beachheads, allowing the swarms to grow, and begin harvesting the biomass they needed to swell their ranks still further. I tried to make my next remark sound like a joke, already knowing the answer, but clinging to the hope that it wouldn't be the one I expected. 'I take it my lift's postponed?'

"Fraid so,' Zyvan said, taking the pleasantry at face value. 'You'll have to sit this one out too.'

But, as I stared at the flickering lights in the sky, I didn't think for one moment that that would be an option.

From *The Crusade and After: A Military History of the Damocles Gulf,* by Vargo Royz, 058.M42.

THE SECOND TYRANID assault hit Fecundia with a ferocity the beleaguered defenders could scarcely withstand, losing several of the lighter vessels to acid or bio-plasma discharges even before the fleets closed. Through these gaps in the defensive line poured uncountable numbers of mycetic spores, each loaded with lethal organisms, infecting the planet below like viruses finding a vulnerable host, while the living starships tried to engage the survivors at close quarters with claws and tentacles, or launched boarding parties in an attempt to harvest the crews.

Though faltering, however, the line did not break, the gallant starfarers of the Imperial Navy retaliating with lance, broadside and torpedo, tearing the hearts out of untold numbers of the void-spawned abominations. Even the merchant vessels still in orbit used their relatively puny armament to good effect, forming themselves into ad hoc squadrons whose combined firepower was sufficient to cripple, and in a few cases kill, those tyranid monstrosities incautious enough to consider them defenceless.

Nevertheless, the battle in space was a close-run thing, and could easily have had quite another outcome had it not been for the unexpected and decisive intervention of Commissar Cain who, at the point the battle began, had more than enough to concern him as the invasion of the surface got under way.

TWENTY-FIVE

'LOOKS LIKE WE'RE a prime target,' I said, trying to keep my voice level, as the number of contact icons grew around the glowing rune marking our position in the hololith.

'We are,' Yail agreed, sounding as happy as a Space Marine ever is when faced with overwhelming odds, which isn't exactly cheerful, but a lot more sanguine about it than I generally am. No doubt because, from their point of view, it'll either result in a heroic victory or a glorious last stand, both of which will go down well in the annals of their Chapter.

'They're targeting the bioship fragment,' Sholer said, sounding almost as concerned about his lump of meat as our own safety, which I have to confess was my main concern at this point. 'What's our state of readiness?'

'As good as it can be,' I told him, knowing he'd be as aware as I was of just how inadequate that was likely to prove. 'The skitarii have finished laying minefields, and are dug in around our perimeter.' Rather them than me, I added silently to myself.

'My battle-brothers and I will be joining them,' Yail added, 'as soon as the tactical situation has become clear enough to know where we will be most needed.'

'What about the Land Speeder?' I asked, turning my attention to the pict screen, across which the darkened dunescape was scudding. The scout vehicle had been flying round in circles for the last hour or so, sending back increasingly pessimistic reports about the number of creatures heading our way from the scattered spores – not just vanguard organisms like gaunts and lictors this time, but scores of termagants, and the larger warrior forms to herd them. This time we'd be facing an army capable of coordinating itself and shooting from a distance, not an instinct-driven swarm desperate to close. There were even a few unconfirmed sightings of larger creatures, capable of taking on an armoured vehicle, if we'd had one, or, more cogently, tearing their way through whatever defences we'd manage to put in place before they arrived. Formidable as the walls of the shrine were, they'd been built to withstand an assault by nothing more threatening than the elements[1], and I couldn't see them holding for long against a brood of carnifexes determined to breach them.

'Standing by to provide fire support,' Yail assured me. After some discussion, we'd agreed that the fast-moving flyer would be best employed once the expected assault began in trying to pick off the larger creatures coordinating the others, in the hope of disrupting whatever strategy they were attempting to use against us. That would entail remaining fast enough, and high enough, to avoid any ground-to-air fire the swarm might bring to bear, of course. We could only hope that the superior range of the heavy bolters and missile launchers, and matchless marksmanship of the Adeptus Astartes, would be equal to the task.

'What about the landship?' I asked, catching sight of the harvester still parked alongside the shrine, like a dinghy bobbing next to a wharf. 'Can we use that to evacuate the tech-priests?' Who would, of course, need a military escort to ensure their safety, a job for which I considered myself the prime candidate.

'That has already been considered,' Sholer said, 'but their chances of getting through are extremely low.'

'I imagine so,' I said, having thought as much, but it never hurt to

---

1. *Which on Fecundia were hardly to be taken lightly.*

ask. The huge, lumbering machine would be an easy target for the swarm, which would simply keep pace alongside, throwing bodies at it until they tore their way through the hull. After that, it would all be over. 'Then what do we do with it?' I added. 'It's blocking our fire lanes, and giving them enough cover to mass for an attack.'

'Detonate the reactor,' Yail said. 'The specimens caged inside will attract others, so if we time it right, we should take out a considerable number of the attacking swarm.'

'The crew's already been evacuated into the shrine,' Sholer added.

'Glad to hear it,' I said, as if I actually cared one way or the other. 'How are you getting on with defrosting the bioship fragment?'

'Slowly,' Sholer admitted. 'It's been dug out of the ice, but we needed heavy lifting equipment to move something that size, and our analyticae simply aren't big enough to get it into. We've had to move our equipment into one of the storage bays in order to study it.'

'Show me,' I said, calling up a three-dimensional plan of the shrine on the hololith as I spoke. It sounded like the perfect place to avoid, and I wanted to make sure I stayed as far away from it as possible. Sholer poked the controls, and highlighted a large, vaulted area near the top of the structure. I stared at it in surprise. 'I thought you'd keep it down in the sub-levels.'

'The higher the better,' he said, 'as the tyranids don't appear to have any flying creatures among them.'

'Not yet,' I said, 'but they will.' One thing certain about the 'nids was that whatever problem you presented them with, they'd have a creature perfectly adapted to dealing with it spawned and ready to go within hours.

'The chamber connects to the main cargo lift,' Sholer said, pointing to a wide shaft extending all the way from the lowest sub-level to the flight deck on the roof. 'We can return it to the cryogenitorium easily enough if we have to.'

'Good enough,' I said, hoping I sounded as though I meant it. If we had winged organisms fighting their way down from the hangars, and the bulk of the swarm scrambling up from below, we'd have nowhere to go in any case. I turned back to Yail. 'Better get all the non-combatants into the mid-levels, and be ready to seal off the lower ones,' I said. That should buy us a little time if the swarm broke through. Or, more likely, I tried not to think, when they did.

'I agree,' he said. 'Although we should arm as many of the acolytes as we can. It will make them feel less vulnerable, and lack of accuracy is hardly going to be an issue if the swarm does gain entry.' Which was an understatement if ever I heard one.

WE DIDN'T HAVE long to wait for the first attack, which came less than an hour later. The night beyond the sheet of armourglass making up one wall of the shrine's main operations centre was suddenly lit up by a series of vivid flashes, like far-off lightning, accompanied by a low rumbling sound which made the window vibrate almost imperceptibly. In fact, I'd never have felt it, if I hadn't had my fingertips pressed against the slick, transparent surface as I craned my neck for a better view.

'Looks like they found the minefield,' Jurgen opined, handing me a more than welcome mug of recaff.

I took it, and nodded my thanks. 'It does,' I said, opening a vox-link to Yail, who was off somewhere in the darkness looking for 'nids to pot. 'Contact in sector three,' I told him crisply, then added 'but I imagine you noticed that,' in my best wryly humorous tone, as though I was eager to be out there with him. But someone had to watch the hololith, keeping an eye on the overall tactical picture, and for that job, to my vastly unspoken relief, we'd had a wide choice of me. I'd fought the 'nids before, and could pick out the patterns of movement that betokened an incipient charge, or a flanking attempt, better than anyone except possibly Yail, and his place was alongside his battle-brothers, not sitting out the fight in relative safety. His sense of honour would never have permitted that.

'We have it covered,' he assured me, although from the hololith display it looked more like he and the rest of the Reclaimers were just offering themselves up as an appetiser for the first 'nid arrivals. His last couple of words were almost drowned out as the speeder howled in from the south, unloading a blizzard of fire into the heart of the milling swarm, and pulled away again in the nick of time, rolling to avoid a barbed strangler pod fired by something in the press below. The living warhead burst in mid-air, spewing out an expanding mass of razor-edged tendrils which plummeted back into the heaving crowd of deadly organisms, ripping those it entangled apart with its fearsome thorns, which didn't seem to disconcert the others in the slightest.

I could make out very little of the horde surrounding us, the encircling mass reduced by the darkness to a single amorphous stain on the landscape, which seemed to seethe like an angry sea as highlights struck briefly from one piece of chitin or another. I found myself obscurely grateful for the lack of clarity, as seeing that unstoppable tide of malevolence for what it was, and being able to pick out individual creatures within it, would have been far more unnerving.

'Commissar,' one of the red-robed acolytes manning the lecterns called, somehow managing to inject a tone of apologetic diffidence into his mechanical voice, 'it appears we have a problem.'

'No, really?' I asked, tearing myself away from the window with some reluctance. The inexorable creep of the advancing wall of death beyond it had become curiously hypnotic. Then, reflecting that sarcasm wasn't exactly calculated to inspire already terrified civilians, I plastered a smile on my face, as though I'd meant it for a joke. 'Are we running out of recaff already?'

'A serious problem,' the cogboy insisted, predictably having had the sense of humour bypass common to his kind. He was carrying a welding torch in his mechadendrites, the makeshift weapon, and hundreds more like it, having been the closest we'd been able to come to Yail's suggestion of boosting morale by arming the tech-priests, and poked at the dials and switches in front of him with calloused and stubby fingers. Something about the intensity with which he was working worried me, and I hurried across the wide, high room, Jurgen trotting at my heels.

'What?' I asked, finding the display in front of him as incomprehensible as I'd expected. Jurgen leaned in for a closer look at the wobbling dials, his brow furrowing in bafflement, and the cogboy flinched, apparently still in possession of his sense of smell.

'I'm getting traces of movement in the cryogenitorium,' he said. 'Something's moving around down there.'

'Frak on a stick,' I said, seeing no reason not to express my disquiet in the most forthright possible terms. If anything, the short burst of profanity seemed to reassure the cogboy, probably because he'd been worrying about bothering me unnecessarily. 'They're waking up!' I retuned my comm-bead. 'Apothecary, we're reading movement in the deep freeze,' I said. 'Is the node waking up?'

'Not as such,' Sholer said, 'that would imply a sense of individual consciousness, which tyranids don't possess.' Not for the first time, I found myself regretting that it wasn't possible to strangle someone over a vox-link. 'But we are registering cortical activity, which is increasing in strength by the minute.'

'Then that's what's reviving the specimens,' I concluded.

'A reasonable hypothesis,' he conceded. 'But most are too deeply embedded in the ice to free themselves.'

'They don't have to,' I reminded him. 'You've got burrowers down there. They'll break it up enough for the others to get out.'

'Then we have a serious problem,' Sholer said.

Before I could congratulate him on his acuity, the entire room seemed to tremble, while a deafening rumble shuddered through my bones. A vivid fireball blossomed beyond the sheet of armourglass, against which debris clanged and clattered, leaving a few faint chips and streaks even in that phenomenally tough surface.

'There goes the harvester,' Jurgen remarked, in conversational tones.

'We're pulling back,' Yail voxed, almost at the same moment. 'We can't hold them any longer.'

'Then don't try,' I advised, after a quick glance at the hololith. The noose was tightening all around us, and unless they moved fast, they'd be cut off within a handful of moments. The Land Speeder was swooping and diving beyond the wide window, covering their retreat with strategic blurts of fire, and by the light of the burning landship I could see an unstoppable tide of chitin sweeping towards our fragile bastion from all directions. 'As soon as you're inside, we're sealing the lower levels.'

'Acknowledged,' Yail said, not bothering to ask why. If he'd been monitoring my conversation with Sholer he'd already know, and if he hadn't, I was pretty sure he'd be able to work it out. 'We'll be with you in ten.'

As it turned out, it was a couple of minutes more than that before the towering bulk of the Space Marine was looming over me again, his Terminator armour looking even more battered than before. Several of the rockets were missing from the shoulder-mounted launchers too, which in itself stood as mute testament to the ferocity of the fight he and his comrades had put up.

'I'm recording more movement below,' the welder-wielding cogboy piped up from behind his lectern, and I tilted my neck to converse with Yail.

'Looks like you got back in the nick of time,' I said. I turned back to the hololith, and called up the schematic of the shrine Sholer had shown us in the conference room so short a time before. Several internal doors were marked in red, to my considerable relief. 'All the doors have been welded shut.'

'That'll buy us a breathing space,' Yail agreed. 'We'll set up pickets here, here, and here.' He indicated a couple of choke points, where corridors intersected. 'Reclaimers here, and skitarii there.'

'This junction would be better,' I said, my innate affinity for complex corridor systems kicking in, and indicated an alternative to one of the points he'd suggested. 'If the 'nids get into the ducting, they can bypass a post here.'

'Good point,' Yail said. 'We'll deploy there instead.'

'Better hurry,' I said, 'it won't take them long to climb half a dozen levels.'

'But they're not climbing,' the cogboy put in. 'Look.'

His instrumentation made no more sense to me than it had done the last time I looked, but Yail seemed able to read it without too much trouble. 'No, they're not,' he said. 'Can you transfer this to the hololith?'

The cogboy nodded, and a moment later contact icons began to appear, clustered in the lower levels of the schematic. 'Best I can do,' he said.

'It's good enough,' I assured him, and turned to Yail. 'They're in the plasma vents.'

'Some of them, anyway,' the Space Marine agreed. 'I doubt many will fit.'

'They won't have to,' I reminded him, the picture of the huge serpentine burrower I'd found myself standing on the first time I'd visited the cryogenitorium fresh in my mind. 'The trygon will leave them a tunnel to follow.'

'Why are they heading for the surface?' Jurgen asked. 'They usually want to attack us as quick as they can.'

'Because there's more prey to be had outside,' I said, with a sudden flare of realisation, 'and the ones attacking us are just as eager to kill the bioship node. We'll keep for both of them.' Which was hardly a comforting thought in the long term, but if it gave us a respite now, I wasn't going to argue.

'There's the first one,' Jurgen said, returning to the window and looking down at the landscape below. Ignoring the sudden assault on my sinuses which joining him entailed, I stood next to him, and followed the direction of his grubby forefinger. As I did so, something fast and scuttling flung aside the grating it had just ripped from the nearest vent, and leapt at the unprotected back of the gun servitor still doggedly guarding it from the encroaching swarm. The construct fell in a flurry of slashing blows, flesh, bone and metal parting like morning mist, and its slayer bounded off into the darkness. "Stealer, you reckon?'

'Could be,' I said, as a dozen more bioforms swarmed out of the narrow opening, and followed their fellow. A brood of termagants, outnumbering them at least two to one, and being herded by one of the hulking warrior forms, turned their fleshborers on them, bringing the first few down, then the purestrains were among them, slashing and tearing at their prey.

'Structural breach,' the cogboy said, and for one terrifying moment

I thought he meant that the swarm below had changed their minds and decided to come after us instead. But the icons on the hololith were moving out, beyond the subterranean boundaries of the shrine.

'The burrowers are loose,' Jurgen remarked, as though commenting on the weather, and a moment or two later I saw something monstrously huge surfacing within the heart of the swarm, knocking uncountable scuttling horrors from their feet. Some fell into its gaping maw, others were mashed to paste beneath its gargantuan coils, then it was gone again, leaving only an eddy of disorientated abominations on the surface to mark its passing.

'They seem to be targeting the synapse creatures,' Yail said, and I nodded.

'Just the same tactics we'd employ,' I agreed, although the two swarms seemed able to exploit one another's vulnerabilities with an instinctive speed and precision we could only gasp at. 'But this can't go on for long.'

'It can't,' the Adeptus Astartes sergeant agreed. 'We just have to hope that the loser weakens the victor sufficiently to tip the odds in our favour.'

'It'll have to tip 'em a long way to keep this place secure with little more than a mob of cogboys waving sharpened sticks,' I said, 'even with you and your men to lead them[1].'

'And you,' Yail reminded me.

'We're just prolonging the inevitable,' I said, switching the hololith back to the overall strategic view to emphasise the point. 'So long as that bioship fragment is here, they'll just keep on coming.' The scrimmage in orbit seemed just as desperate and bloody, the hive fleet pressing the Navy hard, although at least it looked as though no more spores were falling. I switched the view again, to the region surrounding us. 'There are more 'nids inbound all the time.' I zoomed the image, taking in a cluster of contact icons scuttling towards us as fast as their legs could carry them. 'This group could have joined the assault on the main hive, but it's coming here instead.'

---

1. *From the fact that he doesn't mention the skitarii, we can infer that none were within earshot.*

'We need reinforcements,' Yail said, scanning the datafeed for any unengaged units, and coming up as empty as I had.

'Or we need to evacuate,' I added. He looked at me as though I'd suddenly started talking orkish, so I waved an expansive hand, taking in all the tech-priests surrounding us. 'This place is full of non-combatants, whose ministry is desperately needed to keep the forges running. If nothing else, we have to ensure their safety.' And mine too, although I didn't think it politic to mention that.

'Fecundia is being overrun by tyranids,' Yail said, still sounding bemused. 'We are hardly likely to find a safe refuge for them anywhere else.'

'Anywhere else has got to be safer than the 'nids' primary target,' I countered. I gestured towards the tactical display again. 'The main hives are being successfully defended, at least for the moment.'

At which point, I finally heard a welcome voice in my ear. 'Ciaphas,' Zyvan asked, 'are you still there?'

'Hanging on,' I replied. 'Watching a little tyranid civil war from the windows.' It was still raging unabated, although sooner or later the superior numbers of the invaders were bound to tell. Not far away a brood of carnifexes was charging ponderously home against the flanks of a transplanted tyrannofex, which staggered and fell, retaliating with a withering barrage of fleshborers which began to devour its attackers instantly. Maddened with the pain of their wounds, the hulking slabs of muscle and bone staggered drunkenly, and charged again at random, crushing a group of their own hormagaunts as they went. 'Quite a pleasant change to see them ripping into one another.'

'No doubt,' the Lord General said, sounding strained, 'but we're not so lucky. We're barely holding on up here, and the leviathans at the heart of the fleet have just come into auspex range. Unless we can come up with something in the next couple of hours, it looks like we're finished.'

'So I take it evacuating the civilians will be out of the question?' I asked, getting precisely the answer I expected.

'You take it right,' Zyvan said, sounding appropriately touched by my non-existent concern for the non-combatants; but under the circumstances I could hardly ask about being able to make a run for it myself. In the unlikely event of getting out of this undigested, I had a reputation to maintain, and if a chance did come up to save my own neck, it'd be a lot harder to take if I'd undermined Yail's trust in me beforehand. 'The Navy's got its hands full, and even if we could get a shuttle away, it'd be downed before it hit the atmosphere.'

'Then we'll hold on as long as we can,' I said. Which was all good sinew-stiffening stuff, just the kind of quietly understated declaration of resolve someone like I was supposed to be was supposed to say in situations like this. I glanced at the hololith, seeing the swirl of the internecine battle to the death unfolding like a clash between storm fronts. 'We'll upload our tactical data, and keep it coming in real time. If we do go down fighting, the analysts might be able to make something out of it.'

'Standing by to receive,' Zyvan said, and cut the link, rather hastily, I thought[1].

'A good suggestion,' Yail said. 'I'll advise Apothecary Sholer to prepare whatever results his researches yield for transmission too. It would be regrettable if any useful information was lost at the last minute.'

'It would indeed,' I said, thinking it would be a damn sight more regrettable if I was. I spoke absently, though, my attention almost entirely on the ebb and flow of the contact icons in the hololith, as my subconscious struggled to bring something about them into focus. I glanced out of the window, where the epic clash of chitin was still illuminated by the flickering glare of the immolating harvester, translating the movements of the icons into those of the actual creatures, and realisation suddenly struck, like one of the secondary explosions going off around the wreck. 'Look at that!'

'They're giving it some, all right,' Jurgen agreed, completely missing the point, which was nothing new, but Yail was looking puzzled too.

'All I can see is tyranids killing one another,' he said, with a faint air of resentment, as though he didn't see why they should have all the fun.

---

1. *Probably to hide an emotional reaction, although, typically, this appears not to have occurred to Cain.*

'But it's how they're doing it,' I said. I pointed at a particularly egregious example. 'Look at those termagants.' A brood of the invaders was firing its fleshborers at an advancing tervigon, the towering creature's thick armour plating shrugging the incoming hail of deadly beetles off with almost contemptuous ease, although several of the newly-spawned termagants scuttling around its feet fell, while the others returned fire with fleshborers of their own. Abruptly the target brood scattered and ran, taking what cover it could.

'That's typical instinctive behaviour,' Yail reminded me, still none the wiser, and I nodded.

'But they had one of the big warrior forms with them,' I said, pointing it out just before the tervigon bit it in half, chewing and swallowing its impromptu snack with every sign of relish. 'It should have been directing them, overriding the instinctive response.'

'It should.' Yail nodded, in sudden understanding. 'The presence of the node from the bioship must be inhibiting the hive fleet's ability to pass on instructions.'

'Jamming it, like we do with enemy vox-channels,' I agreed. I made for the door, with a fine show of decisiveness. 'We need to talk to the Apothecary right away.'

TWENTY-SIX

Sholer's makeshift analyticum turned out to be pretty much as I'd expected: a large, echoing space the size of a shuttle bay, the cargo pallets usually stacked there either pushed into the corners or pressed into service as improvised tables and workbenches, at which crimson-robed acolytes of the Omnissiah were toiling away diligently, doing Emperor knew what. Cabling ran everywhere, with the typical cogboy's indifference to either trip hazards or the danger of accidental electrocution, although I suppose the latter would hardly inconvenience anyone with so high a proportion of mechanical to organic components. If anything, it would probably perk them up a bit[1].

The middle of the chamber was dominated by the bioship fragment, a vast chunk of necrotising meat, which towered more than twice my height. In fact it would be no exaggeration to say that it was roughly the size of a Baneblade overall, though less firmly defined. Noisome fluids seeped from it constantly, trickling into a hastily-drilled hole

---

1. *Quite possibly, if their augmetics were powered by internal capacitors; a common arrangement among heavily modified tech-priests, particularly if they do a lot of work in the vicinity of poorly insulated wiring.*

in the floor, from which a steady splashing sound indicated that they were being collected in a vat of some kind[1]. Needless to say, the stench was indescribable. The whole thing was studded with metal spikes driven deep into the mound of flesh, from which a forest of wires ran to banks of instrumentation, the displays of which were being intently studied by Sholer and his gaggle of assistants, a few of whom I recognised from the analyticum downstairs.

'Commissar,' he greeted me, with manifest surprise, as I bustled in, Jurgen at my heels. It was, perhaps, a measure of how overpowering the stench was that I had to turn to make sure my aide was still there. 'I assume your presence means an unexpected development?'

'It does,' I assured him. I'd petitioned the machine spirit of my data-slate to keep watch on the tactical information we were uploading to Zyvan's command centre aboard the flagship, and handed it over hurriedly, with a nod towards the kopje of diseased flesh looming over us as I spoke. 'We think this thing's jamming the influence of the hive fleet. I need to know how, and if we can exploit it.'

Sholer glanced at the slate for a moment, assessing the tactical data as rapidly and comprehensively as only an Adeptus Astartes could, then handed it back, with a cursory nod. 'Intriguing,' he said, and turned to one of the flickering data displays. 'The main instances of disruption appear to correspond with neural activity on these frequencies.' The regular wave patterns dissolved into meaningless static, and Sholer frowned. 'Equipment malfunction,' he said. 'Hardly surprising, given how quickly it was all moved and reassembled.'

'Jurgen,' I said, divining the probable cause[2], 'could you find me a recaff somewhere? And you'd better get something for yourself while you're about it. It looks like being a long night.'

'Of course, sir,' he said, and slouched out. The display steadied.

Sholer gave it a couple of extra whacks to be on the safe side, and turned back to me. 'This is a very promising line of enquiry.'

---

1. *Either for subsequent analysis or to contain a potential biohazard, if not both.*

2. *Jurgen's ability to nullify psychic phenomena appeared to have disrupted genestealer brood telepathy, and the ability of individual tyranids to sense the greater hive mind, on several occasions prior to this, although, for obvious reasons, experimental verification was never possible.*

'Which is going to be terminated in pretty short order, if the creatures outside have their way,' I reminded him. 'How can we use it now?'

'We'd need to boost and transmit the signal,' he told me, clearly intrigued by the possibilities; something I'd have found a good deal more encouraging if he wasn't still treating it as an abstract problem to be solved for the fun of it, rather than the urgent matter of our survival. 'Unfortunately, transmitting a psychic signal isn't quite as simple as sending a vox.'

'Use a psyker, then,' I said. 'You're not going to tell me an installation as sensitive as this one doesn't have an astropath on staff?'

The Apothecary nodded.

'Of course there is,' he agreed. 'But I don't see what good it'll do. She won't be able to read a thing from it, let alone act as a relay. The warp shadow's got us completely cut off.'

'No harm in asking her, though, is there?' I demanded, with rather more asperity than I'd intended.

'None whatever,' Sholer said.

THOUGH I'VE NEVER been particularly comfortable in the company of astropaths, I was more than happy to see this particular one, who strolled into the analyticum with complete confidence, stepping over the cables lying in wait for the unwary without so much as a flicker of her sightless eyes. Like most of her kind, her age was indeterminate, the skin of her face etched with faint stress lines, although the faint stubble on her shaven head was dark where it shouldered its way through the tattooed icon of the Emperor, no doubt intended to invoke his protection. 'You must be Cain,' she said, turning her head in my direction, and adroitly sidestepping a scuttling CAT as she did so.

'I must,' I agreed, debating for a moment whether to extend a hand in greeting, before deciding against it. Her preternatural senses would probably make her aware of the gesture, but if they didn't, I'd look like an idiot. Then she extended hers, to precisely the right position for me to take with the least amount of difficulty. 'Good of you to come.'

'It's not as though I had a lot else to do,' she said, with a faint smile, as I released her hand after a perfunctory shake. Even through my glove, I thought I could feel a faint tingling sensation, although I suppose that could have been my imagination. Without Jurgen around I felt unusually vulnerable, even though I knew intellectually that she couldn't read my mind directly. I'd made sure my aide was occupied elsewhere, however, as his presence would have been sure to disrupt proceedings. I'd known psykers have a seizure in his vicinity, and even if our astropath wasn't simply poleaxed by his aura of psychic nullity, she'd certainly recognise him for what he was, a development Amberley was sure to take the dimmest of views of[1].

'Clementine Drey.'

'We need you to transmit something,' Sholer explained, and Clementine's face took on a puzzled expression, deepening the delicate tracery of barely-perceptible lines across her face into full visibility, adding a couple of decades to her apparent age in an instant.

'I can't push a message through the shadow,' she said, as though explaining to a child that space was black.

'We know,' I said. 'We just want you to send it out there regardless.' If I'd said we wanted her to contact the hive mind, she'd probably go completely to pieces, leaving us no better off than we were now.

'Transmit blind?' Clementine asked, apparently unconscious of the irony, and looking no happier. She clearly wasn't an idiot, and probably had an inkling of what we were after. She turned, looking uncannily as if she was studying the bioship fragment with her sunken eye sockets. 'You want me to try contacting that?'

'Could you?' I asked, trying not to sound too eager, and she shook her head.

'There's nothing there. It's like...' she paused, groping for an analogy. 'It's like a hole in the room. There's just nothing to sense, like a fragment of the shadow itself.'

---

1. *Got that right. Jurgen was one of my most carefully-guarded assets, which is why I'd left him in the relative obscurity of his position with Cain, to be used as required, instead of inducting him directly into my entourage. Apart from the inconvenience of my own psyker collapsing every time he walked into the room, I had no wish to be constantly fending off colleagues from the Ordo Malleus who felt a blank would be better employed tagging along on their latest daemon-hunting expedition.*

Sholer and I looked at one another. I don't know how he was feeling, but I was close to despair. How could the astropath pass on the signal from the bioship fragment when she couldn't even perceive it? Then my eye fell on the array of instrumentation, and their scurrying, red-robed attendants.

'Can you read those instruments?' I asked, hardly daring to hope.

'Of course.' Clementine looked puzzled again, though how she was able to perceive them at all was beyond me. 'It's simply data flow. The kind of thing I encode for transmission all the time.'

'Can you do it in real time?' I asked, and her expression began to border on the scornful.

'Easily,' she said.

'Right now?' I asked, thumbing my palm for the answer I wanted to hear.

'Find me a seat,' Clementine said, in a resigned tone. She turned her head. 'And I'd appreciate a little privacy. The process can be unpleasant to witness.' By which she meant unpleasant to experience, if I was any judge, having had more than a little experience of polite misdirection myself. Sholer went off to chivvy the rest of the cogboys away, while I heaved a couple of the smaller crates around to screen off the main workstation from eyes other than our own.

By the time I'd finished, Clementine had settled in a chair before the lectern, staring through the pict screen as if she could see the individual electrons pinging about in it. For all I knew, perhaps she could.

'Commissar,' Jurgen's voice sounded urgently in my comm-bead. 'The 'nids are finishing off the last of the ones we thawed out, and most of them are moving on the shrine.' His words were punctuated by the hissing roar of the melta firing. 'Some have already broken through in the lower corridors.'

'It has to be now,' I said, as Sholer rejoined us. 'The other group's on the way up to kill this thing.' As if to underline my words, the muffled roar of a bolter echoed from somewhere beneath my feet.

'They're in the lift shaft,' Yail's voice chimed in, unnecessarily, as my innate sense of direction had pinpointed the source of the firing. I pictured the wide, deep void, plunging all the way down to the lower levels, providing the invading tyranids with the most direct route possible to where we were sitting.

'How long can you hold them for?' I asked, drawing my weapons.

'Long enough, I hope,' Yail replied, before cutting the link, no doubt having a good deal more to concentrate on than idle conversation.

'Ready,' Clementine said, looking far from happy, as the sounds of distant firing redoubled. 'I'll just keep echoing whatever comes in through the feed, although Throne knows what you expect to pick it up.' Her mouth moved, in some litany peculiar to her caste, then her body spasmed, as though she was throwing a fit, every muscle locking rigid with startling suddenness. She slipped from the chair, smacking her head on the edge of a nearby crate, and opening an ugly wound, which Sholer moved to staunch. A thin trickle of drool, admixed with blood from her bitten tongue, oozed slowly from the corner of her mouth.

'I'll tend her,' Sholer said, looking up, and catching sight of me with my weapons at the ready, no doubt assuming I was desperate to join the fray, instead of just paranoid about being caught by the first 'nids to make it through the door. Come to think of it, there was only one entrance to the chamber. Once they got inside, my chances of getting out would be minimal, and the huge, putrescent mass of their prime target would be drawing them like kroot to carrion. 'You may join the defensive line.'

'If you're sure,' I said, careful not to overplay the gallantry to the point where I'd be incontrovertibly stuck here.

'Completely,' Sholer said, and drew his bolt pistol, more than ready for the fray. Seizing my opportunity, I sprinted from the room.

THE CORRIDOR OUTSIDE was full of panicking cogboys, running around in a fashion uncannily reminiscent of the aftermath of the escape of the genestealers. Confusingly, as many seemed to be running towards the sound of the Reclaimers' bolter fire as away from it, something I at first attributed to a misplaced desire to get stuck in with the improvised weapons most of them were brandishing. Looking around, I saw everything from hastily adapted tools to simple lengths of piping weighted to create heavier clubs, often supplemented with a spike or two, vicious enough to have gladdened the heart of any ork. A few carried more sophisticated armaments, perhaps scavenged from repair shops or hastily assembled from scratch, with bolt pistols and makeshift grenades fashioned from lubricant cans being popular choices. One fellow had even provided himself with a crossbow, which wouldn't have looked out of place in the scavvy camps of the sump[1].

Having no desire to meet any tyranids head-on myself, I forced my way through the crush away from the sounds of combat, only to discover my error, for a living nightmare was blocking the corridor ahead of me, screeching in furious frustration as it battered against the ceiling and walls with leathery wings. It seemed I'd been right, and the invading hive mind hadn't taken long to deploy gargoyles against us. I raised my laspistol, cracking off a couple of shots as it rose above the heads of the cogboys blocking my line of fire, but all that succeeded in doing was drawing its attention to me, which was far from what I had in mind.

Dropping the tech-priest it had been savaging, it swooped towards me, bringing up its fleshborer to vomit a charge of deadly beetles in my direction. Fortunately its aim was disrupted by a cogboy showing rather more initiative than good sense, who flung a weighted line at it, which wrapped around the forelimb wielding the living weapon and jerked it aside at the last possible instant. The rain of frantically chewing mandibles pattered harmlessly against the wall of the corridor, only a few strays and ricochets finding living flesh to burrow into. And, given that it was so liberally laced with metal, much good it probably did them[2].

---

1. *A reference to his origins in an underhive, although on which world remains obscure, 'scavvies' being a common term in such communities for those at both the literal and metaphorical lowest stratum of society, who subsist by scavenging whatever they can from the detritus falling (or being dumped) from above.*

2. *Despite the horrific nature of the wounds they inflict, fleshborer beetles die within seconds, so those injured by them often recover if enough remains of any vital organs attacked, and tech-priests would have had most of those replaced by more robust augmetics in any case.*

The gargoyle screeched again, and rounded on my unexpected deliverer, its stinger-tipped tail thrusting towards his or her abdomen[1]. One good turn deserved another, particularly with so many witnesses around, so I lashed out with my chainsword, severing the barb before it could penetrate and bringing up the weapon on the backswing to slash at the hovering terror's exposed underside. 'Hold on!' I called encouragingly, although the tech-priest showed no sign of letting go, hauling grimly on the line like a fisherman with the biggest catch of their entire life. A gout of foul-smelling entrails spattered the floor and my much-abused greatcoat, confirming once and for all that it was past salvaging, and the gargoyle battered at me with its leathery wings, trying and failing to bring the fleshborer to bear once more. Seeing its head turn, I ducked, letting the crown of my cap take the gobbet of venom it suddenly spat with the intention of burning my eyes out, and retaliated with another swipe of the chainsword. This time the screaming blade slashed the wing open from top to bottom, spilling the air, and the creature fell heavily to the floor, fluttering about in the slick of its own innards like a sparrow taking a bath.

'Finish it!' the tech-priest urged, the even mechanical voice somehow imbued with bloodlust, and leapt forwards, pinning the fleshborer under a mechanical foot with such weight and energy that the sculpted flesh burst like a ripe fruit. That was all the urging the others needed, and they fell on the downed creature like a pack of sump rats on a corpse, hacking and bludgeoning it to paste with club and blade.

'They're almost at the top of the shaft, sir,' Jurgen reported, the sounds of combat echoing hollowly in the background through the tiny vox-receiver in my ear, and I vacillated for a moment before responding. The gargoyle could have been alone, but I doubted it, and if one had found its way inside from the landing platform, the rest of its brood wouldn't be far behind. Even if they weren't, there was nothing on the flight deck capable of taking to the air, and I'd simply choke to death in the miasmal atmosphere[2] if the airborne monstrosities didn't

---

1. *Presumably a particularly heavily augmented individual.*

2. *Clearly an exaggeration, as he'd already been exposed to it for some time on more than one occasion.*

get me first. On the other hand, perilous as joining the defence of the lift shaft would be, at least I'd have Jurgen's melta and the surviving Reclaimers to hide behind.

'I'll be right there,' I replied, as though I'd never had a moment's hesitation, and trotted away in the direction of the shooting.

To my surprise a lot of the red robes surrounding me came along too, their blood and lubricants all fired up, apparently eager to bag another 'nid or two, now they'd had a taste of bloodshed. Which was fine by me – the more the merrier, particularly if they were standing between me and the swarm.

I glanced into Sholer's sanctum as we swept past, but he was still crouched over Clementine's spasming body, partially obscured behind the screening crates. Even if he was aware of my presence, he seemed too busy to acknowledge it, so I just kept moving, my comet tail of cogboys streaming out behind.

'Sorry I'm late,' I said, as I joined Yail, a couple of Reclaimers, and Jurgen, all of whom were lined up along the Chimera-sized doorway to the freight elevator[1], which had been cranked open to allow them an unrestricted field of fire. Fortunately the hive mind was only throwing creatures capable of climbing against us, which ruled out anything with ranged weapons, but for every hormagaunt or purestrain 'stealer which went plummeting back into the depths, another dozen kept right on coming. 'Gargoyle got in the way.'

'I know,' Yail said, 'the Land Speeder's trying to keep them away from the hangar,' which at least accounted for the absence of the other Reclaimers[2].

I don't mind admitting I quailed a little as I looked down the vertiginous drop to the sub-levels so far below. The walls of the shaft were seething with chitin, scuttling upwards with malevolent purpose, their rending and scything claws clacking together in an almost deafening cascade of crepitation. The defenders kept pouring

---

1. *If the bioship fragment was really, as Cain described, the size of a Baneblade, the door would have had to have been considerably larger than that to admit it.*

2. *Apart from the Techmarines that Sholer mentioned at their first meeting, who appear to have been elsewhere throughout the incident.*

fire into them, which I lost no time in adding to with my laspistol, but for all the effect we were having we might just as well have been lobbing rocks. 'Can't we get the platform moving, and scrape them off?' I asked, taking the back of the head off a particularly persistent genestealer with a lucky shot clean through its gaping jaws.

'We already did,' Jurgen informed me, sending a melta blast through the torso of another, the thermal backwash sending a couple of the others tumbling back down the shaft by way of a bonus.

'So trying again would just bring them up faster,' Yail added, punctuating his words with a burst from his storm bolter, which sent half a dozen gaunts after them in bite-sized chunks.

'They seem to be moving fast enough already,' I said, feeling a bit of heroic understatement would go down well about now.

A faint explosion echoed up the shaft. One of the cogboys had got over-excited and lobbed a home-made grenade down it, no doubt having calculated where in its trajectory it was likely to explode[1], showering the 'nids with bits of broken metal.

'Not as fast as they were,' Jurgen observed, as though the matter were only of passing interest.

'They're slowing down?' I asked, a sudden flare of hope rising within me, and my aide nodded.

'They were sticking to the shadows before, using cover. Now they're just climbing straight into the line of the guns, so we're holding 'em off more easily.'

I tapped the vox-bead in my ear. 'Sholer,' I said, trying not to sound too exultant, 'it seems to be working. Is Clementine still transmitting?'

'So far as I can tell,' Sholer said. 'She's suffering continual seizures, each more violent than the last. Any one of them could prove fatal.'

'Then we need to finish this fast,' I said.

'I concur.' Yail's head inclined a little, that being as close as he could come to a nod encased in the clumsy Terminator suit, and he triggered the remaining rockets in his cyclone rig in a single salvo. A second or so later a firestorm boiled up the shaft, crisping the chitinous horrors

---

1. *Or simply not caring; under the circumstances, he was almost bound to hit something.*

clinging to the sides of it even as they were shredded by the hail of shrapnel from the frag charges, and we leapt for our lives as the backwash boiled out through the open door. I hit the metal flooring and rolled, the furnace heat of the overlapping explosions searing my back, and came up, my laspistol pointed at the smoke-blackened portal. Only Yail still stood where he had been, protected from the fury of the blast by the finest armour known to man. After a moment, he spoke. 'We have prevailed,' he said simply.

'We have?' Strangely unwilling to believe it, I moved slowly to the edge of the abyss, and looked down. Sure enough, the only movement I could see was a few wounded stragglers squirming back into the vents at the bottom of the shaft which had evidently provided them with ingress.

'Looks like it,' Jurgen said, sending them on their way with a burst from his lasgun, his unique personal odour already beginning to displace the smell of charred flesh and scorched metal in my nostrils.

'The gargoyles are also fleeing in disarray,' Yail informed us, unable to keep a note of satisfaction from his voice.

'Excellent,' I said, doing a slightly better job of sounding businesslike; but then I'd had a lot more practice at hiding my feelings. I activated the comm-bead again. 'You can tell Clementine to stand down.'

'Unfortunately, I can't,' Sholer said, his voice tinged with regret. 'As I anticipated, her last seizure proved fatal.'

From *The Crusade and After: A Military History of the Damocles Gulf,* by Vargo Royz, 058.M42.

Commissar Cain's flash of inspiration, and Astropath Drey's heroic sacrifice, were to have a far wider effect than either could possibly have anticipated. The inexorable advance of the hive fleet in orbit faltered as the coordinating intelligence lost control of the individual bioships, which began to react instinctively to their current circumstances instead of in pursuit of a wider strategy. The Imperial vessels, on the other hand, were still able to support one another, a tactical advantage they lost no time in exploiting. Rallying as many ships as he could, Admiral Boume began to directly engage the leviathans, which had been left vulnerable, though far from helpless, by the loss of their escorts, killing one and mauling the others so badly that they were forced to flee.

With their loss, the tyranid organisms on the ground reverted to their instinctive behaviour for the most part, only able to act as one in the presence of the synapse creatures sent to herd them, which, of course, became prime targets for the subsequent hunt. Though rumours persist of a few isolated organisms still lurking in the wastelands and the depths of the hive sumps, no reliable sightings have been recorded for nearly three decades, and Fecundia today is officially classified as cleansed. The Imperial Guard garrison established in the wake of the incident, and the indigenous skitarii, remain on the alert, however, for any signs of a fresh incursion.

TWENTY-SEVEN

'ALL RATHER SATISFACTORY,' I said, sipping my bowl of tanna, and regarding El'hassai through the steam as I contemplated the regicide board between us, a delaying tactic I was certain didn't fool him for a minute. He was certainly a more challenging opponent than Zyvan, although whether that was because he simply didn't think like a human, or his profession tended to encourage the use of misdirection and subtlety, I had yet to make up my mind. The Lord General had his hands full negotiating the terms under which the garrison we were leaving behind was supposed to co-operate with Kyper and his skitarii in cleansing Fecundia of the thousands of tyranid stragglers (not surprisingly, he was pressing for full autonomy for the Guard units, while Kyper was equally determined to keep operational matters firmly under his own jurisdiction), leaving him little time for socialising in the relative comfort of the flagship. Though El'hassai would hardly have been my first choice of dinner guest under most circumstances, there were a few outstanding matters nagging at the back of my mind that I felt we should discuss. Partly for my own satisfaction, and partly because I was ever mindful of my covert avocation as Amberley's eyes and ears. If I was right in my suspicions the

Ordo Xenos would probably be quite interested in the conclusions I'd come to in the relatively quiet couple of weeks following the desperate battle in and around Regio Quinquaginta Unus. 'A bloody nose for the 'nids, and the forge world successfully defended.'

'Thanks to your ingenuity,' the tau said, his attention apparently entirely on the move I made. He studied the board for a moment, and turned one of my pieces, with an unmistakable air of satisfaction. 'And that of Apothecary Sholer. Unfortunately we seem unlikely to be able to use the same stratagem in the defence of other worlds.'

'Unfortunately so,' I agreed. The tau certainly couldn't, anyway, not having any astropaths to project a jamming signal with, and Sholer seemed pretty convinced that we needed a living hive node to produce one anyway, which weren't exactly thick on the ground. He was urging Kyper and the Death Korps to round up as many live tyranids as possible, to see if he could make the trick work with recorded or synthesised data, but so far would only allow that it was a promising line of enquiry, which could mean decades of research before anything useful emerged from the analyticum. Come to that, I couldn't see either Guardsmen or skitarii exactly falling over themselves to round up 'nids they could just as easily pot from a safe distance. 'But at least what's left of the hive fleet will be a lot easier for your ships to pick off when it hits Dr'th'nyr.'

'Especially since the astropath attached to the Imperial observers has given them adequate warning of its approach,' El'hassai said. He inclined his head courteously. 'For which we thank our allies, of course.'

'One good turn deserves another,' I said, turning a piece of his own. 'If you hadn't warned us the hive fleet was coming in the first place, Fecundia might easily have fallen.' I took another sip of tanna. 'In fact it almost did anyway, taking a substantial chunk of Battlefleet Damocles with it.' Which would have left half the Imperial systems in the Gulf open to an unopposed land grab by the tau. More than enough to compensate them for the loss of the single world they'd handed back to us on the brink of seizing it, and which they no doubt expected to regain before too long in any case.

'But it didn't,' El'hassai said evenly, studying the board again. 'And your ships are being refitted even as we speak.'

'Quite so.' I savoured another mouthful of the bitter liquid, and held out my tanna bowl, which Jurgen refilled with his usual quiet efficiency. 'Ready for our return to Quadravidia.'

'Quadravidia?' The tau diplomat tilted his head in a perfect imitation of human surprise. 'Surely it's adequately defended by the merchantmen delivering infrastructural enhancements?'

'A burden the unexpected survival of our warships can relieve them of,' I said. 'Just as the unexpected survival of Fecundia can relieve the tau empire of the burden of supporting an Imperial world. I'm sure those resources will be far better employed in defending your borders against the tyranids.'

If I'd been looking at a human face, I'm pretty sure the expressions I'd seen flickering across them would have been surprise, chagrin, and possibly amusement, but then he was a diplomat, and a xenos one to boot, so it's more than likely he was just projecting what he thought I wanted to see.

'Perhaps they will,' he said evenly. 'The tyranids are a greater threat to both of us at the present time, than either of us is to the other. It's in both our interests to maintain the alliance against them.'

'Indeed it is.' I raised my tanna bowl in a good-humoured toast, which, after a moment, El'hassai echoed, with barely a trace of irony. 'You might almost say the Greater Good demands it.'

[*On which somewhat frivolous note, this extract from the Cain archive comes to a typically self-congratulatory conclusion.*]

ABOUT THE AUTHOR

Sandy Mitchell is one of Black Library's best loved authors, and has written fiction set in both the Warhammer and Warhammer 40,000 universes. He is best known for the nine books of the Ciaphas Cain series, along with a plethora of associated short stories and audio dramas. Also known as Alex Stewart, he writes screenplays for film and television.

WARHAMMER
40,000

FIRE CASTE

PETER FEHERVARI

An extract from Fire Caste
by Peter Fehervari

On sale March 2013

SOMETHING DARTED FROM the trees behind him, buzzing like an angry insect. Iverson spun round firing, but the sleek white saucer streaking towards him zipped between his snapshots, skimming high above the ground on an anti-gravity field. The disc was only about a metre in diameter, but Iverson knew that a soulless intelligence guided the machine. It was only a drone, its artificial brain no more sophisticated than a jungle predator, but the very existence of such a thing was blasphemous.

Blueskin technology is a heresy upon the face of the galaxy!

Of more immediate concern were the twin pulse carbines mounted on the underside of the drone. As the disc whirled to dodge his fire those guns rotated independently to lock on him. He dived aside as they spat a stuttering enfilade of plasma. The dive slipped into a fall, saving him from a second burst as the machine whizzed by. He rolled over and fired after it, catching it with a couple of rounds as it banked into a turn, but his shots only mottled its carapace. Chattering angrily the drone soared back towards him.

A hail of las-bolts spattered the machine from the side, knocking it off kilter and exposing its vulnerable underbelly. Careening wildly through the air, the drone raked the ground with plasma, shredding two of the unconscious Konquistadores. Someone roared in fury and fresh las-fire ripped into the saucer's belly. One of its carbines exploded, taking the other with it and spinning the machine out of control. Gushing smoke and burbling in distress it retreated, losing altitude as it limped towards the trees, but Iverson was already on his feet and charging. Leaping, he swung the shock maul down on the drone, smashing it towards the ground. It tried to rise and he struck again and again, elevated by a hatred untainted by doubt.

The machine exploded.

Iverson was thrown from his feet. Falling for what felt like forever he watched a ragged arm spiralling towards the sky, its hand still clenching a shock maul. It was awful and absurd, but suddenly he was laughing and someone else was laughing along with him. He glanced across the clearing and saw Cabeza. The cadaverous Konquistadore was on his knees, cackling through a mask of mud and blood. His lasrifle was levelled at the wrecked drone.

CABEZA DIDN'T KNOW why he'd thrown in with the commissar at the end. He'd already turned his back on the Imperium to sign up with the enemy in the hope of a better deal. He wouldn't be the first Guardsman to do it, nor the last, so why make a bad move now? What could Iverson offer him except more pain and maybe a quick death? Even for a commissar the man was crazy! Just look at him lying there with his arm torn off at the elbow and laughing like it was the best joke in the Imperium. *Crazy!* Except Cabeza was laughing right along with him so maybe he was crazy too. And maybe that was all there was to it.

'For the bloody God-Emperor!' Cabeza cackled through the last of his broken teeth. Then a drone soared down behind him and his chest erupted in a superheated geyser of flesh and blood. Looking down at the sizzling cavity in his chest he frowned, thinking a full-grown mirewyrm could swim right through there. It was a miracle his torso was still holding things together.

But then it wasn't.

* * *

As CABEZA'S CORPSE collapsed inwards like a slaughterhouse of cards the second drone flashed past, homing in on Iverson. Biting down on the sudden agony of his ruined arm, he rolled to his knees. His laspistol was gone, lost somewhere in the fall. It wouldn't have stopped the machine, but it would have given him a stand. Hadn't Bierce taught him that a stand was all that mattered in the final accounting?

But hadn't he stopped believing that long ago?

And if he'd stopped believing it, why was he still fighting? Maybe because Bierce was standing at the edge of the clearing, hands clasped behind his back in that parade ground rigor, watching and judging his pupil until the bitter end.

The drone swept past and began to circle him, chattering and chirping as two more descended to join its dance. The machines seemed to grow more alert and aware in numbers, almost as if they were parts of a collective mind coming together. Maybe it was just a delusion, but Iverson could have sworn there was real anger in that mind. He'd destroyed one of its components and it wanted revenge. And so the drones were playing with him, *enjoying* his hopeless, one-armed struggle against the coral, mocking his determination to die on his feet. He could almost taste their hatred. Wasn't that why the Imperium shunned such technology? Didn't the Ecclesiarchy preach that thinking machines loathed the living and would ultimately turn on their creators? Mankind had learned that hard truth to its cost long ago, but the blueskin race was still reckless with youth. Perhaps that would be its downfall. As the drones circled him Iverson took comfort in the thought.

The machine chatter rose to a higher pitch and he steeled himself for death, but abruptly the drones fell silent and drifted back a few paces. To Iverson's eyes they looked reluctant and sullen, like angry dogs leashed by their masters. And as the dogs withdrew the masters emerged.

They crept from the trees in a low crouch, their stubby carbines sweeping from side to side as they advanced, hugging the coral with a bone-deep distrust of open ground. There were five, lightly armoured in mottled black breastplates and rubberised fatigues. Their long helmets arched over their shoulders, giving them a vaguely crustacean look, the strangeness heightened by the crystal sensors embedded in their otherwise blank faceplates. Iverson recognised them at once: pathfinders, the scouts of the tau race.

Despite their hunched postures the warriors were swift and graceful, fanning out to surround him with the perfect coordination of bonded hunters. Slipping on the coral yet again, Iverson abandoned dignity and faced them on his knees. He could see Bierce lurking at the periphery of his vision, demanding some final caustic rhetoric from his protégé, but Iverson had nothing to say. Glaring at the pathfinders, he noticed one of them was quite different to its companions – shorter and slighter of build, the set of its shoulders subtly wrong. The only one with hooves… Iverson's eyes narrowed as the truth hit him: the odd-one-out was the genuine article.

Under that loathsome xenos armour all the others are human!

The lone alien stepped forward and dropped to its haunches, bringing its impassive crystal lenses level with his face. There was a crimson slash running along the spine of its helmet, identifying it as the leader, but Iverson was drawn to another mark – a deep crack running from its crown to the chin of its faceplate. The damage had been patched up, but the rippled scar of a chainsword was unmistakeable to a commissar.

'Your face,' he breathed. 'Show me.' The warrior tilted its head quizzically at the challenge. 'Or are you afraid?'

'Be watchful, shas'ui.' It was one of the traitors, his voice surprisingly crisp through his sealed helmet. 'This one is of the commissar caste. Even wounded this one will not yield.'

The studied formality of the traitor's words disgusted Iverson, particularly the way he'd spoken that unclean xenos rank, 'shas'ui', with such reverence. These traitors weren't just mercenaries or cowards looking for a way out – they were true believers.

The shas'ui considered Iverson for a moment, then it began to unclip its helmet, its four-fingered hands nimble as they uncoupled the power feed and flicked an array of seals. Throughout the ritual its cluster of crystal eyes remained fixed on him, unwavering until the helmet was swept away and he saw the face of his enemy.

Even for an alien it was ugly. It leathery blue-grey skin was tinged with yellow and pockmarked with insect bites. A rash of boils ran from its neck to cluster around a topknot of greasy black hair, but its most startling feature was the ruination left by the chainsword. A deep rift had been carved into the right side of its face, running from scalp to jaw, mirroring the crack in its helmet. It was an old wound, but still hideous. A bionic sensor glittered from the scabrous mess where its eye had been and the whole jaw had been replaced with a carved prosthetic. The remaining eye, black and lustreless, regarded the commissar inscrutably. For all its mutilated strangeness the creature was recognisably female. She was the first tau Iverson had seen up close and whatever he'd expected it wasn't this filthy, disfigured veteran.

You're even uglier than me. It was such an absurd, irrelevant thought that he almost laughed out loud.

'Ko'miz'ar.' The word sounded unfamiliar on the creature's lips, but he sensed it had faced his kind before… and had the scar to show for it. 'Ko'miz'ar…' It was an accusation ripe with hatred.

Order the novel or download the eBook
from *blacklibrary.com*

Also available from

GAMES WORKSHOP®

and all good bookstores